FANATIC

Thomas Keneally was born i̶̶̶ published in 1964. Since then number of novels and non-fiction works. His novels include *The Chant of Jimmie Blacksmith*, *Schindler's Ark* and *The People's Train*. He has won the Miles Franklin Award, the Booker Prize, the *Los Angeles Times* Prize, the Mondello International Prize and has been made a Literary Lion of the New York Public Library, a Fellow of the American Academy, recipient of the University of California gold medal, and is now the subject of a fifty-five-cent Australian stamp. He has held various academic posts in the United States, but lives in Sydney.

'Enlightening . . . Keneally's descriptive gift comes into exquisite play . . . his prose tempered, characteristically, by an ironic undertone that keeps the narrative buoyant. With Mitchel's protracted, dangerous and endlessly frustrated escape plan, *Fanatic Heart* takes on something of the character of a nineteenth-century adventure novel . . . With this, his fortieth novel, and now aged eighty-eight, Thomas Keneally shows himself to be as adept as ever at converting research into illumination and evocation.' *Times Literary Supplement*

'From the splendid opening line, this novel reads like no ordinary tale of the Irish potato famine . . . In all this Keneally has a lively style as he veers between omniscience and Mitchel's viewpoint, the prose studded with exclamation marks and a winking authorial tone . . . *Fanatic Heart* is a story busy enough never to be boring, even if the details are crammed too tightly. And Keneally doesn't whitewash his man . . . Even by the standards of his time, Mitchel was deeply racist: he wanted to reopen the transatlantic slave trade fifty years after its abolition, and argued against rights for Jews, who suffered similar restrictions as Catholics did in Ireland. That's the problem with a fanatic heart: you never know which way the fanaticism is going to turn next.' *The Times*

'Meticulously researched and full of compelling historical detail . . . Dickens is referenced more than once, and there are times when this compendious novel . . . stands comparison with the master. But in its gripping account of Mitchel's audacious escape in the outback, where he evades capture up to the very last minute, its models are the adventure novels of Sir Walter Scott and Robert Louis Stevenson . . . a gripping and resonant story.' *Financial Times*

'From the Irish Famine to the American Civil War, *Fanatic Heart* is a powerful literary adventure story from a master of historical fiction. Thomas Keneally has created an unforgettable novel about John Mitchel – Irish patriot, journalist, escaped convict, hero, father, husband and, deeply flawed man.' Christine Dwyer Hickey

'A brilliant conjuring of the early Irish patriot John Mitchel. The novel lays out through meticulous research and fine prose the first potato famine and Mitchel's rise to rebellion against the British in the 1850s; followed by his arrest, separation from wife and family, and his forced expulsion along with several famous cohorts to a penal colony in Tasmania. Mitchel's wife, Jenny, also comes to life on the page, bringing her family by sailing ship around the world to join the rebel in exile only to support his daring escape to America and their final road to freedom. Outstanding.' Mark Sullivan

THOMAS KENEALLY

FANATIC HEART

faber

First published in the UK in 2023
by Faber & Faber Limited
The Bindery, 51 Hatton Garden
London EC1N 8HN

First published by Vintage in 2022
Published by Penguin Books in 2023

This paperback edition published in 2024

Printed in the UK by CPI Group (UK) Ltd, Croydon CR0 4YY

The right of Thomas Keneally to be identified as author
of this work has been asserted in accordance with Section 77
of the Copyright, Designs and Patents Act 1988

A CIP record for this book
is available from the British Library

ISBN 978–0–571–38797–7

Printed and bound in the UK on FSC® certified paper in line with our continuing
commitment to ethical business practices, sustainability and the environment.
For further information see faber.co.uk/environmental-policy

2 4 6 8 10 9 7 5 3 1

This book, in case of any doubt to the contrary, is
dedicated unambiguously

And without any desire to plunder the misery of strangers,

To the dispossessed and hunted indigenes
of Van Diemen's Land:

May their Voice be heard!

To the liberty-deprived convicts of Australia, transported
in converted slavers to the earth's end.

And especially to Mary Shields, Limerick waif and
Australian matriarch, and two political rebels, Hugh
Larkin of Laurencetown, Galway, and John Keneally
of Newmarket, County Cork.

All these have been talkative ghosts at our hearth.

But above all,

In bewilderment at the race delusions of Caucasians,

And at the scientific, theological, economic and political
theories that sanctioned taking liberty away from
Melanesian 'blackbirds' in my own nation,

And from Africans in the United States and Caribbean,

This book is dedicated with humility to those
forebears of African-Americans,

Whose ghosts still cry out for the fullness of their freedom.

'Out of Ireland have we come.
Great hatred, little room,
Maimed us at the start.
I carry from my mother's womb,
A fanatic heart.'

William Butler Yeats

'Then die . . . Die in your patience and perseverance, and
be well assured of this, that the priest who bids you perish
patiently, amidst your own golden harvests, under the
gospel according to Downing St, insults manhood and
common sense, bears false witness against religion,
and blasphemes the providence of God.'

John Mitchel

'You that Mitchel's prayer have heard,
"Send war in our time, O Lord!"
Know that when all words are said
And a man is fighting mad,
Something drops from eyes long blind,
He completes his partial mind,
For an instant stands at ease,
Laughs aloud, his heart at peace.
Even the wisest man grows tense
With some sort of violence
Before he can accomplish fate,
Know his work or choose his mate.'

William Butler Yeats

Preface

Famine Epiphany, Summer 1847

This was a hard summer but people were getting used to corpses by the road and along ditches and did their best not to step on them. John Mitchel was shocked himself, at how he could leave home in Ontario Terrace, having kissed his children's heads and absorbed the smell of warm oats they exuded, and then stride down Mount Pleasant Street barely noticing the ragged old man on the corner who might both be younger than him and have typhus. Or the hollowed country girl with her face in a skeletal rictus of pleading, seemingly unable to ask anymore, for anything.

But there was one incident in that year that came to his mind whenever the word 'Famine' was used in later times. William Smith O'Brien, a member of the Irish Party in the House of Commons and the leader of their faction, Young Ireland, that Mitchel himself belonged to, had been in Limerick. There he wanted to give a speech for his re-election to the House of Commons, and he needed conservative votes to bolster his normally progressive ones. He had been embarrassed that John Mitchel, seen as a firebrand, had turned up in town to visit some fellow radicals to talk about necessary matters, like stopping the next harvest ever being shipped out of the country.

Tom Meagher, who accompanied Mitchel, did not necessarily like to stay around in Limerick while Smith O'Brien pretended to be a harmless and hopeful improver of things that Westminster had no intention to improve. Meagher was young and, even with a rough country walk in mind, appropriately dressed and shod and looked the very essence of the healthy and alluring orator unleashed on nature.

He and Mitchel both happened to like those Comeragh Mountains just south of Clonmel, and John said he knew the way to a *clachan* on the southern end, close to the sea and on the banks of a stream, that he had visited in years past. He had for some time wondered how they were faring down there, the people who had been so hospitable in his earlier visit.

When they departed the public house at Knocknacullen, where they had left their horses, John carried some bacon and bread and wine in his satchel, and the two set off over the slopes of Croughaun, from which, that clear day of late April, they hoped to see the coast. A lovely wild scene faced them at each step, a shaggy country of great boulders and scooped loughs under blue mountain bluffs. The white-mantled hawthorn bushes lent a brightness to the scene, though, and reminded John of paintings he had seen of the branching coral of the South Pacific.

After much tramping, they saw the *clachan*, the hamlet, below on the banks of its lough, under the scarps of red and black. Meagher frowned. His riding jacket shone in a brief, light-infused shower of rain. 'Where's the smoke?' he asked. 'Where's the turf smell?'

In fact, there was not a twitch of life. They caught instead what Mitchel thought a particular hellish smell, a stink empty of hope and human expectation. He wondered had he been too optimistic that a village so remote would be exempt from the curse of the times? As if the lack of a post office meant the pestilence couldn't reach them?

'Oh, loving Christ!' said Meagher as they stalked through the little gathering of houses. Meagher was like a young land agent expecting his tenants to emerge. Mitchel walked beside him, heartsick and with swimming eyes. Knowing they would need to examine the cabins, the laneways between each as cold as absence. Though most doors seemed open, or off the hinges, the friends delayed entering the first of them, exchanging wary glances with each other.

Despite their reluctance, the truth was, Mitchel knew, that they felt a powerful obligation to witness for themselves the fate of those whom they considered brethren.

It was as wretched a scene here as it was elsewhere. In one dwelling and then another, the stench they set themselves to endure was a variation on putrefaction. The yellow, dried-out, grinning corpses did not reek like the corpses of well-fed men. It was as if they had been mummified from within – those who'd starved so long that a fever devoured them in the end, leaving little enough for wasting away. The two friends were encountering *that* stench.

As they walked amidst the houses of the dead till they reached the end of the cluster, not one did they dare to enter. Turning around, they stopped now at what Mitchel recognised as the threshold of the house of his host two years before. He shut his eyes and put his head inside the door jamb and stupidly said, with shaking voice and eyes shut, 'God save all here!' As if he were dropping in for breakfast.

There was no answer. Ghastly silence and the subtle reek of starvation and fever dead. Mitchel opened his eyes to see the bodies dimly, spaced around the fire someone had managed to light in the past winter but dead now. They were all dead. The strong man and the dark-eyed woman and the little ones, with their liquid Gaelic of two years ago mute on their tongues. Mitchel met a skeletal child, a mummy, on the floor between the hearth and her parents' bed. He smelt the blinding particular fetor until he turned, saw Meagher's handsome shape in the door, and rushed past him. Out in the laneway, being well fed, he was violently sick and became aware of Meagher beside him, and of his hand on his left shoulder.

Mitchel said, 'This is not human, Tom. Not human that we let it . . . I don't know . . . *take place.*'

'They can't know it's like this, Mitch,' said Meagher. 'They can't imagine . . .'

Mitchel knew Meagher meant, 'Over there. Downing Street.' The British government's imagination seemed able to cross oceans, penetrate Asia and even the Antipodes. But they couldn't ever imagine Ireland.

'They can't imagine,' John Mitchel agreed. He stood upright. The stink of that cabin was still stinging his eyes. 'We can't bury them,' he mourned.

'Oh, Jesus,' said Meagher. 'You know we'd be looking for trouble from fever, Mitch, even had we a shovel. But I'll let my father know, and maybe something . . . pulling the ruins down over the bodies at least, with a priest to recite the rites.'

4

Meagher's father was a powerful man in the county, and mayor of Waterford City. The first Catholic in the post, they said, since the Reformation.

Mitchel knew precisely what had befallen the people in that cabin. They'd shut their door so neighbours did not see the shame of their starving. The other families did the same. On their own hearth, they shrank and grew fevered together and raved with hunger and delirium until they hardly knew one another's faces. Mitchel surmised that at some point, with eyes the fever had made mad, they scowled on each other with a cannibal glare.

The father had scrounged a few pennies on a 'public work', make-work sites for hungry labourers, men, women, children – heaving rocks and moving soil on some vacant place of torn-up soil and rock leading nowhere. There he earned perhaps the sixth part of what would have maintained his family. Not that it was always dispensed by those officials who set up their pay desks on a heap of stones. But when it was, it kept the family half-alive for three months, and so instead of dying in December, soon after the blight struck, they were dead in March. And the agonies of those three months? God would not want to recount them.

'Fatal times!' declared Mitchel.

'It is getting late,' Meagher said. His eyes shone, blue as a wraith's, in the half-light. 'You are hard hit, my good friend,' he told Mitchel. 'I've never seen you so distressed. I fear you can never forget this.'

And that was right.

5

1

Who Will Marry Jenny Verner? 1836 and Times Various

Jenny Verner realised now what many might have spoken behind their hands about her when she was a child. For she knew she was illegitimate, one way or another.

Common people used a crasser, harsher word for it. She understood later the conversations people had under their breath when she hid in corridors to overhear them. Further, there was a story about her father, who had married her – by all accounts beautiful – mother when she was carrying a child from another man, and people thought that very good of him, but their mouths took on tucks that proclaimed him unworldly.

And now the topic was: who would marry the eldest of their children, the girl Jenny? Strangely, since they would say she was a beautiful little thing just like her mother, and it would be false modesty on her part, she realised, to say she was not. Her parents were both considered handsome, and apparently respectable in every regard. It was only later in life that members of the wider family of the Verners let her know that her parents, in fact, had not so much as married, and that *Burke's Peerage* told the world that anyhow, or at least told anyone interested enough to look her father up.

James Verner had been a captain in the British army and resided in the Churchill mansion, where he had fallen for the coachman's daughter, Mary. Mary was now James Verner's companion there at 52 Queen Street, Newry, and had been for decades upon decades. And not wed! Who indeed, consulting *Burke's Peerage*, as reputable people did, would marry her, Jenny Verner? Once she had even heard her own mother ask the question in lamentation. The problem itself asking about the problem.

It seems her father would have been Baron Churchill of Armagh if – as the eldest of the Verners – he had married properly. A younger, capable brother of his had instead been given the title now, and all the Armagh estates attached. Except for Jenny's father's determined love of her mother, he could not only have been a peer, but also elected to the Commons in Westminster. Again, except for love of her mother . . .

They were noble parents. Her father had commanded a company of troops at Waterloo, and her mother was intriguing. Yet the ordinary way the two lived in Newry seemed smaller than such absolutes as Love vs. Power. This Shakespearian tale seemed comprised of characters writ pleasant and small and domestic, and even timid.

The Verners were a family that had involved itself in the founding of the Orange Order at their townhouse in Dawson Street, Dublin. And the Orange Order was the very essence of loyalism to the British Crown and to Britishness as it sat and disported itself in Ireland.

'Well,' Jenny had been told to say by her parents, 'if it is hatred of other Irishmen, that is not what the Orange Order was founded for.'

'Really?' people replied, thinking of fisticuffs between the Protestant Orange and the Catholic Green at St Patrick's Days from Sydney to Toronto, Belfast to New Orleans.

'It is possible to celebrate one's origins,' Jenny would as a young woman maintain, 'and indeed uphold one's freedom from the undue claims of Papism upon the soul, as the Orange Order does, without hating one's fellow Irish!'

It was lesser minds, she believed, who in upholding Protestant ascendency decided that that meant hating and attacking the masses of Catholic Ireland. She had asserted these nuances in front of her genial father and he seemed to enjoy her view as wonderfully daring. It was her argument even before she met her Johnny Mitchel. There were a number of people of Protestant Ireland, not simply her, nodding towards their fellow countrymen then, seeing a unity of interests with the Irish mass, oppressed as they were on the one hand by Catholic dogma, on the other by Britain, both of whose rules were absolute.

The Penal Laws – which served severely to oppress Catholics, denying them an education, land ownership and public posts – were finally revoked by the Irish Party and the Whigs in Westminster in 1829. Still, the Established Church, called the Church of Ireland, actually the Anglican Church in Ireland, raised tithes from Catholics and Presbyterians. Even Presbyterians got into trouble for resisting to pay the tithe proctors, the agents who exacted the payments. As a member of the Church of Ireland, Jenny Verner, Who-Will-Marry-Her Verner, felt embarrassment that her church was sustained by tithes exacted from Presbyterians and Catholics.

But she knew that was not a very common sensibility amongst her parents' contemporaries. Sometimes Catholic peasants would kill a tithe proctor, or at least burn his house, and those who did were either hanged or sentenced for life to Australia. As people seemed to think appropriate.

———

Now John Mitchel, straight from Trinity College in Dublin, had become a bank clerk in Derry, and of course he did not like it, the mean and frivolous arithmetic of it all, and the lack of scale. The way numbers would be the absolution for all sorts of tragedies, for hunger, want, disinheritance. At that stage, prior to his meeting with Jenny, and numb from a hated job, he fell in love with a Belfast girl he met who was six years older than his nineteen years.

John did not fall in love by measures. And this woman, who had relatives in Newry and knew of his much-respected father, the non-subscribing Presbyterian Reverend Dr Mitchel, possessed young John's soul. The 'non-subscribing' sector was a church which refused to sign on to any creed and attracted liberals and improvers.

John, stricken for the woman, rode to Belfast from Newry, where he was being interviewed to become a possible law clerk in the practice of a Mr Neill, to lay his soul before her, plead with her. He was not, though, admitted to her and went into a decline. Ultimately, it was when, after less than a year, John had been somehow cured of this first thwarted and unhappy love, that Jenny would inherit him. She would come to pity that Belfast woman who would never travel with him amongst the volcanoes and wild torrents of the earth!

For she had never heard anyone proclaim like John Mitchel.

———

Jenny Verner herself was said to be talkative. 'Men don't like girls who make their opinions known,' said her mother with her look of bruised prettiness. Yet she came from an opinionated clan. Not so much her father; he was the quietest clansman. Her uncle, her father's younger brother, Sir William Verner, Grand Master of the Orange Order, was vocal in Parliament. Abomination and the defence of the British Protestant inheritance made men vocal, in part because there was great applause in it from their own type; because the humblest Protestant, even the poorest Presbyterian, saw himself as at least above the mass of the disinherited Irish.

She was hungry for talk, this girl whose father could have renounced and exiled her, as members of the gentry did renounce their children of dubious origin. 'Your father gave up everything for you,' her mother told her, as a caution, and her mother was right. Jenny's was the birth he would not cover up, nor would he send her mother away to live in some cottage on an endowment.

But it meant her mother did not want to permit the small rebellions, or to let her daughter hanker for talk of lightnings and revelations, which was the daily talk of John Mitchel, law clerk, when she first met him. Mitchel had a view that to set everything spinning and falling was as much an act of creation as actual systematic building – indeed more so. When a structure fell, he said even then – and as he would

11

later write – the germ of the new building was in the ruin. And Jenny Verner had been from fifteen onwards anxious to be his acolyte in ruin and his abettor.

She had first seen John on his way to work. The girls of Miss Bryden's School for Young Ladies were on one side of the river named Clanrye, proceeding downstream, and he was on a tow path on the far side. He was a God, Jenny thought. He was also a young Wordsworth, a Romantic figure – nearly six feet, with dark floppy locks and penetrating eyes. Mitchel knew a friend of hers in the same class, Mary Thompson, and Jenny treacherously had her contact him in the hope he would go for Sunday walks with her, accompanied by Jenny as a supposed guarantor of propriety.

Jenny's infatuation was apparent to her mother, who was nervous that Mitchel was Presbyterian, son of a minister of that church and of what were called 'the auld lights', who did not subscribe to the general Protestant creed as settled on in 1725 – and did not see it as their duty to preach loyalty to the state, but loyalty to conscience. Additionally, they could be vocal in their condemnation of injustices in a way respectable people rarely heard in the Established Church of Ireland, which let Caesar do very much whatever Caesar chose. The auld lights believed there was a social covenant between the state and the ordinary folk, and that if the state neglected it, it must be challenged for it.

Now, being of the Establishment, the Verners were Britons by vocation. When women of that Establishment asked behind their hands who would marry Jenny Verner, they were not thinking of the Presbyterian, intensely eloquent and grey-eyed John Mitchel. They were thinking of the Church of Ireland. They were thinking as well of acreage.

When – it was the summer of 1836, and John merely twenty years of age – Jenny walked with John Mitchel and Mary Thompson along the Newry Canal, he talked of the three-card trick by which Ireland had been deprived of its own parliament on the last day of 1800, in part in punishment for the '98 uprising.

'Now,' he told them, and the idea had the charm of heresy against the supposed privilege Mary and Jenny enjoyed as members of the ruling and Established Church, 'we Irish are ruled entirely for the convenience of Westminster, our linen industry is run down, and the mass of people are still subject to rules more suitable to the Ottoman Empire. Even now, Catholics are still practically excluded from every profession, except medicine, and from all official stations without exception. They try to serve on juries, and are refused.

'Until I was thirteen' – he spoke of this as if it were an eon ago – 'the Penal Laws still governed Ireland!' There had been amongst other ills the denial of education to children of Catholics, and a place in civil life. There were punishments if they sought education, as some scholars and priests did, in foreign countries. Over time, people, Catholics on the rise, tolerant Protestants, had come to ignore some of the worst: such that Catholics were forbidden to exercise trade or commerce, could not legally hold leases of land for more than a few years, and were disqualified from inheriting the lands of Protestant relatives.

Most interestingly, John complained, a Catholic citizen could not then legally own a horse of greater value than five pounds, and if he did and yet pretended that his horse was worth less than that, a Protestant gentleman could buy it from him for at most that sum, un-horsing the Papist idolater, vaulting into the saddle in his place and riding away with a prime mount. The laws had also decreed that a Catholic child who turned Protestant could sue his parents for maintenance, at a level to be determined by the Protestant-governed Court of Chancery.

How far from the Nazarene, the shoeless Christ, was all this? asked John Mitchel.

It was to abolish these inequities that the Emancipation laws were supported in Britain by fair people – and perhaps by some who took the Duke of Wellington's view, that if the Catholics were not emancipated there would be civil war.

It was a matter of great sadness to John, and thus to her, that because Irish peasants – the so-called 'low Irish' – were repelled by a government which, despite Emancipation, in so many remaining ways was unjust and restrictive to them, the Catholic Church and its clergymen remained the sole area within which the millions of voteless and voiceless souls could find their dignity, their place of hope.

Early in Jenny's association with John, her mother was worried that she was 'catching ideas' from him. Jenny did in a sense catch them, but what her parents did not understand was that Jenny found, half-buried in her nature, the same propositions John so powerfully announced. This was the peril of revealed truth, when it entered not only on the tongue of the prophet, but evoked a hidden, a half-suspected twin in the fibre of the listener. Jenny came to pity the Verner family for the antiquity and staleness of their beliefs.

Her father, gentle, and nearing sixty, spoke sometimes of his younger brother as an enviable hero, adjutant of the 7th Queen's Own Hussars, wounded at Waterloo after having fought Napoleon for some years in Spain. As well,

Uncle William was a Member of the Parliament in London. Everyone called him affectionately 'Taffy', like a Welshman – Jenny had no idea why. He lived over in County Armagh at Loughgall and was said to be a good landlord, and there often were such people. Her genial father's opinions were an echo of his distinguished brother's, and when she met John Mitchel, she was ready for a revision. Could Ireland be a just country when five per cent of the people, including her people, owned ninety per cent of the land? That was a good question.

She needed a revision and that was what she got from Mitchel when they all went wading together, in the Newry River or at the head of Carlingford Lough – an exercise banned by Miss Bryden. For example, her father always drank a toast at dinner to the legendary old Battle of the Diamond, at which, on a crossroads in Loughgall, the young Protestant Peep o' Day Boys fought the young Catholic Defenders in some year God smiled on. 1795 to be precise. Papist blood was spilled in buckets, so it was considered a grand opening round to Protestantism and the Protestant genius!

How John Mitchel narrated the same event, though, was somewhat in contrast, and all the blood let at that crossroads brawl was Irish. Shivering a little in the Norwegian current that came by way of Scotland's upper isle, he explained, 'Irish linen had grown to be the finest in Britain, and under the camouflage of religion, Protestants fought Catholic weavers and linen workers in an industry that was being shrunk by Downing Street's design. The Peep o' Day Boys, and the Catholics who suffered at the Diamond crossroads, were equal victims of British policy. And right on cue, hating and maiming each other for the convenience of our rulers. And going to a lot of trouble too to show – by their very mayhem – that the Irish needed to be governed from Westminster.

'The English rejoice every time the Irish fall on each other,' he declared to her as he finally took his boots off, and went wading, long white ankles shining in the dusk in the sea near Warrenpoint – they had wandered as far as that, out on the open lough. Mitchel's skinny ankles seemed part of a new version of man.

In the 1798 uprising, John's father, the Presbyterian minister, had fought with the United Irishmen against her loyal family and their Volunteers, and against the British Army. As a young man, he had given leadership and comfort to the United Irish Croppies, the Papist foot soldiers. The Reverend Mitchel of '98 had sung, '. . . The mountain Glen I'll seek at noon and at the morning early, And join the bold United men while soft wind shakes the barley!'

Meanwhile, the Verners of '98 sang, 'In our green fields from end to end, although it seldom shows, In every field of Ulster soil, the Orange lily grows!'

And the Verners were determined to keep it so.

But as they walked the hillsides, Jenny and Mary were receiving John Mitchel's vivid reimaginings of Ireland – not as a place of rancours and opposition, of blood curses and turned backs, but of reason. Jenny was utterly enchanted and captured.

2

Jenny: Elopement Play, and Marriage, 1836–37

Jenny's tremulous and aging father decided he would move to France for the sake of his health. Indeed, he had congestive lungs, and his heart palpitated. And the Normandy coast was considered the great geographic antidote. But having heard the news from Jenny, John Mitchel, now a young law student in Newry, knew that her loss was one he could not survive. In fighting for her, he was fighting for life itself.

One day on a walk – with Miss Thompson, at Jenny's sly request, dawdling behind – he said to her, 'England is very close, my Jenny. I am countenancing that we go there and be married. That union of spirits! And so we could present our parents with the established fact.'

She liked the prospect of such an established fact as that! It was an extreme and dramatic proposal, but she felt she was profoundly his companion, so plans were laid for the elopement. He would pretend to be off to Dublin, to clerk on a case at the famous Four Courts, but he would double back and wait for her in a carriage at the crossroads near Bridge Street, where the Dublin Road began.

She would leave 52 Queen Street by the front door, and saunter away, not attending Miss Bryden's School that day, it being her last year anyhow, but already a worldly woman with mysterious fish of her own to fry – as she liked to think of it. She would meet John at the bridge, and they would cut away in his cart together across to Carlingford Lough to meet the regular packet to Liverpool. So she would always live amongst ever-enlarging concepts, she believed, and in a world given meaning by what John Mitchel said and she agreed with. She packed for the adventure in the delight of it, pursuing without the help of the maid the secret and ecstatic diligence of stowing the clothes of her escape.

They had quite a gallop to Warrenpoint, and were rowed out over choppy water by a boatman to the Liverpool ship. She thought in an ecstasy, even if you drown us today, Lord, I shall sing in gratitude for eternity. They weren't drowned, in fact, but boarded the packet up the side stairs in the rehearsed identities of one Lieutenant Johnson and his young sister. Quite worn out at the scope of what they had done, Jenny fell asleep in their little cabin while John kept knightly watch from a chair. He had begun reading her some novel by Benjamin Disraeli, *The Young Duke*, a distracting moral tale about people far from her experience in Newry. As he intoned from the page, this tale of a young aristocrat – despite the drama of the day – unexpectedly put her in a drowse amidst all the fevers of her excitement. It was true that their sharing of a cabin, to those who did not understand their purity of intent, would bespeak moral peril and evoke a coming misjudgement by a mean-spirited world. But her reckless mood said that if this escapade were seen as implying and making certain their ultimate marriage, so much the better!

Next morning, they landed in Liverpool at the new Albert Dock, secure in their virtue still. The masts of Liverpool – a world of them – seemed to offer choices to her widening soul. These were dimensions, she knew, made possible to her by the scale of her desire, and she might move into that world of licit frenzy in hours or – at most – days. She knew as well that she had only the most inaccurate information about how such activities would or should play out in reality.

They landed with their modest baggage and ate breakfast in a little private room at a hotel near the new Custom House. And Mitchel told her that by overnight research, which had consisted of a frank discussion with a sympathetic ship's officer, he had found out that Chester was a much better place for wedding licences than Liverpool. They would hire a carriage straight after breakfast to take them there.

During the journey, they made a good show, had anyone seen them, of discussing *The Young Duke*, of all things, the pretensions of which held no relevance to them. But Disraeli was critical of the political enthusiasms and romantic life of aristocrats like Peel and Grey, and so was daring. It seemed, like everything she saw, to relate somehow to her hopes, which seemed larger than universes.

That delightful freezing day as the coach wheels slipped and bucked on frozen ruts, and she sat half-reclined and encompassed in a cloak against John Mitchel's shoulder absorbing the warmth of his blood, it took them an hour and a half to get to Chester. There, in a dim office in the town hall, they filled out the wedding forms, and found couples wanting to wed still had to wait a number of days – five. It was better than in other jurisdictions, but a near-intolerable delay just the same, given the weight of their affections. But they reconciled themselves to patience, and took a warm room in an inn near the cathedral and city wall.

They were still waiting the next morning when Jenny's mother and father arrived with constables from Liverpool. Lieutenant Johnson and his sister had been discovered. Jenny's parents uttered plaints as expected: 'What were you thinking of? Did you think it cute simply to vanish? You let John Mitchel abduct you. And you know that a lady of your background does not marry like a peasant, at sixteen!'

In fact, she was two years over marriageable age, but there was no chance to say that. John broke in with a little speech about his sorrow for this irregularity, grieving that they were distressed – yet he knew they were meant, by all that was holy, for each other. That made no inroads on her parents' frantic state. Jenny could see that they were driven by a sense of the havoc their own marital irregularity had had on their lives, and a fear too that somehow the pattern of their sins or omissions had driven her on this adventure.

There was no denying her mother's sincerity and terror on her behalf, nor the extent to which Jenny hated it, and wanted to cry, 'I don't need to live by your mistakes!'

She was stopped only by the presence of the constables. But now they all fell into banal roles. She wept for John and reached for him, but from respect for her father he did not presume to reach back. John made another little speech about his sorrow for this irregularity, but assured her parents that nothing improper or damaging to her reputation had occurred. 'Will the world believe that?' cried her father. 'You stupid young man!'

Jenny found herself at one stage weeping in her mother's arms like a penitent child, and felt both comfort and bitter disappointment with herself. She was aware this was the wrong place for her, that she was in a sense betraying John. Jenny did not want to be this maiden she was, a schoolgirl howling in her mother's grasp. John Mitchel would probably write her off now, for reverting to apparent childhood like this, and that made her even more disconsolate.

In any case, in short order, the still mysterious nuptial rites and the resultant freedom to be woman-to-man, a freedom she had intended to use vigorously and learn well, had been denied her. And for now, she was too busy arguing with her parents, and with these constables of the Liverpool police establishment, telling them she had been a willing partner to the elopement and that John was not an abductor. Because her father was demanding that John be arrested precisely for that – that was what the police were there for.

It was futile to argue with her father – his fear, his need to make her safe in France or somewhere else. The constables took John away as he yelled that he would see her again. Then, when there were just her mother and father in the hotel room, she became fully their daughter, and as well as mourning her cruelly abridged career as a bride, she felt a faint but treacherous strain of gratitude the episode was closing. In that, she was sure now – as she would later confess guiltily to John – she had betrayed her best hopes in life. For it was not that she was cured of him. Although the arrival of parents had diminished her frenzy, it meant she was offered the chance to be a child once more and to put more months into her growing.

'This cannot happen again, Jenny,' her mother told her, and Jenny thought, 'That is the first outright truth you have uttered.' Elopement, successful or prevented, was a once-in-a-lifetime experience and either succeeded or failed. She could tell that by how extreme and dramatic an experience it had all been.

As her father started fulminating about when he himself was young – that he had needed to be taught and to have the inappropriateness of his actions brought home to him – her mother gently told him he should stop for now. Her mother was less assertive suddenly, less certain, less loud, and more comforting.

To her father Jenny was willing to be sullen. She told him that if John Mitchel were charged with abduction, she would never forgive him for it.

From what her father said, she found out they had been betrayed by a jealous clerk in Neill's law office in Newry, where John worked. Her father had warned the Reverend Mitchel, who had rushed out and tried to intercept his son before he could take her away, but was too late.

After his arrest, John was conveyed back on that night's boat to Ireland in steerage, under the care of two Liverpool police. It was the same ferry her parents and she travelled on. The journey home was drab and full of disillusion, but Jenny decided despite all disappointment to be dry-eyed, since her parents would take tears as guilt. During the stop in Dublin, she was confined in her cabin and did not see John escorted off in handcuffs to be taken to Kilmainham jail on the edge of the city, to await transportation to Armagh. But knowing he was gone, she was determined to be calm and tell her father she should be arrested too then, since she had come across the Irish Sea with John Mitchel by consent, not as a prisoner. She was desolated, though, and would have yearned for a short, deadly fever had she not advanced from her weeping and fragile mood to one of grim determination.

By the time John was on bail and arraigned in Armagh, her father and mother were seeking out a modest rental cottage in Boulogne. Jenny had in the meantime been rushed away from Newry to a favourite aunt's place in the hills of Loughgall. The magistrate who committed John Mitchel to trial, asserted finding that he was of sufficient age to know better than to run away to England with 'a minor' and a 'gentle lady' and 'without the consent and permission of said minor's parents'. He also made a remark that he could not overlook this case, since the young, influenced by reading vulgar novels, in which elopements were common and daring, too often considered it an exciting recourse, and there was a need to make examples. But then, after the severe lecture, he let John out on bail. He had been assailed by references from clergymen and country doctors and even notable landlords as to Mitchel's character, references gathered together in particular by John's formidable mother. These all asserted that Ulster would be shocked if John were to spend undue time imprisoned.

Substantially relieved at being spared a longer term of incarceration, John's thoughts turned immediately to the young woman he adored. An older schoolfriend of his, John Martin, who had trained as a surgeon but was now a farmer in Down, lived not more than a mile or two from Jenny's aunt's, and helped him find the address at which she was a recluse in the countryside.

A young man, powerful in frame but hopeless and bewildered by love, appeared at the door, courtly and polite. He was told by the maid that Miss Jenny Verner was not there. Ah, he asked, but was she sometimes there?

Jenny heard from upstairs everything he said to the maid. 'Madame, I know you are merely being loyal in saying that, and following your mistress's orders. But I happen to know infallibly that Miss Verner is under this roof, and I wonder could you be so kind as to fetch your mistress so that I might be able to commence matters from that known fact.'

He sounded so respectful and so official she went and got Jenny's aunt. When her aunt arrived, Jenny heard him tell her, 'Madame, I am a worm in your estimation. I am the John Mitchel of whom you have heard. I would understand if you whipped me away from the door. But I beg you not to do that, since I am here only in the role of supplicant to ask you if I could, under proper conditions and supervision, glimpse Miss Jenny Verner whom I adore and cherish. I was involved in a poorly considered adventure with Miss Verner which ended sadly for her through my thoughtlessness. And being at this door, Madame, I must say, under the risk of my being sent hence, that I see the fine Verner features undiminished in your own face, and glowing – as in a however irrational reassurance that yes, indeed, you may consider my plea.'

So he went on addressing her with his level and reverent respect, as he did everyone. Jenny's aunt had imagined a black-souled rogue and not this polite, palavering boy who John the prophet was now, transmuted into John the parlour-room charmer.

Accordingly, and to John's exaltation, she allowed a brief chaperoned meeting in a parlour. Another day, binding John Mitchel on his honour, Jenny demanding to be put on her honour too, the aunt walked with the young pair and listened to all they said, and found it sufficiently tame so that next time, she let the two of them walk ahead. It was a poetic winter's day, the air severe and biting, but sunlight playing games on the hillsides, dodging between hurtling clouds. The massed clear purple of the Mourne Mountains' flanks and their snow-speckled summits hung above their path, then would become wrapped in vapour, and they were both given to loving such manifestations.

Jenny's fear that John Mitchel considered her childish had obviously not been realised. 'I will ask your father,' he told her, 'and if he decides that on balance I can have your hand, there will be a marriage and the little business of elopement can be forgotten. And the trial will die – though that is not a motive for my searching you out. Your splendour is entirely my motive. I am not driven by fear of prison. I am driven by a desperation to join your life to mine.'

Jenny had, since hidden in the hills, felt fevers and dreams even more intensely than before. She had been told by class-mates that these were the kind of frenzies that Papist girls were required to confess to priests, even though they barely had the language to describe what had overcome them. Not for the first time, she was relieved to be a member of the Established Church of Ireland.

———

Jenny discovered that when John had first been brought to Armagh by the police, his own father thought it a lesson that would cure him of his unruly ardours. The Reverend Dr Mitchel always believed John had too much passion, in an Italian rather than a Scottish-Irish and Presbyterian vein. His mother, though, and John himself told Jenny this, was angry at her husband's idea that her boy needed to be taught a lesson in public court. His mother and his young sisters loved John as fiercely as child or brother could be loved. And it was true that, at the same time, Reverend Mitchel's flock were more frightened of Mrs Mitchel than they were of him.

But over such divisions ran the question, now renewed. 'After an abduction, who will marry her?' For now the matter was compounded. And the practical knowledge came to Jenny's parents that if there were a trial in which her abduction was dramatised, she too would be its victim. For every man attracted by the trace of a romantic story, there would be three suitors repelled by it, especially the sort of men to whom marriage was a half-step up, a compact for which they need make no apologies.

There was a problem in that Jenny's uncle, Sir William, Tory member of the House of Commons for Armagh, disliked the whole business, and told his brother so. A woman, however shakily, bearing the Verner name going to be married in a non-subscribing Presbyterian Church! Sir William believed that, even though a lot of decent Loyalist people attended Reverend Dr John Mitchel's church, and swore by its pastor's intelligence and compassion, the Presbyterians were a suspect branch of Christianity.

Sir William would have considered the Reverend Mitchel did not instruct his worshippers as to what to believe, but raised issues created by Scripture, and suggested possibilities. He was not a source of certainty, as were the parsons in the Church of Ireland, but a fellow pilgrim – and in his own humble mind, no more than half a step ahead of his congregation in his search for the meaning of the divine. As well as that, the unassuming but scholarly Dr Mitchel, like many middle-class Presbyterians, had in his remote youth been a United Irishman and transported weapons by wagon for the rebels of 1798. Any marriage Jenny underwent to a Mitchel, said her uncle, should at least be conducted in the Church of Ireland!

So it was all at once settled. John had been to see Captain Verner, *de jure* and by intense affection Jenny's father, and had impressed him with his chastened tone and sincerity and repentance. The business of who would marry Jenny, that cosmic question which had beset her family, need no longer be asked. She came home from her aunt's, and she and her mother planned the wedding, an enterprise in which they flourished together. It was to take place at Drumcree in County Armagh, at the Church of Ireland's Ascension Church, just over the county border from Down.

And so John and Jenny, at the end of weeks of disturbed and unsettled desire, in icy February of 1837, took each other's hands in a town known for its conflicts and contradictions, Orange and Catholic, pledging their love in a shire of hatreds. *And* in a church which was then being rebuilt, so that the marriage actually took place before the Reverend Babington in the porch, which satisfied her parents that it had been celebrated with the proper rites, even as John's unjealous Reverend Mitchel stood by smiling. Only his mother frowned.

3

Early Marriage, Jenny
and John Mitchel

They lived in the early years of their marriage in the Drumalane townland of Newry in the house of the Mitchels. The Reverend Mitchel had visitors all day in his study, but John's mother would collect him for his meals. It was from his mother, Mary Haslett, that John seemed to get his force of character. 'Now, my good man,' or 'Now, my good woman,' she would say to any dallying visitor, 'Dr Mitchel must have regular meals to be fit to confront you and be of use, so you will now excuse himself for the duration of his luncheon!'

If they wished to wait, she would send them to a little lobby until her husband was ready to resume his dialogue with them. Her opinion was that many who came to drink at the wells of the Reverend Dr Mitchel's wisdom had too much time and could think of nothing better than wasting it in the shadow of an eminent thinker.

The Mitchel women, mother and Matilda, Margaret, Henrietta and Mary Jane, were very lively girls, also with not quite enough to fill their time, who exercised their chief enthusiasm for the Mitchel men, and the little brother William. They saw their task as being to keep John and his father, both given to ardours and enthusiasms, tethered to the demands of the earth, and to cosset little William, who seemed a puzzled and puzzling little boy, always drawing diagrams of imaginary machines.

Jenny's instinct told her at once that Mrs Mitchel would be happiest if Jenny lost herself amongst the four daughters. The eldest, Matilda, was two years younger than John, and thought he was the cleverest man ever born and the most charming. His bouts of crippling asthma, which would alarm Jenny, made not a dent in his repute with his sisters.

Once married, Jenny could have fitted into their community, if she chose – like five girls at school under an affectionate but unchallenged headmistress. But Jenny felt that if she did this, blended herself in, she might as well have stayed at Miss Bryden's. For she had an honour they did not – she was Mrs Mitchel the younger. She was not their peer, she was the peer of the daunting and original Mrs Mitchel. And since John had done her the honour of marrying her, she had a duty to assert her status.

One evening John had one of his alarming asthma attacks. He considered the condition a personal enemy, a household demon with a name. He had been suffering it since childhood, although he had surrendered most of his childhood imperfections, she had hoped, by marriage. It was under Mrs Mitchel's authority that Friar's Balsam was mixed with boiling water by the old housemaid Hannah to ease John's breathing. But when Mrs Mitchel reached the kitchen to prepare it, she found Jenny already there, working with

Hannah, the water nearly boiled, balsam standing by for mixing.

'Oh, Jenny,' said Mrs Mitchel, testing the limits of archness as she did with the visitors to Dr Mitchel, 'I am pleased to see that you feel yourself confident enough in my kitchen.'

'Thank you, mother,' said Jenny, addressing her as Mrs Mitchel had invited her to do since the marriage. 'I am preparing a respiration for my John.'

'Well, I shall do that,' she replied, stepping forward in a clearing-the-decks way, as if making Jenny irrelevant to the scene. But there was a bigger issue than the etiquette of kitchens.

'No, mother,' Jenny told her as pleasantly and emphatically as she could. 'It is my duty to do this. I am his wife.'

'As you wish,' she sighed, and glanced at her daughters, beginning to take the reordering of the pantry as a tribute to the status of the young wife. Although accustomed to command, she was a good woman and Jenny found from that day she honoured her authority as that of John's spouse.

Balsam inhalations were the limited measure of remedies when it came to asthma, and Jenny was now the asthma mistress. The balsam was comforting but all too ineffectual. It was, however, the sole succour she could offer Johnny, and as well as that the two women understood each other.

———

While John had his father's probity, he also had his mother's force of character. These two tributaries ran together: fire and honour; intensity and intelligence. Jenny could not imagine living a thousand times over and not on each iteration marrying John Mitchel.

After a year passed and spring of 1838 came, Jenny was showing a child and they took their own cottage in Newry. A little boy was born and named John Charles; and John himself, suddenly John the elder, was admitted to the provincial board of solicitors. Neill the lawyer, of senior years in the practice when John had been a clerk, now depended on him to do a lot of drudge but well-paid work in courts from Belfast down to the Four Courts of Dublin. The routines of family absorbed them. Jenny conceived what proved to be a second boy.

When they had two sons, rugged little fellows John C. and Jamie, John the elder went into practice with a man named Sam Fraser, a member of the congregation of the Reverend Mitchel. Fraser was a lively fellow, a sort of progressive Orangeman, willing to advance the status of Protestants but not at the expense of breaking Paddy skulls.

A lot of John's work had to do with broken Paddy skulls. After assaults or quarrels, Catholics sought the services of Fraser and Mitchel, because they were not ferocious haters of Papists.

Jenny was fascinated by how lively were the Reverend Mitchel's non-subscribing Presbyterians – the parties and debating nights, and dinners and the dancing. In all this she was an accomplice with John's lively sister, Matilda. And the long arguments raged as ever about what is an Irishman, the most vexed question in the world if one were born in Ulster, with power on the Orange side which still left Protestants feeling besieged, and strangely homeless, and exposed to attack.

John's abiding friend remained John Martin. Jenny came to rely on his uncomplicated and immense loyalty and would come to need his friendship too. He was a reserved young man, lank-haired and old for his years. John had first met this careful and sober-minded boy at Dr Henderson's Academy in Newry, and Martin was a surgeon now. He had never practised medicine, but preferred to live on an ancestral farm at Loughorne, just five miles away from the Mitchels.

It was in some ways an unlikely friendship, given John Mitchel's capacity for large gestures, and all the more piquant for that. And though they found plenty to argue about, from philosophy to political economy and the merits of Dickens and Carlyle – John being ardent for Carlyle and not so keen on Dickens – the story of their lives, Jenny and John Mitchel's, would be bound up with the surgeon-farmer Martin. He was a bachelor, and the ambition to be a paterfamilias, a prophet of the hearth, did not seem to be written into his nature, as it was so plainly into her Johnny's.

In those years before John became a figure known to the public, he would show her his letters to friends like John Martin, or else read them himself with ironic inflections. For some reason he was grateful for her approbation, or wanted what he thought were the most pungent bits to be read back to him, and Jenny loved that he was so boyishly vain of his wit. Why he, a graduate of Trinity and a lawyer, should seek the approval of a schoolgirl, she did not know. But he would always be proud and vain about it.

When one had children in quick succession in a young marriage, the woman's attention was to the multiple demands of their young lives, and nature seemed to place the mother into a state of vacant brainless devotion. In the fifth year of marriage, when a girl named Henrietta was born, Jenny decided that nature transformed the woman from temptress to matriarch, and now time and energy had to be found for shared letters and the grace notes of serious prose.

That being so, as much as John *needed* her applause in that time, Jenny felt pleased and elevated to give it. If she was sometimes tired and petulantly delayed reading the letters, that was a rare occurrence. She did not like petulance to start with, and did not forgive her tendency towards it very readily. She believed it was a small, unworthy force. She would sometimes simply set her three little beasts – serious Johnny, who had a tendency to police his younger brother Jamie and the non-walking infant Henrietta – on the maid, and consign them to the nursery so that she could read John's essay-style letters and Carlyle's *Sartor Resartus*, which Johnny the elder and John Martin both made much of. She believed that one fine book, well-studied, was itself a form of education.

She would always remember the artful letter Johnny wrote to John Martin. Martin, with much time on his hands, had said he thought he might register the Martin family arms. Now there were Martens and Martinos everywhere on earth with abundant coats of arms, but he seemed to be seeking a special one for the Martins of Down, and John was willing to mock the solemnity of that process.

'Are you preparing to register your arms at the Newry Sessions? Have you provided witnesses to satisfy the justices of your loyalty? Do you stand well with the police? And do you have any personal enemies amongst the magistrates? And what are your attitudes towards firm oats and dead pigs? Watch how you answer!'

But for John Mitchel, even as a then private man, everything came back to the state of the Union between Ireland

and the rest of Britain. In those days, Lord Devon, whose chief qualification seemed to be that he'd married a young woman from Limerick, was sent to Ireland to enquire into the way land was held there. As John wrote to Martin, his view was that Lord Devon should just write one word in his report, the adverb, 'precariously'; as in, 'the mass of Irish smallholders occupy their land *precariously*'.

'But seriously, Mr Martin,' the letter from Mitchel to Martin continued, 'what do you think of Lord Devon's commission? A commission into an enquiry into a speculation into an Irish poverty that of course must be the peasant's fault if in fact it exists? It is the sort of thing government calls when the facts stare them in the face and embarrass them to put aside pressure for change, and to weaken and divide popular feeling; and then, then – ah, the statesmen are all liars and will go to hell! – then to put the people off with a sham of relief, with the minimum of justice and the maximum of statesmanship . . . But if I run on any longer, I might get intemperate in my language.

'I can enlighten Lord Devon in a sentence. The land system in Ireland is a method of control, a badge of conquest, and a means of holding millions in subjection. I fear that that is not the end of the beast that Lord Devon will choose to inspect. He is all a hoax and a cod!'

———

John did not always like the law, particularly of land tenure, as it was handed down by the court. But there was more protection for the tenant in Ulster than elsewhere, especially if a Catholic tenant was not involved – the jury was almost bound by Protestant solidarity to find against him.

34

John was good at arranging settlements between landlords and farmers of middling or small size whose tenancy had been cancelled for non-payment of rent or other issues.

In Ulster the tenant was entitled to be paid off for any improvements, barns or fences or stables, he had made to the land, as well as for the good repute he had built in the neighbourhood – what lawyers called 'good will'.

In Leinster, Munster or Connacht, the other ancient kingdoms of Ireland, millions existed on ancient leases named conacre – a small rented strip, perhaps a quarter of an acre – and rundale – the right to farm a strip of land on the common ground – and could be thrown off their land at will without legal recourse, even if the peasant could have afforded rent and improvements. The rent was on the onerous side, particularly for those poor tenants all over the country whose landlords were absent in London or France or northern Italy, and needed to soak the small farmer so they could continue themselves to live in uphol-stered idleness. Agents and middlemen ran things in Ireland for these self-exiled souls.

Much of John's clientele, though not all, were small Catholic landholders, and when they went to court he was prosecuting for them, or defending them, in front of Orange judges, and nearly invariably top to bottom Orange juries, despite the fact that Catholics were eligible now for juries. Given his popularity with lesser landholders gener-ally, John was frequently in the saddle riding around Down and Armagh to quarter sessions and assizes.

Fraser, his boss after Neill, had suggested they open the law office in Banbridge, the big town in the north-east of Down. Jenny and John and the children moved off to live in a pleasant little cottage, with some acres as well in which to grow oats and hay. From Newry to Banbridge was fourteen miles, but John C., the elder boy, was impressed enough on the way to ask was Banbridge at the end of the world. They all laughed, unconscious as yet of what huge mileages would come to govern all their lives.

In Banbridge as earlier in Newry, John was such a good advocate for the small farmers, most of them Catholic, that the word got around that he was a secret Papist and no longer a son of Presbyterianism. How prosperous they would have ended had he stuck to the law! But when law is not even, it challenges the practitioner. Indeed, it challenged John Mitchel. It demanded commentary from him.

———

Daniel O'Connell, the Liberator, was a demigod of the Mitchels. As Jenny described it in later years, he 'worked and devoted all energy to bringing about the Emancipation of Catholics in 1829. Then, supported by the pennies of the peasantry, he aimed at the peaceful repeal of the Union between England and Ireland, and thus self-government for Ireland'.

The Liberator was a sturdy bear of a man to begin with, and a landlord, a rare Catholic one, from Kerry, the other end of the country. It was interesting how, as ancestral Catholics, the O'Connells had been able to keep their land in Derrynane. They did it through Protestant trustees, who would have been rewarded for betraying them, but never did. Only if you were trusted by the local community could you get away with using English law to defeat the Penal Law.

In 1828, he embarrassed the government by being elected to Parliament by Kerry smallholders, being unable to take his seat because he was a Catholic. After Emancipation, he was elected to a seat in Clare and became the first Papist to take a seat in the Commons since the Reformation! He led in the Commons a group of representatives named the Irish Party. Those who belonged to the party swore that they would not be corrupted by offers of places in the cabinet and by other British privileges, but campaign ruthlessly for Ireland's interest and for the peaceful separation of Ireland, and the reintroduction of its own parliament.

Since those belonging to that party had to give up many profitable pursuits to sit in Parliament in London, the Repeal Association – of which John and Jenny had become members in Newry – raised money to keep itself viable and to keep its members in Westminster. There were Repeal Wardens in every Catholic parish, who collected the pennies of farmers who believed in supporting Repeal and the Irish Party.

John Mitchel was a member of a committee which had brought the Liberator up to Newry to address a public dinner. As at these sorts of subscription events, the men sat at table, observed by women on a balcony, and from her balcony Jenny saw O'Connell charm the locals with his big, eloquent, fervent features. In his speech he had a gift for impressing his deepest feeling in each listening supporter, as he mentioned those amongst the Whigs and the Radicals who supported the concept of self-rule for the Irish. He carried with him a convincing belief that the British could not resist the numbers he could peaceably gather, the very scale of those who supported him, or, above all, the weight of his reason.

Through O'Connell, a Catholic middle class were now allowed to be full members of the bar and serve on juries, to attend schools and universities and even hold commissions in the Army. At a humbler level the Liberator's reforms moved in the Commons permitted freedom of religion and let Catholics be fully educated.

The reality of this Emancipation had not been quite as golden for Irish of the poorer farmer and labourer orders. But in the minds of the Orangemen it remained a calamitous mistake for the British government ever to have liberated the Papists from the laws that had kept them down – and a lot of the old boundaries still existed in practice.

Yet there was something in their enthusiasm for the Liberator's program which created doubts in the Mitchels. Jenny thought she saw even then in Daniel O'Connell, the *shoneen*, the up-jumped squire, of the kind he himself sometimes pilloried on the platform. He had that smooth complexion of a man who had a certain number of government posts to distribute amongst his followers, permitted to do so as long as he and they did not break the peace by open rebellion.

And, indeed, the Liberator asserted he would never encourage them to break the peace. He believed that he would achieve a separate Irish parliament by mere moral force of politics. Such was his charm that none asked what sort of politics, applied on their own, would make Downing Street give up Ireland when they didn't have to? The Irish thought the world could be defeated by rhetoric and song, even though no great power has ever yielded to such things. But if they ever were to yield, it would be to the charm and eloquence and pungency and influence of a man like this! The Liberator!

Now, John Mitchel began to visit the headquarters of Repeal at the old Corn Exchange – Conciliation Hall as it was now called – whenever he was in Dublin on a case where he was instructing barristers. He spoke admiringly of a young woman named Jane Elgee he had met there. She was the sort of figure men called a 'bluestocking', as they did of women who had an interest in ideas and literature and reform. Jenny watched Miss Elgee, feeling a little envious of her for being a woman who could command her own time. Miss Elgee compounded all her other gifts by being able to speak German, and had translated an enormously popular novel about a courtesan who took revenge on the men who used her.

A considerable deal of what John did at this time was to represent this and that Catholic middling farmer and argue he owned enough freehold to be able to vote. He sat through a session at Downpatrick where the judge cavilled and haggled over title deeds, and cross-examined and brow-beat a string of Catholics who had, by their own talents, acquired and worked their freehold land, and deserved to be enrolled for elections. The fantastical processes of all this, the number of grounds the Crown could find to deny men the vote, made John's brain itch. His idea of Themis, the blindfolded goddess of justice, now was that she plagued his mental balance as severely as the asthma daemon, and was a thoroughly sinister and cynical daughter of the gods.

'You have never seen her as I have,' he told his sister Matilda, John Martin and Jenny, 'loading her dice, poison-ing her sword, setting up her table of hunt-the-pea, at Newcastle and Downpatrick.'

In the midst of court, he told Jenny once, he had a vision of the silent glens that lay beneath Slieve Donard and had a positive frenzy to be there – instead of at the courthouse – to the point he had to ask the court for a recess. He was clearly suffering a panic at the extent to which the man-contrived law departed from the laws of the wind, the rock, the rain and the sun. For the sun shone nowhere, he said, in the hearts of the hard men of the bench.

Mitchel was by everyone's account an excellent instructing solicitor and brought the high seriousness to the law that he brought to all human issues. But because the better-off Catholics came to him with grievances, he brought to the question of juries and jury-fixing the same intense and sometimes morbid attention he gave to Irish history. Not that all his clients were Catholics, and only the most severe Orangemen Protestants avoided him. Though there were a myriad of them.

When he rode off to local courts in Dromara or Ballina-hinch, he would sometimes have a pleasant surprise. If his client were a Catholic merchant dealing with a disputed bill, or a Catholic middling farmer in dispute over boundaries, he came up against juries which did have their occasional just men or their occasional Catholic member. Thus, John's client might win in the courts of Down or Armagh or Belfast or Dublin. For some men could be Protestants, Orangemen and Freemasons, and be broad in perspective and pen to all reason – many of John's friends were, and considered themselves true Irishmen too. Some Orangemen's chief and reasonable concern was they did not choose to be ruled by the Catholic Church, as neither did John himself.

There was a notable case when after an Orange march in Drumcree over in Armagh – Drumcree where John and Jenny had been married in the lobby of the new Church of Ireland – three young Orangemen, who had taken some

40

liquor, called at a Catholic house and one of them threw a stone through the window. If it had ended there! An elderly woman came out, calling down a divine curse upon them in the old Gaelic tongue and smacking them with a broom. A son of the woman emerged from one of the sheds and saw them seize the broom from her, then witnessed one of them picking up a segment of log and throwing it at her, at which she fell to the ground.

After a further exchange of curses, and the Catholic young man chasing them off with a peat shovel, it was found the old lady had died – possibly not from the blow itself but from some fit produced by it. John represented the woman's son, in the case for wrongful death he brought against the assailants. Two of the young Orangemen were found guilty and were in this case sentenced to transportation to Australia for fourteen years. Such were the occasional victories of John Mitchel. Had it been Catholic boys who had in their reckless-ness killed a Protestant grandmother, they would have been hanged, but for the moment some justice was justice enough. After that, though, the undue nickname 'Papist Mitchel' was more generally used, he believed, than ever before.

'But the point is . . .' he argued, coming home one evening to a dutifully cleaned house, all trace of the day's mayhem cleared away for his entry, and he not noticing anyway, '. . . the point is, Jenny, that if Catholics were allowed full justice and fair juries, that will weaken the hold of the Catholic Church on them.'

'Because they would have more trust in the state?' Jenny suggested, nimble as she could be.

'Exactly,' he told her, eyes glittering. 'Exactly! The Orange Order could undermine the very thing they hate by mere democracy. They don't see, our fellow Protestants . . .

every denial of justice, every death like the old lady's of Drumcree, binds those people closer to the Catholic Church. For they still can't look to the state for justice!'

'But Ulster was never a place for calm reason,' she asserted, because it was true.

'No. Reason is reserved for some hearths, or on some private walk on hilltops, or in private drinking sessions. But no-one seems to want to win by subtlety. Everyone wants to win by a ferocious blow to the head!'

Jenny was willing to abandon all reason herself, though, when young Johnny C. caught typhoid in Banbridge. The doctors who visited him and inspected his rash of rose-coloured spots and saw his paroxysms of stomach pain and delirium gave her little hope he would survive. She was not a woman of ideas anymore, not calm as she tore out her pantry, looking for a food that may have caused it, dispensing with items on suspicion. The maid and Jenny boiled water in great quantities, and would not let the other children drink and bathe in water that they had not prepared. As far as Jenny was concerned, the arts and politics could die that week, and justice could languish eternally as long as little John C. went on breathing. She was prepared to sacrifice all the credit of being able to hold conversations with her husband for young John C.'s frightened eyes to be appeased.

But he came through. He was so sturdy a little boy, although he thought he was not and begged pitiably for relief when the fever was at its height. And the games of humans, the hungers for affection, resumed when James, the second son, was soon enough asking, which one of us do you love more? For he could tell, and his mother could not say, that there was something about the oldest child, something novel and compelling, something lacking in the rote raising of second and third children.

Her own father was in less than good health in Boulogne, despite the good the Normandy coast was meant to do him. But in fact John's father died first, a man to the end ferocious for ideas but gentle in his dealings – John and his mother tending towards ferocity in both quarters, and not least in the duties they placed upon themselves. But all the duty Mrs Mitchel could muster, all the regulation of visitors, and the boilings in her own kitchen and all the rest, went for nothing when her husband fell down from apoplexy at the end of the winter of 1840, and died within a fortnight. The celebrated Reverend Dr Mitchel was – with a frightful suddenness – gone from the earth.

John was in a pitiable state of loss and remorse when his father died. It wasn't in his nature to be reconciled. 'I've given my poor father more grief than all the sisters and young William combined,' he told Jenny. John Martin in turn told Jenny that when Johnny took him into the parlour where the old man lay encoffined, he said, 'I put more grey hairs on that fine head than anyone else on earth.'

There was no casual affection in John Mitchel, and Jenny could not complain of that. But her husband became nearly a lunatic now from spasms of guilt. As parishioners lined up in the Drumalane hallway and even down the steps to make a last visit to the Rev Dr Mitchel, John himself, with stricken eyes, could barely restrain himself from telling all of them what a bad son he had been.

One parishioner mentioned how brown the dead man's hair still was. And John answered, 'It's a wonder, because I was bad enough a child to make him grey.' He spoke a great deal to his sisters – Matilda and the others – about how he should have stuck to the banking and about how ridiculous he had been about a certain girl from Belfast. How he had sunk then into a self-regarding decline, when all along God knew, and his father sensed, that someone yet to be met was awaiting him.

Jenny was concerned he might make a further spectacle of himself at the funeral and told him, 'Now, Mr Mitchel, your father told us all he had a happy life, and do you think he was lying? Are you really accusing your father of being a liar in his saying, just the Sabbath before his death, how delighted he was with the life he had led?'

Of course, John denied that his father would lie.

'Then why do you wish to take the grief we all feel for him and make it an issue of what sort of son you are? You have two sons of your own. Your task now is to be a father.'

Whenever he went to speak, no doubt to reiterate what a frightful child he had been, Jenny held her hand up. 'No, Mr John Mitchel, whatever kind of child you were, your task is as a father now. Make sure you are a splendid father, for I don't want you moaning in old age that you failed at that too!'

He looked dismal as if he were about to fall into terminal mopes. But then he brightened, and set his shoulders to the new task, even offering to feed young recuperating John C. his custard and prunes.

John himself was not reconciled to his father's death, as much as swept on from it by events.

4

A Further Account of the Mitchels, 1843

The transformation of John Mitchel from lawyer to writer and revolutionary was not much delayed by his father's death, as intensely as he mourned it. It was put in progress by a newspaper, *The Nation*, begun by Welsh-Irish songwriter and lawyer Thomas Davis and by an Ulster shopkeeper's son, Charles Gavan Duffy. Both men were members of the Liberator's Repeal Association. While on a case in Dublin, Mitchel had met Davis, a young barrister who lived in Baggot Street and who wrote journalism and verse for the paper that would become home, meat and bread for John and for his family. John himself, in writing for this newspaper, became a rebel.

In Banbridge, Jenny was aware of the two-edged business of marriage: how a man who did not look at other women could be considered a drone of a fellow, but at the same time how dangerous a tendency he might harbour. *The Nation*, she thought, was like another woman. Sometimes he would read it to her even when she was too tired to take it in. He thought that that was only generosity, that Jenny could not live another day without being informed by it. He had submitted some reviews to Duffy, on the work of Carlyle, and one had been published!

One thing John Mitchel brought to his engagement as reader and occasional writer for *The Nation* was, again, how Westminster would be persuaded to give up the grand convenience of its power over Ireland on a voluntary basis, and on the strength of the eloquent speeches of Daniel O'Connell and the less eloquent ones of his followers. The Liberator had begun to speak to huge outdoor meetings about the rights and dignity of the Irish and how the Union with England maimed the country, and in answer the British Parliament could think of nothing but strengthening the garrison of Ireland by 20,000 men, all of whom, said the Orange papers John mocked, were 'Protestant regiments'. So much for Irish independence by persuasion! 'Loud seditious rhetoric on our side,' said John in the notes he was keeping for possible later use in *Nation* articles, 'and fixed bayonets on the other.'

He told Jenny about seeing at the Dublin Corn Exchange the main contributors to *The Nation* when a court case took him to that city. And then gradually he got to know his journalistic heroes. At Duffy's table he met John Blake Dillon and an extraordinary young man, dressed in the height of fashion, his talk graced with elements of wit and freshness, Thomas Meagher. But – and this is where a taint of Mitchel's fraternal envy came in – while Meagher still had some of the florid look of a schoolboy, his cheeks still round, he could rouse a room with two sentences.

'Surely not?' Jenny teased him. 'Wasn't he educated by the Jesuits?'

'Not that,' John relented in humour. 'But I tell you, I envy his speaking. My God, he is thirteen years younger than me. Now he might have been too long with the Jesuits in Stonyhurst and sounds more Lancashire than Irish. It doesn't matter. When he decides to speak, he enchants people.'

Thomas Francis Meagher's father was the sort of Catholic merchant one found in the big towns. He had spent his early years in St John's, Newfoundland, where he had built a fortune in shipping. Returning to Waterford to run a trade between Waterford and St John's, he lost his wife when Thomas was only three years old. She perished giving birth to twins, one of whom died immediately with her, the other in infancy. Now he was a widower and lived in a big house on the Waterford docks, served on the corporation of Waterford and had been its mayor.

His son, Tom, a mercurial and gifted boy, had received a double dose of Jesuits instead of going to Trinity College, since Mayor Meagher believed the only Catholics who received academic honours at Trinity were those who gave up their faith.

These days young Tom was supposed to be studying for the Bar but was better at attending the dinners of the Dublin Inns of Court than he was at learning law from observing a senior silk at the Four Courts. In this he was in no way enviable. Given the same chance, Mitchel would have been exemplary and a gift to the Irish Bar. Meagher spent his days working for Repeal.

When John said the young Thomas Francis Meagher was half in love with Miss Elgee, Jenny did wonder if John was part infatuated himself. 'She has big bones and moves like a galleon,' he said. 'Dressed in a rainbow of colourful cloth, like a grand conveyance decked out for a holiday.'

Was she thinking of Meagher when she published the poem signed 'Speranza', not plain old Miss Elgee, in *The Nation*'s pages:

New energies, from higher source,
Must make the strong life-currents flow,
As alpine glaciers in their course
Are the deep torrents 'neath the snow.
The woman's voice dies in the strife
Of liberty's awakening life;
We wait the hero heart to lead,
The hero, who can guide at need,
And strike with bolder, stronger hand,
Though towering hosts his path withstand.
Thy golden harp,
Loved Ireland!

It was not verse like Shelley's, nor did it compel one to an utterly new vision. But thousands loved her striving poetry and the way she took her lyric observation not of the stars but of all the griefs of the Irish. She came from a notable Protestant family in Wexford and had a dour solicitor for a father, but was a free and ardent soul. And she spoke German.

Her poems had been signed 'Speranza' when they first began to arrive at the offices of *The Nation*, and were written on note paper with the motto *Fidanza, Speranza, Constanza*. The covering letter was signed by one John Fanshawe Ellis. John Fanshawe Ellis/Jane Francesca Elgee, you see. She was trying to prevent her family from discovering she was far from being a loyalist of Empire. Duffy had written many requests for a meeting with Mr Ellis in his *Answers to Correspondence* section of *The Nation*. John Fanshawe Ellis

48

ultimately replied, Duffy went to the address and was astonished to encounter not some young male prodigy but the
magnificent Speranza. Jane Elgee herself.

Even though her pseudonym became an open secret now,
her radical verse did not cause her to be charged with sedition,
since she went to Dublin Castle regularly and gave a talking
to to the Lord Lieutenant, supreme in Ireland, the appointee
of Downing Street, Lord Heytesbury, about the condition of
Ireland, the uncertainty of Irish tenancies, and the need for
public education. The authorities chose to be amused by this
statuesque chastiser and decided she was their pet radical.
She complained to John and to Meagher about this unfortunate position, and wanted to show them one day that she
was dangerous enough to be punished in the end. She was a
patriot to Ireland when all her class were patriots to Britain.

Mitchel was fascinated that she had caught the same
Hibernian fury he carried in him. And a terrible thing to
be visited by such a passion as she had, and then when you
spoke of Ireland, of the ridiculous courts, of the encumbered estates under landlords who lived in France and Italy,
and how something must be done, you would then run the
risk of being patronised by others as an amusing arguer for
a new system.

———

When Mitchel sat with them all one evening in Down, Tom
Meagher, the young orator and dandy, had some useful and
illuminating advice for Mitchel, advice he said he had earlier
in the night passed on to Speranza as well. 'I had to ask
her, dear woman,' young Meagher admitted, 'to moderate her
tone towards the average Briton.' He believed that the time

he spent studying with the Jesuits at Stonyhurst in Lancashire had made him an expert on the life of the average Briton, and certainly he believed he had done comparative study into the lives of the English farmworker in the villages around the college, and then into the lives of the Irish peasant.

'You mustn't think that it is merry England over there,' he advised. 'We have, for example, the Whiteboys anti-landlord protesters, ordinary men creating societies to help them hang onto their small tracts of land, and they are transported to Australia for their protests. The British have what are called Swing rioters who have equal grievances against the squire, against his lordliness and his power and his rents. And the Swing protesters too are transported!'

When the farm labourers young Meagher had spoken to from around Clitheroe and Hurst Green, villages near his Lancashire college, attempted to form a sick benefits club for labourers, it was deemed a secret society, and its organiser, a young farm labourer of twenty-four years, a fellow of no ordinary talent, was transported to Australia.

In the village churches, the wives of farm labourers had to go to the front pews to curtsy to the squire's wife and then the parson's, and it was no wonder that dissenters attracted people to meetings in laneways where the service of Christ did not require any bowing or scraping. The Corn Laws designed to keep out cheap European grain, and allowing squires and merchants to profit from high prices, was a constant complaint of the labouring families, a complaint never listened to when uttered individually, or en masse by the Swing rioters, who could also, predictably, be arrested and sent to jail or Australia. The teachers who ran the village schools in Lancashire, said Meagher, were not as clever as the hedge schoolmasters in Ireland, who gave unofficial and sometimes outdoor classes to children. For British farm children were taught as much of the world as they needed for farm labouring, but not enough to give them an appetite for knowledge. In their world the squire tyrannised over the farmers, and the farmers over the labourers.

'And so the labourer's son joins the Grenadiers or the Hussars,' said Meagher. 'Should he because of that be considered as the essence of evil, in himself?'

'Not at the point of recruitment,' John admitted.

'And his officers might tell him that with his smart livery he is part of the majesty of Empire and commit him to charge Irish peasants, who wish to put themselves outside that glorious thing.'

'What a deplorable state of affairs!' Mitchel could not help remarking, a little stupefied.

'Yet it has always been the way of the world,' handsome Meagher assured the company. 'It is deplorable, as you say. In this world the poor are set to punish the poor. And I know you do not hate the poor, John Mitchel.'

'Yet were there a battle?'

'Yes, were there a battle . . . one has to fight. And yet at the end of everything it is not the grenadier from the laneways of the Hurst Wood we hate. It is the mechanism, the machine. If we abominate the English farm labourer along with the great mechanism of Westminster or Downing Street, then we are playing Downing Street's game . . .'

They were all absorbed, all three, by the force of that truth. Mitchel asked, 'What did Speranza say when you told her this?'

'She said, "All true, Mr Meagher, but I do not have the space to mourn the English farmworker. It is the Irish farmworker that is my brother."'

For some reason they laughed at this – it sounded like Speranza. But unless she were bluffing him, Meagher's point penetrated Mitchel more thoroughly than it had that particular dazzling maiden. And sometimes, Jenny noticed that John might adapt his rhetoric to what Meagher had told them of the labourers of that part of Lancashire where the Jesuits had nested.

5

Hectic Days in Banbridge and Dublin, Mid-1840s

Jenny liked to continue to think of herself as an independent woman, a bluestocking or would-be smart moll who had found her man and, while still young, borne her children. But later she wondered whether she would have been quite as ardent had she never met John. She found it testing to think of her life in those terms. The niceties and prejudices of her childhood had certainly been swept away by John Mitchel's enthusiasms and arguments, which would become in time ever more markedly his own, the opinions of a prophet and leader rather than of a mere partisan. Was Jenny independent of him? Indeed, what human spirit is as independent as it thinks it is? The fact that John presented reasons for a different Ireland, and that some notable newspapers did the same, and that it was all radiantly eloquent, and a beloved voice on top of all – that itself changed her, even as she suckled babies.

Daniel O'Connell, the Liberator, began holding his great Repeal meetings around Ireland, attended by 300,000

Irishmen of all classes. Such numbers, you could see why they made Dublin Castle uneasy! And always, the meetings were at significant places, at Tara, the hill of ancient kings in County Meath, and then at Mullaghmast, where in 1577 the interloping English slaughtered a number of invited Celtic chieftains. O'Connell must be altogether a larger being in the open, said John, amongst thousands, than he was when seen closely in a dining hall. Surely his authority expanded in the open air. O'Connell made the illegitimacy of rule from Downing Street so apparent that the British might yield it up in pure embarrassment.

———

John began his career at *The Nation* by submitting book reviews. Its bright-eyed editor, Duffy, was impressed by John Mitchel but was wary of him. Duffy asked him as a test of seriousness to go all the way to Galway by coach to attend the Liberator's monster meeting there. And if due to mud and broken axles John missed that, then to attend and write about one of the others the Liberator had planned at Loughrea or Tuam or Clifden.

John took this up with huge enthusiasm. It was not that he wanted the renown of that famed, most incisive newspaper, many of whose contributors were revered nationally and even referred to, with approval or not, by the London papers. But he did nonetheless have undisguised literary vanity.

John initially went to Dublin on some routine matters of inheritance and voter enrolments. When he was finished with that he rattled west to Kildare, where the best roads beside the Grand Canal gave out. From the window of his coach he saw every degree of middle-man and agent riding busily about, and small farmers and peasants on foot, standing still in that sage way of the bystander to see the coach go by. The crops which the Irish peasantry grew but did not eat were vivid on the landscape – barley, oats, wheat.

It was uneasy country and Mr Robert Peel's government in Westminster had been rendered so mistrustful of the Liberator's purpose that they had brought in a new arms law. If anything that could be used as a pike or a spear was found on a premises – which could be searched at will by the constabulary – the householder would receive a seven-year sentence of transportation to Australia. All arms were to be registered with the police and all blacksmiths to be registered, given their historic contributions to making pikes in the uprising of the United Irishmen some forty-five years ago.

John wanted to write for these people, the suspect masses. *The Nation* was read aloud to the peasantry by travelling readers. To write for that paper was to be an Irish influence for freedom, as John had an ambition to be. But to be one of its voices was to be a voice for European freedoms in general in an exciting age of dissent.

The coach rolled into Galway on the afternoon before the meeting, and the preparations for the next day's great Repeal event were evident. Men with their Repeal membership cards tied to their hats with green ribbon bustled about the entire area of the market square, and some of the trades who meant to march in the meeting had unfurled their banners just to make sure that they were in good trim for the next day. In the long twilight, outside the hotel where Mitchel had taken a room, excitement filled the evening air. An intoxicating perfume of hope. Even he could almost feel the imminence of the liberation, the government having greeted O'Connell's earlier meetings at Tara and Mullaghmast with great seriousness, as if they had been conventions of declared rebels.

John was about to encounter the mystery, the sacrament of O'Connell – yes, the sacrament, even if that was nice talk for a Presbyterian! In the morning air, Repeal Wardens were everywhere around the square, calling on groups to gather, telling the fisherwomen where to stand, empty baskets – they had already sold the overnight catch – on their hips. There was a phalanx of fishermen lined up in the street on the north-east side and decorated, as if they were ivory turners or some other fashionable trade, with rosettes and sashes and ribbons. Mitchel introduced himself as from *The Nation* to a harassed warden. The man stopped frowning and his face took on an unseamed boyish enthusiasm. 'Well, God aid you in your hearing, sir. Sure, if you line up with the tailors there, you should be well able to hear the man himself!' He pointed to the banner of the Galway tailors.

In the marketplace the temperance bands from Oughterard and Sligo Town, and from Castlebar in Mayo, were striking up in competition with bands from Portumna and Tuam, and with a number that had come up from Clare. Serious brass sounded everywhere in experimental forays. The mayor went by in his chain of heavy office, a number of aldermen trailing him. Everyone was in the full flower of sobriety, since the march wardens had the most severe orders to exclude anyone who was inebriated that day and on whom the drink was obvious. For O'Connell was willing to be dismissed by Downing Street, but not on the dubious basis that his audience was a drunken horde. This march was to be in no way the dissent of tipplers, but of the purposely sober.

All the bands struck up at once, and an enthusiastic tailor slung a fraternal arm around Mitchel as the air filled with music, some of it set to the lines of Thomas Davis, the rather prolific *Nation* poet whose lines were never far away from anyone's lips. John's brotherly tailor sang

And Hark, a voice like thunder spake,
The West's awake, the West's awake!

'Indeed, it is awake today,' Mitchel assured him.

On his other side was a thirty-year-old or so journalist from the *Tuam Herald*. 'How many do you think?' he asked.

'It is hard to say,' said John. 'But it seems that half the west is here in the square. Perhaps we can have a better idea when we get to the meeting place.' It was to be a farm at the place named Shantalla.

'I think,' the Tuam man confided, 'we'll have half a million in the end. All, not to hear, but to *see* the Liberator, and know that he exists!'

John asked, 'There must be a journalist from *The Times* of London here. You don't know who it is, do you?'

'I do not. I am sure, however, he will find much to disapprove of amongst us. He won't be telling his readers, "These are the people we condemned to ignorance. And look at what a fountain of rhetoric they now drink from!"'

John liked this man and secretly wished him well.

They marched off through the town and out into scattered cottages and countryside. An hour went in that sweet country and so they entered a second hour, and with the bands playing without respite, even on the hills. They marched through Oranmore, and old men and old women were brought to their doors to see the miracle of the mass passing by. In their faces John fancied he saw all the wrongs and indignities of a subject people. At last they reached Clarinbridge, to the south of the town, and there, in a carriage, stood O'Connell and some priests and his right-hand man, Tom Steele. The Liberator wore the many-coloured cap an artist had placed on his head at Mullaghmast. He was Seer, he was Doctor, he was Pope, he was Doge and Master and Wizard.

Thus now, an about-face for the mass as, greeting the Liberator with cheers, the thousands, if not hundreds of thousands, of marchers wheeled back, the end of the line becoming the first. Mitchel drank water passed around by the tailors. What amiable fellows! The evening continued casually as all followed the Liberator's cart into the fields of Shantalla. Still an extraordinary press of humans, the biggest that John had ever seen to that stage of his history, and perhaps the biggest he would ever be amongst.

A platform had been built atop a number of rocks, and a warden invited the crowd forward to make sure all heard what the Liberator actually said. Unlike his friend from the *Tuam Herald*, Mitchel had no shorthand to let him take down his long speech verbatim.

And then the moment came to him to speak, and even for those who could not possibly hear him, in the extensive corners of that field, there was a surge of enthusiasm. The great roar was directed his way and then it broke into silence, and he said, 'We are engaged in a struggle to liberate the slave from the hand of the stranger.'

'The slave . . .' Even though in Parliament ten years before he had helped end slavery in Britain, and so was a hero in America, he still called the Irish slaves.

Perfect, crystal words followed, all true to purpose. Downing Street had conveniently placed a warship so that it could be seen in that 'V' of hills from where they stood. O'Connell wondered why martial naval means were directed towards him when he was a spokesman of moral force, which had no steel to present in answer but had merely the wishes and hopes of the people who had joined him here at Shantalla.

Nothing more was needed, and he could have left the platform then. But he had much more to say. And so next he denounced Prime Minister Peel. He denounced evictions from Irish farms which had given the tenants no choice but the workhouse, creating a rural resistance which meant that young men were shipped to Van Diemen's Land, or risked a journey to America which they knew would commit members of their family, if not the entirety of them, to the sea. They wanted the children of the soil of Ireland to vanish, said the Liberator. The Irish were to possess no rights except those of subservience, the workhouse, or exile!

The oratorical periods flowed on, and were all germane. He began to speak about Ireland's lost Parliament, which it would take only the Queen's own writs to put into session. He denounced absentee landlords and, once again, the habit of evicting tenants – had not one hundred and three families been thrown off their land, ejected from their hearth, this very year? None of it would happen if there were universal suffrage, the right to vote by ballot, and an Irish parliament in an Irish state.

John could hear him well, yet tens of thousands of the Shantalla gathering could not, who nonetheless stood there all over this vast meadow in silence, men and women and their children who knew from reading and being read the Liberator's parliamentary speeches, his speeches at other meetings, and thus knew from his annunciating presence what was being said. They heard their hopes released into the air like freed birds. It was as well that he wore the many-coloured Mullaghmast cap and the red cloak of a Dublin alderman, for he was both wizard and high priest of liberation, and the warship out on the 'V' of ocean seemed a laughable blot of inhibition on the grandness of things and of the dreams he was uttering.

John wrote, fast as he could, what was being said, even though Duffy had said to him, 'Write something along the lines of the event itself, even for the majority who can't hear a word.' But the Liberator was speaking in the confidence that all journalists had shorthand and that these people who were present would very soon be by a fire somewhere in the west, reading or having read to them the precise wording of what he'd said. Thus John was under the onus not to misrepresent anything that was uttered, since like the last hundred who had entered the farmer's gate, he was there to watch the phenomenon itself.

And he did.

———

Within three months, in early autumn of 1843, the Liberator had intended to hold a monster meeting at Clontarf, out beyond North Dock – a place bound to figure sadly in John Mitchel's own history – but that had been memorialised as the place where, nine hundred years past, the ancient king Brian Boru defeated the Vikings. This proposed meeting, and the expected crowds, were all too much for Dublin Castle. The meeting was proclaimed – that is, it was prohibited – and even more soldiers were brought in from England. The Liberator could have gone ahead with it, and he had the power and influence to assure it would assemble. And then God help any army that tried to disperse the horde of his attendants and the splendid hosts of his adherents!

But rightly or wrongly, he obeyed the letter of the confected law, and called off this supremest of all the rallies of the summer. It accorded with his non-violent propositions, and his care for his own crowd, since there were both British cavalry and artillery posted on top of Clontarf; and out in the bay, not one but a whole flotilla of ships, prepared to open fire.

And, despite his forbearance, a number of Repeal men, including the Liberator himself, were arrested and charged with conspiracy by Lord Clarendon, the Chancellor of the Exchequer. For planning peaceful assembly! Repealers, and John was one, were willing to resist the arrests physically, but O'Connell advised that he would face the charges in court and that he did not want a confrontation, that he had already shed enough blood, when years before he had fought a duel with a gentleman named D'Esterre. A bullet from O'Connell's pistol had hit d'Esterre in the groin and he bled to death from the wound the Liberator inflicted. So, for d'Esterre's sake, Daniel O'Connell called off all spirited resistance and would now, on top of that, be found guilty of conspiracy.

As the Liberator served his term in Richmond Bridewell on the South Circular Road, Dublin, there were rumours that his passion for Repeal had been chastened out of him in his imprisonment. He was now a man of nearly seventy who had lived on his nerves, and he was feeling his way now, some Repeal men said, not to rebellion but to an alliance with the Whig ministry in London, in the hope they would reward Ireland in some way. Or, said the doubters, reward him by giving him the power to make appointments of his own supporters to posts in Ireland.

John Mitchel, on a journey to Dublin to carry a motion of solidarity from the Repealers of Down, visited the charged men within the forbidding-looking walls of Richmond Bridewell. O'Connell and the Clontarf organisers were in fact kept in comfortable rooms set aside for prisoners of means, his supporters picking up the cost, and where, amongst excellently tended garden beds in the yard, a tent had been erected for his use. John had already, in the role of an admirer, met Davis, the same poet whose verse the warden in Galway had recited, and who as one of O'Connell's lieutenants had been found guilty of conspiracy too. The Liberator was now, in the summer of 1844, serving the first few months of their combined sentences with his chief officers.

Davis told Mitchel sadly, in the garden of the prison, the government did not have to worry further about how many thousands of people might meet peacefully and legally, or in what trappings they dressed themselves, or in what shoes they marched, or what banners they might flaunt. Not while there were 50,000 rifles in all Irish garrisons now, besides the Orange yeomanry.

When the House of Lords, the court to whom O'Connell had appealed, decided that the charge of conspiracy against him could not be sustained anymore, it seemed a bad day for Dublin Castle. On the news of his release from prison that morning, the Liberator was drawn by a coachman and six grey horses on a carriage made as if for an Emperor, with carved figures of Hibernia Triumphant on its sides, through Dublin to his house in Merrion Square, before a crowd that did adore him for taking things so far, and which probably still believed, unlike Davis, that he was on a tangent to end British rule.

Davis, also released, directed John to copies of *The Artillerist's Manual* and told him that that was what they must study now. For if Downing Street met peaceful assembly with armies, was not the one remaining dialogue a military one? Thus John began to research articles on warfare as waged by banditti or irregular foragers or Spanish guerrillas.

———

In the autumn of 1845, Davis, whom Jenny had heard of only as a noble being and songwriter, suddenly died, killed by scarlet fever. John was possessed now by a greater urgency to communicate via *The Nation*. He was aghast at the wrongful ordinariness of Davis's death. The poet had been a hearty strong fellow, complained John to the heavens. It was hard to think he had fallen to such a banal foe. Though they were in Banbridge at the time, John Mitchel mourned for all that was going wrong in Dublin, from the passing of Davis to the new timidity of the Liberator.

In early autumn, Mitchel had gone walking in County Down with Martin and Duffy the editor, a solemn Irish trek to honour their friend, the great lyricist. Duffy and John would never quite get on – he did sneer that since John's journey to Galway he believed he knew how to speak for the small tenants and farmers. But they were friendly enough to make the journey credible.

The two walked eastwards from Loughorne, where they collected Martin, intending to reach the sea at Newcastle, and, on the way, ascended Slieve Donard, for which John had a passion and from whose top on clear days Belfast could be seen, and even Dublin. That is, if the clouds parted they could as good as see Ireland as one. The walkers discussed the new Dickens, *Nicholas Nickleby*, along the way, and agreed it was not his best. Yet certainly it served as an essay on the dangers of sectarian feeling.

As a result of this journey they'd taken together, Duffy asked Mitchel to move to Dublin, become a more regular contributor and to take over some of the editorial tasks as a full-time manager-editor. Duffy offered a salary considered liberal at the time, though it would not make up for the loss of the law practice Mitchel had built in Banbridge. It had always been thought that once the Banbridge office was running well, John would move back to Newry. But now Duffy offered Dublin.

At first Mitchel thought that, despite all, he should settle for his law practice.

'Mr Mitchel,' Jenny instructed him, addressing him formally, 'you have no obligation to Duffy. You have made a splendid and solid career. And I like that solidity.'

'I would not mind a destiny that was practising the law, imperfect as it is, until I am old,' said John. 'And old men saying, "I must have my Mitchel, he helped me last time."'

'And where would farmers unjustly kept off the electoral rolls go for comfort if John Mitchel left?'

'Indeed,' he agreed.

'And yet,' said Jenny, because she felt she must.

'Yes,' breathed John. 'Indeed, and yet . . .'

They both knew that should he write for *The Nation*, his name might become renowned, a pledge to the Irish people, so that in furthest North America the Irish would know it as the name of a new thunderbolt. And a Presbyterian who spoke for the masses – doubly honoured for that! On the other hand, would she and Mitchel ever have those things that men and women wisely desired? What if they would not be allowed the simplest fulfilment? The household. Its rewards came from growing and maturing and eventually fading far from the regard of strangers.

Both of them possessed an appetite for large events. And yet Jenny loved and was riveted to a fellow named Johnny Mitchel, who was ill-designed for stasis and made for lightning change! She sensed there would be more lightning, should he take the job with Duffy, more change perhaps, than she could ever desire. That was the risk. But the air seemed to demand he take it.

John seemed to have accepted that the offer would have been good for a man of no responsibilities to a wife and children, and did not try to convince her that he must go to the newspaper. She might have felt its inevitability more than he did.

And then he had a particularly poisonous trial to cap things off. The land agent for Lord Glenmachan came to a tenant farm up near Belfast in a small carriage, and told a boy, who happened to be the son of the tenant, to mind the horses. The boy, being no lover of land agents, let the horses wander. Having had an acrimonious meeting with the father over barley, the agent came back to find the horses grazing on the road verge, and the carriage half tipped over. He took to the boy with his riding crop, and when the boy resisted, drew a knife and skewered him. The boy died, and the tenant farmer brought the case against the land agent, and consulted John Mitchel as his lawyer. John went to argue the case at the Downpatrick Assizes, but through a series of dodges and mitigating factors, the land agent was exonerated. Mitchel's children had gone to bed when he got home to Banbridge from the trial, dizzy with tiredness and disgust.

And Jenny thought then, for forty years more John would take such cases, if spared, and for forty years more would come to her bewildered by the obscenities of Irish justice, by jury packing and by false witness. Or worse still, he might come to her accepting it all as the norm, and accept his role as a servant without finding daily honour in it — as Dr Mitchel had found honour in his days.

From that land-agent case onwards, Jenny was secretly in favour of his taking the Duffy offer, but could not say too much, for his own enthusiasm for the idea was growing fiercely enough for both of them. He could say what he believed in *The Nation* and, once put in print, it would not be denied or overturned. It could not be done away with, in the way the county judges dismissed a pleading.

At *The Nation*, Jenny and Mitchel realised, he could speak as he wished to without reference to judicial permission; the permission, that is, of some self-glorying county court judge. At *The Nation*, all that was swallowed down within him and repressed by legal custom could be let free. At *The Nation*, he could speak for Thomas Davis, this compelling and now vanished voice. Jenny remembered that when John began to write for the newspaper, his hands would tremble as he opened its pages to show his exuberant reviews of Leigh Hunt's poetry or of Carlyle's *Cromwell*, as if even his reviews had, coded within them, some galvanising manifesto, some version of 'Harken to me, all ye people'.

So it was decided. Jenny would stay behind with the children until there should be a house in Dublin ready for them. He should go and find that house.

The property he took within ten days was at Upper Leeson Street. It was no castle, he warned her by letter, but civilised and suitable for such polished souls as Jenny and the children to live in with esprit.

There were other developments. 'Yesterday's edition of the *Pilot*, published by Repeal,' reported John to Jenny, 'has, through ignorance, committed the blunder of giving a most glowing review of my life of Hugh O'Neill, which it praises in most rated, though somewhat ungrammatical, language.' That was the case: he had written in his spare time a book on Hugh O'Neill, warrior, a fellow torn in pieces by the subjection of Ireland, who died in exile in Rome. Suddenly, John was a man with a book, and a job, and a house in Dublin.

And a woman with child. Jenny was just quickening and thickening with another life, the fourth to go along with the boys and Henty. She would be named Mary when she came, but soon after she was forever known as Minnie. When Jenny gave birth to her, there was a physician present, so it was a fashionable birth, if birth is ever fashionable. The contractions and struggles were not fashionable: they were of the elements, a great storm on a dark sea. Yet Jenny smiled when she saw the stubborn little face. The wearer of that face would not easily surrender the earth. She was determined not to go to Heaven early.

6

Dublin Life, 1845-47

They were fully settled in the house at 1 Upper Leeson a considerable time before Christmas of 1845 and joined the Unitarian congregation, whose pastors were friends of the late Rev Dr Mitchel. On a more martial and revolutionary front, John was also a member of the '82 Club founded by the late Davis. This was the armed corps of the movement dubbed 'Young Ireland' by the Liberator. Their uniform was green and gold lace, like that of an officer of hussars, and which John sometimes wore to Repeal meetings – but not as much as Tom Meagher, the envied young orator upon whom Jenny now clapped eyes for the first time.

Well . . . Mitchel was one kind of phenomenon, Jenny saw. And Meagher another! It wasn't right to look at the vests and hats and pomade he wore socially and call him a dandy, as there was something dismissive and vapoury in the term and Meagher could not be easily dismissed and was far from a vapour. But he certainly looked elegant and was determined to be a finely-dressed rebel. Talk seemed to bubble out of Meagher's lips like water from a fountain; not under as much force as John Mitchel's pronouncements, but every sentence had a casual polish and allure to it. And he was as good-looking as an actor – and was himself an actor to an extent.

And Jenny also met Miss Jane Elgee, often found in Meagher's company, and rumoured to be 'soft' on him. Jenny liked her and they became friends fairly readily. Indeed, Speranza was tall – she was a large presence – and wore vivid casings of fabric and lace, in combinations of colours some mothers would advise against, but which in her were appropriate to her vivid intelligence.

Jenny, who was flattered by her willingness to converse, still referred to her simply as 'LG' in John's company, as a just-in-case antidote to any charm she might exert on Mitchel, whose admiration for her was considerable – though Jenny had to admit, no greater than the automatic awe Speranza imposed on all, as she strode across the small living room in Upper Leeson Street.

She was, Speranza, in some ways simplicity itself, though willing to spin ideas out in men's company. As far as Jenny was concerned, she was discriminating, not least in her seeing a contrast between Mitchel as fulminator of *The Nation*, and home-and-party Mitchel. Speranza confessed in her sonorous voice, 'I did not know what a good man your husband is for a party and a dinner. He seems an austere man, but at the dinner table he is sociable and there are no long lectures. He is friends to all. Again, no disquisitions. No rancour. Aphorisms, perhaps. *Bon mots.*'

Dinner, as Speranza further reassured Jenny, was not a political exercise for Mitchel. Wit, briskness, unlaboured satire and conversation – that was John's menu. Everyone said that, praising John's table and thus Jenny's. Carlyle, the great author of the day, had said it when he was in Dublin and had visited John. It was a gift John had, and of which Jenny was proud.

The poet also made an impression on the young Mitchels – when Speranza visited the children's rooms between courses, she told them a story about Irish magic which gave John C. nightmares. Was he a changeling? John C. wanted to know, and how could he know if he was one? This all came from the stories that Jane Elgee, who was about to produce a book on Irish fairytales, let slip in the nursery. Thank you, LG, Jenny thought, I'll visit your house when you have children and keep them up half the night with tales about malicious fairies and little people and changelings! Aye, and she'd throw in a few banshees as well!

Henty said, 'I don't want to hear any more stories from the fairy lady.'

'You think she's a fairy lady,' Jenny was tempted meanly to mutter, 'with such hips?' But thus women corrupted their daughters, and she did not choose to corrupt Henty.

Speranza was a larger character than Jenny. She translated books from the German, she could speak Italian, she could scare children. Still, she wished no malice and had no designs on Mitchel. Her complexion was not marred by care, though if she were to marry Meagher, Jenny thought, he would cause her a few frowns.

Duffy, a charming enough man himself, considered Speranza the greatest poet of the age, higher in the canon even than Davis. Jenny had read her, and she did write fierce stuff, always seeming able to fit more words in a line than there should be. That did not diminish Duffy's admiration.

'By dungeon walls,' went one of her brisker poems

By scaffolds, chains and exiles' tears,
Slow marking as the shadow falls
The mournful sequence of the years;
By genius crushed and progress barred,
By noble aspirations marred,
Till with a smouldering fire's life
They burn in deadly hate and strife –
I ask you, Rulers of our land,
Have you done well for Ireland?

At one of the Leeson Street get-togethers, Speranza told Jenny she had been visited by an uncle, a major in the artillery, who saw a copy of *The Nation* she had not remembered to tidy away before he came. He launched into a diatribe against it as the ultimate weapon of sedition, and then, given her literary tendencies, said with frightened awe, 'You're not writing for this thing, are you?'

She confessed that she was doing so, and the uncle went off with every intention of telling the family, and seeing what could be done for her. The uncle had said, before departing, 'You will never find a husband writing for such a disgraceful rag.' She would claim she answered, 'Certainly not one like you, uncle.'

———

And now John made his first visit to London, to the core of the problem, and it happened in this way.

O'Connell had said in the previous term of the Parliament in Westminster that he and his party of politicians were so appalled by British policy, and lack of care for Ireland, that the Repeal politicians – the Irish Party – would oppose government business and refuse to sit on the Select Committees of the House. For the impact of the winter, after the potato crop turned to black pulp in the autumn, would be cruel amongst the landless and near-landless millions of the Irish labouring classes. 'You must look at this year's crisis in Ireland before any of us look at any other improvement' was the argument of the Repeal politicians. The black blight struck in England and Scotland too, but the crofters of Scotland had, as did the labourers of the Midlands, north and west, a broader range of foods to call on and generally earned cash wages and were able to purchase food in the market. It was in Ireland, though, with its limited diet that the potato blight would become a famine and then *An Gorta Mor*, the Great Hunger.

So, Repeal members standing aside from their committee duties was a stratagem to make the Parliament in Westminster look at an Irish calamity. When it came to it, however, only one gentleman dared stand by that decision. It was William Smith O'Brien, son of the baronet, and himself a County Clare landlord, who went so far as the Liberator had suggested, and declined to sit on a Parliamentary Committee he had been appointed to – the Committee on Scottish Railways.

The time would come when the Mitchels would see Smith O'Brien at the end of the earth, so it is worth telling the story now. He had nothing against Scottish railways, but they did not present the needs Ireland did. So he as good as went on strike.

He was a cultivated soul, William Smith O'Brien, a Protestant, father of a family in the west of Ireland, and a man of probity. In the face of that first winter of the rotting death of the potatoes, he refused to do anything in favour of

Scottish railways until something was done to relieve the Irish condition. The Speaker of the Commons called on the House to vote him in contempt and to have him disciplined. The House debated Smith O'Brien's refusal, and the Liberator argued in favour of his countryman, that Parliament had no legal rights to compel Irish Members of Parliament.

That hungry year of 1846 was now moving towards a fatal spring in which the Irish would have no money to buy grain – a spring in which the Commons voted to commit Smith O'Brien to the Sergeant-at-Arms of the Commons. William Smith O'Brien, so went the judgement, was to be confined to an improvised dungeon in the lean-to shed against the wall of the chamber, a small, sad, damp, miserable room with a trestle bed and a deal table. O'Brien's diet, though he was descended from Brian Boru, king of all Ireland, was to be water and dry toast. In those days, Parliament met in the St Stephen's Hall, the home of the Commons until a new Palace of Westminster was built, and it seemed all Westminster was still a building site, and the shed drafty and half-made.

In Dublin the group around *The Nation*, including Meagher and Speranza, Mitchel and Duffy, voted to support Smith O'Brien, but the other members of the Repeal committee merely voted a motion of sympathy with him. The token of support from Repeal and the Irish Party made Smith O'Brien, a very measured fellow, extremely angry at the Liberator and his followers. A delegation was raised into being by the '82 Club to present an address of support to Smith O'Brien in person. John Mitchel was selected to be a member.

The party that set off for London had time to get there, given that Smith O'Brien would be kept in his improvised dungeon a full twenty-five days. Mitchel went in the night boat out of duty rather than friendship. At that stage he considered Smith O'Brien a subdued, cold and rather timid man. But after John arrived and saw the man in his cell, in the lean-to against the wall of St Stephen's chapel, his collar in disarray and him staring and hungry but impenitent, he grew to have a better estimation of him.

In spite of his situation, Smith O'Brien was delighted they'd come to visit him and that they wore the uniform of the '82 Club and thus all looked like hussars – Thomas Francis Meagher most of all, in some regiment in an opera whose costumier favoured green. This made the Sergeant-at-Arms of the British Parliament, the imprisoner of Smith O'Brien, with his long old-fashioned coat and his ruffed collar and sword from beheading times, very nervous.

Smith O'Brien told the delegation that ordinary Irish people were writing to him in Westminster in numbers to tell him that his choice of the Irish Famine over Scottish railways was the right one. The Liberator agreed with him but dared not say so.

Having displayed his solidarity with Smith O'Brien, John did not loiter thereafter at the centre of Empire and all its marvels, but caught the railway back to Holyhead and then to Leeson Street and his desk at *The Nation*. And that was not because he did not have things to see in London and people he might have encountered with enthusiasm; above all, with whom he'd exchanged letters. For it was not the English who were his enemies. It was the English 'thing', the contraption of government – as much an enemy in many ways to its own people, but an outright blight to the Irish.

Smith O'Brien was released and returned to Dublin to speak about his experiences of imprisonment at the hands of the Sergeant-at-Arms of the House of Commons. John saw O'Brien again at Reconciliation Hall, where they had both been taking a more active part in debates.

Meanwhile, Speranza came back to impose another frightening story on the children. She had some new tale from Connacht about the evil eye; indeed, of old witches who learned to say, 'God bless the child,' though it actually burned their mouths and blistered their lips. They bore it because the sentence gave them access to houses from which they stole the infants. Jenny thought her insistence on the telling of bedtime tales, which without any intention on her part frightened little Henty in particular, had something to do with impressing Tom Meagher that she had a way with children.

In this desperate era, when many in Ireland, including the Irish nobility, were predicting famine as a result of the potato blight and being ignored, it was nonetheless thought something must surely be done, even by Westminster. And if Westminster and Downing Street did nothing, Mitchel, Smith O'Brien, Meagher – the men of the '82 Club – believed the Irish should do it by rising, and installing their own righteous governance.

Those peasants who entered Dublin were falling to the street as if hunger had stopped their hearts. And it was known that 'beyond the Pale' – that is, beyond the city and out in the counties and even in the outskirts of the capital – middling farmers were these days forced to eat turnips because of a blight that had hit the potatoes in the autumn, and the malnourished were yearning for the berries and even the thistles that would come up in spring. It was reported that many small farmers were secretly eating colecannon made of turnips, a stockfeed they were ashamed to devour. In Malahide, on the sea at the north-east edge of Dublin, women were collecting kelp on the beach for feeding their families. God knew what was happening in far Connacht!

Meantime, Jenny felt she could achieve a brief amnesia of the dreadful politics by spending time with the charming infants John and she had begotten. However, she also read proofs of *The Nation*'s pages, and met and ate dinner with all the sages of Young Ireland. As for John, in March he was elected to occupy the chair at a Repeal meeting, a considerable honour in everyone's estimation. He would be, in that time in Dublin, as vividly present in the world as a man could be, his affections for his wife, children and the cause as intense as his writing. He told Jenny one day that he was not living anymore – he was alive!

Mitchel had never had a happy time with his public oratory, though. His speeches were workmanlike and lacked the power of his written words, though he found it hard to assess why he lacked the verbal flow of Meagher. There was a social night which they attended, a conversational soirée, at the Unitarian congregation of a Dr Drummond in Dublin. Dr Drummond, like everyone else, was an admirer of the late Dr Mitchel, whose memory he invoked every time he saw John and Jenny.

It was suddenly announced at this particular event that impromptu speeches were to be made, and a number of young men distributed cards with topics written on them. For no reason that Jenny could identify, John expressed a great sense of humiliation about his speaking skills, and he felt positive irritation if not outright anger when he was handed a card with the topic printed on it: 'All men, including people of no property, should be given the suffrage.' Jenny would have thought John could have spoken at length on the subject.

It was transparently a trigger to get the notable John Mitchel of *The Nation* to speak about anything, but when his turn came he rose, read what was on the card, and then excused himself and Jenny, and took her out by the elbow. All the way home to Upper Leeson Street, he fumed uncharacteristically about the presumption of the young man who'd given him the card.

His anger and confusion had grown from the time he'd been asked by the Repeal committee to give a speech at the Corn Exchange in memory of Davis, and had prepared it exhaustively. When he rose on the day, he'd thanked the chair, and commenced

Thomas Davis died in September 1845 full of foreboding and despondency as he watched what he considered the decline of that Repeal Movement which had at first so many elements of power!

Before the grave had yet closed on him, began to spread rumours of a dreadful hunger . . .

And then to his own surprise, he burst into disabling floods of tears.

The court system had rarely given him a chance to make speeches, given that he was usually instructing a barrister who made the speeches for the client. Tom Meagher said to him while comforting him the night of the Davis speech, 'Give over with the lawyer style of speaking, Johnny. Forget you were ever a lawyer in Ulster. Speak in absolutes, not in conditionals. Ireland has no time for the conditional.'

In London, the Prime Minister Peel had just the one splendid policy, which was to create university colleges where Irish of all religious backgrounds could attend. The Liberator irrationally opposed them, because he seemed to believe Catholics would be contaminated by the secular, or at best Protestant, ideas they would encounter in a non-Catholic university college. So, as a whole, did the Catholic clergy, who, it turned out, could be accused of rather having their brethren ignorant and poor than expose them to 'heretical' ideas. It was all part of the plan of the Liberator, and his son John, to make Repeal a Catholic fortress, with the very occasional Protestant here or there, like a raisin in a cake.

John Mitchel wrote, 'I am one of the Saxon Irishmen of the North, and you want that race of Irishmen in your ranks more than any others . . . Drive the Ulster Protestants away from your movement by needless tests and you perpetuate the degradation both of yourselves and them.'

———

For millions of Irish in every part of the country, the calamity of the Famine had taken on its own vicious momentum. At first, they tried to eat the loathsome mass, and some of the first of the victims died, caught between hut and privy by the resultant violent diarrhoea which further weakened the hungry.

Mitchel and other Dubliners, travelling out of the city, began now to see corpses of the famished beside the road, in ditches and by hedges, as winter progressed on its way towards spring of 1846. And, aghast, the city people noticed them with shock at first, until they became so common a sight even in the capital that passers-by learned indeed to pass them by, step around or over them, because through no fault of theirs the failing had somehow become less visible and less than human.

The early victims had had a part in the previous summer of producing barley, corn, pigs and cattle to be sold at market, but buttermilk and potatoes, with oatmeal in good times and bacon in glorious ones, were what they ate daily. Imagine a man sitting on a three-legged stool, one leg of which was the potato, the other buttermilk, and the third the occasional luxury of bacon. The potato leg had been knocked out from beneath him – that is, from beneath the five to six million who lived by it. A stool could not stand on two legs.

There was some hope that government could help, but, typical of the mood, in the London *Standard* one writer suggested that before any assistance was to be offered, first the ungrateful Irish demand for repeal of the Union should be suppressed, and the railways should transport British troops to the Irish regions to crush such agitation.

In answer, John wrote in a fever of outrage at *The Nation* office. Can a man become a dangerous rebel while simply sitting at his desk, John wondered. Can he become a Bolívar or a Garibaldi in the minds of his opponents and his supporters while simply writing? Mr John Mitchel tried to manage, of course!

'It might be useful to promulgate through the country, to be read by all Repeal Wardens in their parishes, a few short and easy rules, as to the mode of dealing with railways in case of any enemy daring to make a hostile use of them against ordinary people.' So wrote John in *The Nation*. Railways, he believed, though inconceivably valuable to many people as highways of commerce, were better dispensed with for a time than allowed to become a means of transport for invading armies. 'First, then, every railway within five miles of Dublin could be in one night totally cut off from the interior country. To lift a mile or two of rail, to fill in a perch or two of any cutting or tunnel, to break down a piece of an embankment, all seem obvious and easy enough.'

When Jenny read this article in proof-form before publication, she thought, with wonder, he must have been studying the manuals of Kossuth and Garibaldi and others, who wanted to wreck Austrian railways. As well as the shining exemplar of Hofer, who, before the age of railways, was executed only after driving Napoleon out of the Tyrol in Austria twice over by catching columns of troops in ravines. And he had taken Thomas Davis's advice and studied military manuals of irregular ambush. Lying at Jenny's heart, John Mitchel's head had been full of detonations for the sake of the starving.

'Second then,' wrote John, 'the materials of railways, good hammered iron and wooden sleepers – need we point out that such things may be of use in other lines than assisting locomotion? Third: troops upon their march by rail might be conveniently met with in divers places. Hofer, the Tyrolean rebel against Napoleon, could hardly have desired a deadlier ambush than the brinks of a deep cutting on a railway. Imagine a few hundred men lying in wait upon such a spot, with masses of rocks and trunks of trees ready to roll down; and a train or two advancing with a regiment of infantry, and the engine panting near and nearer, till the polished studs of brass on its front are distinguishable, and its name may clearly be read . . .'

Having raised the possibility, he backed away from recommending such action directly. 'But it's a dream,' he wrote. 'Surely no-one would force us to employ these schemes in reality. But let us all understand what a railway may and what it may not do.'

Some people might have said John was being speculative or at most uttering an exhortation against conspicuous railway movement of unneeded soldiers. But the Tory government in Britain had the luxury of hysteria, and saw what he wrote – despite the qualification at its end – as a threat. So, in another sense, did many Irish. The article made Mitchel an instant hero amongst them, as one who had answered back. Wherever were Irish, his defiance was reported and celebrated. For he had reminded everyone that the people were not impotent there.

But the Liberator visited *The Nation* office, where John was so much of the time just then, Duffy being absent on leave, and complained. The newspaper must make it clear in the next edition, said O'Connell, that it had no power to compel Repeal Wardens to do anything such as was suggested in the article.

In the excitement of the idea that people could if necessary curtail the movement of soldiers, and of John's whimsical reminder to Downing Street of that fact, he believed he would not be punished. He was merely reminding the government there was such a thing as 'popular power', and making a little display of bravado in sour times. How dangerous could that really be in an age when all daring was being sapped by Irish hunger?

But for whatever reason, it caused a reaction.

Not many days passed before a prosecution for sedition was issued against Mr Duffy as proprietor, based on the two railway articles Mitchel published. It was a British paper which first raised the issue of the railways as weapons of offence, and Mitchel was responding to that, so neither Duffy nor John was chastened. The case would take six months to come on. In the meantime, there had been news suggesting that there might be war between Britain and the United States over the Oregon border. John wrote in *The Nation*, 'Bring us war in our time, O Lord. If there be war between England and the United States, it is possible for us to pretend sympathy with the former. But we shall have allies, not enemies, on the banks of the Columbia, and distant and desolate as are those tracks between the Rocky Mountains, even there may arise the opportunity for demanding and regaining our place among the nations.'

Of greater issue to the ordinary people, Gaelic speaking, was that they were already locked into the Great Starving. What would the government in London do? Some members of the Commons said that the Famine might be a providential instrument to thin out the Irish population, considered to be too large. That is, that God and the economic benefit of others meant that God and government let the hungry die!

Prime Minister Peel repealed the Corn Laws, which made the importing of cheaper grain from the continent possible, and so helped the British poor. However, it did not help the Irish as much as the Prime Minister hoped; for five million at least of them rarely used money, often paying the rent for their quarter acre or more of ground through the labour they did for the landlord, and coming to deploy cash only when they bought oatmeal. In their close to money-less world, how could they replace the potato by buying grain?

Peel promised the Irish a supply of Indian corn imported from America. This was a grain not traded on the European market, and thus if it was dispensed cheaply to the Irish peasant was incapable of unsettling that market in any way. It was to be sold from depots in Irish towns at a penny or two per quart, and the peasant could buy it with the pennies he earned on public works designed to keep the masses diligent. But often it was not ground to flour, because it needed heavier millstones than European grains did – and, eaten as it was, it caused mayhem in the stomach. Many died of the resultant gastric illness. People called it 'Peel's brimstone'. As the Indian corn became available, with it came a proposed new Coercion Act to crush discontent.

In time, Jenny would hear the ignorant say many offensive things: such as that the Irish grew potatoes out of laziness. In fact, they grew them out of lack of land, their imaginations and survival wrapped up in that one small plot – with, of course, no compensation for improvements they made upon it. Nor was Ireland full of agronomists teaching Irish peasants the wisdom of other usages. And to propose that God, the capital 'P' of Providence, would delight in their deaths! That was a further slight, and Mitchel burned at its evil slickness, and so did Jenny.

But others accused the Irish of wilful starvation by not eating fish. First, the fish in streams belonged to landlords, and millions did not live on the coast and there were no salting works, and so the fish would rot on their way inland, on the bad, gouged and rutted roads of Ireland. In fact, the Irish were fixed on and determined not to ignore any source of food, including fish and even the nettle and the shamrock. The scarecrow corpse with green grass stains on its mouth could be encountered in legions on the road out of Dublin.

'The Irish people,' wrote John Mitchel in the spring of 1846, 'always half-starved, are expecting absolute famine day by day. They know that they are doomed to months of a weed-diet next summer . . . They behold their own wretched food melting in rottenness off the face of the earth;

and they see heavy-laden ships, freighted with the yellow corn their own hands have sown and reaped, spreading all sail for England. They see it, and with every grain of that corn goes a heavy curse.'

———

Mitchel was appalled when the Liberator himself made a speech in the Commons, worthy of a Crown Prosecutor not of an Irishman, about the subversive nature of *The Nation* since Thomas Davis had died. He said he did not want to be identified at all with the newspaper's attitude to tearing up railways. Because, he said, proving his respectability, he was number one shareholder of the Cashel to Dublin Railway. O'Connell was aware that his liberation of the Irish had come to him by way of an alliance with the Whig majority of the House of Lords, and hence cherished the idea that the Whigs were a safe cohort to which to attach the Repeal wagon and with which to seek an alliance all over again. It might ultimately lead to genuine relief of the starving.

John Mitchel had complained that the Liberator was pretty much urging the British to go after *The Nation*. And so it happened. Charges were levelled at Duffy and the newspaper, and Mitchel himself acting as solicitor.

Jenny went to the trial in Green Street, Dublin, wearing a sombre purple dress to convey her seriousness and her pride in the solicitor for the accused. Mitchel had brought out of retirement a man of over eighty years as the barrister. He was not a perpetually practising barrister but a member of the outer courts, the sort of barrister they called for some reason a 'stuff gownsman'. Old Robert Holmes had been married to the daughter of Robert Emmet, the great massacred hero of the United Irish – hung, drawn and gruesomely quartered in 1803.

Holmes, as instructed by Mitchel and recognised by the court, presented in defence of *The Nation* a history of the occupation of Ireland, and from this as template, why would the Irish not have concerns that the railways would be used against their interests? The Chief Justice didn't think much of Holmes's argument, but the sheriff had made the great mistake of allowing some three Catholic gentlemen of property on the jury. Meanwhile, said old Mr Holmes, if *The Nation*'s railway articles were seditious libel, they were no more so than the satirical work of Jonathan Swift and William Molyneux, philosophers and wits.

Holmes certainly had a line in oratory: 'Where a people is subservient to the will, mocked by the pride, and ruled by the caprice, the passions, and the interest of another state, that people will inevitably portray the vileness of its condition,' he said. And the railway article had merely done that. 'National independence does not necessarily lead to national virtue and happiness, but reason and experience alike demonstrate that public spirit and general happiness are looked for in vain under the withering influence of provincial subjection.'

A conviction had been confidently predicted before Holmes spoke. But the jury was locked up without food for twenty-four hours and could not reach a verdict, and was then discharged.

Mitchel and Duffy were free and exultant.

In London, Robert Peel was also beaten on his Coercion Bill. It was out of the pure bloody-mindedness of those landholders in the Commons and the Lords who now got less for their grain than they used to, and according to the conventions of the Parliament, which said a Prime Minister must resign if defeated on a bill, Peel withdrew from leadership as required. Lord John Russell, the Whig, became Prime Minister.

The Repeal Association had now split. Various supporters of the Liberator wanted the young men around *The Nation*, and Smith O'Brien who was now associated with them, to renounce all physical force in their service to the well-being of the Irish. It seemed to John and his comrades, however, that this was all because Repeal itself, knowing it could not liberate Ireland, had fallen back on an alliance with the Whig party and Lord John Russell.

They suspected that O'Connell's ambition had shrunk: that what he wanted in old age was to be able to hand out the patronage of various Irish positions under the Crown, and that alliance, Mitchel thought, would bear little fruit, though it might enable the Liberator to nominate his people to posts all over Ireland and they would love him for it. Mitchel and other Young Irelanders saw this as a lame substitute for independence, and in the office of *The Nation* they did not trust the tame path which bound Repeal closer to Downing Street rather than to a genuine liberation.

And indeed Lord John Russell, who needed the support of the Irish members to survive, would be grateful for the Liberator's backing, but not the reforms he suggested. John Mitchel would write in *The Nation*: 'There was an end of the Repeal Association, save as a machinery for securing offices for O'Connell dependents.' Then he wept and raged in private, safe with Jenny. She was, Mitchel told her without male artifice, 'the hearth for his tears'.

———

Everyone in Ireland awaited the October crop of potatoes, the failing and starving more intensely than others. Everyone knew that the only mercy under the sky was a crop of healthy tubers. When the potatoes proved healthy they sung praises. When stalks were still green, and potatoes revealed themselves plump in the soil, some began harvesting and left off for joyous sleep but woke to corruption and blackness and pulp like the year before, their hopes reduced to muck by their own doorways.

'A thousand farewells to the white potatoes,' the poor folk wailed in the old language. 'For as long as we had them a pleasant hoard. Affable, innocent, coming into our company, as they laughed at us from the table's head.'

But for some in the city, life was near-normal, and even though Mrs Mitchel the elder and some of the Mitchel sisters were often in Newry, to their delight and wonder they could travel back and forth to Dublin on the Ulster railway that had opened five years past. So there was much sisterly aid to make it possible to satisfy the Mitchels and their infants, a brood of hungry talents.

And amongst the guests at the dinners to which the Mitchels invited the *Nation* gang were not only Meagher and Jane Elgee, but a passionate adolescent named Devin Reilly. With an aching ambition to become Meagher or Mitchel, he was always willing to help out at *The Nation*. There was also a priest named Father Kenyon from Templederry in Tipperary, who occasionally snatched an evening in Dublin.

He told all the heretics to call him 'John' and he was a great talker; one could imagine him in another life being the owner of a musical pub where Gaelic songs and those of Thomas Moore and Davis were sung.

Kenyon was the sort of priest who told you frankly that there had been many like him in 1798, officers and counsellers in the army of peasant, or, as they were called, Croppy rebels. But now that the Catholic hierarchy had, like the Liberator himself, made their arrangements with the British government, Kenyon was an outsider, caught between his own rebellious soul and the orders of his bishop. If pushed, he would concede there were larger authorities than bishops. There was the authority of the people's suffering, and that spoke to him, he would say after sherry, louder than cardinals.

Then there was a young journalist named Patrick Smyth, who wore a theatrical moustache, and whom Speranza considered a vulgar and conceited fellow. He had been a classmate of Thomas Meagher's at the Jesuits at Clongowes and he would play a great role in the Mitchels' future.

Above all, there was the reputed genius, a strange fellow named James Clarence Mangan, the poet and librarian in his ratty coat who seemed to conceal in his pockets fragments of meals forgotten, and occasional bottles of tar water tonic he swigged to help his chest and still the malign spirits evoked in him by his drinking. He had written the supreme verse 'The Dark Rosaleen' – 'Rosaleen' or 'Roisin' being a word of code standing for Ireland itself; favoured as it was, at least in Irish dreams, by many European admirers from Spain to Russia.

There's wine from the Royal Pope
Upon the ocean green;
And Spanish ale shall give you hope,

My dark Rosaleen.
And gun-peal and slogan-cry
  Wake many a glen serene,
Ere you shall fade, ere you shall die, my dark Rosaleen.

Even Speranza was a little in awe of Mangan, though not in the self-interested way she was of Meagher and Duffy. But with his tortured features, his tenement of an overcoat, and his home in some squalid courtyard of the Liberties slums to the west of the Castle, she had no intention of courting him. She had thoughts of courting Meagher, and, if he failed to co-operate, Duffy.

Duffy's wife, Emily, had died a few years back, and his lovely departed spouse seemed to last longer in song than in the heart of the widower. There was a period when Speranza did indeed switch her attention from Meagher to Duffy, who was of a calmer disposition than the younger man; even if he were two-faced, criticising Mitchel behind his back for his self-supposed capacity to understand what the millions of landless folk felt in their misery.

Jenny heard an exchange at one of their soirees in Leeson Street. It seems Speranza said, 'I cannot forbear telling you, Mr Duffy, how deeply impressed was I by the opening lecture at the club.' She meant by this the '82 Club, and Duffy had given the said lecture. 'It was the sublimest teaching, and yet the style so simple for all its sublimity. It seemed as if truth passed directly from your heart to ours without means of any other medium. I felt that everywhere the thoughts struck where the mere words cannot. It was a case of soul speaking to soul.'

'I had not known you were there, my dear Speranza,' Duffy had replied.

'Actually, Mr Duffy,' Jane Elgee disclosed while her whole face coloured, 'I must admit I was not. I read your speech. But . . . but I hope to hear you in the flesh sometime soon.'

Charles Duffy tried not to laugh. Soon, it was discovered that he was engaged to a Catholic girl named Susan, and Speranza grew less impressed with his capacity to speak soul to soul.

Few other husbands could have ever brought such prize spirits home, genial even in their vanities. Sometimes John Martin was in town, staying at the house of his sister, Mrs Simpson. And now and then Jenny met the illustrious Smith O'Brien, a very sober man, soft spoken compared to Meagher but able to cast a hushed regard over any room he entered. Smith O'Brien was leader, and since he would not rule out the use of physical force, he was therefore seen, with varying degrees of hope from some and condemnation from others, as the 'physical force' leader.

7

The Further Story of the Mitchels in 1847-48

The great Thomas Carlyle, the Sage of Chelsea whose *French Revolution* in three volumes was essential reading for men and women of the age, came to Leeson Street too, along with his remarkable wife, and Mitchel was fond of telling people about the honour of it. Indeed, *The Nation* was becoming such a significant journal that the English papers had taken note of its reaction to Carlyle's new book on Cromwell, and Carlyle had been motivated to seek John Mitchel out.

He sat with his feet wrapped around the legs of his chair in the Mitchels' dining room, leaning forward like a handsome owl to discuss the age in which new revolutionaries like the Young Irelanders found themselves. In Jenny's dining room, the Mitchel sisters flitted about to anticipate every stray desire of the great talents there – and of the greatest of Britons, who was Scots. Carlyle even made a fuss of Mrs Mitchel as the relict of a brave Presbyterian non-subscribing pastor.

This was in the second beastly year, when the potato fields growing through the summer looked emerald and without blight, and indeed would survive on a considerable scale, though not enough had been planted by a hungry people. Was it an omen when Carlyle said, 'Dear Mrs Mitchel, you present at your table a truly noble potato. God bless the memory of Sir Walter Raleigh, who brought us the potato from South America. Without it we would be stripped of half the charm of the physical world, wouldn't you say?' Jenny gloried, even while she knew that, for the starving, the physical world itself was being stripped away.

Carlyle said he admired John and what he called his 'elastic spirit'. He opined that Mitchel was 'a Scots type the English have no time for! Don Quixote, though . . . Don Quixote is not a figure the English love. They don't tilt at windmills. They sell them out from under a miller who is behind in rent.'

Typical Gaels they were – he and Mitchel – mocking away gently at the Sassenach, the English Saxons. Did the great Scottish writer and his brilliant and quick-witted wife Jane endow the Mitchels with a sort of deathlessness and invulnerability? John and Jenny thought so! Like the Carlyles, Mitchel had contempt for political economy, the doctrine of not feeding the Irish with state-bought European or even Irish grain, for fear that would affect prices. Because that would affect the market, and the market was the very child of God for those who preached what Carlyle called 'the dismal science' of economics.

In this view God was the ordainer of markets and smiled on the men of the market who sometimes shelled out cash for a spire or stained glass in his honour. However, for Carlyle as for John Mitchel, God was not in markets at all, but in dreams and aspirations, in visions of an amended future.

With Carlyle's blessing and with the strength of their imagery, they would send the invader reeling. Scots people and Irish were notorious in thinking that England would be beaten by the graphics of their speech. The Liberator had believed it. The concept of a rational future was the 'Everlasting Yea' of which Carlyle had written, and Coercion bills and such were the 'Everlasting No'.

The Everlasting Yea bloomed in the winter. The Mitchels had moved now to Ontario Terrace in the city, and John returned home to share that his friends had come back from a mission to visit the French revolutionary government, the one that in February that year had overthrown the monarchy and caused the undemocratic lump of the king to flee to Surrey. How potent would it be if the French devoted their army to Ireland's liberation. The revolutionary group in Paris was in part led by the poet Lamartine, who was the new French Foreign Minister, and all over Europe, in hopeless monarchies, people were saying, 'Look at that – a poet Minister of State!' A dreary king fallen and a poet and other democrats bloodlessly – *bloodlessly* – elevated in his place.

At the start of the revolution in Paris, students and the workers put up barricades, and the king's men sent the National Guard to attack them, the regular French Army having already fired on and killed some protesters. But then the National Guard sided with the rebels. A prodigious and bloodless revolution resulted, and King Louis Philippe escaped to England in an ordinary hackney coach disguised as a Mr Smith! This was intoxicating stuff for the Mitchels, and caused amusement even amidst the children in the nursery.

Could any of the British Army, the Irishmen who served on it, side with the Irish in the French manner? Could there be a similar rebellion in Ireland? All of John Mitchel's friends, none more so than Meagher, excited by the pattern that had been set, were taken by the concept. And if there was to be moral force rebellion – though not without arms and barricades – why couldn't it be tomorrow? Not simply Ireland, but the world was ready for revolution and an enhancement of citizenry. In the two Sicilies, in Vienna, Berlin, Milan and Budapest, ordinary folk were ready.

Meagher, who had learned his French from the Jesuits of Stonyhurst, was disappointed in his conversations with Lamartine, the Wordsworth of France and now its Foreign Minister as well. The man who as a poet had once said that 'poetry was the voice of those who had no voice', was now as a minister wary of the Irish question. His government was anxious for Britain's recognition. If the British recognised the new French regime, the world would.

He and every right-thinking Frenchman, he assured young Meagher, felt the British administration of Ireland had made gross mistakes. Every Frenchman was sentimentally persuaded Ireland should have self-government – that at least. But being anxious for Britain's favour and recognition, Lamartine could not support an Irish rebellion by landing French troops in the west as Napoleon had in the 1798 uprising.

However, given Lamartine was such an adorer of the French tricolour, he gave Meagher a tricolour flag a woman friend of the poet's had given him. Of course, the gentle women needle-workers and revolutionaries would choose Meagher the *beau* as the fit recipient of their gift. Mitchel was taken with it when Meagher showed him. It was green and white and orange. Yet, both of them knew that under whatever colours, the Irish people continued to starve.

Thomas Francis Meagher was, by now, in the press of Britain and the world not simply Meagher, but Meagher of the Sword. Little Irish boys as far away as New England recited his Sword speech from the dock. He had transformed himself in the eyes of people with a speech that was the envy of young Irish orators, when Repeal and the O'Connells – the Liberator and his son – tried to force Repeal members to renounce any possible chance of any physical resistance in Ireland. Returned from Europe, impressed by uprisings not only in France, but in Belgium and Switzerland, Meagher had taken rhetorical wing in a speech that transcended other speeches.

'No, my lord,' he addressed whoever was the chairman of the meeting that day. 'No, my lord, I am not ungrateful for the man who struck the fetters off my arms while I was yet a child, and by whose influence, my father – the first who did so for two hundred years – sat for the last two years in the civic chair of an ancient city. But, my lord, the same God who gave to the Liberator the power to strike down an odious ascendency in this country, and enabled him to institute in this land the glorious law of religious equality – the same God gave to me a mind that is my own. A mind that has not been mortgaged to the opinions of any set of men – a mind I was to use and not surrender.

'I dissent from the peace resolutions of Repeal because I should have thereby pledged myself to the unqualified repudiation of physical force in all countries, at all times, and under every circumstance. This I could not do. There are times when arms alone will suffice, and when political amelioration calls for a drop of blood, and many thousand drops of blood. The soldier is proof against an argument – but he is not proof against a bullet. The man that will listen to reason – let him be reasoned with! But it is the weaponed arm of the patriot that can alone prevail against battalioned despotism. From that evening on which, in the valley of the Bethulia, God nerved the arm of the Jewish girl Judith to strike the drunken tyrant Holofernes in his tent, down to this day, in which he has blessed the insurgent cavalry of the Belgians, His Almighty hand has ever been stretched forth from the throne of light, to consecrate the flag of freedom and bless the patriot's sword.

'I hail the sword as a sacred weapon and if, my lord, it has sometimes taken the shape of the serpent and reddened the shroud of the oppressor with too deep a dye, like the anointed rod of the high priest, it has at other times, and as often, blossomed into celestial flowers to deck the freeman's brow!'

One could hear the cheers in the hearths and *shebeens* of Ireland as newspaper readers recited this speech to audiences of Irish. But only now did Meagher really take flight.

'Abhor the sword? Stigmatise the sword?' he asked. 'No, my lord, for in the passes of the Tyrol it cut to pieces the banner of the Bavarian, and through those cragged passes struck a path to fame for the peasant insurrectionists of Innsbruck! Abhor the sword? Stigmatise the sword? No, my lord, for at its blow, a giant nation, the United States, started from the waters of the Atlantic, and by its redeeming magic, and in the quivering of its crimson light, the crippled colony sprang into the attitude of a proud republic – prosperous, limitless and invincible!

'My lord, I learned that it was the right of a nation to govern itself not in this hall but upon the ramparts of Antwerp when Belgians displayed their arms, sweeping the Dutch marauders out of the fine old towns of Belgium, and demanded their recognition as a nation! This, the first article of a nation's Creed, I learned upon those ramparts, where freedom was justly estimated, and the possession of the precious gift was purchased by the effusion of generous blood.'

Thrilling music this was, and acclaimed by many honest Britons as well as Americans and French, Austrians and Hungarians. Published in *The Nation*, Meagher's 'Sword Speech' resonated around the world.

Although the harvest of 1847 had largely escaped the disease of putrefaction, there were still not enough potatoes since the sick and the starved and despairing, and those who in a desperate winter had eaten their seed crop, had not planted potatoes as normal. It was a deadly season with infections going on in the fever ships crammed with Irish eking their way across a winter sea to North America.

————

In the Easter of 1847 John and Jenny were invited to the opening of a wonder of the age, a stratagem against famine after so many Irish had died and others fled. Out in the centre of the nation, and in the south and the west, millions were frailer than a babe, and while few actually starved to death they were beset in the meantime by fevers when they were weak, fevers that took them away and left their shrunken corpses in ditches along roads, or in cabins where no fire burned, and no food graced the hearth.

But behold, their masters had thought of them and had brought to Dublin that Easter their very own version of resurrection, a novelty which John would consider one of the most ignominious of contraptions ever exhibited under the sun. On an esplanade outside the Royal Barracks in Dublin was erected the National Model Soup Kitchen, a marquee with as many laurels and banners and decorations as a circus tent. Amongst the parties who had been invited to this event, the military was very obvious, Mitchel saw, with plenty of officers from the garrison, and their ladies in satins.

In lines outside the marquee, guarded by police, were drawn up in orderly manner the impoverished class of Dublin and its surrounds – broken tradesmen, ruined farmers, destitute seamstresses – held back by a rope until the invitees had all had the chance to prowl around the humiliating interior of the soup pavilion. Some were allowed to stay inside, as John and Jenny did, and saw the police march in the paupers to various places along the walls, where from a central boiler they would be offered a fragment of bread and thin serving of soup, and would eat it using spoons that were chained in place. There, the poor of Ireland gulped down food crafted for the desperate, while the genteel people within discussed how appropriate all this was, and while John and Jenny shared an awareness that this was where the occupying power had Ireland, its hand locked on the spoon, driven to gratitude for the soup and bread slice.

That was a grim and humiliating day, even more so for the fact that appropriate satirists equipped to deal with the phenomenon of the soup kitchen and its chained soup spoons would be Dean Swift of Dublin or, in the modern era, Carlyle, who would have seen it as ridiculous and futile, apart from a minority of folk temporarily fed, in the name of the political economy he hated. Downing Street had answered the massed death of thousands of Irish with a trick, a gesture, a circus sideshow.

——

In that terrible year too, the Liberator went to London and found out again in conversation with the Whigs that nothing fresh, a mere reordering of the already failing policies, would be applied. He was in bad health himself, and the doctors recommended he go to Genoa, where indeed he would die in May 1847.

Jenny thought, 'Poor old man!' At the moment when he could have changed all, his courage let him down and he must have known it in some parts of his soul, and been inwardly chided and haunted by it.

Meanwhile John's own chiding eloquence manifested itself thrillingly in *The Nation*. 'Now, if the island does,' he wrote, 'as I think it plainly does, yield food, and enough for all its inhabitants, then I think we ought to be taught, as a fundamental postulate, that we have an absolute right to be sufficiently maintained out of that produce first. Not that any individual has a right to take another's property, but that the whole community has, and ought to exercise, that clear right, no matter what legal, social or physical obstacles may be in the way. For I do think it is still in the power of the aristocracy to save this nation and themselves at the same time, by letting the starving avail themselves of the harvest.'

Jenny was now in reverie and in every breath a rebel woman. A new Coercion Act of late 1847 allowed the Lord Lieutenant to proclaim any district he saw fit to, and to throw into proclaimed districts any number of police, and to levy rates on people for payment of all expenses and to suspend *habeas corpus* and other basic rights. The police were to go into any man's house in search of arms, and, as well as that, men between sixteen and sixty years could be called on to help track down persons suspected of crime. The people had asked for bread and were given an edict.

The landlords were relieved to get this new protection, for there was a considerable level of agrarian crime at that time – that is, small tenants pleading, threatening and knocking down doors to deliver ultimatums on the doorstep. And then being arrested and sent to Australia.

As Mitchel had it, 'A kind of sacred wrath took possession of a few Irishmen at this period. They could endure the horrible scene no longer, and resolved to cross the path of the British car of conquest, though it should crush them to atoms.' Jenny felt herself one of those, restrained from folly only by her care for the children.

Meanwhile, Duffy increasingly found John's writing too baiting. The end of the connection came in December 1847. Speranza wrote a grand dirge as grievous as the times.

> There is a proud array of soldiers – what do they round
> your door?
> They guard our masters' granaries from the thin hands
> of the poor.
> Pale mothers, wherefore weeping? – Would to God that
> we were dead,
> Our children swoon before us and we cannot give them
> bread.

———

Duffy almost regretfully called Mitchel's general tone 'mischievous' when asking him to leave *The Nation*. O'Connell's people complained that his writing was too mockingly seditious. Other papers reported on John's dismissal, which in many quarters made him even more a hero. So pleased was his mother that she travelled to Dublin to stay with John and Jenny – the mere fifty-nine miles including crossing the river – and with a brittle positivity tried to talk him into going back to the law and ceasing to stir the wells of his ironic – and not that she would call it that, but some said 'insurrectionary' – commentary.

At first, he did think of resuming the law, perhaps in Dublin, perhaps back in Newry. But it was clear that this was a far too expectant moment of history, and he told Jenny that if she could bear it he wanted to be making journalism until it was resolved, when he would either bow to the terrible absurdity or try to eliminate it.

In any case, John Mitchel would not retire now, when his voice had reached its apogee. A number of influential men sent him messages backing him financially to start a new paper. Jenny could see it was the only thing for him – how could he go back to being a County Down solicitor? She had even felt sure that her mother-in-law and the sisters would take over the raising of her children, should John or she be punished some way. Punishment was in the air, after all.

Mitchel rented a new office in Trinity Street, a very short walk from home, and gathered all the talents he could still muster, including his old friends John Martin and Clarence Mangan.

On the February day in 1848 the *United Irishman* edition number one appeared, Jenny went to the office in the narrow street. The print run was not arriving fast enough from the nearby printers to keep the paperboys and women supplied. People were paying many times over the price to get a copy. The price during the day rose to a shilling, and when the second batch was printed at about four o'clock, the crush at the office door was so terrific that one poor news seller, a woman, was carried away in a faint.

This popular acclamation of John's arguments was piquant and wonderful, and Jenny felt it filling her with the idea that alterations would be now made in tyrannous things such as Coercion and Famine Poor Laws. The Irish hated the work-houses but sometimes in desperation left their children at the gates in the hope they would survive on the just-enough-to-survive-on gruel. In any case, John's view in the *United Irishman* was for not-so-passive resistance: 'I had come to the conclusion that the whole system ought to be met with resistance at every point; and the means for this would be extremely simple; namely, a combination amongst the people to obstruct and render impossible the transport and shipment of Irish provisions; to refuse all pay in its removal; to destroy the highways, to prevent everyone, by intimidation, from daring to bid for grain or cattle if brought to auction under distress – in short to offer a passive resistance universally.'

This was a cry that bespoke largely peaceful means. But the call for resistance continued to resound in other editions of the eighteen days it would be published. Jenny agreed with him that every other option had failed, but had been fearful about his editorials. In them he espoused defying of the authorities and the destroying of highways to block the export of food and the movement of the military. Jenny reassured herself that Duffy and Mitchel both had survived the earlier trial concerning the matter of railways.

On one editorial in those bitter days, John defied Lord Clarendon, Lord Lieutenant of Ireland, across the river in Dublin Castle, to charge him with sedition if he wanted to, and boldly pack a jury against him, 'or else see the accused rebel walk a free man out of the Court of Queen's Bench, which will be a victory only less than the defeat of Your Excellency's redcoats in the field'.

So many Irish were so responsive to John's eloquence on paper that he did expect to be immune. Even were he ultimately proven innocent, though, what worried Jenny was how being arrested for sedition might upset the children. She did not know the government in Westminster were manufacturing a special law for John Mitchel, an obscene law that would remove from the prisoner the option of pleading the past mistakes of government as any defence.

Spring broke and the buds broke in an Ireland dominated by the phenomenon of death, and grass grew up around the corpses on the roadways. Many of the starving had taken to the roads and the tracks these past springs, hoping to encounter unspecified mercy. Fevers dropped them before they reached it. On 13 May, John went home with his younger brother William, who had been his representative with the printers and remarkably useful, and with loyal young Devin Reilly, and sat down with Jenny and the older children for dinner. During the meal the maid answered the door and met two policemen with a warrant for his arrest.

8

John Mitchel, May 1848

John Mitchel, condemned on a Saturday and in his cell in Newgate in Dublin, was aware that his Irish Confederate brethren were restraining their club members in the city and elsewhere from any attempt to rescue him. They had been honest with him on that. A delegation from the '82 and Confederate clubs had visited him the day before his sentencing and told him they wanted to keep open the possibility of an autumn and harvest uprising – it not yet being even high summer. They would be ready then, their message was, and when they succeeded, they would have him brought back in honour from whatever penal settlement he was in!

But when John had been arrested he found he had rather depended that his allies would not be quiet if he were to be shipped out of Dublin for a convict enclave. Penal settlements were all in other hemispheres, the western and southern, far off. He had not thought the reaction to any sentence he received would be as restrained as Smith O'Brien and others seemed to want it to be.

On that Saturday, old Baron Tom Lefroy – a suitor of the novelist Jane Austen in his youth – condemned him without any subtle conversation at all. It had been a harsh punishment for his forays into defiance – fourteen years of transportation, from 27 May in 1848. Mitchel had until now believed he was right in predicting to Lord Clarendon that it might be dangerous to arrest and find him guilty; that there would be resultant acts of insurgency. It was true Jenny had been invited out on most nights of his imprisonment to march with this or that Confederate club through the city's streets and past Green Street. His cell was on that side of the prison that was by the square, and he could hear the tramp of men, whose solemnity was itself a warning to the Lord Lieutenant, and their three cheers for Mitchel. That was the extent of what had happened so far. And it might be all.

But, given that under the new and special recipes for treason felony John realised now he could not have been found innocent, Lord Clarendon had taken the marching of the clubs to heart and meant to ship him off at once – the same Saturday of the sentencing. He was slated to be hurried away before dusk to forestall any massed intent by Mitchel's colleagues or their said Confederates.

Lefroy, narrow-faced and handsome in a judicial fashion, and a supposed historian of Ireland, was opposed to any liberation of Catholics, given the massacres French Catholics had carried out on Huguenot families like his two centuries earlier in France. Thus, between the letter of the Treason Felony Act and mercy, he was happy to steer clear of any potential tenderness in the legislation. The Treason Felony

Act of 1848 had declared that it was a statutory offence punishable by up to twenty years' imprisonment even to 'imagine' let alone to 'compass or devise' that the British monarchy would ever lose sovereignty over Ireland, or any other part of Her Dominions. Thus, to foresee a republic of Ireland achieved even by peaceful means was a transportable offence. One of its provisions was that it violated the law to stick the Queen's likeness upside down on a letter!

Lefroy was willing as a sectarian too to condemn anyone who claimed kinship with Papists. Since Mitchel had represented Irish Catholics in the courts of County Down and in the Four Courts of Dublin, as well as at Newgate, and since he did not consider them a debased form of humanity, he was as good as and no better than a Papist and ripe to be condemned by Baron Lefroy. Nonetheless, the British newspapers reflected on Lefroy's moderation in merely condemning Mitchel to a fourteen-year sentence. It would do the trick, of course, and send him home, a weakened force at the age of fifty-two, a man with coughs and a stoop, unfit for revolution.

How many of Austen's young men, with whom she danced and whom she viewed as gentlemen, were 'moderate' judicial assassins like Lefroy? How many colony-based monsters were in their youth the object of her smiles? And how lucky was she not to have given up her pen for any of them. Lefroy had tried, for one thing, to convert the Jews of Dublin to the Church of Ireland, which would certainly have created a flurry over the reserving of pews in the Cathedral itself.

In the court there had been three tiers of onlookers – balconies crammed with spectators – and when the specially selected jury made up of friends and dependents of the

Castle brought down the verdict, Mitchel was returned to his cell. He had been allowed to see his wife and two poor boys, ten-year-old Johnny and eight-year-old James, the childhood of both darlings intruded upon by Lefroy – and, some would say, by their father as lightning rod as well. His heart yawned for Jenny in a terrible, doleful, prohibited way. What God had joined together let Tom Lefroy tear apart. Jenny whispered, 'I have spoken to Smith O'Brien. I consider your friends disgraced if they let you be sent off!'

She meant, of course, sent off out of the city, for transportation. Mitchel spoke into her hair. 'Tell him if he is thinking of uprisings, the city is indeed the place. Not the villages but the city! Remind him that is the doctrine of the French.'

Her hair smelled of rosewater and from her face a delightful smell of patchouli and nutmeg. She was dressed and scented for a reunion. But for fear of her and of others, they were getting rid of him, and he was still in a suit, not prison clothes! There was clearly time for other servants of Downing Street in other places to attend to that.

'We will meet, Johnny of mine, sooner than Lefroy thinks,' Jenny said as they had the ultimate hug. John told his eldest son, John C., that it was unjust but he was now the family's man. Then Jenny and the boys went, and from his cell Mitchel sensed an ongoing stillness in the city, no cries of outrage indicating his rescue.

Quite early in the afternoon, his jailers rushed him out to a small stone yard to put him in fetters. There were three of them, one armed with a shiny new carbine. Another asked him to put his foot on the stone seat that was by the wall so that one of the bolts could be fastened on Mitchel's ankle. They were in such a hurry they told him to take the other one of his fetter chains in his hand, and like a bride carrying her own train he obeyed their order to come along. In the tense calm that surrounded the prison, he heard an occasional military command and tramp of instant obedience from beyond the walls. These were not sounds made by his people but by regular troops. The stillness of the air depressed Mitchel. He doubted there would be any rescue in the street, yet who knew? So he followed his jailers through an empty hall of the prison to the outer door.

He stepped out on the square into a host of men and horses and saw lines of police in the streets and along the railings. All he could see at first were police capes with the sheen of a minor downfall on them. And beyond the capes, across Green Street, more of them were along the pavement by the boarding house where country lawyers like himself had stayed when in the city on court matters. But there was cavalry as well, black-helmeted, scarlet-coated and cuirass-chested in the streets and at the intersections, the horses nickering and tossing their heads to make the chief noises that could be heard. And blotting out the other side of the square, like a ceremonial hearse for a European king, nothing other than a large black omnibus.

Across the way, men and women gazed over police shoulders in perfect silence, so that the clack of his chain and an occasional hoof-clop was the chief noise in the street. He walked a little way, scanning the crowd for Jenny, who would be there even if no other rebel was. But it was too packed out by police and cavalry to see. Then, at the command of uniformed police, he turned up the steps into the interior of the omnibus. Constables and two detectives awaited him inside. He was flattered that in their faith in his demonic powers, they had decided his strength was equal to a full company of police, who sat around the walls and seemed pale and large-eyed. The door was instantly slammed shut outside, and a commanding voice cried, 'To the North Wall!'

He was being taken straight to a ship, and somewhere in the way he could not help hoping there might be a demonstration, planned or impulsive, and he be shot, or rescued! If the latter, by tonight the fire of revolution would burn garish outside the courts. Dublin would be choked with barricades. Or, to its peril, not.

9

Jenny on Eve of Sentencing, and Sentencing Day, 1848

Jenny's bewilderment the night before sentencing, as she settled the boys and girls to their rest, can be imagined, and she may have wished she had John's mother and sisters still there to respond to the questions. But they had taken their own house in the city and if things went badly – as all expected, given the strictness of the legislation and the narrowness of the especially selected jury – she would have to answer the children there. 'But why is Lord John Russell so angry with Pa?' 'Why is Lord Clarendon so mean?' 'Can we see Da tomorrow? I can show him my new book.'

Prior to the day of sentencing, every evening some of the Dublin Confederate clubs marched to Green Street in their green ranks in excellent order, and gave the prisoner three almighty cheers that he must have heard. And on that Friday night, six hundred members of the Dr Doyle Confederate Club reached the steps of number 8 Ontario Terrace by way of the Grand Canal. Jenny had heard them coming, and welcomed them, since they seemed to offer unexampled possibilities. They told her they had every intention to resist any deportation of their heroic brother, her husband.

'Madame,' intoned their captain, 'however some of us Irish citizens may have disagreed on abstract questions, we have now but one absorbing duty to perform – namely to prepare night and day for the purpose, should he be convicted, of restoring him in triumph to liberty and to you!'

Jenny stepped into the modest little garden in front of the house and delivered the answer she had prepared. 'I have not hitherto allowed any fears I might feel for my children's safety, or my own, to interfere with that line of policy which my husband thought it his duty to pursue, and I do not intend to do so now. I believe it would be a fatal madness to let any Confederate, including my husband, be shipped away, simply shipped away, without our intervention! This is a moment when those who preach the sword cannot carry it merely sheathed. If such a statement is conspiracy or treason felony, the authorities know where I live!'

She had not made such a reckless invitation without being assured by Mrs Mitchel the elder and the four sisters, and by the O'Hagans, and a dozen other noble couples, that they were ready to raise the children if she herself should be charged for this brief defiance.

The delegation from the '82 and Confederate clubs that had visited Mitchel in Newgate the day before his sentence had asked him to confirm their decision that they hold themselves ready not for his rescue – should he be sentenced on the Saturday – but for the coming harvest rebellion in the autumn. However, Mitchel believed that not all the Confederate clubs agreed with waiting for autumn; certainly the company that visited 8 Ontario Terrace didn't. He therefore refused to sign a paper deprecating all attempts at rescue. He did so on principles he believed in. All the rebellions that year, from Budapest to Paris to Rome, had occurred in cities.

'He may be home tomorrow night,' she told them. 'Mr Holmes his lawyer thinks he might well be. Then there will be no need of your gallant intervention.'

But in the middle of the night, Meagher hammered on the door, and the maid in her night clothes invited him in and then called Jenny. Jenny had till then thought it might be the police. If they arrested her too, the Confederates – the whole Young Irelander apparatus – could scarcely avoid rising in outrage!

Meagher, though, was very grim all over his young face, all flirtatiousness and teasing gone. As they drank tea in the small hours, he filled her in with intelligence from one of the constables who guarded the jury: the verdict seemed to be going the Crown's way. It was only if the jurors thought the law so absurd that it could not mean what it said, for example – that it was a felony to be punished by up to twenty years' transportation to claim that a time in the infinite future might come when Ireland might not be subject to the sovereignty of the Crown. If such a clause were to be taken literally, well . . . John was guilty. But such a law was an indecent intrusion on the mere speculations of Irish people. It was invalid to make the wish into a crime itself, except as a pretext to net a man like John Mitchel.

John's brother Willy had been assuring her all week there would be a hung jury, but when he talked to others she sometimes heard even him mutter that Baron Lefroy had a solid jury this time – not even one sentimental Repealer on it.

Jenny thanked Meagher and told him optimistic forecasts, rather than realistic ones, were better not encouraged. But if John were found guilty and sentenced the next day, when the jury came back, and was moved out of the country, surely there would have to be resistance.

'I'll be at the Rotunda early to confer with O'Brien,' Meagher told her solemnly. She could tell there was no shrinking in him. Merely wise caution.

Before breakfast on the Saturday, Jenny went to the half-empty court – Baron Lefroy had called an unexpectedly early appearance for his jury so that they would not be booed. She heard the jury bring down the verdict and be booed in any case as Lefroy thanked them for their service. For the moments after the sentence there was no breathable air and as if that tower of time, fourteen years, had fallen about here and all was dust.

Jenny decided then, after she and the boys had seen Mitchel in the prison, and everyone was feverish – including Mitchel and herself – with all the possibilities of the day, to take the children to the O'Hagans' where they would spend the coming hours. She felt she must go to link up with Meagher to add her voice to the clamour she expected to rise that day throughout the capital. In other separations from John there had always been a projected date and acceptable hour of homecoming. But not this time.

———

So she took a cab from the O'Hagans' over the steely river to the cake-shaped Rotunda and its colonnade, the headquarters of Young Ireland located by the laying-in hospital for women with child. The Confederates were said to be meeting there early to discuss John's case and the contingencies of the day. Perhaps three dozen members were already there when she arrived – as if news of the verdict had disturbed their Saturday lying abed.

Meagher came out to meet her. 'Is it true the verdict is in,' he asked, 'and has gone against us?'

Jenny confirmed it had.

'Oh, God,' he said. 'What is to be done?'

Meagher and Jenny met up with the young man Devin Reilly. With boyish naivete, Devin took hold of her wrist and looked her in the eye. 'He cannot be let go, Mrs Mitchel.'

Others were beginning to arrive, but the agenda did not commence until twelve, said gentlemen in the know. Jenny asked Meagher and young Reilly would they accompany her to a tea house, which they did, and the men in the smoky interior cheered them as they came in and sat. It was all very well, Jenny decided, but would they still be drinking tea as John was taken away?

A gentleman she vaguely knew came up to her to make a speech, but Meagher intercepted him.

'Let the poor woman be, there's the fellow!' He lowered his voice. 'There's nothing you can say. Leave it to the Europeans and Americans to mock this sentence!'

Indeed, Jenny wasn't very patient to be so met and accosted either. What once might have looked like support now seemed cheap sentiment. As soon as the tea was ordered, she regarded Thomas Francis himself.

'I feel it here, Tom. This is what it was all for. All the talk and drilling with weapons. John discussed with me the very plan to follow if a leader was silenced by a fraud of a jury.'

Devin Reilly pecked at his tea excitedly. 'She's right, Mr Meagher,' he said. 'John has brought this on as if to plan, and the plan should now be followed. We have Confederate clubs all over the city, groups of two hundred to six hundred men. What is all their drilling for, as well as all the argument? If not for liberating John Mitchel . . . and starting things at last.'

Jenny began to tremble, to hear from young Devin what she had told herself since she'd seen John an hour earlier in prison.

'You said, Mr Meagher,' Devin continued, 'in the debate after you got back from Lamartine: "If the Union will be maintained in spite of the will of the Irish people, if the Government of Ireland insist upon being a government of dragoons and bombardiers, of detectives and light infantry, then up with the barricades, and invoke the God of battles." Your own words, sir.'

Meagher was nodding. His rhetoric was plush but so was his resolve. 'I am sure, my dear lady,' said Meagher, 'that there is no unwillingness in our Confederate clubs or amongst the '82 clubs. Reilly, let us take our proposal to Smith O'Brien.'

Meagher was no longer blatantly handsome as he normally was, for yesterday's cologne water was drying and turning sour on him and he had not slept. Jenny had an impulse to kiss him now, nonetheless, for his willingness to press Smith O'Brien towards the unavoidable issue.

She found, however, that like any woman who set the hares running, she was then put in the corner while men consulted about where the hares' run would end up. She was then in fact, with every courtesy and guarantee of support, put in a coach and sent back to the O'Hagans' in Mountjoy Square, to see the children again as she dearly wanted to. After telling them that Mr Meagher and Mr O'Brien were discussing to see if anything could be done straight off for their father, she sat in a very pleasant corner by the standards of most days – the conservatory of the O'Hagan house, where she drank tea in what was developing as a bright Saturday.

'One way or another, your John will not be long imprisoned,' Mrs O'Hagan asserted. 'O'Hagan and I talked about it half the night. Lord Clarendon has gone too far! Strangely he is not a bad fellow face-to-face, a friend of playwrights and all the rest. But it is – as always – a matter of what his orders are, and how he obeys them!'

Jenny was tempted to utter the most base insults to Lord Clarendon's name, the kind that a carter might use if he combined his cruder imagination with that of a poet like Mangan. Poor Mangan today shaking his head after some opium drench in one of the squalid laneways behind Dublin Castle. Mangan already mourned for all Ireland's lost centuries – and if the '82 clubs called Ireland to arms today, he would himself probably be lost in dreams.

At O'Hagans' after noon, the men of Young Ireland all bustled into the house. Smith O'Brien was there now – he looked like a man awaiting a blow. Having arrived, they announced little to her. However, Meagher and other men were carefully speaking to him in conspiratorial voices, which Jenny thought boded well.

Mrs O'Hagan vanished when it became clear that O'Brien wished to sit with Jenny and address her. He entered and sat down across the little tea table in the conservatory's pearly light. There were shadows of exhaustion in his face. There had not been any such greyness in John's face when she last saw it – there had been expectation.

'Mrs Mitchel,' Smith O'Brien told her, 'it has been a hard business repressing the Confederate clubs from taking to

116

their weapons' stores and marching upon Dublin to liberate your husband. But I think you should see this.'

He showed her a letter from her John addressed to a range of Young Ireland notables, saying that he left the issue of his rescue ultimately to the leaders on the ground.

'He only wrote that,' Jenny said, 'because he believed you would see in any case the absolute . . . the imperative need to prevent him being sent out.'

Smith O'Brien explained to her that as much as all Ireland wished Mitchel instantly free, there could be no uprising today and no rescue. But he would surely not expect one. The Confederates and the '82 Club should hold their resources for the coming crisis in the autumn, at the attempted shipping out of the harvest. O'Brien opined there would be a plan in place by then. Then he said something similar to that which Mrs O'Hagan had said. 'John Mitchel will not be long a prisoner of the British Crown! Despite my arguments with him, he will be President of a new Ireland, uniting Protestant and Papist.'

She waved John's letter and said, 'This in no way exempts you, Mr O'Brien. By the date, it was written some time ago.'

'If they ship your husband today, we are short in all regards. We are short of time and weapons and plans.'

'And valour too, it seems,' Jenny accused him. 'I am the mother of five children, the eldest being an adolescent, the last a young girl named Minnie barely eighteen months. What will you do, Mr O'Brien, about restoring John Mitchel to those children?'

'All our efforts,' said O'Brien almost wearily, 'all our efforts, all our plans, are bent upon an uprising at the time of the shipping out of the harvest.'

'The autumn,' Jenny challenged him. It was too far off and too speculative.

'That is the time to which all our actions and plans and best hopes are directed. We have a good chance of bringing down the British dominance of Ireland then. And your husband – he will be the first state prisoner released, and will come home, madame, to acclamations and all the honours of the new state! And he will be nothing less than a consul of the people.'

Jenny had by now stood up. Her anger was vast, but she was not sure where to address it. O'Brien seemed too calm, as if he could not understand the mortal enmity she felt for him. Revolution by evasion. The French hadn't done it that way.

'Mr O'Brien,' she challenged him, 'what would you like to happen if you were the prisoner? Remembering always that John gave comfort to you in your imprisonment in Parliament!'

'But I wouldn't have wanted my confreres to try to liberate me by stratagems with no chance of success,' he replied. 'When he is taken to his ship it will be under the most dense conditions of security, amidst unassailable phalanxes of police and cavalry. To be honest, we fear the casualties the people would suffer attacking such a column without preparation.'

'Since you have all met Lamartine,' she accused him, 'you want to choose an hour when no blood will be spilt! That revolution . . . It was a fluke! Even the French them-selves were surprised by it. You have the masses, and the masses will be on the streets. They are fuelled with anger over John's sentence. The revolution itself declares its hour. Its hour is today.'

'We will not wait much longer, Madame Mitchel,' said Smith O'Brien. 'But we must have time to marshal without catching the eye of Dublin Castle. And inviting a massacre!'

'But,' said Jenny, 'if even you have not ruled out blood, any who bleed today will be honoured and rewarded by a new Irish state . . . When you invoke blood, sir, you must be prepared for it to be shed. Otherwise, you'll never pass from poetry to acts!'

'You are quite right,' he said, as if given suddenly the debating points for her consolation. 'But preparations are also essential.'

'You must not patronise me. These are easy choices for you, Mr O'Brien. I am the one who lives with them.'

'We all acknowledge that. You and your children will never want . . .'

'Except for a husband,' she challenged him.

He seemed very tired by this mess, of the exercise of calming the wife. He wanted to get back to discussions with his lieutenants.

Jenny said, careless of how her words might spread in the room, 'All I know for certain is that John foresaw an uprising at a time one of the leading men was arrested. If John is not a leading man . . . who is, Mr O'Brien? I reserve the right myself to cry out for his release.'

'As do I!' called a contralto voice from amongst the crowd looking in from the dining room, which Jenny had till that second presumed entirely male. It was not like Mrs O'Hagan to make a demonstration amongst men. But it was not her. It was Speranza, who had somehow arrived, and her voice swelled with intentions.

Smith O'Brien ignored this outcry from the Castle darling, and took Jenny's hand, seeking it as if for his own comfort. 'I must ask you to believe that everyone here wants your husband freed forever and honoured. The question is, can he most effectively be liberated a little later than today?'

'I cannot believe he would not say, "Free me now, brother!"'

'Then we must look at that, dear lady, one last time and see if there is a chance of success.'

He looked across the room as if someone else were awaiting his attention.

'Am I to be privy to those discussions?' asked Jenny.

'Dear lady, you are not a member of the Confederation. But I promise I shall convey our decisions promptly.'

'Is it because of your earlier arguments with him?' Jenny asked. 'Is that why you will make no attempt?'

To his credit Smith O'Brien answered without apparent distraction.

'We did not argue. It was all a difference of strategy. He was trying to win Northern Protestants over while I tried to win the landlords.'

'I don't care whether it's landlords or Northern Protestants, I want my John back.'

Jenny stood and looked at all the men on the edges of the room, crowding in from the dining room. Some hung their heads. Devin did not. Meagher was holding his opened hands up.

Speranza towered behind some of them. 'I have my carriage here at your disposal,' she cried out. Jenny felt a profound warmth for her she never had before.

Then Smith O'Brien suddenly declared, 'Be assured, Mrs Mitchel, our men will reconnoitre the path between Newgate prison and the docks in case unexpected opportunities arise. But I know your husband would say, do not strike when they are all prepared. Strike when they are not.'

'Miss Elgee,' Jenny cried. Smith O'Brien stepped backwards, ceremoniously, a little too much like an undertaker. 'Miss Elgee,' Jenny repeated, 'we believe in possibilities today. Don't we?' Speranza said she did, and Jenny was her friend for life.

———

Now, putting on again her shawl and hat, Jenny found Mrs O'Hagan was with her all at once as if by family agreement, accompanying her to Speranza's carriage to visit the jail, to get a last view of John Mitchel. The only man in history, she would say, transported on the day of his sentencing! Meagher followed them out, and given that the street was crowded with carriages went and fetched Speranza's carriage and driver a little way away.

He said to Speranza, 'You will be careful, Jane.'

'As careful as you and Mr O'Brien clearly intend to be,' she said, giving him a dose of his own passionate indifference. He was clearly offering himself as a male guardian for the expedition but could see they had chosen not to ask for one.

Off they rolled on what would be at most an easy drive, but was slow because of traffic once they crossed the river and its sickly reflections of that day of loss and dishonour. They could not get near Green Street and the jail, even though Speranza in her deepest Castle-style voice told the police at a barrier that Jenny was the prisoner's wife and that, by the way, she herself was honoured to be there in such company.

A senior policeman of some sort appeared and Speranza honked in a way that could not be ignored that he must as an Irishman know the state Jenny would be in. He nodded as if he did, and when he saw Jenny's half-crazed face, he bowed.

But then he vanished and there was a large black wagon creaking across the little square, John in it, turning into Dorset Street, and turning again to approach the North Circular Road. It was at first as if they were taking him home to Newry, her John – or so she thought in her madness.

Speranza told her coachman that they could intercept the great juggernaut at Henrietta Street, and they thundered off and turned right and approached a great barrier of police and cavalry again at the junction before the black wagon passed. There were also men from the clubs, some of them wearing uniforms, gathered to watch the thing grind by, as if they longed for a word, a clarifying command. Most wore no uniform, having been ordered off doing so by Smith O'Brien, and again Speranza leaned out of the carriage window and communed with them about that – the question of whether action should have been taken, as a matter of honour, successful or not.

And Speranza's wagon did see quite close John Mitchel's great, black vehicle, which seemed designed to carry the most gigantic animal ever to walk the earth. And while she loudly promised to give the men of the Confederation a stern talking to, somehow the comfort offered by Mrs O'Hagan's firm hand around her waist saved Jenny from losing her hold on the day and leaving the carriage and ranting in the street to amass these gentlemen whose clarity had been sapped by O'Brien.

Speranza said what Jenny already perceived – that a genuine assault up any crossroad before Great North Road would have drawn off great numbers of police and cavalry. A second attack then, back at another point, might well have routed the thinned-out column, and a rescue might have occurred – and though some rebels might have been dead at the end of the day, what honour there would have been in that, and what grave lessons it would have given to Downing Street!

At last, without any rescue being attempted, the caravan turned south-east towards the North Docks. Any fantastical dream of a return to Newry and every plan of battle fell flat there. Jenny roared, 'Johnny!' It was piteously loud and some people averted their eyes.

They took her back to O'Hagans' then, where the children were. Even Speranza seemed altered, strangely reduced so that Henty did not fear her anymore.

Jenny knew John's sisters were coming down from Newry – where they had been protecting their mother from becoming enraged in a court – to take up their new address. She would rest after they arrived, she promised herself, and had welcomed their willingness to help.

10

Mitchel's Transportation

The noise of the enclosed tumbril rolling forth from Green Street was enormous. John Mitchel could tell, and see through barred window slots, that the cavalry had come up on either side and that they were travelling on the North Circular Road towards the quays. He sat on a long bench, either side of him a plainclothes detective – one of whom held a pistol, cocked and with a cap on the hammer, and its barrel to Mitchel's heart.

When they got close to the river, there was no demonstration. No outcry from the crowd. For all he knew, though, there might be an explosion; a bomb or other infernal machine might go off in front of the great wagon, and another behind. There might be sudden chaos amongst the horses, fallen police capes, stunned police. Then a party to extract him from the great black conveyance! Meagher had spoken thrillingly of the sword, but swords would do nothing in the modern scene. Stunning detonations would do the job. Mind you, with all that drastic noise and jolting, the detective's pistol would certainly go off, and he be blown to fragments. But if that had to happen, so be it.

Instead, however, the wagon made a painful turn clockwise to the quays and continued at an increased pace – accompanied by the cantering of the hussars. It was not long until the huge wagon drew up suddenly, and Mitchel was grateful that the detective failed with that shock to shoot him dead by accident.

When he dismounted, the pistol-holder and his companion accompanied John down the steps and out of the apparatus. He found himself by the quay wall with two ranks of soldiers guarding the path to and through the dock gates. No turbulent citizenry were anywhere in sight. So, it was as Smith O'Brien and Tom Meagher and the rest had warned him: they would lead the countryside in rebellion at harvest time in autumn. And when they controlled the country, Meagher of the Sword would bring Mitchel home with brass bands. He'd damn well want to.

Jenny would not be satisfied by this day, though. John felt her disappointment acidly in his own mouth. Poor Jenny of the five little Mitchels. Advancing in his fetters, holding half the chains cradled in his arms, John saw through the gates on the pier a large cutter full of armed sailors below the stone dock, manoeuvring in the water. A standing officer ordered him by bullhorn to descend by ladder, which was not easy given the chain. The detectives kept their pistols on him as he went down, and then followed him aboard.

As ordered, Mitchel sat beside the naval officer, and the marine guards averted their gaze and the oarsmen began immediately taking him out over a grey-brown River Liffey, with the corpse of a dog floating on it, to the trim government steamer *Shearwater*. A man on the quay called out across the water, 'God bless you, John Mitchel!' And Mitchel heard the naval officer gasp, and saw an inspector of police warning the man not to create a disturbance.

The officer at his side was short and dark and about forty-five years of age. He said, 'You'll find yourself comfortable on *Shearwater*, Mr Mitchel.'

At the ship's landing stage, some of the marines went first, then he followed up the stairs in the gravity of his chains. Mitchel arrived on the open deck and officers there nodded and took note of him. The short, dark officer was right behind him and exchanged salutes with his brethren on the deck, saying, 'Come with me, please, Mr Mitchel,' and John did so in a daze.

Mitchel was led aft and conducted down a companionway to a good cabin – not the chain-hold, as he had anticipated. At the officer's signal, the purser had followed them up with a case of tools, and once they were in the cabin, the officer ordered the purser to remove Mitchel's fetters. So their weight came off and Mitchel felt he might, if admitted to the deck again, waft ashore. The officer called for a steward and asked for sherry and water to be brought in. They sat together, Mitchel and the officer, at the unreality of a polished, neat table, waiting for it to be served.

When it arrived, and the officer had himself prepared a glass, he told Mitchel he was to be taken that night to the infamous penal structure in Cork Harbour, Spike Island. He himself would only go as far as Kingstown on this vessel, since his own ship, the *Dragon*, lay there, and, after the pleasure of escorting Mitchel, would assume his own command.

Then that chap ventured to say that Mitchel must have heard of the unfortunate ship *Nemesis*. 'I was her captain,' he told him with a restrained pride.

'Oh, then you are Captain Hall,' Mitchel surmised. 'We took note of your adventures in the literary pages of my own seditious newspaper.' For Captain Hall had written a passable book about his adventures in China. 'And your earlier work about the Peruvian and Brazilian revolutions,' Mitchel added, and saw on the captain's face the delighted vanity of the author whose work has been read.

However, the captain declared, 'Your mind is said to have been running too strongly on revolutions lately.'

'Almost exclusively,' Mitchel told him.

'You'll be amused to know I've been invited to dinner at the Castle tonight,' the captain informed him. 'I'll come up to the Castle from Kingstown. I have you in the afternoon, and the Lord Lieutenant in the evening. Both sides of the Irish equation!'

Mitchel was not as tickled by this as the other man. But both of them said it was surpassing strange, and then the captain–author declared he had heard Mitchel's father was a very good man.

He led Mitchel on deck again and shook his hand. Accompanied by echoing commands he descended the ship's stairs to his boat, and John thought at once of his family: his mother being brought back there now, just where the estuary narrowed, by Claremont Bridge, in the house she and the sisters were renting. And Jenny, in Ontario Terrace, off in the sunset murk. Jenny would probably need to leave her house and move in with his sisters and mother. She wouldn't be delighted. As for the children, even the boys were perhaps a little too young to know the nature of his crime and that there was honour in it to answer the false thunders of government. They would be fed and nurtured in sacred trust, Mitchel was sure, by his confederates. But John was sure his newspaper office had been ransacked already, its contents seized, its print scattered, its printing press draped like a corpse, and its door barred. No income there for Jenny.

He felt sourly after Captain Hall had left him. He, Mitchel, had gestured, the nation had listened, given him ninety-five per cent approval for effort. But he had achieved precisely nothing. He had made tyrants fearful for some six months, he told himself. That was all. It was not enough. And the tyrants had him well and truly now.

Mitchel still stood on deck and no-one forbade it as they picked up steam again, making a fair way. They passed Bray Head. The mountains of Wicklow showed up to the west in a profound melancholy purple. The two detectives had been in the background all this while and suggested, as if it were not an order, that they might go down for tea, since darkness was at last dropping, and Ireland of the saints and plentiful martyrs could no longer be discerned.

11

Mitchel – from Spike Island to Bermuda, 1848

The detectives showed him to the cabin and its good bunk, and a meal was brought to them. They all ate functionally and then the plainclothes men left him and went into an adjoining cabin. They told him – as if at his service and not at the service of the court – one or other of them would be at the door all night. After they left, Mitchel felt so pleased to be alone again that he was struck by a sudden mad comforting certainty that he would see Jenny again, and it was on that unreliable basis that he fell to sleep.

The next morning in his cabin he found that someone, an officer or one of the detectives, had left a copy of the final edition of the *United Irishman* in the cabin. Issue 16 was the last one the world would see – the proprietor and editor being under transportation, but his friends John Martin and Devin Reilly faithfully getting the edition into print and to the streets as a genuine act of defiance. Reilly, young and as volcanic as Kossuth or Garibaldi; Martin staid and the most unlikely rebel. It was likely they too would be transported for producing their paper. Sedition was sedition! God bless it. They could be charged under the treason felony law that had first been used on Mitchel himself.

———

Mitchel was invited to breakfast by the lieutenants and the surgeon. Over the meal in the officers' mess, one of the young lieutenants who had been cruising in the Pacific and had a robust tan tried to cheer Mitchel up by saying he would acquire the same sub-tropic tint as he had to bring back to Ireland one day.

All morning and afternoon, the coast of Ireland was hidden in mist. Beyond those banks of condensation lay the same afflicted land, and laneways scattered with corpses, green stains on their lips. And typhus and relapsing fever kept their headquarters in the hungering, weak flesh of the people.

When they were making north-east past the estuary of the Blackwater, the peaks of Slievenamon, the Knock-mealdowns and Comeraghs emerged from strata of cloud, and within half an hour they were inside the spacious harbour of Cork, one of the earth's largest harbours and a few hundred yards from the unforgiving demeanour of the buildings of Spike Island. A boat was lowered and manned, and the detectives told Mitchel solemnly they would 'take it on their own responsibility' not to chain him on his journey ashore. It seemed he was not as daemonic as he had been the day before.

Once landed on the island dock and on the way up hill towards the long prison walls, they passed over a drawbridge and many sentries and grating doors, one after another, and so entered a small square courtyard. Here they were shown by a turnkey to a dim room with a bed, table, chair and basin stand. Mitchel was told by the two police officers who had brought him ashore that their association was now at an end and they would report his co-operativeness to the authorities. 'Please don't,' Mitchel suggested. 'You realise I despise their approval.'

But though having been willing to shoot him for the Crown's sake the day before, they said this day that they hoped to meet him under happier circumstances, and so left him to possession of his cell, and the little yard beyond.

Since Mitchel was still a novice at the business of being transported, he took special and fuller note of all that happened, looking to learn of his new situation as quickly as he could. The solemn older jail governors and officers he would meet in his career and who always seemed to carry in their faces a grey regret and a certain scepticism about the redeemability of men would turn out to be numerous – and the one he met at Spike Island was the first of the series.

This solemn, older man arrived in the cell, introduced himself, and told Mitchel he could write home to Ontario Terrace, but the letter would need to be submitted to him before it was sent. Mitchel sat down and wrote, confessing to no discomfort or misuse, telling Jenny he was in Spike, the last Irish station before being finally shipped off and out of the way of things. He asked Jenny and his sisters for a trunk with some clothes and books. He knew Jenny would read the reasons for his lack of desperation and wailing. First, he would not give them the satisfaction of confessing to regret or pain. Secondly, he would not state his sacred love of Jenny in front of the grey man's jaded eyes.

The old governor left, but a turnkey in his navy-blue jail uniform sauntered into the room to take his place and lounged on a chair. At the clang of a bell, he departed and locked Mitchel in, and Mitchel felt the full weight of where he was. The truth is he would not have been human if he did not weep a little for the coming convict regimen.

———

The ship of his transportation fetched him the next day. It was a smart naval vessel he was rowed to: the *Scourge*. That senior old official he had met in his cell had told him very cheerily that it was to be Bermuda for him, and Mitchel thought that at least, unlike New South Wales and Van Diemen's Land, Bermuda was in the right hemisphere.

And so, though restless about that smart vessel, he found the atmosphere not punishing but very kindly. When in the Celtic Sea he dined with the handsome young captain, Wingrove; they talked about Thomas Babington Macaulay, former politician and historian. Macaulay riled Mitchel and thus piqued his spirits. And Wingrove was an intelligent man, and would as good as admit that the Empire was an empire like others, and at least the work of man and not necessarily that of Providence.

Mitchel was still a little dazed by his two departures, the unreality of Green Street prison, the high-ceilinged court, the rush to the docks, Spike Island. He argued, as if in sleep or a fever, that Macaulay admired *this* barbarous mechanical century above all centuries. In fact, both century and Empire were God's will. 'And if this is,' Mitchel dared say, 'the greatest century of humankind, with its mines and its mills and its murderous market in grain, then I would rather die now, like the millions of Irish who died for the theories of political economy!'

As Mitchel expatiated to Wingrove and other officers, who were very tolerant of his views and did not combat them very hard, he was feverish then, at the same time, with too much and too little hope. In the mess with its good silver and pictures of famed ships, and with the Atlantic brightening outside the ports as they reached south, Mitchel felt himself a lost soul, wandered from some just century – although whether that century was in front of or behind him he could not tell. He was being punished, he felt, for finding himself deposited in the wrong time. And yet he had his own cabin and was well fed. This bewilderment occupied all the days at sea.

Perhaps a day or so outside of Bermuda, in the South Atlantic, and the closest shore being North Carolina, a terrible heat fell on them and reduced the ship to silence. There was no slap of sail, no creak of timbers. Nothing lay in sight, no bird to offer the imagining of an arrival. Humid clouds obscured the horizon. Wingrove let him sleep on deck without guard or any restraint. Mitchel feared that the poor fellow might not go unpunished for such kindness, but the captain said he had been ordered to treat him like a gentleman.

When the morning arrived, the land of Bermuda was visible as a mulberry smear on the discernible horizon, but the land grew whiter and whiter as they got closer, an archipelago of white rock, white cottages, green cedars, and that ungodly shrub of spiky leaves named the yucca.

Mitchel saw some splendid-looking beaches and he tried to imagine his sons and daughters tumbling and running there – that is, if the delayed rebellion itself were defeated, and he must live through his time, and be pardoned in the end but restricted to the island. So they too might indeed have to live with him there.

There were fertile little groves that seemed to be producing a staple vegetable – it was arrowroot. And there were plentiful orchards too. Pigs rooted along round the aisles between trees. He was not in despair that morning, given the freshness of the scene, but he wondered practically how to put together a menu for his children and Jenny, should they come to join him. Pork and plaintains. And limitless other fruits.

Wingrove invited Mitchel onto the quarterdeck as they approached the navy yard. Mitchel hesitated.

'The government might not approve of your leniency,' he said.

Wingrove again insisted. Uneasily, Mitchel complied.

They could see a fort ashore with army guards patrolling it. This was an island of Bermuda, said the captain. All the islands were jammed close together and this with the fort and main naval dock was named 'Ireland' Island. Out of delicacy, he did not labour the irony. The landlocked masts of a vast ship were visible. Wingrove mentioned the Bermudas were a set of connected islands in the shape of a fishhook, and they had reached the eye of the hook. On one side of them the vast ship proved itself to be the huge *Great Western* – the first great steam ship – working, Wingrove told him, around the Caribbean. In his voice a tremble of love, a man comfortable in the age of steam and starvation.

The moorage of *Scourge* was a little way offshore and the sun went down suddenly. No-one came for Mitchel and he enjoyed the evening with Wingrove and his officers, still looking through the telescope at various points ashore, taking it seriously. The naval headquarters above the dock were as sturdy as the Tower of London and protected by terraces of artillery.

Inside the embayment, Mitchel could see three prison hulks, roofed over, and men in white linen blouses and straw hats moving on the decks. If they paused, the broad arrow of criminality could also be seen, stamped on the fabric on their backs. Would he be required to wear that, instead of the suit he had stood trial in and still wore? All possibilities were in the air, even as softened by Wingrove's etiquette. Mitchel knew he was already summoned by the admiral to report and this was certainly the last night on board the amiable *Scourge*.

Mitchel woke early next morning in a mauve dawn and saw another West Indian steamer in the anchorage, and one of the officers visited it to see if it had newspapers. He brought back the London *Morning Post* of 29 May, the very day after Mitchel's sentence some weeks earlier. There was a notable headline – 'THE CONVICT MITCHEL'.

He was delighted to see that his friends Reilly and Martin were reported as setting up a newspaper in his honour, which they would name *The Irish Felon*. In spite of the reality that he would not soon be going home to Jenny, despite the denial even of touch, this gave him great cheer. His friends, including dear old Martin, an unlikely figure of defiance with his unassertive physique and lank hair, were determined that every moderate resister to British rule should become charged and criminalised, and thus all Irishmen would discover that they had no recourse but subservience or rebellion. But of course, Reilly and Martin would be first amongst them. Even then he wondered whether their argument was the work of a season or of centuries.

Wingrove approached him as he walked the deck and said, 'Mr Mitchel, I hope you do not mind accepting my best wishes as you commence your sentence. You are a man whose conviction is international news. The notable figures in society are now the political activists, and unlike other people enduring punishment for, say, murder or highway robbery, you are known the world over. I make no remark on your sentence except to say what is obvious – the political prisoner is often a weight on the system of justice and attracts from his admirers a persistent campaign for his release. I expect that in the end you will be pardoned; I hope it is earlier than later.'

Mitchel felt endeared further to the man. He did not want to cast a shadow over this kind impulse to console him. But he was forced by principle to dissent from the sentimentality. 'I may perhaps be rescued in some way, captain, and I have to thank you for your gentle sentiments. But you must be aware I will not be in a position to accept any pardon, for to do that would be to accept I had committed a crime, which I do not. I hope you understand my position.'

Wingrove then murmured that, whatever the case, Mitchel should find a way to accept whatever dilution of the sentence arose from his reputation. It was kind of him to say 'reputation' rather than 'ignominy'.

It was as if the people ashore had been surprised by Mitchel's arrival, for he remained on *Scourge* until four in the afternoon, when boats were seen coming off from the hulks, rowed by men with the broad-arrow apparel. The hulks will be my portion, Mitchel pronounced to himself. How strange, it struck him. Such a peculiar habitation, a ship with no destination. Or a ship that measured its destination, anyhow, in years and in supposed rehabilitation.

They could keep him there a century, he could have told them, and he would not be rehabilitated! I am thirty-three years. Unless rescued by events, I will be a man on the verge of turning fifty before I could seek a cottage in the hinterland. He hoped these calculations would enrage his friends in Dublin and help them at the harvest uprising.

A cutter came out to fetch him, and three men came aboard the *Scourge* and stood like a committee on the main deck. Wingrove presented Mitchel to them for all the world as if he were a guest of the state. An official in a blue uniform introduced himself as superintendent of convicts. The second was a commander of the hulk Mitchel would serve his sentence on, and the third a doctor, Dr Warner – of whom, said the superintendent, he might see a considerable amount, since Captain Wingrove had reported he suffered asthma. The words between the official party and the convict then were terse: did he have luggage? And so on. The superintendent gave Wingrove a receipt for Mitchel's body, and then he stepped forward to descend the ladder behind Dr Warner of the hulk *Dromedary*. Once in his boat at the bottom of the steps on *Scourge*'s side, it pulled itself away for the closest of the three hulks.

Mitchel boarded the *Dromedary* when, after a few minutes transit, across dazzling water, from the *Scourge*, they gained it. The *Dromedary* seemed to Mitchel a venerable old full-bottomed Napoleonic ship. Under a huge canvas canopy which seemed to shade the main deck, an ancient mate took possession of the three shillings Mitchel carried on his person, and gave him a receipt.

Dr Warner rattled through the limits and the privileges of Mitchel's situation: he was to wear his normal clothes for now. He would not be sent forth on labour. The surgeon told Mitchel earnestly that nobody wanted to add to the annoyances he was suffering and that no severity would be used towards him, provided he was amenable to the rules. But, above all, he was to have no connection with public affairs or politics, and was not to address or tamper with any of the prisoners on board.

These gentlemen bade him farewell for now, and he followed the old mate down the ladder to the half-deck, and in the very centre of the hulk, opening from a dark passage, there was a sort of cabin a little wider and a little higher than a dog box. It was, in fact, the hole through which the mainmast formerly ran down into the ship, and it was very dim, even though two bull's-eyes in the deck above gave some sunlight. John could not stand quite erect under the great beams that used to hold the mainmast in place, but half of the floor was raised a further nine inches still, and on that part he could not stand at all.

His small portmanteau was sent down with the message that if he wished to walk on deck or on the breakwater alongside the hulk, he might do it by arrangement with the mate. So he decided to go for a walk that very evening. He had taken a turn or two on the pier, but as the gangs of prisoners began to come in from their work yards amongst palm trees, the guards asked him to retire to his quarters. A cup of black tea and a slab of bread were delivered and he was locked away for the night. Downing Street had made him exempt from work! Look how generous we are, they would say to the world.

He was woken at dawn and taken to bathe down the steps of the hulk on the starboard side away from the pier. He could hear the riot of breakfast time on the convict decks, mysterious shouts and cheers and groans, a greeting to a new day of incarceration. After he swam alone in the sea, long before the gangs went out to work, he dressed and walked on deck in the shade of the canopy. In this part of the ship he was separated from the mass of convicts, who were in a communal space forward on the main deck. It was the servants who shared the cabins aft, where mates' pantries and accommodations, as well as the surgery, and his own obscure hutch, could be found.

The second night, asthma, the beast, kept him panting on his side, like a landed, suffocating fish, till dawn. Then and later, he felt grateful for the morning and evening murmur of felon talk from below and forward, and the occasional bark of laughter. That Sunday there was a service on deck, and he was directed to a seat near the blue-coated guards and mates on the quarterdeck. He saw some of the convicts look at him, as if to wonder why he, being such a notable enemy of the state, a uniquely tried and uniquely condemned man, by a statute tailored specifically for his case, had the privilege of standing and kneeling where he did while clothed like a free man. The convicts as a group looked weather-beaten, and the faces of some had that look of being aged from birth, aged by fortune. And Mitchel was sure it would have shocked the worthies on the quarterdeck had they seen in visible form the daydreams and yearnings of the imprisoned that morning.

After the service, the chaplain came to him in his cell and offered to lend him books, and procure any titles he wanted from others. Mitchel liked the man. He did not preach esoterically, about such subjects as, say, Pelagianism or free will or predestination, nor about what a peril one John Mitchel was to the soul of the average British convict, but about patient service and the privileges of freedom that follow it: good, practical, if forgettable urgings for Her Majesty's felons.

The private anguish of another night passed. His old demon-friend asthma liked his low-roofed mouldy cabin.

On the first Monday of his sentence in Bermuda, they gave him a new cabin, elsewhere, aft. This one he could stand upright in, and it was fourteen feet long, with a table, chair, a washstand and a full window, heavily cross-barred, but which nonetheless gave plenty of light and air. And there were two shelves for books.

The old mate said to him, 'You seem a peaceable enough fellow, Mr Mitchel. Before you came to this hulk, they removed every last Irish prisoner as if they were likely to burst into flames at the sight of you.'

John had only a few dragging days in his new cabin when Dr Warner came to him and said there were orders to remove him to the hospital ship.

'But I'm quite well,' Mitchel told him, although he thought at once that that old mate was more observant of his cramped breath than Mitchel had given him credit for.

'Even so,' Dr Warner informed Mitchel, 'the order has come from the Governor, which means that it has come from the authorities at home. You are to go this afternoon.'

'What is the meaning, though,' Mitchel asked, 'of sending me to a hospital ship when I'm quite healthy? I am no invalid.'

Warner said Captain Wingrove had reported that Mitchel had suffered a cruel fit of asthma aboard the *Scourge*. And now it had been observed he had had similar fits on *Dromedary*. So Mitchel was rowed out to the *Tenedos* hospital ship, larger and cleaner and not as ancient as the *Dromedary*. *Tenedos* was a mere quarter of a mile from the land in a pleasant bay named North Lagoon.

Mitchel's cabin had two windows and no bars, an iron bed and table, and other appurtenances. Here he settled himself to write an account of what had happened since Spike Island, in a letter for Jenny's perusal, and while he wrote grew more content in soul, more patient for the wheels of history to turn. Because the uprising was to come and God knew the popular fury was intense. As well as that, the doctor on *Tenedos*, Dr Hall, was a genial old man who thought Mitchel suffered from melancholy and who had a shaky hand. He did not know Mitchel was anxious to discover whether he was to be in this place for the term of his sentence or would be liberated soon by the actions of his brethren in Ireland.

———

Sometimes Mitchel thought he should resist every kindness from Downing Street, and from genial Dr Hall, and that he should do it to evoke severity which could then be condemned in the leading articles in the liberal and the American and French press. But the poor surgeon would be so confused. He came to Mitchel's room and talked to him at great length in the evenings. He knew Ireland very well, and particularly Down and Armagh, and said he had been very affected by the articles and images of famine in the *Illustrated London News*. The Famine had been very perplexing. A terrible act of God, he said. Mitchel could not help but say, but very forgivingly, since there was no triumph in flaying the poor fellow, 'I'm here because I dared say it was an act not of God but of man.'

A good-looking fellow of middle years wearing convict canvas came into Mitchel's bright little hutch aboard *Tenedos* that same day. He said, 'I trust, sir, that you will find every-thing as you wish here. If I can do anything for you, I'm sure I shall be happy. My name is Garrett. I repeat, Garrett!'

The last two words he said with such an emphasis that Mitchel suspected he was meeting a man of renown, with whom many readers of *The Nation* would be familiar. Mitchel's reaction was not clear to the fellow, and he went on again, '*Garrett*, sir, yes, Garrett. You must have heard of me at length? It was in all the newspapers. I say Garrett, sir!'

Mitchel told him that he was sorry, but though his visitor was obviously a man of some note, he, Mitchel, had never heard about that. Garrett, however, kept on prompting Mitchel. 'The railway affair, sir? A matter of £40,000, sir? Left it behind me, sir, with Mrs Garrett, who lives in Broad-stairs in a very handsome style but is speaking of going to France, sir, to Bordeaux. I have been here now two years, as orderly, and I like it very well – now devilish fine brown girls ashore here, Mr Mitchel. I have to say I created a great sensation when I came here. Nearly as big as you.'

Mitchel rose and bowed to him. 'Sir, you do me too much honour, for I never saw such a sum as £40,000 in my lifetime.'

'But, my dear sir,' said Garrett, admitting what the court in Ireland would not, 'you are a prisoner of state. You are a patriotic martyr and all the rest! While for my part, my little affair was made a concern of state too. Lord John Russell, when Home Secretary, made an appeal to me to disclose my method – the way I had done it, that is.'

Mitchel said, 'I trust, sir, you treated the man's applica-tion with the contempt that it deserved.'

Garrett laughed and told Mitchel that he might be sure of that. Meanwhile he was a mender of things and an orderly on *Tenedos*, where men were often very sick and beyond low tricks, he said. But it seemed that he went across a few days a week to an island where Dr Warner lived, and had some ducks that needed looking after. There, he said, he had made the acquaintance of two or three splendid coloured girls.

And there it was. There seemed to be always men who found female company wherever they were sent. And, Mitchel acknowledged, he was not one of them, because he had not stolen £40,000 and also, at however a painful distance, because he possessed the majesty of Jenny.

'Do you smoke tobacco, Mr Mitchel?' Garrett asked.

'I am an asthmatic, Mr Garrett,' Mitchel told him.

'I could find you asthma cigarettes,' he suggested.

'I fear they make things worse. But newspapers . . .!'

'There, sir, we hit a sensitive matter.' He touched a finger to his nose. 'But let me see what my coloured girls might do . . .'

'Don't take risks,' Mitchel warned.

'Rest assured, Mr Mitchel, on that score.' And he winked.

12

Mitchel in Bermuda, 1848-49

The surgeon came to Mitchel's room on *Tenedos* after he
had spent a month or so there, and told him they were
sending him back to his cell on *Dromedary*. 'Something has
happened,' John thought at once. Had the Irish uprising
begun? Spontaneously? It was still too early for it – not
harvest time yet. But in any case, he needed to be put in the
greater security of the prison ship.

In a few minutes he had to pack up his portmanteau and
books, say goodbye to a very melancholy Dr Hall, and was
carried across to the *Dromedary* rowed by a gang of silent
convicts who did not look his way. He saw in the blur of
light the prisoners' cemetery on Ireland Island. It made him
think of useful allies and he thought he should have said
goodbye to Garrett.

––––

Back on the *Dromedary* he was welcomed by the old mate and was told what his transfer meant. The New York Irish had heard of his conviction, and there was a story the Irish Directory of New York, a recently founded body full of escaped Young Irelanders, had started to raise money to equip a vessel to rescue him. Therefore, the government's steamer that patrolled the islands was to have all the guns she could carry to repel the Yankees. Or was it all just gossip? The bay where the *Tenedos* hospital ship was moored was a considerable way from the naval yard and the shore cannon, and was not considered a secure residence for him in case the New Yorkers did come. This news, indicating many parties being unhappy at his imprisonment, of course cheered Mitchel. And through the window he could look out at the government steamer and its array of guns, and on sailors cutting new cannon ports in its flanks. The soldiers of the 42nd Highland Regiment had come in from their barracks and were camped along the shore to keep watch day and night so the Americans might not bear him away.

———

Was poor John Martin a prisoner by now? His loyalty to his friends was enormous, and he and Devin Reilly, the enthusiastic young journalist Mitchel had brought with him from *The Nation*, had announced the very day Mitchel was spirited away from Dublin the publication of a new paper, *The Irish Felon*. And Mitchel had no way of telling if, for such defiance, those gentle friends were in the dungeons of the Carthaginians.

Later that month, he discovered from a newspaper supplied to him – after the officers had read it – to relieve his solitude, that John Martin had indeed been charged with treason felony, a crime until now attributed entirely to Mitchel himself. He remembered a young doctor from the fever hospitals in Dublin, Kevin O'Doherty, a member of the Confederation, and was sad to hear he had been arrested on that charge and sentenced as well.

There were even charges against Tom Meagher and he appeared in court in Limerick and Dublin, having given seditious speeches in both regions. He was bound over for trial for treason in both, but was still at large and apparently in the countryside gathering support. Mitchel read that a warrant for the arrest of Smith O'Brien had been issued as well. Smith O'Brien had refused to surrender to an arrest and was at large, somewhere in Munster, consulting the people. It was not harvest time yet. The authorities had moved earlier than O'Brien wanted them to.

Another newspaper reported that Meagher, charged but not yet detained, and at work in Tipperary, had led some tens of thousands of angry men up the mountain of Slieve-namon, the Celtic giant Finn's mountain, and from the summit asked seditious questions, such as, 'Are you content that the harvest in this land, which you see from this summit, and to which your labour has imparted fruitfulness, should again be reaped for the stranger?'

And amongst other things, he invoked on top of Slieve-namon the 'Bermudan prisoner', as the newspapers reported it. 'Then a gallant man, young and brave,' cried Meagher, 'with a young wife and young children who, if they were not made of heroic material, would have clasped him to their breasts before he went forth to preach the glorious gospel that says the life of a peasant's was the same as the life of the lord. That gospel went through the country, and was acclaimed the true one. For which Mitchel was sent to Bermuda!'

There were cries of 'So it is!' said the journalist, and God bless those who uttered them, thought Mitchel, for he felt the mighty unease of Ireland must soon break free and things would be settled. Thus, irrationally, he felt nearly liberated. Unreason, anything that lightened the brain, was welcome in a sentence of fourteen years. Cries, according to the journalist, of 'We'll bring him back!' – these were like opium to a prisoner who had been skewered like a butterfly by Lefroy's sentence, so that the next fourteen years would, without some crisis, be all *served* in near-isolation and not lived.

Cries uttered no doubt with ignorance of Atlantic shipping, or even where in God's name Bermuda was.

———

In Bermuda itself, the prisoners were now not permitted to walk on the breakwater. Mitchel heard them complaining on the convict deck, wishing either for the arrival of the Yankee filibusters to take him away, or for his death.

Martin awaiting trial! Meagher with promises to two courts but unrestrained for now! No wonder my breath is uncertain, thought Mitchel. Through the wooden walls that separated him from the living quarters, he heard the prisoners lamenting further, 'What is he but a convict like the rest of us, a damned bloody convict?'

It was such a reasonable question that it made him consider whether he should suggest to the authorities that he be thrown into the cage where men at least lived together. These men, who needed to take their hats off when they spoke to the guards, and who dared not set foot on the quarterdeck, even if they were sent there, without making a low obeisance, saw Mitchel, himself exercising up and down the same deck, with his hat on, and the guards and officers, now and then when meeting him, touching *their* own caps. He must, he decided, tolerate the other convicts cursing him – their black looks and the shaven heads and faces, and doing their best beneath their amorphous brows to look like burglars and swindlers from the womb.

John began to suspect that as much as some information had been fed him, even more recent papers were being kept from him. He was aware from the brief, weighing-him-up looks the guards gave him that something strange had happened in Ireland. They hushed their conversations when Mitchel drew near.

He said to the old first mate, 'The guards seem to be protecting me from something. If it is that *habeas corpus* has been suspended in Ireland, I already know it.'

The first mate said, in a sentence utterly unlayered with mystery, 'Right you are, Mr Mitchel.'

And so Mitchel discovered, when the newspaper drought ended, that Martin had been sentenced to ten years' transportation for treason felony. However, it was expected he would serve it, not in the Bermudas with his friend Mitchel, but in Van Diemen's Land itself, the very capital of transported Irishmen and Irishwomen at the other end of the earth, in Australia.

Mitchel could blame himself for Martin, for the fact that Mitchel's own arrest and transportation spurred him to publish seditious sentiments, but then for all he knew, Martin and the others might all be liberated by some uprising and sudden success of a revolution begun in Munster. It might occur, and Martin might even be delivered from the Bastille of Green Street while the ship he and the young surgeon O'Doherty were to be transported on was still being filled with felons from Cork or Dublin. But rebellion should arise soon, for Martin was not a sturdy man and had not been at school a boy for rough games.

There was a mysterious passage in one paper, the London *Chronicle*, concerning a daughter of the gentry herself being under house imprisonment in Dublin, not on the orders of Lord Clarendon but by her own family. So much for Speranza, sat upon by broad-based deans and officers and lawyers and military of the Elgee kin.

Even she had been brought down and confined.

———

When Jenny had read all this, back home in Newry in the Mitchel household, she rushed to write to Mitchel and plead with him not to despair. For, with him and Meagher and many others on the run, the famed Irish uprising, for whose sake they'd decided not to try to rescue Mitchel on his journey to his boat, occurred in late July. Smith O'Brien and Meagher and other Young Irelanders, fleeing unexpected warrants for their immediate arrest, had escaped Leinster and Smith O'Brien had taken to the road as rebel chieftain.

He progressed at last into western Tipperary, gathering recruits. However, he then had them melt away under the influence of priests – under orders from their bishops – who told their flocks that those who went with O'Brien and Meagher and the others would be denied the sacraments of the Church.

With the best of the priests, it was concern about the starving facing up to a well-fed army, perhaps, but with the bishops it was also their need for the British government to go on paying them the amount required to run the seminary at Maynooth. So, for mistaken love of peace or from convenience, the priests disbanded each army built by O'Brien and his entourage.

By every sunset, O'Brien and Meagher – Meagher being sometimes with him and at other times trying to raise rebels elsewhere – had recruited a peasant army. By every dawn it had melted away under the authority of priests who guarded the door of heaven and of hell.

The Confederate clubs could also not be roused – those in the solid town of Callan in Kilkenny had been willing to march, while others whom Meagher secretly contacted pleaded for a week to organise kit and ammunition. They too had been planning to be ready when harvest came.

For this sputtering rebellion, O'Brien had delayed a rescue – or an attempted rescue – of Mitchel, saying the clubs had not been adequately armed and supplied. So now there was a poor extemporised mishap of a rising for which the Confederates were not prepared, while those few, some of them miners who closed their ears to the priests, came to a battle under O'Brien for a house in Ballingarry, in the south of Tipperary, against a garrison of police and then late-arriving cavalry. It was a small battle but not a grotesque or fatuous one, although *The Times* made it seem so. But after the action at the house ended, it was said that Smith O'Brien showed himself to the enemy, the police and cavalry, in the hope of a redeeming bullet that no-one would fire. Thus he escaped in disguise but was arrested on Thurles railway station some twelve or so miles north of Ballingarry. He had not seen himself as defeated, even after Ballingarry. He'd had plans – he was going to Dublin at last to try an uprising there, where he should have started! But all was negated by the constable who'd arrested him.

'Beloved John,' Jenny wrote from his mother's rented house in Dublin after she had read of Smith O'Brien's capture. 'For my sake and that of the children I remain hopeful for you and your rescue. As we knew almost by instinct, deliverance won't come from Smith O'Brien, though he states that the reason he tried to escape and catch the train to Dublin was to rouse the city as we told him he should have done in June. Bitterness is an easy drug to suck on, but I will not yield to it. All is still so volatile that you have no grounds to give in. It is clear there are multitudes in Ireland and America who care for us, and for your freedom and the welfare of the children. We will not want while ever you are serving your sentence. I am aware that even members of Repeal are unofficially raising money. I would rather pay our own way, but . . . Many people here told me they have signed a giant petition, or one of a number of great petitions for your release. Of course, Downing Street will assert its advantage by trying the rebels first. But no one seriously thinks you will need to endure Lefroy's dreary sentence for the full length of its term.'

Jenny did not tell her husband how cheap such talk was when folk had a comfortable home to go to and were not members of the starving classes. She did not tell him how desolate she was herself. Her mother-in-law and Mitchel's sisters kept her going, as did many friends. Mrs Mitchel had an air of fierce unapology for her son – for her *sons*, for that matter – and it gave positive comfort to Jenny.

And for the sake of this poor thing they had produced, this bare stutter of rebellion, O'Brien, Meagher and men who had fought with them – Pat O'Donoghue and Terence MacManus, an Irish wool broker from Liverpool – were all in Clonmel jail and to face . . . not treason felony, the notional treason Mitchel was suffering, but high treason and the ceremonious disembowelling associated with it.

At least, Dublin Castle and Downing Street would shame themselves by killing the poor fellows, but Jenny wondered were they made for such agonies?

And if only it wasn't that amiable, handsome Meagher had to endure that death too! If it happened, what would Speranza do? And Thomas Francis Meagher heard the same sentence at last. Did Speranza wail? Jenny wailed. He was close enough to being a mere boy, and his obliteration was a dreadful thing! And all the press, Tory and Whig and radical, recorded Meagher's speech before sentencing, which was a noble thing, given that Meagher was a young man of twenty-five and had not lived in the sense that Mitchel had lived.

'My Lords, it is my intention to say a few words only. I desire that the last act of the proceeding which has occupied so much of the public time shall be of short duration. Nor have I the indelicate wish to close the dreary ceremony of a state prosecution with a vain display of words. Did I fear that, hereafter, when I shall be no more, the country I have tried to serve would think ill of me, I might indeed avail myself of this solemn moment to vindicate my sentiments and my conduct. But I have no such fear.' He was cheered a little to think of his mother wearing his crimes without apology. 'I might, indeed, avail myself of this solemn moment, to then dictate my sentiments and my actions. I have no such fear! I am here to crave with no lying lip the life I consecrate to the liberty of my country. Far from it!'

Meagher was not going down abashed into the grave. If only oratory itself were king, their side would win by streets, roads, avenues, boulevards and oceans.

Mitchel received the letter from Jenny at the same time as one from his young brother William. At least William had got away. He was an unworldly dreamy creature as if all the metaphysics from the Reverend Dr Mitchel had settled in him. He had collaborated with dear Martin, but then had had the wit to go to Cobh on Cork Harbour and leave for America.

Willy was a man who liked to collect small mechanisms and ponder how they would help printing presses and textile machines. A man enchanted by devices, he had in a way been considered younger than his years. Mitchel was so pleased that at least his brother was safe, what with disembowelling and the sundering of limbs on the imperial menu.

The American rescuers had failed to arrive in Bermuda and snatch Mitchel away. The great Irish rebellion, of which Smith O'Brien made so much in refusing to rescue him on that last day in Dublin, had now occurred. And the Irish were all losers, Mitchel too. He felt he dare not swallow or twitch – like a tightrope walker, he believed slight movements would pitch him into eternity. But so also for those benighted still walking the earth, those poor souls who would perish in the coming Irish winter, even if the crop returned to the normal scale, which it might never do.

Mitchel wondered if he must consider suicide. Things were so bad that he could not listen to the overall air of doom. Better to think like a man making a decision to buy more land or acquire a public house. For the truth was unscalable. The events of the past few months had promised little except that he would serve the whole fourteen years, every otiose, bloated day of it. And Jenny was condemned to that same term too. And on top of that, did he have the right to expect his sons to become big-hatted, shoeless farmers of Bermuda, and his girls the wives of merchants in the town of Somerset further south?

First, he decided, he could not kill himself, as much as he and the others deserved self-extinction for their incompetent rebellion. If he did so, apart from the issues of Jenny and the children, he would be a co-conspirator with Baron Lefroy, the sheriff of Dublin, and with the ministers of the Crown. He could not admit himself to be a felon. If he took his life, apart from all the pain he should unleash on them, he would scandalise his children and teach them the evil lessons of despair.

Besides, there might be other chances to have his part in the business of Ireland. By serving his span of years, he could stand as a spur to the apathetic, and continue to rouse the young, perhaps, to a perpetual disaffection. Everything he did and wrote would soon be forgotten if he recklessly ended his life. His flesh crept at the idea of being buried in the convict cemetery, amongst the gimcrack graves of pickpockets and fences of stolen goods. So, one fragment of reason at a time, he condemned himself to life.

———

In November came the story of Smith O'Brien's August trial in Clonmel. Yes, the fools condemned him to the barbarous punishment. Chief Justice Blackburne intoned at last, 'The sentence is that you, William Smith O'Brien, be taken from here to the place from whence you came and be thence drawn on a hurdle to the place of execution, and be there hanged by the neck until you are dead; and that afterwards your head shall be severed from your body and your body divided into four quarters to be disposed of as Her Majesty shall think fit. And may God have mercy on your soul.'

Then Mitchel discovered that Downing Street were chastened by the brutality of what they intended to visit upon handsome young Meagher. In any case they passed a law to make high treason punishable by the same means as humble treason felony; that is, by transportation. Smith O'Brien, Meagher, the wool merchant MacManus and O'Donoghue, a rather cranky paterfamilias and Dublin clerk who had had the courage to stand with O'Brien – both of whom having been O'Brien's lieutenants in Tipperary – would be deprived of their graphic mediaeval death and instead sent into transportation for life. Not to Bermuda but to Van Diemen's Land. One afternoon Mitchel was walking on the P deck, a straw hat on his head because, although it was now meant to be winter, and there was a wind which the guards said came from Canada, the sun was still vigorous. There was a cry from the sea beyond the *Dromedary* announcing that a prisoner was being returned from the hospital hulk *Tenedos*. First came a soldier, then the recuperated felon, and then, with quick eyes that encompassed the deck, the convict orderly, Mr Garrett, the legendary thief. He took his canvas hat off, but his eyes lingered on John Mitchel, as if summoning or at least heavily suggesting that they converse. As the old mate and the soldier took the returned prisoner below, Mitchel walked down the companionway to the main deck and crossed to Garrett. He had already removed his canvas hat and his bow was commanding in its casual irony.

'Mr Mitchel, sir,' he said confidingly. 'I hope you will have been free of asthma while awaiting your deliverance.'

'I am much better,' Mitchel told him.

It was a lie. On a characteristic night, like the night just past, he ended half-conscious over the back of his chair, his limbs leaden and his brain dizzy from the night's struggle with breathlessness. With dawn he found himself better able to breathe. It was as if the promise of light induced in his body some remedy for the gasping horror of it all. The asthma preferred to work in darkness like Satan.

'Forgive me, Mr Mitchel, but I think you tell a little untruth there, surely to save a friend distress.'

Mitchel laughed. 'You have caught me out, Mr Garrett,' he said.

Garrett lowered his voice. 'There is a transport meant to be coming from England, and full of new felons. It is said that when it arrives here and discharges its people, a number of those already here, such as myself perhaps, and ditto yourself, will be dispatched on it to Africa itself, to what they call the Cape. The men so shipped will – on landing – be granted tickets-of-leave.'

'I doubt that would apply to me,' Mitchel told him. 'Even if I were put aboard such a ship.'

'Believe me, Mr Mitchel,' Garrett told him, 'my intelligence on this matter is of prime quality. I must speak to our surgeon, dear old Dr Hall.'

'Africa,' Mitchel said.

'Yes, Mr Mitchel. Bermuda is such a rum place. There is a woman in Georgetown who believes I have somehow engaged to marry her. I do not think Mrs Garrett would much like her husband turning bigamist.'

Mitchel said he didn't think she would either.

Garrett whispered, 'Let me see to this for you.'

———

By 1 December, it had been six months since Mitchel left Cork Harbour on the *Scourge*. One twenty-eighth of his sentence was served. It was quite chilly in a humid way, and he had had constant asthma. But the 42nd Regiment were concentrated around the pier, and their bands started up about dusk and were pleasant to listen to.

Dr Hall, the medical superintendent of the hulks, came to visit him on the report of the *Dromedary*'s surgeon, Dr Warner, who was worried about him. He asked if Mitchel had been ever so consistently ill before, and Mitchel told him no. The doctor told him in return and with an air of infallibility that he could not expect to survive in this climate, which was notoriously bad for asthmatics.

Mitchel thought to ask, 'Sir, is it a settled part of the transportation system that an invalid be confined to that place which is most likely to kill him?'

'It is not policy,' the surgeon replied. 'With respect to you, something might be able to be done. If you write to the Governor.'

'But why can't you write, doctor?'

'It's not the way it is done. But you can say in your letter that the chief surgeon has announced to you that you cannot live under these conditions.'

'My dear doctor, I've never asked for any mitigation, and don't want to start now.'

'But I cannot circumvent the normal channels. The form must be complied with.'

Tears had now appeared in the amiable doctor's eyes. 'You are still young. Write to the Governor in some form – a simple letter will do. Take your pen, for God's sake, and think of your children. And so write.'

Mitchel was so affected by the sight of an old regimental surgeon with tears in his eyes that he said he would write something acquainting the Governor with his condition. He reasoned that, after all, he was not sentenced to death. He did not want, however, to be humiliated by their mercy, and he would rather their kindnesses were as consistent as their cruelties. In some mental confusion on these matters, he wrote to the big fellow himself.

To his Excellency the Governor of Bermuda,
I wish to take the liberty to bring to your notice a state-ment about my health by the medical superintendent. As I am not sentenced to death it might be well to get some change made in my position, either by removal to a more healthy climate or otherwise, so that I may be enabled, physically, to endure the term of transporta-tion to which I am sentenced. [Mitchel quoted the last sentence directly from Dr Hall himself here.]

He did not end with the normal slavish palaver or promise to pray, as he had always prayed, for his Excellency's prosper-ity and the efficacy of his power. Dr Warner made sure the letter was sent, as soon as finished, to Government House ashore.

Waiting for a reply from the Governor, Mitchel did not hear till about mid-December that, as Garrett had said, there was indeed a ship travelling from London with a cargo of convicts, and that, upon landing its felons in Bermuda, it would go on to the Cape of Good Hope with a select cargo of 'recommended prisoners'. On arrival in South Africa, they were to be set at liberty by ticket-of-leave.

How wonderful, Mitchel thought, firstly if he could go, and secondly if he was able to get that certificate of semi-liberty, and live ashore with Britons and Boers and Kaffirs. He now – with some irrationality, anticipating the Governor's mercy – began to daydream about, at some stage, growing South African vines with the help of his sons. Prior to his Irish return, that is. The grand return. The takeover. The redemption.

On Christmas Day, Mitchel ate alone in his quarters but heard the noise of a convict theatrical below decks, attended by the guards and the mates, and gales of seasonally humane fraternal laughter, from which he was as usual excluded. It bore on him that day that the crossing of the Atlantic would also take place on his continuing exclusion from many contacts. That day he had an appetite to be loud and companionable, lost in a fraternal mob.

In February, a sort of commission made up of Mr Hire, the commandant of hulks, Dr Hall and several other authorities sat on the issue of who was to go in the transport to the Cape of Good Hope. The orderly Mitchel had acquired who did his bed each day told him he too, the orderly, had been placed on the lists and intended to go, saying exactly as Garrett had that Bermuda was 'one of the rummest countries as is!'

Mitchel was separated from the convicts by two walls, but he often heard them when they spoke aloud. Gambling was common amongst them and so was as much obscenity and blasphemy as could be fitted into the span of a sentence. His hearing had become trained to their muffled voices. He had been told tradesmen amongst them sometimes did jobs for people on the island and acquired gambling money by that means. They talked a great deal about the black women who visited their work sites, peddling fruit and tobacco. One of them cried, to a young man who had developed an affection for a black woman and wanted to stay in Bermuda for her sake, 'You ignorant shit-face. Don't you know there are black women by the million in Africa?'

They gossiped about one convict who had a black sail-maker's wife ashore in Bermuda in love with him. She had plans to escape Bermuda and so he too was terrified of being put on the list.

Mitchel was aware that Irish country boys of twelve or fourteen years, his son Johnny's age, had been shipped there for taking sheep or poultry to keep their families alive, and were receiving the initiation of the convict deck, their baccalaureate in depravity. For the simple truth, and no-one said it explicitly but only by reference to 'abominable prac- tices', was that convict boys were desired for buggery on the hulks, and it had always been so.

———

The sapping minutes and hours eked away. Each left a scar on his soul. It was, for dear God's sake, 1 April, the day of the fool, and the promised convict ship had not yet arrived. Dr Hall and Dr Warner began to discuss taking Mitchel back to the hospital hulk, for there was a withering wind blowing from the north.

The vessel appeared on 5 April – Eastertide. It was said by the old mate that the authorities hoped it would be turned around in two weeks. Its men were landed, some onto *Dromedary*, and Mitchel heard them being hooted, chaffed and teased in the convict mess.

The new-arrived ship was a fine old solid sort of vessel in very good trim. It was named *Neptune* and more than six hundred tons. Mr Hire and his friends, the doctors – poor old Hall and Warner – visited Mitchel to tell him he had indeed been selected for the Cape. He was very excited, and as Hire spoke earnestly to him about the possibility of his getting a clerkship ashore, he savoured secretly the fact that escape from the Cape would be a possibility. There were Spanish and Portuguese possessions, and regions under chiefdoms he could possibly flee to if given a ticket-of-leave to live within a certain district and occasionally report to police. In his mind, escape, rather than a ticket-of-leave, was the only fit response he could make to Lefroy's sentence. In any case, his health would be better, ashore, at the Cape. In the meantime, he was more than sincere in thanking these good functionaries of the convict system.

Dr Hall was very worried, however, that he might not last the journey to the Cape. Mitchel, though, told him to be assured that he was motivated to live, and had no desire to be an Atlantic Ocean wraith. Mr Hire then mentioned – as something marginal – the fact that there was some resistance amongst the citizens of the Cape against the landing of convicts, but said that prejudice should not operate in Mitchel's case.

Regarding the *Neptune* itself, Mitchel heard there was a separate little cabin fitted out for him and an opening on the quarterdeck where he could enjoy boredom with dignity throughout the journey to Africa. On his last Bermudan Saturday, he was anxiously awaiting the mail from England, which had been due two days before. If the latest news from Newry did not arrive, God knew when he should hear of Jenny and his brood again.

During his last Monday on the Bermuda hulk, the mail ship scuttered in, and he had his letters, instantly sacred to him. A boat was to come for him after breakfast the next day, and he wondered would they take his journal before letting him go. But in fact they suggested he bring along records and books, and they let him take it all, and daguerreotypes of the family too.

Strangely, Mitchel felt he must make a proper farewell to the dear old mate, for after all, there was no escape for him. Some officers shook his hand, and the convalescing convicts on deck, returned from work, scowled at him as if from habit and then decided on balance he had not caused them excessive misery and he had fought those who had condemned them and broke into cheers as he moved amongst them. He was transported to *Neptune* in his own cutter, though, for fear he might infect any Irish convicts.

His wrists were chained for the walk to *Neptune* inside the dock, during which he was escorted by a sergeant and two soldiers of the 42nd, in their kilts and checked stockings. He felt privileged by comparison with them – he was going, they were staying. It was as simple as that. He was exhilarated. He rose to the deck of a live, working ship, with its cargo of already loaded fellow felons vocal below decks.

––––

The captain, a red-whiskered Scot, was phlegmatic as one might wish a captain to be, and Dr Dees, the surgeon superintendent, greeted him. Dees was a young man whose professional passion seemed bright in him still.

'We've appointed you, Mr Mitchel,' scowled the captain, like a punishment, 'the best quarters we can.'

Dees said brightly, 'I fear, Mr Mitchel, you are to live quite solitary and have no access to the cuddy, the cook's galley that is, nor intercourse with the officers of the guard.'

Mitchel told him he understood. 'If it were not so, the fact is that you and they would be dragged before Parliament and disciplined.'

Dees smiled broadly, as if relieved to have the harsh news dealt with. Indeed, the captain and his two mates gave Mitchel a wide berth on the quarterdeck, knowing that there could be a criminal offence in getting to know him.

A young officer and a warden were called on to take Mitchel to his cabin. The warden carried his valise, and the young officer was permitted to be polite. As they progressed to the companionway, sailors were running about the deck on maritime tasks preparatory to the *Neptune*'s weighing anchor. The voyage to the Cape was calculated to take two months, the young mate told Mitchel.

His cabin was a filthy little thing with a window that looked over the section of the afterdeck where a few off-duty soldiers sauntered about, smoking and chatting. Beyond the gangway forward, a squad of prisoners stood, in their Bermuda uniforms. Mitchel was delighted to see amongst them the unmistakable frame of Mr Garrett. Perhaps canvas adorned with the broad arrow was meant to take identity away from the prisoner, but it had no power to erode Garrett's casual style and his exact unrepentant slouch. So, he had escaped his marital dilemma in Bermuda!

Mitchel was appointed a convict servant to look after him, a likeable Manchester thief named Decker, and with his help he began arranging things in his cabin. That dusk, he watched, from a section of the quarterdeck where he was permitted exercise, the cedars at the topmost of the Bermuda archipelago sink down, bearing the sun with them.

Signor Asthma became a less frequent visitor from that very night.

13

Mitchel to the Cape

By the time they had been three months at sea, and it was July in the calendar, perverse winds meant they were not halfway to the Cape, and had tacked back and forth across the equator three times in that tedious region of heavy air and mid-Atlantic calms. On his walks on the quarterdeck with Dr Dees, the doctor told him, his brow clenched, that a number of the prisoners were getting ill with scurvy, the lethargy of that disease claiming them, their mouths foul with spongy teeth. The entire journey had been along the equator without any islands to replenish them. So Dr Dees was a prisoner too, to the well-being of the convicts.

As a matter of health, Mitchel drank all the grog he was given. The young ship's parson, oppressed by the struggle the ship was having in progressing, and the ill humour of the convicts as a result, took him aside despite potential punishments, and said with stricken eyes, 'We shall have mutiny and cannibalism and everything horrifying here. We shall have murder!'

Mitchel knew how quickly a change of weather could alter spirits, and assured him, 'No, you shall not have cannibalism.'

Finally, during this grim tussle with the contrary trade winds and uneasy airs, the captain decided it was time, instead of fighting with the trade, to travel with it westwards. After a week, they reached Pernambuco – which British sailors called Penny Booker. Many ships were moored there, and one of them flew the yellow flag of plague. Mitchel was permitted only to survey the town from on board. It was a city of 120,000, but where it ended in the foothills the jungle that set in looked utterly impenetrable.

The trade wind shifted. Mitchel was asleep by the time they sailed out, and he woke at morning to find South America receding in his view. The sea imposed its own sense of dreaming and languor, and he was lazy and wrote less, whether in his journal or in terms of letters. When he heard one day that they were still more than one thousand miles from the Cape, he went into a short slump in which, for a few days at least, he tried to sleep away his fourteen years.

Suddenly, though, in an instant or two, as if all the atoms of air had conferred and come to a majority decision, they were galloping now before a westerly, bucking down into the swell of the Atlantic, and hurling spray right and left. And within a handful of days, so it seemed anyhow, they were in sight of the long grey line of Table Mountain. About noonday the great mountains were all clear to them as they approached, Table Mountain closest and clearest. In the convict quarters, Decker told him a number of men were fitting on their good suits kept in store since they were first arrested in England, in expectation of landing and walking in medium freedom on this shore.

But on Mitchel's part of the quarterdeck, the young officer who first escorted him to his cabin on board told him that – as earlier reported – the colonists were not content that their country should be turned into a penal settlement. Even New South Wales in far Australia, designed for the purpose, had already rebelled, it seemed, and rejected the landing of further convicts. And here in the Cape, the people who opposed the landing of Britain's wrongdoers had captured the legislature and formed an anti-convict association.

Mitchel discovered from the papers printed ashore that it demanded residents of the Cape would not employ any convict, that no citizen would sell anything to any convict, give a convict a place to lay his head, or give any citizen the necessity to deal with, countenance or speak to any convict.

A brisk little Scot, Dr Stewart, the health officer of the port, told Mitchel on a visit from shore that none of the anti-convict sentiment was directed at him. He was known to be on the ship, and given the trouble he had imposed on the home government, Mitchel was very welcome to try to settle amongst them. The settlers of the Cape were completely in the right, said Mitchel, and he himself hoped they would stand up to threats of invasion by redcoats, as much as he would have enjoyed a stroll on the shore. But for now, still being a prisoner until landed, even he was not free to leave the ship.

So the *Neptune* cargo settled uneasily on that Simon's Bay water, surrounded by huge mountains, and beneath the mountains many eyes trained on them. Mitchel went on reading, writing and drawing his grog.

It had always been a matter of wonder to Mitchel that free immigrants and their families went voluntarily to live in a penal colony and adopted it as their country. And at the Cape, he found himself quite fascinated by the contest that was going on there, given that if the colonists went on preventing the landing of the convicts, the Governor would have to wait for orders from home before he knew where else to send *Neptune*. Mitchel enjoyed the utter and glorious uncertainty almost as a stimulant.

It was not a stimulant for Dr Dees, however, who was feeling the weight of it and of his own concern about some patients. He complained to Mitchel that having successfully got the convict components here without deaths, he was now being treated like the captain of a Malay pirate ship, and made to keep clear of the port and its hospitals.

The bells in Simonstown, one stroke every half minute, rang to mourn the arrival. A committee of vigilance, appointed by the anti-transportation forces, kept a constant eye upon the *Neptune* and the boats that travelled to shore and back. Even from the quarterdeck of *Neptune*, Mitchel could see continual traffic on the road between the little port and Cape Town itself. There was much riding at an urgent pace.

The quartermaster-general came on board with two medical officers to inspect the boat. As he was speaking to Mitchel, a small length from them, poor Dees fell to the ground and did not rise. At first it was thought to be an epileptic fit, but it continued after he was put to bed unconscious. He had sacrificed himself for . . . duty? . . . or for the pleasure of men in London who never left the Home Counties unless it was to go to France or Italy.

Dees was carried to the hospital where 'golden' Garrett, the bullion thief, would tend him. Garrett was in a fever of excitement to land and test the new horizons of South Africa.

———

Dr Dees recovered somewhat but was distressed and had fits of great agitation, worrying how his ship could be supplied and fretting about the health of his felons, some of whom were sickening again with stomach diseases on the convict deck. An old frigate named *Seringapatam* was commandeered by the chief naval officer in the port and more than a hundred prisoners were transferred to it. With the summer coming on, it was important that every prisoner had as much air and space around him as possible. Sickest was still the poor doctor himself, who was taken ashore in one of the frigate's boats, and to the naval hospital.

The next day he died. It was some sort of paroxysm or apoplexy. He had been hoping to be relieved of duty and replaced with another surgeon. But his duty had now killed him. Mitchel found that it had been hard not to honour his professional earnestness, and that he had still not lost a single convict, but that he had himself perished for that principle.

The officers who attended the house of the Governor in Cape Town, Harry Smith, came back with stories of his marked ugliness but also of the splendour of Lady Juana Maria Delores de Leon Smith, who famously he had met at the end of the battle of the Badajoz in Spain. She was so admired even by the English colonists that they had named one of the new inland cities Ladysmith, to honour her.

———

In Cape Town, the approach of Christmas actually stiffened the settlers' resolve. They burned the Secretary of State Earl Grey – determined to send convicts willy-nilly – in effigy. Mynheer Smuts, a Boer leader, and a British newspaperman named Fairbairn jointly presented a great new motion at a crammed meeting at the Town Hall: '. . . that all inter-course and connection between private individuals and his Excellency and heads of the victualling departments shall be dropped from this day.' The motion was passed unani-mously. No-one consulted the black people in all this. They lived beneath the level of opinions.

Would Smuts and Fairbairn be Africa's Washington and Jefferson? Given each night some excellent Cape wine for dinner, Mitchel drank the health of the future of the South African Republic!

They were there, within the breath of Africa, but not permitted to land, for a further three months throughout the middle of 1849. Then Earl Grey's despatches arrived, and in them, everyone aboard seemed to know, were new orders for the convicts. Mitchel, anxious to find out what these imperial decisions were, could hear the felons discussing it through the walls, as if they had been selling watercress in Downing Street and had thus discovered the cabinet resolutions.

Some speculation on the main deck during exercise seemed to run to the likelihood they might be returned to prisons in Britain, or promptly pardoned, and returned to their homes. The idea cheered the darkest convict faces. But all this seemed an unlikely arrangement to Mitchel, and was not an expectation he held seriously as he stood on the poop watching the men surge aft to stand before the Commodore of the Navy's flagship, who had come aboard to announce the future of the prisoners. The men grew subdued, some visibly holding their breath.

The Commodore read an Order in Council. After various where-to-as-es and invocations of Majesty, a meaningful sentence in all the palaver was reached and announced that the ship would go to Van Diemen's Land. On arrival there, the prison population, excepting the prisoner Mitchel, were to receive, in compensation for their hard passage, Her Gracious Majesty's Conditional Pardon (the condition being that they never return to Britain in the course of their lives). Special instructions would be sent to the Governor of Van Diemen's Land about Mitchel.

All the eyes of the officers and men swung to Mitchel. He tried to convey a demeanour of scorn. He was oppressed by the thought that now, in the end, he would need to bring his wife and children to that notorious place, that outer darkness! There, as he knew, one out of two of their companions would be felons or the children of felons, people who congenitally felt their hand must be against everyone's, since everyone's hand was against them. Some would be Irish, of course, condemned by packed juries. Like Mitchel himself.

Helped by a ration of grog, the convicts adjusted themselves to the new reality. Families could be shipped out to join the reprieved convicts! Mitchel wondered if his would be permitted. Could he become an assigned convict servant to Jenny? Stranger things had happened in the Australian colonies.

There were now some days of urgent activity on *Neptune*. Ashore, the settlers were planning a dinner of congratulations, with a fireworks display and illuminations of all main buildings. Cape Town had – after all – beaten Westminster!

Mitchel walked a great deal on the deck that last night. There was no secret they were turning to sea in the morning.

Indeed, a war steamer pulled them out of the bay, to what cheers ashore Mitchel could but imagine. Another continent had put its breath on him but exhaled him in the end. The massive geographic arms of the bay receded. A wind, uninterrupted on its way around the globe, cracked fully open the mainmast shroud, and it would not deflate for weeks.

14

Mitchel Nears Australia, Late 1849

On the parallel of 46 degrees south, having sought the gales south of Africa and found them without much trouble, the *Neptune* was sped along by the most strenuous winds in the world, those called the Roaring Forties. Mitchel was ill with a ship's fever but when he came back on deck he could hear the convicts laughing in the high wind on their exercise strip amidships, pausing and discoursing in clumps, like lawyers on the concourse of a court. Their spirits were high for they foresaw freedom. And only the ship's timbers groaned and howled under the forces of sea and wind.

Off the western coast of Van Diemen's Land, the famed convict hell, he saw the comfortless rain-hazed mountains of the island, beyond which he would deliver the daily breath of his sentence. And beyond those shaggy mountains somewhere, Meagher, Martin and O'Brien were already getting on with life under servitude. The idea did not comfort him at that moment. His arrival would deliver him, ultimately and in whatever condition, to Jenny. The mountains remained perpetually visible on the windy south coast. Closer to shore they could see the great crag – named predictably for Wellington – lowering over the land. There was great beauty, but great oddity too, in this place. The forests on either side were of the eucalyptus, which shed no leaves but instead dropped its bark. Australian forests, as he would soon enough find, were littered by sheaths of bark, like rolls of paper torn off the trunks of trees by some demented editor.

They proceeded up a broad and noble estuary and by late afternoon were all at once at anchor a quarter of a mile from the quays and customs house of the town of Hobart. The settlement lay on slopes running down from the hills, with church steeple, a battery, a windmill, merchants' stone warehouses along the quays. It was, Mitchel had to admit to himself, a rather lovely scene, if you abstracted from its chief, penal purpose.

He noticed that the captain and the new surgeon superintendent were now dressed in formal uniform to greet the visitors from the Van Diemen's Land convict department. After so long at sea, Mitchel found that the hills invoked in him a strong desire to go rambling. But not today, for the doctor had told him that the Governor, Sir William Denison, had a special dispatch regarding him on his desk. However, he had gone off into the bush with a hunting party and might not be back even tomorrow.

'They are not hunting the natives?' Mitchel asked.

'No,' said the doctor. 'I think they have done that in the past. The kangaroo is good hunting.'

Mitchel now had a visit from his friend Garrett, who on whatever pretext was permitted to come up from the convict deck and knock on his door. Indeed, Garrett was already wearing a tailored brown suit like a citizen and was full of this moment of deliverance and its omens.

'I trust you have at least a ticket-of-leave, Mr Mitchel,' he said. 'Some sort of rusticating Vandermaniac life!'

'Very kind,' Mitchel told him. 'I hope you find an existence, a reasonable existence here.'

'In that regard they tell me the Old Lady can join me here. We'll soon see if she loves me . . .' Garrett lowered his voice. 'If she brings her great wealth with her . . .'

He laughed like a god at the potential comedy and promise of this.

'And you will not believe what prospects the colony has for me, Mr Mitchel. It's genuine gravy and you wouldn't believe it!'

'I can't guess,' Mitchel admitted.

'With ten others, or eleven, is it? In any case, *we* are to be sworn in as constables.'

That genuinely did amaze Mitchel, a sign the world was turned upside down. 'Perhaps they could swear me in,' Mitchel suggested. 'I could be their constable to hunt down radical force.'

'No. I think I am notorious, but here you are certainly too notorious for that caper.'

'So you will be a police officer?'

'Purely because it wouldn't even happen in Hades,' Garrett told Mitchel, tickled extremely.

Mitchel wished him well, as he had already wished Mitchel.

The doctor later told him that nearly all constables on the island were former felons. 'A dozen of our worst ruffians you will see, in a few days, dressed in blue and armed with

175

carbines and in a position to dominate over you and your gentlemen friends who arrived here before you.' He reassured Mitchel, however, that he had heard that the orders were that he should be treated with some consideration. He offered to go ashore the next day to fetch the Governor's order if he could. If Mitchel was assigned to a residence in the hinterland, he would use his influence as a surgeon to place him, in view of his recent bad health, with his friend John Martin.

———

When the Hobart Town newspapers came on board, Mitchel found that O'Brien was in very close confinement on Maria Island, a rugged place twelve miles in length further up the Vandemonian coast. The convict authorities were very much irritated by his determination, and as far as was known, his health was not good.

From the quarterdeck an officer on watch pointed out no fewer than five ships due to leave for California. Because of the Californian gold, he said, Hobart and San Francisco had become sister ports. And as a miner might go, perhaps O'Brien had thought, or been advised, to try it himself. Apart from that, there were great reefs of gold across Bass Strait, the body of water between Van Diemen's Land and the mainland. A convict whose time was up could, one way or the other, go straight to El Dorado.

A young clerk went aboard, an official of the convict department, and gave Mitchel a communication from the grandly named Comptroller of Convicts, one Dr Hampton. Mitchel was much cheered to find that Earl Grey in London had decreed as prisoner he could be allowed to reside at large in any of the police districts he might select. He could now escape confinement, subject to no restrictions, except for the necessity of giving his parole and reporting himself to the district police magistrate once a month. John Martin, wherever he was in the bush, was of course the one he would go to.

This almost genial situation Mitchel had been offered – his ticket-of-leave – had been given to the other prisoners of *Neptune* too: they could live in the community as long as they did not offend again. The idea was that Van Diemen's Land itself was the prison. The ordinary convicts would be under no pressure to give words of honour, but it was true that if they tried to escape and were recaptured, they would be treated malignly. Best to stay at their assigned labour. But if the chance arose, through bribery or other means, they could try to go to California if they felt up to the punishment of discovery.

But Mitchel was required to keep his word of honour, a pledge based on all that was sacred to him, on all he loved, and on his own validity as a writer and a moral being. So it would be necessary that if Mitchel wished to escape, he must first withdraw his parole and then give the authorities a fair, gentlemanly chance of catching him. If he did not do things according to his solemn word, he would be libelled by his captors throughout the world and would have no honour in international discourse. That is, he could not escape secretly. He had to escape publicly. Smith O'Brien had refused to give his parole and so was imprisoned in near solitary confinement on Maria Island off the east coast of Van Diemen's Land.

But though Mitchel did not recognise the validity of his original sentence, he was nonetheless largely pleased, after all this time at sea, that he must give his parole and live in the colony where allowed, and since every departing ship seemed to be searched many times over, it seemed as well he had no proximate means of escape.

The surgeon of *Neptune*, replacement for tragic Dr Dees, urged him earnestly to take his ticket-of-leave since he said, and believed, that after Mitchel's long separation from solid earth, the close confinement of Maria Island would kill him with prison fever before long. After all, he had been ten months in solitary confinement in Bermuda and a few days short of a year aboard *Neptune*.

'You were not condemned to death,' he reminded himself again. At a profound level, though, he thought he was giving in and going mildly to become a district-wide gentleman lag. He must now renew himself by a sane life.

Mitchel knew that in Van Diemen's Land he was now as far from Jenny's smile and the play of his children as it was possible to get on earth. That awareness tempered any exhilaration he felt in saying goodbye to the officers of *Neptune*, and in being taken ashore, amongst the stone warehouses, beneath the great mountain, and then transported, the ground reeling beneath his feet, to the hotel from which a coach would take him to Bothwell, the town where Martin also lay under the stricture of a parole. John still wore the tattered suit in which he'd been condemned and it might have seemed ragged by Dublin standards. But there were many ragged men, free and convict, in aged suits on this version of the earth.

And so, after a pleasant journey, Mitchel found himself by 12 April in the year of our Lord 1850, sitting on the green grass of the bank of the clear, brawling stream of freshwater in the hinterland, in a valley framed by mountains. The sunshine was streaming upon him and his company through the branches of trees. They were on the outskirts of Bothwell. Opposite him sat John Martin, former farmer and physician of Loughorne, smoking placidly. The journey up here by coach and cart had been less than a day's run.

It was delicious to be here, so encompassed in terrain, though his head still rocked from the implanted motion of the ocean. Martin, he was pleased to say, seemed the old, fussy, reliable bachelor that ever he was. He was necessary, after Mitchel's long time at sea and in prison, to teach the prisoner to live in a world where criminals lived in town, and you needed to commit a new crime to be sent to jail or to the hard labour of one of the Port Arthur establishments. These latter unabashedly described themselves as a place of 'secondary punishment'. But here in rustic Bothwell, in a southern version of Scotland, Mitchel was such a lag still he was always waiting for ship's bells and klaxons to tell him what to do. He even found himself looking for the conversational hubbub of the main prison mess. So he watched Martin for cues to his own life, the pace and timetable of living it. And so they were both still in the world.

———

Bothwell was a pleasant little town remarkably like towns the world over. So, for all else that Mitchel might have sought on earth, he even had a rudimentary golf course if he chose to use it. Convicts could not play on it, but perhaps a ticket-of-leave political who had given his parole might be permitted. Mr Reid, the chief citizen, had a fine house and was a man who had a subscription to *Edinburgh Review*. Mitchel met him at kirk, or at least at the church where clergymen of the Church of England performed morning services on the Sabbath morn, and ministers of the Church of Scotland performed services on Sunday evening, all despite the semi-Papist decorations and stained glass the Anglicans went in for.

There were four large public houses in Bothwell, which were better supported on the voluntary system than the church. The pub was the place where the convict and former convict and free settler would meet. There was a post office and several carpenters' and blacksmiths' shops, a police office and police barracks, and the police magistrate to whom John was to report monthly. He believed he might see the natives of the country, but, for good or ill, said the Scots, they had been already driven off into the north-west of the island.

Even the signs of convictism were muted here, in this valley, which despite the eucalyptus trees could have been mistaken for some fair valley in Europe. You could not tell which of the shepherds, drovers, farriers and so on in this place were free men and which were assigned convicts. The secret was that Bothwell was very beautiful but not made a fuss of by its present inhabitants. This was something Mitchel noticed about colonials: again, that beauty was never robustly extolled in a convict settlement, as if for fear that it would all be negated by some brutality – the slaughter of masters by convicts on the loose, the latter called bushrangers, or the flogging and immolation of convicts in their turn. Everyone, in the meantime, was concentrated on getting along with their convict servants, and letting them have their space as long as that did not coincide with one's own.

The little cottage Martin rented, Nant Cottage, was one thousand feet above the sea level and through the valley ran the river. It was fast, and near the town of Hamilton a little further south-west, became rapids. Hamilton and Bothwell were both Scots names from Lanarkshire, and Lanarkshire people had first settled here as free souls to whom any river must obviously bear the name Clyde to honour the one back in their home county.

There must have been many natives here, though, for it was a lovely place. And there must have been a native name for the river. Martin had made up his mind about these things. 'I cannot for the life of me,' he said, 'disprove that the remaining Aboriginal natives of Van Diemen's Land must have a lien on the country. I cannot prove we had no need to make a treaty, and we did not make one. I believe it will turn out the settlers will need to one day.'

When Mr Alex Reid invited Mitchel and Martin to his house to talk about the history of Jacobinism or the English wool market or whaling in Bass Strait, you would not know, sitting in his parlour, that you were not in Scotland. There were Highland prints and good wallpaper and plaster mouldings (possibly done by a felon with that background). The Reids had come close to making Caledonia in another place here. Indeed, he, Mrs Reid, their son and their daughters had returned to Scotland for some years before realising that the homeland they wanted was here in Bothwell in Van Diemen's Land.

And yet they had needed to live in a frontier cottage for some years before the fine house was built. Mrs Reid could tell you, too, of the time bushrangers took over the cottage, called the men in from the field and made them prisoners, and then began to attack all the household furniture with axes. One of the Scots the bushrangers had trussed up suggested under his breath that Mrs Reid should make laudanum-laced tea, but the head bushranger (Irish, of course, one of the sons of banditry) guessed the purpose, said it had been tried on them before and that there would be a vengeance if he were to be found sleeping about the place when the constables came searching for them.

That was twenty years ago or more. Now Alex Reid, a sturdy man of about fifty years, wore at that age merely the trace of pain suffered in the past (not least from the death of two daughters). Jane, the daughter who lived at the house, no older than Jenny, was herself a widow who had left behind, when very young, a deceased husband and a fever-extinguished baby in Bengal.

All these folk made Mitchel very welcome and expressed the honour of meeting him, and Alex Reid's Jacobite tendencies fitted well with Mitchel's Hibernian ones. As well as this, conversation did not proceed far before the Reids told you that any enemy of Governor Denison, Lieutenant Governor of Van Diemen's Land, was a friend of theirs.

Alex Reid told Mitchel, with his wife and daughter and friends listening with approbation, that the great Scot who had written *The Wealth of Nations* had nonetheless gone wrong in his theory on colonies. Adam Smith had gone so far as to say the colonists should pay the mother country's expenses in running the country, since the money was poured out in their interest. He seemed to believe like George III that the British had run the American colonies purely for the benefit of the Americans. Yet an empire acquires colonies, said Reid, for nothing but its own aggrandisement.

Just the same, Governor Denison was a disciple of the idea of a benevolent empire and wanted the colonists to meet the expense of the penal colonies throughout the island, precisely as if the colonists desired and enjoyed them. He had convened a Legislative Council of whom Mr Reid was a member, but they had all resigned, to the applause of their fellow settlers, when Denison tried to get them to legislate taxes – their only attitude towards the penal system being that they wanted it to end, and they wanted self-government.

Mitchel would find these sentiments existed in other members of the Bothwell community, and they expressed delight that someone had turned up so well known that his story might cast light on Denison, a creature of darkness.

Mitchel was exhilarated to hear all this, and felt a warm friendship for the rugged colonists who seemed to be approaching a state of resistance like that of the Cape.

———

Twenty-four miles north of the Clyde, Martin would tell him, up on the shores of two mountain lakes, Lake Crescent and Lake Sorell, their territory met up with the territory of O'Meagher and O'Doherty, who regularly wrote to him by common mail; though for special letters, such as planning a meeting, O'Meagher always used a reliable Irish rider. O'Doherty, the young doctor transported with Martin, went sometimes there for reflection and recreation and of course to see the magnetic O'Meagher. They called him that. Why not? There was a courtesy of calling a fellow what he wanted to be called, and he probably wanted to use 'O'Meagher' in honour of his Gaelic forebears, the O'Meachairs of Tipperary.

The authorities supposed the Irish state prisoners would not be demented enough to ride to that wild westerly rim of the wilderness, but Martin had himself already been up there to meet the others. The British Empire's supervision did not quite reach the westerly banks of that mountain lake.

Meanwhile, Mitchel told Jenny in a letter, the terrain and the elements did their best to charm him. The fragrance of the gum trees combined with that of the native tree called the wattle, and laid a perfume into the air. There were many parrots and parakeets, which went flashing amongst the green like winged gems where he and Martin rode or went tramping. He felt he should try to evince a furious and chronic indignation at being a prisoner, but the place subverted him and made him forgetful of the fact in a way that Bermuda never did.

As well as that, he had a cow to milk every second day and Martin was running a flock of two hundred ewes on the two hundred acres over which the Nant Cottage farm extended. And in the farmhouse they had so much room they could each have a separate office. But Mitchel also had Martin to speak to, and he could educate the newly arrived felon on three months of Irish history that had followed Mitchel's transportation.

Martin also resolved to take Mitchel up to Lake Sorell the next week – the milking could be done by a ticket-of-leave woman who lived nearby, and Martin knew a man in Bothwell who would rent them a horse.

Nearby the cottage, at the edge of the village, was a lady who conducted the singing in the church on Sunday. She came to Nant Cottage once a week, along with a convict maid, to clean and to leave delicacies such as apple pies for the delectation of the convict politicals of Bothwell. She sought Mitchel out very early and told him that she 'came out free'.

To have 'come out free' was the patent of nobility of Van Diemen's Land, and meant you had the chance to employ anyone who came out convict. However, she too was afflicted with dislike of Sir William Denison and his no doubt splendid spouse, Lady Catherine. Of course, she admired Mr Reid who rebelled in the Legislative Council against Sir William's estimates.

On the morning of the planned reunion day at the lake, the two Irishmen rode forth at eight o'clock from Nant Cottage, and the morning presented itself grey and grim. What was rain in Bothwell's valley became snow on high points of ground. Their good chorister saw them ride past her door, and she and her husband came out and exhorted them to the best of their skills not to venture forth. The streams further up the mountains around the lake might be in flood. But Mitchel and Martin said they must press on.

'I have not been astride a horse for two years, madam,' cried Mitchel through the downpour. 'I don't want to give it up. So I must take my chances.' They followed the valley for four miles to a place call Quoin Hill, where Mr Philip Russell, a Scottish settler who had 'come out' at the same time as the Reids, occupied a fine stone house. It was not a day to be sociable with Mr Russell, so the two horsemen kept on and beyond his pasture.

It was as they ascended a boulder-choked gully that the rain turned into snow. They kept their heads down and were aware only that they were rising up through the blinding tempest. At every mile the forest became wilder and the track harder to read and more encumbered with fallen trees. Martin kept on assuring Mitchel that when they were halfway to Lake Sorell they could turn back if the going got too rough. But at last they came to a level plain scattered with majestic trees, like someone's park in Ireland.

Martin said, 'We are on the plateau, young John, and we will soon be at the most companionable fire you could think of.'

He led Mitchel over a rough wooden bridge built by the settlers for their stock to come down from winter pasture. They went on in hard country and saw occasionally a few sheep cowering under a honeysuckle tree. And then they could see Lake Crescent, like a great field of slate under the scowl of clouds, and followed its grassy shore, then crossed a short stream and were on the shore of Lake Sorell. Martin told Mitchel that they were about to meet a hermit named Cooper who occupied a hut up here and who would feed and restore them for the last effort to get to O'Meagher's.

Mitchel was by then feeling utterly fatigued, having been far too long on a ship. When they got to Cooper's log hut, they could see Lake Crescent to the left and the vastness of Lake Sorell, that huge mountain tarn, to the right. Cooper, Mitchel would realise later, fitted the role of Vandemonian hutkeeper: a man of about forty years, with a sharp, intelligent face and wearing a blue woollen shirt. He told them he knew that Mr O'Meagher and Mr O'Doherty were at Townsend's just four miles further on.

And yet Martin and Cooper could see, as Mitchel sat by Cooper's fire, that he couldn't go any further. So Cooper borrowed Martin's grey and set off to ask their co-conspirators to come to them. Leaving, he cried, 'Just keep the fire up, gentlemen, that I may get the chops ready when I come back.'

Mitchel did not envy Cooper his afternoon ride. And it was dark as they heard the gallop of three horses and a loud laugh which they knew belonged to O'Meagher. Mitchel wondered could O'Meagher actually exist there in that blizzard, or if someone beyond the log wall was impersonating him. But seeing his large handsome face, enhanced by a beard – the face of an urban sybarite impersonating a man of the wilderness, a bandit chieftain – Mitchel himself began laughing like someone possessed and kept laughing till birds rose from the reeds on the foreshore and flapped complaining away.

After O'Meagher, Mitchel embraced O'Doherty, a fine erect-looking young physician. He and Martin then attended to the horses – Mitchel was now refreshed enough to do that – Martin giving them two handfuls of oats each, and the pair setting them loose to forage – the bush everywhere providing close shelter, whether the wattle-gum or the honeysuckle tree.

Meanwhile, Cooper was in his hut roasting mutton chops, boiling tea in an open tin can slid over the fire, and cutting the bush flatbread called damper into thick slices. Back in the cabin, they dined primitively, since Cooper had only one knife and one fork. But the meal was exquisite.

The talk was all of Smith O'Brien, who that night was still on Maria Island and as isolated from the other convicts there as Mitchel had been on the hulks. Smith O'Brien had been subjected to the most rigorous and capricious behaviour by Comptroller General Hampton, who was galled by the fact that O'Brien never showed him respect. Only at the insistence of a prison surgeon was he allowed to go roaming about the island for a time each day, always attended by an armed constable.

As O'Meagher informed Mitchel, he began to think it might have been better for Smith O'Brien had he been shot dead at Ballingarry last July. O'Meagher also had heard a great deal about the factions of Irish in the US who supported this or that inglorious Irish hero of non-heroic 1848 who had fled to America. O'Meagher had his partisans in New York, and he said that Mitchel certainly did too. If they could see us now, he said, huddled so happily around the fire in this antipodean hut, with snow outside, what would they say?

Mitchel had an answer. 'The Americans . . . Aren't they saying, why not send a ship to get them out?'

'Though that is the dream,' said O'Meagher, 'there is the question of the parole and how to withdraw it. And then get away with speed. We would need many friends here, as well as in America.'

Mitchel thought of Alex Reid and wondered would he, if it came to it, hide any of them from constables. Actually, Mitchel concluded, he probably would for the sake of spiting Denison.

'It seems to me that many here like us for not being friends of the Governor.'

'A very promising crowd, these Vandemonians,' said O'Meagher. 'The secret meanwhile for us is: not to be caught in marriage by any of the Irish girls. Then, if an American opportunity arises . . . Well, one is unburdened and better placed to simply go! Now, Mr Mitchel, in that regard, will you bring your divine wife all this way?'

Jenny had written to Mitchel raising the issue, but details were inevitably uncertain. O'Meagher, seeming to contradict his counsels against being charmed by anyone here said, 'I am not a fellow for long courtships when left to my own devices.'

'O'Doherty is comforted,' said O'Meagher, 'by the way his betrothed maiden, the great Eva Kelly, forges poetry specifically for him.'

Eva Kelly was a young woman from Galway who had contributed poetry to *The Nation*. O'Meagher threw his head back then and recited reverently

Yes, pale one in your sorrow
– Yes, wronged one in your pain,
This heart has still a beat for thee,
This trembling hand a strain.
Come wild deer of the mountainside!
Come sweet bird of the plain.
To cheer the cold and trembling heart
That beats for thee in vain.

During the recital young O'Doherty looked aside as if better to listen to the metre of the poem and respect it.

O'Meagher saw this. 'That is poetry, O'Doherty, no? That is the real product!' And so he chose, standing, to move on to a further verse of Eva's.

How I glory, how I sorrow,
How I love with deathless love;
How I weep before the chilling skies,
And moan to God above.

O'Meagher had recited these verses conscientiously and without irony, and at the end said, 'What man could be indifferent to such sentiments? What man could betray them? Certainly not a decent fellow like Doctor O'Doherty.'

O'Doherty looked over at Mitchel. His eyes were moist.

'Eva may come here,' he said. 'As your own wife might, one day.'

'Mitchel's wife is a priestess and a woman warrior,' said O'Meagher. 'Perhaps even I would behave for a woman of such stature.'

Martin's eyes shone. 'I don't think so, Thomas,' he said, and all laughed.

———

Mitchel had indeed thought how Jenny might enjoy the community of Bothwell and, such was her robustness, how she would enjoy a company like the one at Lake Sorell. But he did not praise the country around Bothwell with the idea of baiting her, as badly as he wanted to see her and as biting as might be the demands of the flesh.

These were the sorts of questions upon which he slept, and in the morning the landscape around Cooper's place was white, and they went ploughing out in their boots to find their wandered horses. They discovered them by a native honeysuckle tree, nibbling the branches, and drove them in, and after Cooper's breakfast, they rode on with O'Meagher to the snug cove by the Dog's Head Peninsula, where O'Meagher's stone habitation stood.

The day became bright and the snow melted before their eyes and the lake was as smooth as a mirror, and still moored, though full of snow, a little skiff was tied up to a pier – the *Speranza*, as O'Meagher had entitled it. Beyond all that glassiness of the lake, the tiers of Van Diemen's Land wilderness ran away to the west like godlessness.

In the afternoon they rowed round O'Meagher's inlet and out to an island, sailed back on a westerly and ate and talked and drank. Would Ireland rise? Would American Irish add their numbers? The talk was energetic. Grand alliances were conjured up in the dense and brandy-laced air of O'Meagher's wilderness living room and its giant fireplace. France might speak again and America had not spoken at all. It was not impossible that an army of Irish–Americans might one day invade Ireland, perhaps even along with the French. That was the shorter-term aim for France, and the longer term was to destroy Downing Street's imperial sway.

The next morning they parted, promising to rendezvous again the week after next, and so Mitchel and Martin rode away southwards in inclement weather. Having met O'Meagher, and finding him and O'Doherty unreduced, Mitchel had been refreshed by the idea the game was not over yet.

15

Living as a Bothwell Convict, from 1850 Onwards

John's letters to 'Beloved Jenny' became richer in detail and observation. She could tell he liked Van Diemen's Land and knew it would be a habitable zone, at least until the currents of the earth began to move again, and the forces smashed down by regimes in 1848 – in Prague, Vienna and Ireland – could rally themselves again.

'In other directions, John Martin takes me riding and so we meet one Kenneth McKenzie from Ross Shire, who brought us in after sending our horses to his stable and introduces us to his wife, a McRae who speaks Gaelic Erse better than she does English – though she has been some quarter of a century here. By the time their children had come into the hut, I was convinced that I was in some brae in Scotland. Except their children had that colonial flatness to their vowels and they lament before the hearth like magpies.'

By July, when he was living entirely absorbed in farming in Bothwell, he had been in Van Diemen's Land and had his vigour back after the year at sea in *Neptune*. That month, Jenny decided they must be together and for the first time expressed her ambition to see him in person.

He was careful in his reply. 'So, my jewel, I acknowledge your desire to come here, despite the exercise it will be with the children, and so I will study if by any means it is to be achieved.'

For it was a place of condemnation.

'I have received a letter from Smith O'Brien himself. You may very well know more of him than I do these days, although I suppose your newspapers there are also full of as much gossip as fact about him. We are all famous for having been sentenced by order of Downing Street, and no-one more than Smith O'Brien. If in vanity we had hired a friend to make us notorious he could not have done as well as our enemy. Imagine if we had succeeded! In any case, the O'Brien letter was headed, "Darlington Probation Station, Maria Island". It seemed that he wanted to explain to me his decision to refuse parole. The said parole, he told me, would only give him a sort of mock liberty, he said, in a district about the size of two parishes. I am tempted to tell him an ordered life is still possible in our little region, and he might find a like place. "I do not regret, but on the contrary rejoice, that I refused the pledge required," he assured me. But Comptroller Hampton and his Excellency the Governor had earlier made things hard by depriving him of exercise, and subjecting him to an unlimited period of absolute silence and solitude. In reality some of the Commandants were a little more lenient on him. If the solitary treatment had been continued to be enforced, he says he would long before now have been either in his grave or in a madhouse.

'Obviously he cannot bear this torture much longer and Martin and I smoke the pipe of deliberation over this matter, sitting in the bush at sunset upon a prostrate gum tree, and find no solution. We put aside a book to be sent to him in his exile, but I, the fire-eater, am in comparative liberty and he, the moderate man, is being worn down by penal silence and devices.

'The Comptroller General, Dr Hampton, had clearly read Smith O'Brien's letter to me, since his seal was on it. Martin and I were rather depressed by this missive of O'Brien's and wondered how we would survive in Smith O'Brien's situation listening to surly jailers and hearing only the birds calling, and the bolts tightened at our door.'

But the letter to Jenny Mitchel did not end there and he did return to the issue of Bothwell's notable charms.

'We in our turn were soon comforted by pleasant nights in the surrounding country, not least the house named Ratho by that witty, dry Scot named Alexander Reid, who had a splendid house with books and an amiable family. Convicts were excluded from his house except as servants, and yet he didn't count Martin or myself under that heading and he would have preferred entertaining us than the Governor. I felt quite grateful, and not for the first or last time, to that former engineer officer, the Viceroy William Denison, for the more unpopular he becomes to O'Brien, the more authoritarian he becomes, the better the more discriminating people in progressive newspapers, to whose pages he is elevated only by his connection with O'Brien, consider him a cheap colonial tyrant. Not that Reid wasted large amounts of breath on his Excellency. He was a good conversationist beneath his dryness and proud of the Scots of the New Enlightenment, including my revered friend Carlyle.

We have agreed with the great Carlyle that having hypo-critically condemned slavery, the British really merely introduced a white version of it, called industrial slavery. You see how solemn we get about the great machines to which so many Britons are themselves slaves. In any case, I walked home from Ratho feeling blessed by normal discourse.

'And yet, my beauty, my lovely Jenny, are there enough Rathos to make this a place as yet for you and the children? The truth probably is that I have not yet seen enough of the place to risk your happiness here, or to reconcile myself to the fact that my sons and daughters will grow up in this society which still has the Denisons and the Hamptons to deal with, and where the kindness extended to me may not automatically be directed to my children. If I could only be reassured on these matters! I go about seeking that reassurance, and if I can only get that, I would ask you to come at once. This quiet, golden valley would be enhanced and brought to the summit of charm if you live within it, Jenny, and if we walked through it together. You know these things, and what delays my welcome to you. Love delays it, I hope, not pride. And the burden of time I still need to serve.

'Love of all loves,' Mitchel felt bound to tell her, 'penal colonies are not normal places to live. Amidst pockets of civilisation, much is off balance . . . Now we called in at a stockman's hut on our way home, and were served a stew by the former convict wife, and chatted with the time-served, that is, former convict husband. Even at Ratho they would have to say that that fellow has grown at least halfway human. And to be fair to Ratho, Mr Reid wants the vote to go to former male convicts who own property, such as the man I refer to, as well as free settlers.

'Martin teased me about the man: "He has gone all the way human, John. It is peculiar to me that you are the greatest wrecker of society at least in your intentions, and yet you have less time for your fellow convicts."

'It is true that I have bourgeois attitudes even to Irish convicts who may well have stood up to landlords or burned down a tithe proctor's house, resisted paying tithes.

'So John Martin went on laughing to himself in his private way. "You are even worse to the Irish, I think. You were willing to die to have them rise up against tyranny. The ones who did, the ones who stole a little of the harvest or a calf, are here! And they invoke our names kindly. Even if you were the Comptroller General . . ."

'But he did not finish the sentence because he realised it might be far too insulting. And as gentle as this chiding was, I saw that it was accurate. I did harbour the morality of the Protestant gentry, combined with a desire to bring the entire temple down.

'The hutkeeper in question who had been so kind to us was a London East Ender and Van Diemen's Land shepherd, and it had been explained to me that East Enders made the best stockmen because the animals seemed exotic to them. The hutkeeper and his Highland wife had a rather tall child of about six. Who would that child become? Would he ever dine at Ratho? Or go to Port Phillip across Bass Strait and make a fortune from gold, and become a big name anyway?

'I made the point that as excusable as their initial crime might be, I've seen in Bermuda and on the *Neptune* what Britain's corrective system does to men. It renders them beasts if they were not already, and you can see in their eyes that only instinct, a gift for beastly opportunity, remains.

They are preter-human, I would say, or sur-human. This is what Britain's correction does to men. I would be remiss not to remind you.'

Even so, this had become something of a repeated objective of John Martin's, an argument for John Mitchel to let his wife and children come. There was room for them at Nant Cottage. And if Mitchel did his remaining twelve years here, his children might stay on, considering it theirs. And then, how could they leave? And mingling in the society of the good quiet colonists here, he and Jenny might almost forget at times the outrage their enemies had put upon them in keeping John here at all, and might begin to enjoy this matchless climate, and a landscape which seemed designed for sport.

And so one evening, Mitchel wrote to his mother's house in Newry, inviting Jenny and the family to the Antipodes without reserve. He hoped this decision might not turn out cruelly or absurdly. That he needed Jenny, he could frankly admit. The earth would never cease rocking from his voyages, he believed, until she steadied it.

———

They had a visit from Terence Bellew MacManus, the charming young man who had stood with Smith O'Brien at Ballingarry. Like O'Meagher, he had a somewhat Lancashire accent from the Jesuits at Stonyhurst, and the two were about the same age. He was a well-made, muscular fellow, not as striking perhaps as O'Meagher, but he looked so valorous he cheered Mitchel up: a wool merchant in that great all-but-Irish city of Liverpool, he'd given it all up to take his role in the uprising.

He rode by stealth up the valley of the Derwent and Clyde from New Norfolk to see Mitchel and Martin in Bothwell. They began to prevail on him to wait for the next ride up to the lake, and then there would be five rebels in the one hut, a circumstance that would eat the heart out of the Comptroller General if he knew of it, or so they liked to think. But MacManus had other plans.

When Mitchel and Martin got back to the lake in clearer weather, their chief sport was shooting ducks, which cooked up very well. Having written off to Jenny, all John could see in the landscape were now things that negated his invitation. He noticed that the birds had a foreign tongue, and that the very trees whispered in foreign accents. The gum trees had hard, horny leaves which had neither upper nor underside and which were vertical to the wind. Thus they rattled and never let a breeze through them in the European way – never could they whisper, quiver, sigh or sing, as did the beeches and the sycamores of old Rostrevor.

The Tropic of Capricorn had too much influence there, as did the Antarctic Circle south of them, and between those two they were captured in a space called Bothwell. Only the river spoke like the coastal streams of Down. Yet the day Mitchel wrote the letter of invitation to Jenny, he saw a platypus – a true, amphibious quadruped with a duckbill that slipped into the water of the Clyde, not far from where Martin and he were inspecting a site for a larger potential home, which would include Martin as the kindly uncle.

Would this place talk to and recompense beloved Jenny? Recompense her fully? She suffered so bitterly from sea sickness to begin with. Was he selfish? He missed his woman. He needed his wife. Whereas John Martin seemed complete unto himself as he was.

On their way home to Nant Cottage they overtook a man and woman. The woman was hideous, with a brandy-bloated face, and wore a white satin bonnet adorned with artificial flowers. The constable told them she was legitimately at large, with a ticket-of-leave that allowed her the entire island. She had been honourably discharged from a remote settler's house and was going to Hobart for reassignment, so that the benefits of her company and services could be spread around the whole island. She beamed at them. 'Gentlemen,' she addressed them as a form of farewell.

The man with her was a convict constable of the kind Garrett and some other members of *Neptune* were enticed to be. He carried a musket on his shoulder and there was a display of keys at his belt, and as Mitchel and Martin turned off, he saluted and called to them, and they heard his Irish intonation. And into such company Mitchel had beckoned Jenny.

But at least there was a local mare he intended to buy as a gift for her – a very pretty chestnut mare, Fleur-de-Lys.

———

In early summer he rode into the police station in Bothwell and got permissive documents from Police Magistrate Davis to meet Jenny's ship, which carried their five children, as well as a young girl from Banbridge to mind the children, when and if Jenny was too ill. He was full of expectation and dread as he rode to New Norfolk and then down the Derwent Valley.

In Hobart itself, he lodged with the young doctor John Martin had nicknamed 'St Kevin' O'Doherty. The real St Kevin at Glendalough had had his rest disturbed by a maiden, and so was the Van Diemen's Land St Kevin's rest by dreams of his Irish fiancée. They went out on rides that showed in full bloom all the British and Irish flowers that in the home hemispheres only survived in greenhouses. Men who were doing well in the new colony surrounded their houses, amidst the native trees, with mimosa and with the golden gorse named whin, and with the sweet briar that did so much better here than it ever did in the land where Robert Burns sang of it.

Mitchel was, botanically at least, a Vandemonian patriot. As well as flowers, beehives had been brought in, and the air sang with the bees who took nectar from a variety of plants, chiefly antipodean. One man in Bothwell had advertised three tons of honey for sale. Mitchel could say the bees had made the transit of the globe, and hoped his family would as well.

Occasionally, they saw a clan of the natives crossing the valley, tolerated upon their way. There was a time when they attacked places like Ratho and shook the Scots presence and took their vengeance upon shepherds for invading their land. Yet they were, in their remnants of settler clothing, the least offensive figures in the landscape.

———

Riding with Kevin O'Doherty around Hobart, Mitchel became aware that the surgeon was indeed a captive to an Irish beauty, a woman quite young, a Galway landowner's daughter named Eva, as O'Meagher had said. Mitchel had read her poetry. Duffy had dubbed her *Eva of The Nation*, and she was a champion to the Irish. The point was that Eva was only now nearing eighteen. O'Doherty's doubts were very much like Mitchel's. Could he bring a bard of national-ism, a rare girl who barely, nonetheless, knew the time of day in Galway, to a place like this? He found it hard to imagine.

The surgeon was also not good at confiding his own doubts. Mitchel did not know why. But Mitchel did begin, at least for O'Doherty's sake, to praise Van Diemen's Land and the future Tasmania as an amiable place for any woman – a place temperate, calm and pleasing as it might be. He did not mention the ticket-of-leave woman Martin and he had met on the road back to Bothwell.

To add to Mitchel's own confusion, Terence Bellew MacManus had escaped from the island. Since Launceston had been his district, he operated in the north of Van Diemen's Land – as Martin had reminded John once, more than two-and-a-half times the size of Belgium – and he had his own cabal of allies. Now they had helped get him away on a New Bedford, Massachusetts, whaler.

That was one of the things that had worried Mitchel about Jenny and the children. He said to Kevin O'Doherty, 'I feel I have been desperately foolish in inviting the family here just as MacManus demonstrates that one might get away.'

The authorities had let MacManus live in Launceston because he could get office work there, but he had had trouble when he needed to go to Hobart on business. He was tried for leaving Launceston without a pass, and then, the great Denison not being satisfied with that, for being in Hobart without one.

At last they sent him back down to Hobart, to the pris-oners' barracks, and dressed him in the grey fabric of the convict gangs and shipped him by steamer to a convict timber camp in the Port Arthur region, to do three months' probation and labour to get back his ticket-of-leave.

A company of three hundred progressive souls marched to the prisoner barracks in Hobart while he was still there and gave three loud cheers for Mr MacManus, whilst a band played rousing Irish music. Before the steamer took off for the camp the next day, he wrote to O'Meagher and told him very cheerfully that he'd look a very reduced chap when they next met, since the ration there was a pint of skilly, a thin oatmeal broth, morning and evening, and some mutton broth at noon.

But his secondary punishment did not last three months, for MacManus and some of the supporters brought an appeal against the sentence in the Supreme Court in Hobart, and the appeal was upheld, the courts being somewhat more independent of mind than those in Ireland. The point was that at the end of the trial, MacManus was free, but did not yet have a new ticket-of-leave, and thus his parole against escaping no longer existed.

It was believed he was now well on the way to San Francisco. The police had been set to hunting for him in the north and south of the island to reimpose the parole. At last they believed they'd found him in his lodgings in Launceston but badly stricken with a fever. They telegraphed Hobart for instructions. The government said to remove the sick man to the government hospital and guard him until he was well enough to come to Hobart.

However, the man in the bed was not MacManus but a friend of MacManus's, one John Galvin, a free citizen and immigrant from Cork. MacManus had escaped out of the estuary of the Tamar, and was picked up in Bass Strait by an American ship bound for golden California. At last Galvin disclosed his true identity, but by then MacManus was far gone out into the Pacific. Galvin said that having been a free man arrested by mistake while ill was an outrage. When he was now threatened with a fresh arrest, in return he threatened the Governor with a damages suit for wrongful detention, and for the serious outrage of which the police were guilty. The Governor let the matter slide, fearing amongst other things its risk of all seeming comedic.

But Mitchel could not have used MacManus as a reason for Jenny not to come. For a letter arrived nominating January of 1851 as the date of departure, from Warrenpoint to Liverpool, in an echo of their elopement. Another letter came from Liverpool – they were on a smart ship for Golden Melbourne, the *Condor*.

In the Van Diemen's Land summer with some vivid bush-fires on the western mountains, the family were underway. And many supporters made sure she and the children travelled in the saloon, with the better food and cabins. A letter arrived from her towards the end of the antipodean autumn, that is May 1851, and it was posted to him from Adelaide on the Australian mainland.

———

They were *all* in Adelaide, just the length of the Bass Strait away from Van Diemen's Land! Seven of them, including an Irish servant girl named Mary Laffin, who had a brother in the colony. Mitchel was now afflicted with a delicious fear he would not recognise the children after two years, all of them grown of course and Johnny and James close to twelve and thirteen.

They then arrived in Melbourne aboard the *Condor*, and took passage for Hobart by way of Adelaide, where it also had cargo to drop, but they did not know the ship would be a month unloading and loading in that port before coming on.

A ship's captain of a vessel named *Maid of Erin* found Mitchel, where he'd been permitted by police indulgence to lodge with O'Doherty in Hobart, and told him Mrs Mitchel and the children would have come on in his vessel – except that it lacked accommodation for such a big party. Instead, they had taken passage in a particular brigantine bound for Launceston.

The captain told him further that he had better get moving to Launceston, in the north of Van Diemen's Land, if he wanted to see them step ashore. He rushed to the Comptroller's office, and was interviewed by one of his deputies, who was amiable towards him just as he needed amiability – though in other circumstances, his consideration would have disappointed Mitchel subtly and on principle. His authorisation to go north would be posted there by this office, for Launceston was far outside his region and far, of course, from Hobart, where he was presently licensed to be.

So John took a seat in the overnight stagecoach, with one hundred and eighteen miles to travel. As the coach groaned away into a dusk gale, he prepared himself for a hard night followed by great exhilaration.

At nine the next morning the stage arrived at the Cornwall hotel in Launceston, and he heard the ship had not come in. He was so anxious for his tribe and for his beloved that he went up the hill in an absolute tempest to where the signal flagstaff stood, and waited around all day to see the reports of the signal master. But there seemed to be no movement on the Tamar estuary, beneath the skeins of rain blown across the water.

Next morning, John felt he must report himself to the Police Magistrate. He found the police station very crowded, with businessmen getting permits of all kinds, and even masters arranging matters for their assigned convict workers. He asked a policeman whether the magistrate was in and he pointed to a tall, disappointed-looking man listening to rival claims between two gentlemen at an elevated bench down the room. The gentlemen moved away at last, and Mitchel approached the bench.

'My name is John Mitchel,' he told the man, omitting the descriptors 'prisoner' and 'ticket-of-leave holder'. 'I have come to tell you that I am now in Launceston and that I stay at the Cornwall.'

Mitchel saw straight away that the man was in dreadful agitation, and knew why. For Mr Gunn, the magistrate he presented himself to that rainy day, had barely recovered from the MacManus escape. He asked Mitchel with great anguish why he was in Launceston, and Mitchel told him about his family. He asked if Mitchel had permission to be in Launceston.

'Yes,' said Mitchel.

'I have had no notification,' Gunn informed him and there was clamminess to the hollows of his blue cheeks.

'I can't help that, sir. I did not come to discuss the matter, and my papers are on the way from the deputy Comptroller in Hobart. I hope they haven't forgotten to send them.'

This whole idea of papers coming from Hobart made Gunn waver, and Mitchel nodded politely and repeated where he was staying, and then left.

—

Out on the stormy street, Mitchel then ran into an old class-mate from Newry, a man named Pooler, the chief grain merchant in Van Diemen's Land. They were walking amiably in Brisbane Street when a man in a good suit approached Mitchel, said he was the chief constable of Launceston and asked Mitchel to come with him to the police office.

Mitchel excused himself from Mr Pooler and accompanied the man back to where he had already been, where Mr Gunn was moving about, very flustered. He said Mitchel had been haughty and insolent an hour before and that he would teach him to show greater respect to the bench. Gunn requested the chief constable to read the charge against John. He obliged. The charge declared that Mitchel, a convict holding a ticket-of-leave, had come from his registered residence, Bothwell, to Launceston without a passport. More constables appeared and took Mitchel away to the cells behind the police station. He found himself in a plain cell that might have been in Newgate or anywhere on earth.

As the rain fell outside, he was there through the day, but the chief constable had given him a copy of the Launceston paper to read, and the jailer kept giving him reading matter as well. That cold night he supplied Mitchel very adequately with blankets and steaming cups of tea. Within the interstices of the machine, there was fellow feeling and fraternity. Why the machine was not all fraternity – that baffled Mitchel. Human kindness grew in the crevice of the rock, as poorly valued as moss.

He was a little relieved that the brigantine had not yet arrived – so had the jailer told him. And along came the chief constable just after breakfast to release him, for if the man at the Comptroller General's in Hobart had missed one or two mail coaches, he hadn't missed the third, and Mitchel's authorisation to be in Launceston had now arrived. He was released and as the chief constable walked him back to the Cornwall hotel, he told him that his friend the influential Mr Pooler had got permission for him to go to Longford, a little south of town, where he could just as easily await the arrival of Jenny and the children.

The next day the *Colonial Times* in Hobart lambasted Governor Denison for his cruelty towards Mitchel, and petitions had been drawn up both in Van Diemen's Land and on the Australian mainland praying for a pardon for all Irish state prisoners. Mitchel was so delighted that he wrote a characteristic Mitchel letter to the newspaper.

'Sir – I have just seen a paragraph in your journal, commenting on the short interruption of my "comparative freedom", which has occurred in this place. But for the kind feeling which prompted your remarks, accept my thanks; but as to your suggestion that the inhabitants of the Australian colonies petition the Queen of England to pardon the Irish State prisoners, I must take the "comparative liberty" of requesting that my name may be excepted from the prayer for it. I have no idea of begging pardon, or of permitting anyone to beg pardon for me, if I can help it. In arresting me, I presume the worthy police-magistrate did no more than his duty . . .'

And so on, mocking the pardon in part because Mitchel thought that if it was mocked, the more likely it was to seek him out unbegged, like a cat one treated with contempt.

So much for the chancy information about ships. Because he received, by the same coach as the newspaper, a letter from the young surgeon O'Doherty informing him that the brig *Union* had arrived in Hobart with his family and that he was at the wrong end of the island! He was able to send a message saying he would meet them at Green Ponds, the point on the coach road closest to Bothwell.

And there, on a rainy day mixed with snow, he encountered them. He was rendered near dumb by what he felt on seeing Jenny. He could barely greet her in anything other than clods of syllables incapable of bringing anything close to joyous welcome. How cherished she was, yet every more recent nuance of her features arising from the separation forced on them. And with each one of the children he laughed as heartily as if he thought growing was a comic stunt. Johnny, Jimmy, Henty, Willy, Minnie – a new exciting survey of them had to be made, remarks on their height and their march towards adulthood.

John C. was near fourteen now, with his mother's all-observing eyes and considerable gravitas. Jamie looked the same age as his brother, and more muscular. And according to Jenny, an understander of mechanical parts like his brother, William Mitchel. Henty held Minnie as if she did not quite know whether to introduce her to her father or not. And Minnie, in whose babyhood he had been imprisoned, frowned operatically and shrieked lustily when he came near.

Jenny. Jenny was a complete woman, ageless, sturdy and beautiful – though thin from the journey – grace and warrior at the one time. He was delighted to see her, a woman who should have been reduced by history, but unreduced in essence. You could tell these things, he was convinced. Unchastened, a woman still in the war!

He ordered a spring cart for the family so they could all start out together for Bothwell, and they rode there the first night to stay at the boarding house of Mrs Beech, an incomparable cook of kangaroo haunches. For Nant Cottage was still short of some furniture, due to be delivered.

John Martin was waiting for them at Mrs Beech's and they had a joyous meal. The boys wanted to go kangaroo hunting the very next day, and Mitchel said he could not see why not. The children were excited, and Jenny expounded on the beauty of the country, to the extent that made Mitchel's heart ache, given that he understood and was humbled that she would try to love any country where he was – as he would try also to do for her, but not with such energy and instant goodwill. He knew too that she would have made, on lesser grounds, the same hopeful sounds had she come to Bermuda!

And when next day they arrived at Nant Cottage, from its windows she saw and extolled the three-mile view of the valley and declared she had not expected such splendid pasture in a place set aside as a penal colony.

16

Mitchel with Jenny, Jenny with Mitchel

James, the second son, proved a mad-neck rider. He didn't want to chase kangaroos; he wanted to overtake them, and turn on them and make them chase off in entirely different directions. In fact, Jamie and John C. had used the mishap of Mitchel's being sent away to become independent rovers on their own instigation, and would make excellent bushmen. The elder boy, John C., was competent, but appropriately careful, given that Mitchel's imprisonment had made him feel a poignant responsibility for Jenny and the other children.

It had been the greatest pleasure getting to know his children again. Henty was heart-breakingly serious and maternal, again under the pressure of the strange family imposed on them. She had accepted her task as a deputy mother in charge of Minnie, who was rebellious and spiky, as a younger sister often is. Henty was his sister Matilda reborn, and Minnie was of all things his mother.

Little William had such an air of inquisitiveness about him, and a scholarly frown, and collected leaves and blossoms and the colonial insects. He took them home to John Martin who looked them up in Brown's *Prodomus* to find the official name for them.

They dined with the Reids and their friends, who were charmed by Jenny's frank and handsome demeanour, as by her conversational gifts appropriate to a woman who was admired by Carlyle. Jane Reid in particular believed her a great augmentation to her circle of friends in female Van Diemen's Land.

And John Martin volunteered to mind the children while the Mitchels struck out, man and wife, on good horses, side-by-side, to half-traverse the island and visit an old friend.

Jenny and the children had not been in place long when it was announced in the press that Smith O'Brien had accepted parole. He had been moved from Maria Island to the penal peninsula named Port Arthur, and had lived in solitary confinement in a hut there. Eminent Frenchmen like Alphonse de Lamartine and Alexandre Auguste Ledru-Rollin had appealed for his release, as had even the Whig President of the United States, Millard Fillmore. To Downing Street, the French were decadent and the Americans squirters of tobacco juice. Yet the time would come when they would be forced to listen to them.

Smith O'Brien thus took comparative liberty for the same reason Mitchel had – he declared he had not been condemned to death in the final decision of the law, and he had now moved to a doctor's residence at a place named Avoca, where he was to tutor the sons. A scholar, and Member of the House of Commons for so long! Lucky, lucky colonial boys.

'I have bones to pick with that man,' said Jenny. But given where they all were now, Mitchel asked her to be easy with him.

Now that John had his family with him, he was considered riveted in place against escape. He was allowed to journey anywhere he chose as long as he asked permission and reported to the police at his destination. And so they set off, Jenny and he, to ride out and visit Smith O'Brien, Mitchel on a new horse named Tricolour, and Jenny on Fleur-de-Lys.

Smith O'Brien, having given his parole, was now under the limitations of it – as to where he could travel. Most ticket-of-leave men in Van Diemen's Land could go anywhere they liked on the island and were not bound by any word of honour not to attempt to escape, as Mitchel still was. Gold had been discovered on the mainland and ticketed men, given a rare chance of hiding or bribing their way onto a ship, did so without a troubled conscience. Though Mitchel was still controlled by the burden of surrendering his parole, Jenny was finding the colony so habitable that they might be content to grow old there.

Mitchel had a great amount of stored news for Jenny and they discussed it as they rode east, a civilised ride into, not out of, more or less cultivated and unthreatening places. The news was that Tom O'Meagher had written a half-demented letter to John Martin, saying he intended to marry. O'Meagher had, foolishly Martin believed, pledged his hand to the daughter of an Irish highwayman who had achieved his conditional pardon, one Bryan Bennett. Martin and Mitchel both felt that it was a matter of O'Meagher's desire to fill the nothingness of his imprisonment.

He was one of the best fellows you could meet, but had little in common with this girl. Her name was Catherine, she was perhaps only nineteen and she was comely. She was governess in the town of Oatlands for the children of a respected surgeon named Hall. She was clearly earnest and intelligent. O'Meagher had always had an eye for such girls as her.

Yet he now needed to announce his preference for Miss Catherine Bennett to the Governor and the Comptroller to get permission for this colonial marriage. They would make vulgar and unfounded assumptions about the girl's condition. And it might be that if the union was permitted, the girl would nobly fulfil the role of being Meagher's companion – Mitchel did not know what her virtues were, and her strength. If she had grown, in the shadow of her father's crime, to be an equal for O'Meagher, she might bring him happiness in a Van Diemen's Land future. The Mitchels discoursed on these things as well, Jenny being dubious about miracles occurring in Thomas Francis O'Meagher's case.

Mitchel waspishly asked Jenny, 'What do you surmise Miss Elgee will think of this?'

Now that would have been a marriage worth believing in – the great orator and the magnificent Amazon of a literary maiden! How brilliant would the children have been?

'You did not hear?' asked Jenny. 'Miss Elgee has given up hope of Meagher and married a brilliant fellow called Dr Wilde, a man of medical knowledge and investigator of Celtic barrow tombs.'

At Oatlands they stabled their horses and caught the coach into the hilly, not to say mountainous, north-east of the island. Everyone on the coaches seemed so English that Mitchel was forced to remind himself that he was stuck in a small, misshapen, transported, blasted England, and the legitimate version was not so dear to him that he could love a convict facsimile. And they rested in a hotel in Campbell Town their first night of the excursion, so that he was again the reckless Mitchel, and she was the girl being rowed out on Carlingford Lough for the Liverpool packet.

The next day they were to take a public conveyance, a sort of tarpaulin-covered wagon, out to where Mr O'Brien would meet them at Avoca. In Campbell Town, though, they became aware by various posters that the election of the first legislature of the island was approaching. Two-thirds of the legislature at least would be elected, while great Denison in his vice-regal wisdom would appoint one-third. This was seen as the island's first essay into democracy, and there were tables in the streets for citizens to register their support for one party or other, and blue and red rosettes for the purchasing to suit the worthiness of this or that candidate.

There seemed to be one question of politics that mattered – the transportation system, which progressives were in favour of abolishing. And male suffrage on a very modest property value of £50, on the basis of which many former convicts with a small farm would be able to claim the vote. This was so much more liberal than Ireland's franchise that it seemed clear the home authorities were willing to experiment with Australia, and Jenny found all this wonderful – that democracy and opposition to the desires of Westminster were so rampant in a famed convict island. If this were happening in Ireland, she said, there would be a new Coercion Act passed and twenty thousand new soldiers shipped in. She became so tickled by the election scene that her mood infected Mitchel. Jenny was particularly amused to see the government candidate, Mr Allison, in procession through Campbell Town. She was delighted to find that there was an Australasian League in existence, involving all the colonies. Its flag was five stars on a blue ground and it existed to make progressive demands of Westminster.

The supporters of the official side were those with government contracts, people who wanted to continue with cheap convict labour, and sycophants of Government House in Hobart. And it was funny how politics made strange bedfellows, in that the Governor himself had in the past been anxious that there should be social distinctions against children of the convicts, as – he had said now – there must not be, if there was to be a united society into the future. Mitchel doubted a desire for future unity kept his Excellency up at night, fretting.

In that election frenzy, they moved on to Avoca by spring cart. It was magnificent, mountainous country. They were already at breakfast in the hotel there when Mitchel saw Smith O'Brien – much changed but still recognisable – pass outside the window. He heard Jenny growl, as if at the prospect of challenging Smith O'Brien over his failure to act more than two years past, when Mitchel was transported, when there was a chance of insurrection in the streets of Dublin itself, and Jenny had begged Smith O'Brien to take it.

Mitchel went to meet him at the door of the dining room and they took each other's hand in silence and, instead of speaking, gazed in each other's faces for their histories since they'd last met. Smith O'Brien did not appear to be well. He was grizzled, and his cheeks looked hollowed.

He was a man in need of a family, and said family were back in their home at Cahermoyle in Limerick, where he and his wife had been exemplary and paternal landlords. He must sometimes have wished the authorities had executed him, for there was some great disappointment in his face.

215

'O'Brien,' Mitchel said, and he replied, 'Mr Mitchel.' Mitchel now led him in to Jenny. She wanted to say, even if in good humour, 'Are you happy you let John be shipped, so you could save up a rebellion?' And then, 'Were you happy to take it to the countryside, where none of Europe's revolutions that year had been won?'

But, kind woman as she was, she could not say it to this man, who seemed actively tormented by that and dozens of other self-quarrels. She rose with an unqualified and exquisite smile to greet him. They were all here, in a place that looked like Donegal with gum trees, and beneath a peak the locals had tried to tame by calling it St Paul's. And that was that, however Jenny might argue with smooth O'Brien about lost opportunities in Dublin and the failure of the later uprising he'd promoted amongst farm labourers and smallholders.

O'Brien's family were well, he told them, and Dr Brock his employer was an amiable fellow and let him have access to all his library. But then he said, as if he knew Jenny had grievances, 'All is not mended yet, John and Mrs Mitchel! Ireland is its own spectral shadow.'

'I know,' Mitchel said consolingly. 'I know.'

'There are,' he said, 'barely half the people on the ground as before. It is an island of absences.'

'Yours as well,' said Jenny softly.

O'Brien told them his father, the Baron Inchiquin of Dromoland, the O'Brien, Chief of the Name, and Prince of Thomond, had employed his tenants on building a great wall around the castle, Dromoland. Even so, he admitted, whenever the Mitchels went back they would still find Ireland half-abandoned. The *clachans*, like the one Meagher and Mitchel had visited, full of their fever corpses, were vanished. The people who lived there had died of fevers which struck them when they were weak with hunger, or were now in the Atlantic, afloat or inhabiting the deeps, or settled on the Saint Lawrence or in New York.

'We must not forget that some of the convicts are men who raided the food shipments on road or canal,' said Smith O'Brien. 'As you believed and told them they were entitled to.' His tone was pensive, not accusatory.

Fortunately, he recovered from the gloom of all this and wanted to take them walking, and so all three set off, up the narrow valley of a river dubbed the South Esk (Scotland again being invoked). As they advanced, he filled Mitchel in more exactly on what had happened to him in Tipperary, when he and the others had attempted to rouse a battalion or brigade of rebels.

O'Brien described men presenting themselves when he was gathering in force, men with tears streaming down their faces, pledging to follow him to the world's end and swearing they had been praying for this day – and swearing too that God knew it was not life that they valued!

But afterwards, the priests – as ordered by their bishops – would tell them if they intended to shed blood they would be denied the sacraments, lose their souls and die unabsolved. Many of these men returned and now begged Smith O'Brien's forgiveness for their abandoning him.

And yet some had stuck with O'Brien and the others and travelled on until, in the mining town of Ballingarry, they'd become locked in combat with a police contingent who sheltered in a widow's house there, and were ultimately outnumbered by the arrival of British regiments. O'Brien described that his own forces had been overwhelmed, and then reflected on his own capture on Thurles railway station.

He was observed by a station manager, a class of man who was always a loyalist and possessed so much intelligence about passengers' coming and going.

Jenny made consoling noises and gestures, but both she and Mitchel could think of a better rebellion: broken rail lines at the edges of the city, and barricades within it.

Mitchel noticed, though, that Smith O'Brien, at this global distance from his Irish campaigns, seemed now to have accepted this defeat. It had settled in him – a challenge that had been tried and thwarted once – and though he had not said he would not try it again, it seemed less likely. Indeed, if Smith O'Brien thought a better chance might come, he might surely have looked better than he did.

He informed the Mitchels that various members of his family had told him if he would bow the head and make a submission and beg pardon, Downing Street might let him go. But he refused to court their good opinion.

Smith O'Brien told them then about his failed escape from Maria Island some months earlier, along whose coast he'd been allowed to walk in the company of an armed constable. Irish friends in Hobart had planned that a ship would appear off a certain point of the island, and that it would send a boat ashore. All he'd needed was to escape or overpower the constable, wade out and throw himself into the boat.

But there were delays. O'Brien walked to the same point each day without knowing with certainty whether or not the ship of escape would appear. He did not know either – nor did his Irish contacts in Hobart – that the captain of the schooner had found it profitable not only to take the money from O'Brien's friends, but to sell the news to the great Denison.

O'Brien would set off daily to the possible point of encounter, a beach some two miles from the penal station, always dawdling to allow the ship to get near inshore if it were coming, and then sauntering down towards the beach to see if the ship's whaleboat was closing towards him.

On the day it finally appeared, with its three-man crew, it would not or could not get quite close enough to the beach. Instead, it ran into a nearby cove where the water was calm, though covered in reeds and seaweed. O'Brien waded towards it in his only suit, but, coming closer to the whale-boat, he found the water was so much deeper than he'd imagined that he'd have to depend on the crew if he was to climb over the gunwale.

The constable had by now arrived, waded partway himself, with his levelled weapon above water. With O'Brien floundering away beneath them, the sailors all cried that they surrendered. But they were permitted to pull away to their ship, which was probably hidden just around the point. At first O'Brien was concerned for the crew, believing they were innocent and anonymous sailors risking their lives for him and not wanting them shot. Thus he raised his arms in breast-deep water.

But then he realised, given the constable's quick reaction, and the man's lack of interest in firing on the three in the boat, and the appearance on the beach of more armed guards who had been hiding until now in the bush, that he had been betrayed by the double-dealing ship's captain. He was aware that his attempted escape would give Dr Hampton a pretext to place him in stricter confinement still; probably down on the Port Arthur peninsula, the geographic punishment quarter of Van Diemen's Land.

On the beach in his sodden suit, O'Brien refused to move, hoping the guards would shoot him dead. They had orders not to oblige him and fortunately did not. His resistance was to collapse to the sand and continually refuse to stand up, and so the constables carried him along the beach and back to the Darlington Point convict station.

Smith O'Brien was then put in the most severe form of shutdown punishment, in which all were forbidden to talk to him. Soon after this, he *was* sent to Port Arthur under the same conditions of silence and isolation, though perpetually supervised in all movements by sentries who never spoke – an experience which did indeed wear him down.

On the way back to the Avoca hotel that evening – for Smith O'Brien was allowed to stay overnight – they were on a track that would only accommodate a line of individuals. Jenny, allowed to go ahead, was about to step on a black snake which lay across the path. The red-bellied reptile possessed robust poison glands, so Smith O'Brien bounded forward most gallantly and tried to kill the thing with his staff, but it slithered away into the grass and a dense clump of native iris.

Jenny was not put off bush-hiking by her encounter with this serpent, though she said she was shaken by the thrashing noise of its escape amidst long stalks of vegetation. Yet she had become used, she said in veiled reference, to snakes in her path.

The Mitchels spent a further day talking with Smith O'Brien in the hotel and elsewhere. And the following day, Monday, when O'Brien set off up the valley to Dr Brock's, he recommended that Jenny and John walk two miles up the way with him. He showed them a beautifully situated farm and cottage and advised Mitchel to rent the place, since he could apply to live now wherever he chose. This would be a genuine farm, with plenty of employment for the sons, said O'Brien. Mitchel, the Bothwell patriot, told him though of Ratho and the good Scots of Bothwell.

They sauntered around the area and talked further, but then it was time for the Mitchels to catch the spring cart to Campbell Town, while he had to return to his post. When they parted and left Smith O'Brien standing a moment in the bush, a great public man reduced to the scope of a children's tutor, he looked so wearily brave and so put upon that Jenny wept for him, and all his flawed decisions were forgiven.

———

On the way home they called in to a Cork family O'Meagher swore by at a high place named the Sugarloaf. The family who occupied that exquisite point were the Connells, and the sons of the family had already fetched their horses for the Mitchels from Oatlands. As survivals of the old Ireland, they shone forth, the man Connell and his *vanithee*, the woman of the house, in their unaffected way, and having been already in Van Diemen's Land had not had their souls harrowed by the Famine. They had green cornfields and sheep huge with wool, and their days of fighting bushrangers in these ranges were over.

Mrs Connell confessed she had once, when home alone, dealt with four bushrangers. She had conveyed one up to a closet where the family treasure was supposed to be, then locking him inside, wrapping up the guard downstairs in her muscular hold while her children disarmed him, and then all of them opening fire on the two in the yard, who decamped after an exchange of three or four shots. She was a notorious Titan therefore, a good thing for an Irishwoman to be.

The two that Mrs Connell had captured on her own with the help of the children were hanged. Her proud husband made sure to tell all visitors and then made a hearty joke about every guest being sure not to take a teaspoon with them, for fear that Mrs Connell would take to the vengeance trail.

The black Van Diemen's Landers had been driven away north before they'd arrived here, but Mitchel wondered what Mrs Connell's demeanour towards them might have been. It was a matter he would like to look into, and would have if he had been a permanent resident rather than a convict. For, again, as Martin had said with some amazement, there had been no treaty made with these people, as diminished as humans as they might be.

———

Within a few weeks O'Meagher wrote to the Mitchels and Martin to announce that the wedding between himself and Miss Bennett had taken place in the town of Richmond. Martin visited the house on Lake Sorell where they lived, and came back to tell them both bride and groom seemed congenial, though he thought Thomas O'Meagher bewildered his new bride with his energies and enthusiasms. However, O'Meagher wanted to see Jenny and Mitchel – he said he wished for Jenny's imprimatur on his marriage.

Thus, a few weeks after, they left the children in Martin's care – in fact, in that of Mrs Beech's convict housekeeper. They again took to horse, setting out by way of the Sugarloaf to Lake Sorell, where, if she chose, Jenny could interrogate O'Meagher on his marriage to the Irish highwayman's daughter.

From the Connells' farm the Mitchels rode towards the deep purple reaches of what the colonists called 'the Western Tiers', guided by the eldest son of the Connells who put them on the route to the lake. Soon, all the pleasing plants like mimosa and the wild iris appeared, and they found themselves among stringy-bark trees. They rode on assiduously until they were so high they had a view of the farms of Ross and the far-off valley of St Paul's, where they had left O'Brien.

Mitchel was leading the horses up a remaining steep incline when they saw on the track above them a man, a cabbage-tree colonial hat on his head, a rifle in his hands. He looked like the wildest of wild colonials and reinforced the impression by crying 'Coo-ee!', a sound like a whip crack that was the native greeting. Mitchel replied in the same form as a dog came plummeting enthusiastically towards Jenny and himself. He recognised it as one that had belonged to MacManus.

The colonial man – which he had succeeded in becoming because of his gifts of mimicry and thespian improvisation – turned out to be O'Meagher of the Sword himself. He had come down off the high lake to meet them. And then, as he led them, at more than three thousand feet they met the lake lapping on its shore, a full, vast cup of water contained by mountaintops.

O'Meagher conducted them past what he identified as the Dog's Head Promontory and so to a wonderful embayment where his house stood, the one Mitchel had earlier visited with Martin. Jenny noticed at anchor, near the end of the jetty, the *Speranza*, surprisingly elegant at its jetty, and for a second she had a picture of Miss LG as they knew her, flamboyant and large in great swathes of fabric, progressing down this lake shore, reciting verse. She had seemed drawn to O'Meagher, and the name of the little sloop argued that the sentiment, the affection, might have been reciprocated.

As they gave their horses to a handsome Irish lieutenant of O'Meagher's, Tom Egan, the head of O'Meagher's navy, named Jack, was summoned from a nearby hut to meet Mrs Mitchel. O'Meagher then introduced them to his own wife, who had come forward out of the house.

Catherine was tall in the colonial manner, with bobbed hair and strong features. She was pale too. O'Meagher called her 'Benny'. Mrs O'Meagher and Jenny made an initial conversation, trying doggedly until Jenny said, 'We are nervous coming to meet you. We hope you approve of your husband's old friends.'

This idea that it was Mrs O'Meagher's business to approve or not of Thomas's past friends, rather than them arriving to weigh her, was a generous one, and typical of Jenny, who had a sense of how women addressed things. 'And what in God's name do your parents think of your husband?' Jenny asked further. For she knew what a startling entity, as famed orator and young comet, Tom O'Meagher might be for a normal Irish convict family.

'Oh,' said Benny in native-born, Vandemonian accent, 'they think he is an Irish marvel. But, Mrs Mitchel, they also think it a wonderful thing for you to join Mr Mitchel here. It must have been a day of rejoicing when you saw each other.'

'It was a day nearly beyond description,' murmured Jenny.

Benny seemed a good woman, trying almost piteously to measure up to the great felon, her husband.

Mitchel attempted to guide the conversation away from the wedding and doubts about it, to the issue of how Smith O'Brien looked, and to say Smith O'Brien had told them what his rebellion had been.

O'Meagher said, 'On the day you were shipped away, Mrs Mitchel said something to O'Brien. That we were too influenced by the French business, which was a revolution that raised itself like an act of chemistry, without damage to anyone.'

'But,' Mitchel felt bound to say, 'the French Revolution happened in the city of Paris!'

'We were seeking cities. We as good as had the revolution ready to go in Callan had we seized the time – the townspeople were drowning out the priests.'

'Callan is not, however, a European capital,' Mitchel argued, bound to do so in logic. Callan was not even the main town of Kilkenny.

O'Meagher shrugged. 'Fair enough of you to make that and other observations,' said Tom. 'I will not insult you, Mitchel, by asking forgiveness for doing nothing the day you were shipped away. We did not exactly justify – by later events – our lack of action in your case. And we are all embarrassed by that.'

Jenny, out of the depths of her discussion with Catherine, said, 'Rebellion that day, Mr O'Meagher, made sense, and would have had the people in assent. And even if we had been crushed, think of how it would have been for the Castle to resume control of Ireland the day after! Nothing would ever have been the same!'

'You're probably right,' said O'Meagher with his rich, oratorical dolefulness. 'More than probably . . .'

As a distraction or not, O'Meagher began to speak of his own movement around Munster at that time of supposed revolution, sometimes in company with Smith O'Brien and MacManus and the family man O'Donoghue, sometimes visiting the clubs in other towns, organising men to light beacon fires in the summits of the Comeragh hills, a traditional way of achieving a gathering. But whatever support escaped the net of the priests was rarely immediately available to march out straight away.

He told of how he had ridden back to O'Brien and his small force of followers – those who were not scared of the priests' sacramental threats – and they approached a police station in Mullinahone, Tipperary.

'We called on them to throw their weapons out the window and come out,' O'Meagher said, 'that they should have their lives, of course, for it was not their fault they'd taken up such a dark profession. And it was not their children's faults likewise, or that they should go starving because someone – because we – shot their father. In fact, there was a man inside, a sergeant or some such, but I could tell at once that he was an absolute gasconader, an utter sprouter of cockalorum, a blatherskite of the highest order.

'He cries out how he is the commander of the force and how much he admires O'Brien, but pleads that if they abandon the police station and its weaponry they will face expulsion from the force. Now I begin telling O'Brien that the good sergeant is playing him for a fool, and I make the point that we have come into Tipperary to raise a war, not to bring peace, and that we need weapons, that the stand must begin somewhere, and that we must knock down that wall of balderdash by which we all excuse our slavery to ourselves.

'But . . . William Smith O'Brien is so tender that he lets them all leave and carrying their weapons as well. They were praising O'Brien, praising me, invoking you. Poor little O'Donoghue tried to argue with O'Brien, but O'Dono-ghue had the weakness that he always felt that he was a mere office worker by comparison with the O'Briens, who were the gentry of the gentry. But he is not a warlord, our Smith O'Brien! And you need not tell him I said so, because I have told him myself in dark moments in the past.'

Jenny looked at her husband and made an ironic mouth. Mitchel could see those policemen would have not talked her out of their surrendering their weapons.

But then when the question moved on to the Australasian League and the coming Van Diemen's Land election, Mitchel found O'Meagher much engaged, and in fraternal sympathy with the progressive colonists. No overturn of the system would bring them freedom, since even if transportation ended today, they had their sentences still to serve, ten years left of Mitchel's, and life for the grand declaimer. But of course Mitchel's interest grew as he thought of what an inconvenience these out-surgings of liberty must be to Downing Street. The colonists were in a happier position than the Irish in this: that to bring the overwhelming force of Britain to Ireland was an easy business for the govern-ment in London, whereas to bring an army to bear here would involve huge plans and provisioning and massive ocean passages.

Mitchel decided then in that happy, shared hour with O'Meagher, the women listening, that he would write an account of the anti-convict resistance in Cape Town for the

Colonial Times in Hobart. He picked up from O'Meagher's side table *An Address to the Electors* by one Mr Kermode, who sounded interesting and was standing for election in the Ross area.

'Born in the Isle of Man,' it began, 'Mr Kermode first came to the colony as a supercargo on a merchant ship. Having suffered bankruptcy from his genial reposing of trust in gentlemen unworthy of it, he settled at the unpromising farm he called Mona Vale in tribute to his home island and turned his establishment for Saxon sheep into the most excellent sheep run in the colony. He showed his universal beneficence even to the remaining Tasmanian natives, one of whom he once took to London and introduced at Parliament, to the great enthusiasm of the Royal Society. His record has rendered him a public figure, attracting smiles and gratitude throughout the colony, except only in those corridors of special interest where the convenience of another place, rather than that of the future Tasmania and its enlightened brethren, is served . . .'

Mitchel looked up. 'You wrote this,' he accused O'Meagher. 'This is *your* style. *The convenience of another place . . .* That's the fine touch of your claw!'

O'Meagher winked at him.

Later in the evening, Jenny said, in Benny's presence, 'Now, you must treat your wife augustly, Mr Meagher!' She didn't bother with the pretension of O'Meagher. 'She is a fine young woman.'

Benny cried, 'Mr O'Meagher treats me as kind as any woman could want.'

But Jenny insisted. 'Make sure it is always so!'

For there was an assertiveness in Jenny that young Mrs O'Meagher would find hard to acquire.

The next day, the Mitchels and O'Meagher delightfully sailed around the various points of the lake in *Speranza*. The Mitchels did not – in case of distress – tell him that in Dublin, Speranza was reported to have married a surgeon named Wilde, said to be a very small fellow by comparison to dazzling Mr O'Meagher. Dr Wilde was also reputed to be the leading eye doctor of Dublin. In a sane Ireland, an Ireland that was allowed to be itself, it was likely Meagher and Speranza would have been man and wife of a dazzling household. Naturally, they did not ask him if he had himself heard the news of the marriage, and therefore had his decision to marry 'Benny' been influenced or not by the fact of it.

The lake was so charming that Mitchel could not prevent himself expecting to see Elizabethan or Gothic or Grecian villas and colonnades around the shoreline, and temples to Apollo or Minerva, but of course such sites failed to present; only the great ongoing tiers beyond. The possessors of Lake Crescent, along with O'Meagher and his young wife, were the black swans, and the ducks that sheltered amongst the tea trees along the foreshore.

They reached towards the Bothwell side of the lake, to the south of O'Meagher's place. And here was the log hut of Cooper who had been kind to Mitchel once before when he was here with John Martin during a snowstorm. Along this shore, they had imagined, Martin and he would build a place, a retreat of sorts, on the narrow strip separating lakes Sorell and Crescent. He had mentioned that a number of times to Jenny, who approved of the impulse. In the stern Benny and Jenny sat together, holding hands, as O'Meagher and his admiral worked the sails and the boom swung back and forth energetically every time the sole vessel in Tom O'Meagher's navy tacked.

When at last they left Lake Sorell, Jenny had been so invigorated by the visit that she rode like a young girl on Fleur-de-Lys, leading the way round the west on the shore of the lake. In Mitchel's saddlebag, he carried an orphaned baby kangaroo which was a gift for the children from the Connells of the Sugarloaf, at whose house they had again stopped briefly. They made extraordinary time down the hill, once crossing the upper reaches of the Clyde, and it was still early in the day when they reached the lovely three-mile meadow near Quoin Hill where the Scotsman McDowell dwelt. Jenny did not slow as they entered the Bothwell Valley and the two horses seemed conspirators in elation, galloping across the open ground till they could bury their muzzles in the cold Clyde water and, over there at Nant Cottage, Mitchel and Jenny saw John Martin and the boys and all the dogs out for a walk.

There was joy at the cottage over the little kangaroo. Minnie danced for it, and it watched her with limpid dark eyes.

17

Nicaragua Comes

Mitchel now lived for the better part of two years the life of a Van Diemen's Land small farmer, causing few problems for the great Denison and his Comptroller General, except perhaps when he wrote his anti-transportation piece on South Africa for the *Colonial Times*. He gave up all writing, even a prison journal he had been working on assiduously since he had arrived in Bothwell. Months went by without his adding a sentence to it: in fact, it was nearly two years before he approached it again. Half-pleased with himself for serving time so pleasantly, he blamed Bothwell, for its charm and its languid weather. John Martin and he had discussed this matter earlier and now took up the debate with Jenny. But there was very rarely a lightning bolt around Bothwell. There should have been electrical storms over those mountains and yet by an oddity they did not occur. The air was unelectric and it left the population lethargic, according to Martin, he and the Mitchels amongst them.

Mitchel occasionally went on a kangaroo chase with the boys and Henty, and hard riding was good for them all. The children flourished here in regard to their health and in many other ways as regards their education. Young Johnny was nearing fifteen, James was thirteen, and Henty, at eleven, too vocal to be ignored and riding without a lady's saddle. Willy and Minnie were far too young to be galloping through the Antarctic bush of Van Diemen's Land, but they would not be told. They insisted and rode rough like the colonials, Minnie barely more than five, but a bush-woman in the making.

Mitchel kept up their schooling, while sometimes John Martin gave them lessons and sometimes Jenny. If they were doomed to be colonists, they would be literate ones. And Willy, a collector of barks, leaves and the carapaces of insects, was a young Vandemonian Linnaeus.

And here was Mitchel, mowing hay in January. With sometimes the weather so hot that they waited with longing for the breeze to come up from Hobart. Sometimes, though, like a dallying constable, it lost its way.

In the time Mitchel had been absent from his journal, Smith O'Brien had given up the tutoring and moved in with the family of a wealthy Irish officer at the nearby town of New Norfolk. He was well looked after there, had his own quarters and was a gentleman of the house. O'Doherty was at Hobart Town, resident surgeon at St Mary's Hospital, and sometimes he sneaked up to see Smith O'Brien and then came on to Bothwell from New Norfolk. He was such a pleasant creature and though often beset by settlers' daughters, he stayed faithful to his Irish poet, Eva of *The Nation*, who must now have been a woman in her prime and approaching twenty years.

But the most amazing thing that had happened was that, after being determined to marry into Van Diemen's Land, Meagher (no longer the more Celtic-aggressive O'Meagher, given he had no Convict Department to report to anymore) had fled the place, admittedly having been given the chance, and was believed to be the Irish sensation in New York these days. The marriage to Benny had not calmed his rest-lessness in any case.

He'd sent a letter down to the police magistrate at Ross, withdrawing his parole in proper form, and declaring he would not leave his house at Lake Sorell until police had had a chance to recapture him. In the mountains around the lake it might have taken some courage on the part of the police, and when three mounted constables arrived, they found Meagher surrounded by tall Irishmen, including the Connell boys, whom one would think at a glance had weapons somewhere on their muscular persons.

The policemen chose not to take the chance, instead camping and watching him ride away from the lake and from Benny, who was with child, whom he had sent to Dr Hall's house in Oatlands, to follow him off if he made a success of the escape that filled his dreams. He seemed to have made the flit by way of Launceston, and was picked up by a Yankee whaler, contracted to the Irish Directory in New York, off Waterhouse Island in Bass Strait.

Some months after her husband's escape, Benny had given birth to a boy child. He was born amongst her people in Richmond, but he died there in babyhood as well. Seen off by her highwayman father and her mother and fellow Bennett children, she went first to stay with her father-in-law in Waterford, who nursed her around to be fit for her further journey to the United States. He then accompanied her to a reunion with her husband in New York. Thomas's and Benny's first child slept on in its little grave by the wall of the Catholic Church in Van Diemen's Land.

Jenny wanted to hear that Mrs Meagher was taken into Broadway in triumph and celebration on Meagher's arm. She declared, 'Having married Miss Bennett and given her a child, he had better bring her as his adornment in New York. She was his when he needed her, and now the reverse will be true!'

But after some months, it was reported, given Meagher was a darling in the press though they were sometimes a little snide with him, Benny had returned from New York with her father-in-law to Waterford to prepare for the birth of a child conceived in the vast American metropolis. Jenny surmised that, despite the new pregnancy, the New York reunion had not been happy, for surely New York had adequate doctors, midwives and nurses to deal with the birth of a small Van Diemen's Lander. However, the press said she returned to Waterford because her husband was to take a lecture tour around the United States, and that such a journey would be inappropriate for his wife.

Meagher had now reminded all of them of the abiding duty to escape, but Mitchel was alarmed by the journey the fugitive felon must take to reach New York. There was no direct route to the city from San Francisco, which shared the Pacific with Van Diemen's Land. Californians had to travel south to Nicaragua, which they'd have to cross, and then take a steamer to New York from the Atlantic side of Central America. Otherwise, one could round Cape Horn in distant and unforeseeable oceans. Mitchel did not think he would ever want to subject his young family to such a regimen; particularly not, as he imagined, to the fevers and bandidos of Nicaragua.

His mother and the four sisters had recently crossed the Atlantic and taken a house in Brooklyn. They had followed his brother Willy who had escaped earlier and was working in the New York Patent Office. As delightful as such a reunion might be, New York seemed impossibly distant, and not least because Jenny had conceived a child – yes, a sixth, the Tasmanian Devil Isabel, or as they called her at Minnie's mysterious insistence, Rixy.

———

Helping Mitchel with his hay harvest at Nant were three hulking men guilty of Ribbonism; that is, of harassing land-lords, a not uncommon crime amongst the Irish. These sons of Ireland had declared their own individual wars against landlords, and had of course, under the Coercion Laws, lost grievously. They worked well in the fields of Nant and then came in and smoked and chatted with one another in the farmyard and went to sleep in their opossum skin rugs in the barn. They were civil and good-natured, and did not thieve. Indeed, they were making themselves into a new model of humanity, and with these supposedly desperate men around the family, the Mitchels kept the house windows open, and felt as secure as they would be in Banbridge. And apart from one double-barrelled gun that had disappeared a few years before, the Mitchels had never suffered the loss of any household item.

So the men finished the hay, and when it was all stacked they went to be paid. One of them, a Limerick man, asked

Mitchel to sign a certificate that he had been in his employ and had behaved well. He smiled at his former employer. 'I am off to the diggings at Port Phillip,' he told Mitchel, 'and my conditional pardon is in to be collected from the magistrate. But I'm sure he'll be tickled to see this one come in as well.'

'I wish you well, Mick,' Mitchel told him. 'Don't spend all your money at Maskell's public house tonight.'

'By my soul, sir,' said Mick, 'I must drink tonight to old Garryowen and the sky above him.' Garryowen had grown to be a sort of Celtic Bacchus invoked in the song of that name. 'Beyond that, I shall spare my swallow for the gold-fields. Good night, sir.'

So Mick was going to the mainland to fossick for gold, and in that sense was a happier convict than Mitchel, even with Jenny, would ever see himself to be. 'I am here into the future,' he pronounced to himself, 'into New Year's hay making, and the next, year after year.'

And even as Mitchel cherished the new child, and even as his gratitude and veneration surged for Jenny – his dark Rosaleen, whose beauty she had passed on to their children – and even as Mitchel foresaw Van Diemen's Land venerability as he aged in Bothwell, and no chance for rebellion presented itself . . . all was suddenly changing beneath his feet, and he did not know.

———

Mitchel received a letter from Dr Kevin O'Doherty in Hobart, asking him to visit the town urgently. This latter term intrigued Mitchel. The doctor could not visit Nant Cottage (although he secretly had done occasionally) without risking jail for moving outside his area. Mitchel started in the small hours and reached Hobart by early the same morning.

He found young O'Doherty in his normal place, at St Mary's Hospital, looking through a glass at a lupus on a woman convict's face. When he had given her a salve for her condition, she left, half-covering her features. Kevin's smile grew wide when he saw Mitchel, and he dragged him out of his laboratory and into a small room full of pieces of beds. He asked him did he know who had turned up in Hobart? Well, of course Mitchel didn't.

'Pat Smyth from New York,' said Kevin. 'You know him. A famed journalist.'

'I knew him in Dublin. Has he been transported?'

'No, sent by the Irish Directory in New York.'

This was P. J. Smyth, who had sometimes come to Mitchel's house parties in Dublin.

'He's here to get one or more of us out. Smith O'Brien, if he can. He has the means to get hold of the ship and take us to San Francisco and then New York. Imagine the triumph! The Americans themselves will rejoice. Along with every progressive European heart.'

Mitchel absorbed this. The escape of Smith O'Brien would be world news. Smyth rescues Smith!

'Smyth is travelling today from Launceston,' said O'Doherty, 'and is going to meet O'Brien and me tonight at Bridgewater. You must come too, that's the point. We have to discuss how we might revoke our parole in the proper form if a number of us escape at the one time!'

'What an astounding prospect!' Mitchel said, but it was like a call back to duty and Bothwell had blunted his desire for it.

O'Doherty had borrowed his horse from one of the priests, and he and John rode to Bridgewater together. They reached the Black Snake Inn in good time, and met up with Smith O'Brien, on his horse Old Squirrel, some hundred paces from the public house. They went sauntering in the garden around the pub that warm evening, and bees transported in from Europe, like them, worked at the equally transported hollyhocks and fashionable geraniums and carnations.

Smith O'Brien told Mitchel with a small smile, 'P. J. Smyth is known in America as "Nicaragua" Smyth. He rather enjoys being addressed as such, rather than as plain "Pat".'

The coach with Smyth had not arrived yet, and indeed two hours passed, and still it did not. They went inside for brandy and discussed, in the uncrowded parlour, how they could, all of them still serving time, withdraw their paroles in the proper form. If there were anything improper, the convict authorities would advertise it throughout the world and be in a position to consider them, and advertise them, as men with no honour, and thus men incapable of forming a government for Ireland. In taking up residence in a district, they gave their solemn word of honour not to escape! That word had to be taken back, or else in escaping they'd be condemned before the world.

Tom Meagher should, in Smith O'Brien's opinion, have presented himself to the police magistrate in Ross. So, it was decided, they would have to withdraw their word of honour, each in his official district, in front of a police magistrate, who must have some plausible capacity to arrest them. This would have to be done, therefore, simultaneously in normal magistrate business hours between ten and three o'clock. But Smith O'Brien surprised Mitchel by saying he thought it was very proper, if Smyth had brought the means, to bribe the police magistrates. The corruptibility of officials was the concern of the Crown, not of the prisoner. Any resistance the prisoner was able to offer when the officers of the Crown tried to arrest the escapee while they were still withdrawing their words of honour should also be permissible – though killing them was out of the question.

Mitchel was astonished at Smith O'Brien's calm practicality about all this. But, if they were to escape in a group, he said, the problem was how, in a number of different places in Van Diemen's Land, they could simultaneously make their local magistrates fully understand that they were not joking, that they were putting an end to their parole, abandoning their ticket-of-leave, and that they intended to do their best to escape from that moment.

John made it clear that he was talking in theory. 'I am not suggesting myself as a candidate for escape,' he told them, though they did not seem to believe him. He further suggested they could all assemble in the one place and commit some minor crime – they could not immediately think of what – and altogether, when arrested, renounce their paroles in front of a magistrate. But, with some reason, Smith O'Brien and O'Doherty didn't think it practicable. In any case, Mitchel said, he had the delightful problem that his family had joined him, that they and Jenny had been welcomed to Bothwell and they could not now, having made that trans-global journey, be asked to make it again.

Soon the time came, without Smyth's coach having appeared, for John's friends to go home, especially O'Doherty, who had a long ride to his registered lodgings. Smith O'Brien was also forced to leave, while Mitchel, based on the fact he had broad permission – given that his family had arrived to rivet him in place – took a bed in the inn for the night.

Half an hour after the others left, the coach pulled in, and all the passengers climbed down from it and walked into the hallway, where Mitchel could hear them talking. He dressed, left his room and placed himself against the wall in the corner. Although he didn't recognise Smyth straight off – he had been much younger when he came to the Mitchels' house in Dublin – he saw a tall man in a good suit with a half-cape over his shoulders who could possibly be the mature Nicaragua Smyth.

When the man turned, he showed himself to be youngish looking but weathered. Their eyes made a sort of infallible contact. Even so, Mitchel stood aside as the man went into the office to arrange a bed for the night. John walked into the inn forecourt and when the stranger came out again to get his portmanteau from the coach, he was sure it had to be Smyth – but he doubted himself. He was the only passenger who was not going on the last stretch to Hobart, so Mitchel followed him to the far, darker side of the coach.

'Mr Smyth?' Mitchel murmured.

He spun around – clearly he thought Mitchel to be some sort of detective.

'It's all right,' Mitchel told him. 'Don't you recognise me?'

'Mitchel,' he said, 'Christ, man, they have changed you a little!'

'Follow me into the parlour,' John suggested.

Mitchel strolled inside and sat down and, as the coach took away again, rattling towards Hobart, ordered some brandy.

Smyth came in and had his bag taken to his room, sitting down with Mitchel at once. He began by introducing himself formally, in case the maid or hotel owner was watching, as Mr Nicaragua Smyth of the *New York Sun*. He winked and gave Mitchel a card with all that inscribed on it. So they talked loudly about the New York press, but when it was obvious no-one had any interest in them, they began to discourse more intimately, and Mitchel said he could certainly take him to see Smith O'Brien in New Norfolk tomorrow.

They talked for hours in that room. Smyth told Mitchel about Meagher, who now lived in the Metropolitan Hotel, a massive palazzo on Broadway. Here he took his normally spacious view to the phenomenon of America, and America spaciously responded. Mitchel chuckled at this idea, even while making plans to meet up with the other Young Irelanders in Van Diemen's Land.

Smyth, who had once been an overanxious boy at the Mitchels' table in Ontario Terrace, now looked worldly, John observed, thin in the face, well-barbered and with a trim beard and elegant waist. His own beard had grown thick and rustic at Nant Cottage. So he surmised that their conversation would have seemed to any outsider to be one between a hayseed and a man newly arrived from some metropolitan centre.

Smyth told John that in New York he was considered the President of the as yet unproclaimed Republic of Ireland. He had earned that potential role by the martyrdom of his shipping out without any uprising occurring.

Mitchel wondered about Smith O'Brien then.

'Oh my heaven,' intoned Smyth, 'he will be the Civic Pope and Monarch still, all in one.'

'Then,' Mitchel said, 'Smith O'Brien should escape first. Because he would have immediate power to quell the envies

241

between parties and to lead the New York Hibernians as well. And on top of that, everyone, including the President, would want to speak to him and make some sort of compact.'

As for himself, he explained, his wife, who was not a good sailor, had for his sake undertaken shipping the family here to Van Diemen's Land two years past, and it would be cruel to impose on her another great passage across the seas.

'Not even for the future justice and grandeur of the thing?' Smyth asked, his eyes glimmering. 'From what I observed of your splendid wife in Dublin, I think she might be keener than you.'

———

The next afternoon, having slept a little late that morning, they rode on up the river to the pleasant town of New Norfolk. It took them the better part of four hours, and by that evening they went to O'Brien's lodgings, which were in a part of the house of a hop-growing gentleman named Captain Fenton.

On the way, Smyth reminded Mitchel of his own background, for Mitchel had not known him as well in Young Ireland as others had. He had gone to school with the Jesuits, in fact, and been in the same class at Clongowes as Thomas Francis Meagher, even though he seemed younger. After escaping to the United States in that fatal year, 1848, disguised as a peasant on what came to be called a coffin ship – since coffins were the more likely destination than Quebec or Boston – he had worked as a journalist for the *New York Sun* and frequently been to Nicaragua, whose name was now synonymous with him. It was the place where, if ever there was a canal dug across a Central American country to take ships from the Atlantic into the Pacific, and the other way about, that canal should be.

'For look at the map!' he invited Mitchel. 'That big lake in the middle!' Indeed, he thought the United States should annex Nicaragua.

'The way England annexed Ireland?' Mitchel asked.

'Except that the United States spreads freedom,' said Nicaragua fervently, 'and England spreads tyranny.'

'Is that always so, Nicaragua? With the United States?'

'In my experience, yes,' he insisted. 'But let me tell you I have met a fine girl here, name of Regan. A veritable tulip of a woman. I suggested to her, Mitchel, that she will be much freer there, where her parents having been transported will be seen for what that is – an act of oppression rather than a stain upon them. In America, you will find, I hope, one day, we are permitted to think of the world in true terms. Indeed, it is taken as a national duty in New York, amongst the Irish, to think these things, and when they say what the truth of the world is, they are applauded, not transported.'

'Where does she live, that fortunate young woman?' Mitchel asked.

'In a town almost entirely Irish,' he said. 'With Gaelic the chief language. Westbury, to the north of here. Many people there we could enlist in our escape plans!'

Mitchel and Smyth rode along the pleasant valley and crossed the bridge that divided the town of New Norfolk. At last they rode in through the gates of the estate that harboured Smith O'Brien. There was a smell of hops in the air from nearby ovens.

Captain Michael Fenton was a good host to Smith O'Brien. He had had his own democratic tussles with

Governor Denison, and had brought out six families of Irish to work on his estate, Fenton Forest. Mitchel and Smyth stopped at O'Brien's part of the house, and his Irish house-keeper answered the door. She invited them in and they could see the great man at his desk in a further room.

Smith O'Brien greeted Smyth with his normal restrained urbanity. He offered refreshments to the pair, and sherry and some cuts of meat were brought. Then he asked Smyth to explain his mission.

'Well,' said Smyth, composing himself and crossing his slim legs, 'our friend Devin Reilly and other leading spirits in the Irish Directory in New York have sent me to rescue both of you, or either of you if both of you cannot go. I myself am ready and willing to take the principal risk in any enterprise of that nature, and at the end to rescue you by force, if force be needed.'

'Since you have a sentence for life,' Mitchel told Smith O'Brien, 'it is imperative that you be rescued.'

'I agree entirely with that,' said Nicaragua. 'As well as your capacity to accelerate support for Ireland's freedom, it will be a welcome outcome to the children of the Irish, and to Tammany Hall and the Democrat Party to which Tammany is home.'

Smith O'Brien sighed. It was the most natural and unaf-fected sigh. 'You know that I have already had my chance to escape at Maria Island. I chose to avoid slaughter – I turned back and gave myself up. I fear I would do so again, Mr Smyth, if there was a choice between surrender and blood-shed. Even though I'm conscious that much money from ordinary Irish folk has poured into these rescues.'

Smith O'Brien turned to Mitchel. 'John, then, this is *your* chance. You have youth on your side, a stronger constitution, and stronger motives to escape than I have. And you will be more at home there, in New York, than I.'

Mitchel thought of Jenny again, having adjusted herself to the life of a felon's wife. Must she now be uprooted again? But the truth was that from the time Smith O'Brien had nominated him, Mitchel wanted to go – more accurately, he burned to go. He felt the necessity of America now to reveal itself as more than a destination – instead, a geographical destiny.

Smith O'Brien held up a hand. 'As well as everything else, Mr Smyth, I have been advised the British government might one day soon enough find it is good policy to set me free as a gesture. And without my having to make any submission to them, and without my offering to do it. In that case, I can return to my family in Ireland. But if I escaped to the United States, Ireland would forever be closed to me.'

They argued further. Smyth made the argument that if Ireland were ever to achieve independence, it was essential that the Irish had a sort of corps of government ready to join anyone, Irish-Americans, French, who invaded Ireland. Now Mitchel wondered, could it be at all true – the rumour once let slip, almost reluctantly, by Martin – about Smith O'Brien's being enchanted with one of the Fenton daughters? He could not believe that. But what was obvious to Smyth and Mitchel was that the indulgent life of Fenton Forest had rendered O'Brien in his middle years perhaps a less suitable escapee than Mitchel himself.

'I ask you to do it, John,' said Smith O'Brien. 'You have the instincts to best serve the Irish.'

'You did not always think so.'

'We were separated only by a matter of degrees. We shared a desire for the same outcome.'

'I must test if it is at all possible,' Mitchel announced. 'We have six children now, O'Brien. And they like Van Diemen's Land.'

In the meantime, Smith O'Brien had a room set for Nicaragua and Mitchel to share. As Mitchel lay down that night he began to imagine freedom, thorough freedom, unqualified, and realised how he had become slowly accustomed and reconciled to his own enslavement – something a prisoner of principle should never be reconciled to!

The most direct route back to Bothwell was across country by way of a disorderly town called Hamilton, which had some thirty notorious grog shops. The rough track broke down Nicaragua's horse, and he had to put it in the livery stable there; for the ride on to Bothwell he could hire only a driver and a small screen cart. The journey was wild and thickly forested as only Van Diemen's Land could be, and though Mitchel rode alongside him, the driver restricted their conversation for the last twenty miles to Nant Cottage. As they rode through Bothwell, Mitchel turned aside to the post office in case there was mail from friends in Down or from Brooklyn. As he did, Smyth sent the cart and rider back and walked into the post office with Mitchel. 'Where is this formidable police station?' he asked.

'Just around the corner,' Mitchel told him. 'Part of the same premises as this.'

And while Mitchel waited for the letters to be handed to him through the hatch, Smyth went round the corner and walked into the police building, and even into the doorway of the magistrate's room. Seeing that gentleman sitting at the desk with his police clerk, he crossed the hall into the chief constable's office. He counted the muskets in the racks there, then came out and assessed the watch house opposite, and the constables walking lazily about, one of them leading a horse.

When he came back to Mitchel, he whispered, 'I think three or four men, or at least half a dozen with Colt's revolvers, might sack the township and kidnap the police magistrate. A great fellow is Mr Colt, one of the finest minds in the country.'

Back at Nant Cottage, Smyth was delighted to see John Martin, whom he had met once in Dublin. And everyone, even Jenny, was delighted to have a visit from a New Yorker who was also a known Dubliner. Jenny liked him and showed it by being a jade, ordering him about the kitchen.

After the children slept, but with the eldest, John C., still listening to the older men talk, Smyth discussed how long he had been on the run in the Irish countryside back in that dreadful summer of 1848, trying to urge rebellion to take hold though it never did. In the end, he'd disguised himself as a frieze-coated peasant and went to Cork, made the passage, was hard up in New York, then editing a Pittsburgh paper and contributing articles to the *New York Sun* on the Nicaragua question, an exercise which made his name if not his fortune.

And at the same time, he and Devin Reilly argued in the New York papers against the more facile English lies about Ireland. He repeated how Thomas Francis Meagher, formerly of Dog's Head Bay on Lake Sorell, was surviving now that he was ensconced in the Metropolitan Hotel on Broadway, being wept over by joyful former Young Irelanders, being disapproved of by the more straight-laced priests, and above all, being smiled at by young women.

'Oh dear,' said Jenny. 'He liked to call himself O'Meagher here and that was just one sign he was slightly tetched.

Because, you know, he acquired a wife here? None of us thought the marriage wise, but he did insist on proceeding with it. Mrs Meagher is the daughter of an Irish highwayman and had delivered a son who died in infancy. He has by now surely called for her to join him. He had better, should he wish for my respect.'

Later that day Mitchel told Jenny without equivocation – the only decent way to do it – that Smyth wanted him to escape. You could tell Smith O'Brien was not up to the adventure, Mitchel said: the hiding in forests, the hectic riding to one coast or another. Mitchel admitted he was the one who had invited and enticed Jenny here, and now he was suggesting a drastic change again.

She took thought and turned to him with a half-smile. 'You must go,' she said. 'Of course, you must go.'

Mitchel pushed himself into her arms, very much a man who wanted an excuse to stay where he was. If he were not an angel of disruption . . . he could make a happy settler.

In the next instant Jenny voiced her echo of the thought. 'I wish you could be happy here. A man of lesser destiny could be. But yours is not to be patient endurance.'

'I did not know I'd shown any impatience.'

'Impetuosity then. Since Smyth came, Bothwell's no longer sufficient unto itself. Tell Smyth. You must go! It is obvious. If we assume the bigger stage, we might have peace. We never will have a final peace here.'

And it was true. John's dreams had changed and were now interrupted by insomnia bouts, all since Smyth had brought the concept of escape here.

Mitchel told Smyth the next morning. He looked at his baby, Rixy, carelessly flinging porridge by the spoonful, some of it fortunately entering her mouth. Five of the children had been one thing in Dublin, had been required to become another thing in Bothwell. And now they would be required further to become a third thing. Americans. It seemed an insult to their alacrity, their pliable natures. And yet the boys! Up for anything, endowed with inventive natures by Jenny and – he would hope – himself; but unsure what those natures were for. Johnny, the eldest, like a young Irish volunteer with piercing eyes. After being Irish and Van Diemen's Land colonials, Mitchel would owe him and his siblings a level and stable America. He would surely not be an instrument of chaos in that happy republic!

———

Smyth rode off for Christmas, up north to visit his *inamorata*, Miss Regan, and was then going on to Melbourne to negotiate a rescue ship. John Martin was willing to try to escape also. If Mitchel was able to get away, Nicaragua himself could escort Jenny and the children to San Francisco, giving her every assistance. This is what Smyth had assigned himself to.

Jenny was aware of everything that could go wrong but she remained ardent. Here she would always be the wife of the state prisoner Mitchel. She would rather be the wife of Citizen Mitchel. She was due to visit her friend Jane at Ratho, the best house in the locality, tomorrow. At which levels did these two women meet and speak, with Jenny knowing she was now a transitory character here? The Reids were here forever, it was their Eden. They drove the Aborigines off and then swallowed the wrong of doing that, and had made their antipodean Scots barony here. They intended to lay down centuries of colonial progeny, and to go on into a future in the extreme south of the earth.

But the Mitchels were no longer subscribers to the antipodean version. They were to vanish.

———

Oh woman, mourned Jenny secretly. I do not want or choose the other form, I do not envy men. But sometimes there is envy, as they move history along, and yet we are still captive to the baby in our stomach. They who are babies at our breasts, who make babies at our breasts, who nakedly whimper, but who then, not subjected to the same terms of trade as us, recover from their infancy each morning and attend to adult things that must be done within a week or a month! Were women made dull and stupid and unsatisfactory for history by their nine-month day, the conception in peace, perhaps, the birth in war; the conception in certainty, and the birth in ferment?

Her best friend in Bothwell, Jane Reid by birth, Jane Williams by brief marriage, returned here as a widow from Calcutta at nineteen. And as mother of a dead baby, poor child. She had long needed to find a further life, and was trying to find some revelation about her situation through her fellow countryman Macauley's writing in the *Edinburgh Quarterly*, until Jenny warned her off him. He was a mere guard dog of the ruling power, and implied that God ordained the British Empire, and therefore Macauley polished the present hour over all previous hours.

But Jane had also been reading Dickens. If there was a bard for the poor, Dickens was it. Yet there was – few with the power to honour what had happened to her – a Caledonian maiden who had consented to the experience of empire, who had married a man devoted to Indian conquest and pacification, who had borne children, one stillborn, one dead within days. She was a servant of the Britannic machine and had come from Bengal where her efforts to produce young servants of the imperial concept had run tragic and required the burial of both her babies. And all Jenny's babies were still living, five and then, through the *irrelevant* intervention of a spate of acute and unutterable pain, a sixth, a girl, God love her! Little Rixy. The convict.

In a world in which half the children died before five years, Jenny had been more lucky than her friend, Miss Reid, or Widow Williams of Ratho in Bothwell. How was Jenny to celebrate the mercy of God to her without vainglory, and without inviting disaster? She did not like even to commit it to paper. She simply fed them, and they grew.

Though James had suffered pneumonic fever, he had grown sturdy now and the antipodean and Antarctic woods of Van Diemen's Land suited him. There was for a time a proposal John Martin might escape, but in fact it was Martin who looked a little bent and narrowed down these days. John Mitchel, not given anymore to bad asthma, was, from labour and riding about the country, sturdy as an ox.

18

Mitchel: Waiting for Nicaragua, 1853

It got to be February, and nearly two months had passed but Nicaragua was not back. That, however, gave Mitchel time to refine things. He knew that the escape from here would indeed be testing. If they went north they had to go via Lake Sorell and all the wild country up there. Travelling south would also be a test. Concealment was possible but only in the wildest approaches to Hobart. And Mitchel needed a good horse.

Now, the average mount of a policeman was generally an undistinguished creature – Her Majesty's government liked its officials to manage great mileages in its name, but not at the expense of giving her servants good horse flesh. Mr Davis, the very police magistrate of Bothwell, had advertised a mount named Donald he wanted to sell; however, it was one personally owned by the magistrate that promised much better than the average. It was a half-Arab, and with a lot of endurance in his frame.

Buying the magistrate's horse to escape from the magistrate? That seemed to Mitchel a wonderful impudence. John made a bid for the horse and Mr Davis himself delivered it to Nant Cottage. He was not a bad chap by his own lights, which were not the brightest lights in civilisation.

He said, 'I have to warn you, Mr Mitchel, that if you attempt to put Donald into harness, he will smash everything. I tried it once and it should never be attempted again. I think it's fair to mention it to you, since I don't know what sort of work you want to put him to.'

'Well,' Mitchel told the man, 'just to take me on his back. Having the liberty of the island, I might need to go on long journeys.'

The police magistrate told Mitchel that that was all to the good, that Donald was up to it. And so by transaction, Donald, spirited and strong, became Mitchel's horse, and he kept him well fed and well exercised, and Donald liked it all and was eager.

It was after St Patrick's Day that Mitchel next heard from Nicaragua. Smyth sent a letter at last, saying that he had made up his party to go to the gold diggings over on the mainland, and that everything was well with him. By this Mitchel knew by pre-arrangement he had managed to procure a ship – or better still, a captain. He would, he said, meet the rest of his party of diggers at Bendigo Creek in three days' time. Again, code! It meant Smyth was riding south to come and meet John Martin and Mitchel at Lake Sorell.

It was late March when Martin and Mitchel rode up to the lake and met up with Nicaragua at the house formerly used by Meagher. Nicaragua was accompanied by amiable old John Connell from the Sugarloaf, the husband of the Cork woman who, amongst other gifts, made wonderful mead. Smyth told them that the brigantine *Waterlily* was to come into Hobart and take on a cargo for New Zealand. On its way there, it would wait two days off the east coast by Spring Bay, while the crew cut timber. Now there was a police station round there, but never more than three or four constables, whom Smyth could bribe or intimidate. Mr McNamara of Sydney, the owner of the ship, would be aboard to receive Mitchel and Martin and see them safely on their way. Indeed, Nicaragua intended to depart for Hobart straightaway for a conference with McNamara, who had an office there.

By 9 April, the Nant Cottage folk were told by a messenger riding up from Hobart that all was ready and that the ship should be in Spring Bay by Sunday night and at anchor, with Mr McNamara's flag flying – a red cross with the letter 'M' in one corner. Meanwhile, Smyth and Mitchel, first thing Monday, were to go to the police office in Bothwell, where Mitchel would withdraw his parole.

Nicaragua himself would be with Mitchel when he withdrew the parole, and he said they would be observed by a number of armed locals to whom he had appealed, and whose support he had organised in local pot houses and *shebeens*. So many haters of Denison; so many haters of Downing Street, for that matter. The escape party would ride away during Monday night to Spring Cove, and Mitchel be ready to embark at dawn. If the police boat got in the way, said Nicaragua, McNamara was willing to ram her.

In prospect, it all seemed so easy. And the escapers had friends not only willing to ram police boats, but also watching what was happening from Governor Denison's side and willing to warn Nicaragua and Mitchel about his intentions as well.

For example, a Scots gentleman at Bothwell who had just been in Hobart on business rode into Nant Cottage, and his knocking brought Mitchel to the door with Jenny. He informed the Mitchels not only that a new detachment of constabulary had turned up to reinforce the Bothwell police, but that the *Waterlily* had been allowed to clear out of Hobart Town without examination, bound for New Zealand, specifically because someone had informed on the plan. They would have been ambushed had they tried to hand in their parole to Magistrate Davis.

They had good horses, and if necessary people would hide them all year in the remote country, but dealing with the parole was the only path even to those outcomes.

Nicaragua had ridden south with three Irish friends, one of them the brother of the beautiful Regan, whom Nicaragua meant to wed. By the time they heard from the Scot who'd visited the Mitchel cottage, it was not Mitchel, but Smyth and Regan and Connell who started out for Spring Bay to signal the *Waterlily* on its way, and warn McNamara against trying a rescue.

Mitchel remained, meek as a curate, at Nant Cottage. All this delay, and Jenny and he now burning with an urgency that could not be answered! But John Martin, who was such a calm soul, seemed philosophic about it, and said, 'I am too old and settled for this uncertainty. You must try it without the complication of myself. Because you are the one, above all, they want to reach America.' He used both index fingers as he did at times of emphasis, waving them up and down significantly in emphasis. 'I will be here to help your dear wife. I would happily be of service to help her get away when it is time.'

And that was decided and Mitchel, who had had some concerns about his friend's stamina, was relieved to hear it.

A few days later they had a note from John Connell of the Sugarloaf. It said, and there was no reason to doubt it, that Nicaragua had been arrested under suspicion of being . . . *Mitchel*! He had been surrounded by police the moment he rode up to the hotel at Spring Bay. Fortunately, Connell had separated from him as they approached town; otherwise he would have been detained too.

Now, convinced they had captured John Mitchel, and without Nicaragua being able to prove otherwise, he was locked up in the watch house for the night and could see from the window of his cell the *Waterlily* waiting in the bay. With the signal lamp at her masthead, she lingered futile hours and, receiving no answering signal from shore, at last turned to the east and New Zealand, without her cargo of escapees, but with enough stores on board to make the journey profitable for McNamara.

Nicaragua Smyth was carried in custody overnight, through the bush and in an open cart, to Hobart, where the police magistrate in that town knew Mitchel by sight. Smyth got a cold from travelling in that spring cart and was feverish by the time he was discharged and sought shelter in a sympathiser's house.

Mitchel drove down there after a few days to visit him and found him somewhat better than was to be feared. John then went in solemn mischief to the police officer and told the clerk of the court that he understood there was a warrant against him, and so here he was. He wanted to know the reason for the warrant. The clerk said it was all a mistake and pretended that they should have a good laugh over it.

Mitchel told him he didn't think it was so funny, and neither could the eminent Mr Smyth, an American visitor, express amusement over it, and that his arrest had been an insult to both of them. They were all aware, Mitchel said, as touchy as he could be, that he had promised not to leave the island without first giving the proper authorities the chance to arrest him, and they had arrested Smyth believing him to be Mitchel. And thus they assumed John Mitchel would be willing to make his escape dishonourably!

The clerk then went and fetched two well-dressed men, who introduced themselves as the chief constables of the port of Spring Cove. Mitchel invited them to have a good look at him. His aim, and in his then state of mind it seemed a serious one, was to make the Van Diemen's Land constabulary feel more tentative in future. And to have the pleasure of exacting an apology from them. But he did not get one, as apparently respectful as they were. Above all, Mitchel was hoping that his protestations would cause them to stop watching Nant Cottage and Bothwell, if he emphasised he would not think of absconding without letting them know.

When Mitchel visited Smyth in his sick bed in Hobart, he told him what Martin had finally declared: that Mitchel should escape alone. So they began to devise a new plan involving at its initiation fewer people. Nicaragua and Mitchel would, one morning soon, both armed, go to Mr Magistrate Davis's office and surprise him, and thereafter take their chance for a ship – whether Nicaragua had contracted a particular vessel to the enterprise or not.

In languid Bothwell, Mitchel held Jenny in his arms and told her of all the shifts that had sent the earlier plan awry, and that a plan of different scale would be tried. But she would know when it was happening. And until that day came, he said, they should rest on each other's company and be at their ease and, as far as they could, imitate colonial farm folk.

———

Nicaragua, however, developed pneumonia, and it would be early June before he came up from Hobart to Nant Cottage. His inflammation of the chest had reasserted itself, and the fair Miss Regan had needed to come down from the Irish town of Westbury to nurse him. He was, if anything, thinner that June than the stylish fellow who had descended from the coach at Bridgewater six months before.

Restored to health, he told Mitchel that in two nights' time a ship whose agents were sympathetic would leave Hobart for Sydney, and that they would let Mitchel aboard at the river mouth after all customs and police checks had been concluded. Nicaragua declared the biggest peril would actually be in the Bothwell police office, since by bribing the constabulary here, they would give away their plan. John Martin was now earnestly committed to helping Jenny in her own ultimate departure – her setting out for New York, which seemed worlds away. With the six children.

Martin said, reasonably enough, that if by chance Mitchel missed the ship, he would need to spend several weeks in hiding on the island, and keep moving, which in this country, he wisely said, would be a hardship Martin doubted he could face. Even Nicaragua, he added, must be prepared for hardship if he and Mitchel were on the loose, and Mitchel had withdrawn his parole yet was still hiding in the countryside.

Mitchel listened, but did not think Martin as prophetic as in fact he turned out to be. John Martin was only three years older than him, and a fellow asthmatic, but there was something about him that had always been the aged, wary bachelor.

On the day Mitchel was due to withdraw parole and he and Nicaragua were to depart for Hobart, the town of Bothwell was full of police. They did not know why, but rumours were rife. Mitchel sent his second oldest son James, an energetic rider, down to Hobart Town to ask the agents if they could delay the ship for a day more.

Whatever they said, Mitchel intended to make the escape official tomorrow, for by some means Nicaragua had paid money to an official in Hobart to ensure there would be no more than the normal police complement in Bothwell that day. That is, there would be Mr Davis and his clerk and at least two constables, who would probably be ordered by the magistrate to do their duty and arrest Mitchel. He hoped they could be dissuaded by the idea of big Colt revolvers, which Nicaragua had discreetly shown around in local pubs, so that the word got round that he had them.

Thus, on 8 July, Mitchel had his last night with Jenny and woke to think that from now she would know him only as a potential New Yorker, or else as a chastened escapee resigning himself to further expiatory years as a convict and, at the end of the sentence, colonial farmer. He lay in her arms as ever a half-finished man, since all was to be redefined that day. She, too, would be redefined. They woke as well the eldest boy, sharp-eyed young John C., and gave him his duties for the day of escape. Mitchel had every confidence in him. His piercing eyes barely blinked as they absorbed what his father had to say.

It was mid-winter cold with the breath of snow from the Western Tiers reaching them as Nicaragua and Mitchel set out. Jenny, tears in eyes, punched Donald on the shoulder as if to evince the best of equine courtesy and speed from him. Two of them mounted up at Nant Cottage – Nicaragua on Donald, Mitchel on Fleur-de-Lys – while John C. had walked through the fields to Bothwell ahead of them so he would be ready at the police-office door to hold their horses. In the meantime, before they had ridden a quarter of a mile from the house, they met James, the second son, coming at the gallop from Hobart Town. He handed Mitchel a note that said the ship had sailed – it had been impossible to delay it.

So now they knew there was no escape plan as regards to getting off the island. Frustrated, Mitchel began to discuss calling everything off. There were other possibilities in the north end of the island, said Nicaragua. If Mitchel went ahead and withdrew his parole and survived that, it made no difference now whether he rode north or south or to the east coast. Only west was out of the question, for the Tiers lay there, beyond the lake, impenetrable to horses and without a track to take them through, even had there been shipping that way.

Tom Meagher, Mitchel knew, had had a certain time in the wilderness before he got away, hiding in the north with sympathisers. Mitchel decided he must not torment himself and Jenny with the project of escape anymore.

'I must embark on it then!' he told Nicaragua.

'Very well,' said Smyth. 'I thought you would say that. This day has the decisive feeling to it.'

———

They overtook a Scots neighbour of theirs, Mr Russell, on the way into town, and he asked Mitchel with some interest what prices he got for the grass-fed wethers he had sold at Nant Cottage a few days earlier, and whether he had planted another winter grain crop. Mounted and like a model farmer in the midst of his endeavours, and without any thoughts other on his mind, Mitchel discussed all this with Mr Russell. From a distance, Mitchel meanwhile saw John Martin and James, who must have been riding most of the night, hurrying along the riverbank to be there ahead of them, catching up with John C. Mr Russell was a very handy delayer, but at last he turned off at a house he was visiting, and Nicaragua and Mitchel were left to ride like casual visitors down the main street of Bothwell.

At the police barracks up on the hill they could see eight or nine constables, all armed and performing a kind of military drill. Because some of them were former convicts, the drill lacked enthusiasm – they had had enough of it in their old life and could not see the point now in tranquil Bothwell. The latter was a hopeful sign that they would wait for orders before they intervened. At the police station itself, there was as usual a constable on guard within a few yards of the gate which led into the courtyard.

They dismounted. John Mitchel saw Johnny and Jamie and John Martin standing by the bakery ready to take up their position. Nicaragua and Mitchel had three friends to take control of the horses – they pretended not to be connected with them and let the reins dangle free a while before securing them. Nicaragua and Mitchel moved through the gate, into a hallway and then into the courtyard. Ahead of him and Smyth stood the office where the magistrate could be seen sitting at his desk, and the police clerk at his by the door.

Mitchel had refined the method by which he would manage the withdrawal-of-parole business. That morning he had given John Martin a letter addressed to his Excellency Governor Denison, which Martin would now immediately consign to the post. And so as Nicaragua and Mitchel entered the magistrates office, Mitchel was able to say, 'Mr Davis, I give you a copy of the note which I've just sent the Governor by mail. I have thought it was necessary to give you a copy of it.'

Mitchel immediately placed it on his desk. He could have recited the contents.

'Bothwell, 8th June 1853,' it said.

To the Governor, etc., etc.,
Sir
I hereby resign the item called a 'ticket-of-leave' and withdraw my parole. I shall forthwith present myself before the police magistrate of Bothwell, at his office, hand him a copy of this note, and offer myself to be taken into custody.
Your obedient servant,
John Mitchel

When Mitchel plopped the letter right side up and in front of him, Mr Davis rose, in his dual roles as imprisoner and horse dealer, and only then took up the note as if to read it. But he did not do so. He could see Nicaragua, and Nicaragua's hand inside a kangaroo-skin coat. He asked with a quaver, 'Do you really wish me to read it?'

'That's exactly why I brought it,' Mitchel assured him.

He read through the note and then stared at Mitchel, and saw Nicaragua keeping one eye on the clerk at the door. Yet the confident way Nicaragua planted himself had actually implied that he was merely one of a gathered crowd of desperadoes, most of whom were waiting outside. Mitchel felt Davis must have thought that was the case, because he seemed so faltering that Mitchel prompted him.

'You understand what my note means, don't you, Mr Davis? It's very plain. I am resigning that thing called "ticket-of-leave" and revoking the pledge I gave when I first took it up.'

Nicaragua went on dominating both men with his eyes, left and right. He was a tall, frightening presence. There was no move from either Davis or his assistant.

'So,' Mitchel further explained, 'my parole is at an end, and I came here so that you could take me into custody pursuant to my note to his Excellency.'

Mitchel could hear a constable stamping about in a nearby room. And Davis could call to him or the sentry at the gate to resist any exit Mitchel and Nicaragua tried to make, or to come running right now. But Nicaragua was, of course, fondling the handle of his Colt in his breast pocket.

'Good morning, then, Mr Davis,' said Mitchel. 'If you do not avail yourself of the chance to retain me, I believe I am now entitled to escape.'

Davis now began to move around his desk, and cried, 'No, stay where you are! Guard!' And louder still then, in the hope of being heard up the hill, 'Constables!'

Mitchel and Nicaragua marched out, staring at the police clerk who had no ambition to endure sudden death in Bothwell for the interests of Downing Street and the Queen, given she might not even notice. The guard at the gate happened to be holding two horses – not theirs, but as a favour to someone – and the two passed him as if he were not there. As they got out into the street, there were Johnny and Jamie holding their mounts, and Martin nearby, mildly smiling.

'We are not finished, my dear John C. and Jamie,' Mitchel told them. 'We will meet up again. Soon.'

And feeling light as a feather, he vaulted into the saddle, while Nicaragua was quickly into his. Some visitors to town paused outside the shops and stores opposite and smiled, some waving. Mr Davis's orders could be heard from inside the station, yet the guard holding the two horses looked around as if he were utterly puzzled as to who the miscreants in the scene were. From the entry to the courtyard Mitchel heard Davis scream, 'Stop them in the Queen's name!' Some shoppers across the street could be heard laughing.

'Go!' shouted Nicaragua.

Mitchel nudged his horse with his heels, too good an animal to subject to spurs. There were a few Irish and Caledonian cheers as they galloped down the main road, and some colonial brats ran after them, with one of them, a natural tout, yelling, 'Three to one the white!'

19

Vandemonian Running, 1853

They were soon riding south-west to cross the river just below the town, and held to full speed, not pulling up until they were deeply in the bush, amongst the scattered shadows and high canopies of rainforest. Here they exchanged coats with each other, and the revolvers they each held, and so Mitchel got at last onto Davis's wonderful Arab, Donald.

Nicaragua had already set up the neighbourhood sympathisers to ease Mitchel's escape. A young Englishman – an anti-Denison, anti-transportation and hence devoutly colonial settler – introduced himself only as J. H., so that they could split up if necessary and Mitchel be able to swear he did not know his name. If J. H. and Mitchel headed north towards the Westbury area, they would ride through unfrequented country to begin with and then be surrounded by helpful people. There they would be within a day's ride of the Bass Strait, which separated Van Diemen's Land from the mainland. Nicaragua and Mitchel said goodbye then, and Nicaragua

Smyth rode off to Hobart to attend to his attempt to set up a ship in Hobart to round the island and pick Mitchel up at the other, more sparsely populated, end.

In the grey-blue scattered light of the rainforest Mitchel felt excited, stimulated and, above all, liberated. The rigmarole of the parole was off his shoulders. And then on top of that, if for any reason Nicaragua on his separate tangent were stopped by the police, he could swear that he did not know what direction Mitchel had taken, and tell them then that the escapee had roped him in to visit the police magistrate by threat.

The young colonist J. H. led Mitchel through into a tangle of wooded hills studded with grand slabs of rock. After ten miles of hard riding, they came to the track leading from Bothwell to the Shannon – the Vandemonian version of it – a wild rocky river descending from a tier.

They crossed the Shannon, as hectic and white-foamed as it was, and plunged into wilder country, denser country, still. A marsh they crossed was frozen, the horses' hooves skittered at its edges, but they got beyond it. They had hoped by night they would get to a hut shelter near Lake Sorell. But they rode on in darkness along its shore on the off-chance there might be a police party, despatched from Ross to the lake to see if Mitchel had come up to hide in Meagher's old residence.

J. H. knew they were getting close to a hut belonging to Mitchel's friend Mr Russell, and occupied by Mr Russell's shepherd. They found three men in the hut when they reached it, the sort of men you met in such places, who desired isolation and the freedom to ride round as they pleased, as long as they dissuaded Mr Russell's stock from wandering into the profounder wilderness and perishing.

They told Mitchel and J. H. that ahead lay a mountain which would ultimately take them down by a pass to the low country, but that it was a dangerous ride in darkness. They suggested the visitors stay and share the floor and spare opossum skin rugs. However, since a conscientious patrol could reach them there, J. H. insisted on going on, though with one of them as paid guide.

Governor Denison might have been the King of Van Diemen's Land, but those convict hut-men were the kings of Tasmania. Following J. H. and the hut-man up stony hills riddled with wombat holes, Mitchel found himself at last descending, but on such a rough and rock-cluttered track that they had to dismount and lead their horses. So they came into a country of broken boulders and unexpected little cliffs in all directions, but all of it dense with gum trees. They led the horses, who were uneasy and tossing their heads violently, their jaws occasionally knocking against the riders' brows as hard as a punch.

By midnight, neither the riders nor the horses could move without danger of breaking a leg on icy ground, so they made a wretched camp in the open, compiling a fire with some dead branches. They tethered their horses to a nearby honeysuckle, checked their pistols, then they sat down on a rock and started smoking. They would slip into sleep, though, and wake up when the fabric of their pants was close to the fire, or when their spines were so cold they threatened to crack. This was liberty, Mitchel's first night of it in more than five years.

They finally stood up in despair of warmth and started smoking. *Lib-er-ty!* He hoped that Jenny was warm and undisturbed at Nant Cottage as all around her the two hundred acres silvered into a murderous frost. A closer worry was whether their horses could live through such exposure, since J. H.'s mount and his were usually well stabled at night.

But dawn, bringing back the excitement of escape, also revealed that the horses were in good condition, and nodding their heads and snuffling with appreciation in the first rays of the sun. And it was just as well they had travelled on the previous evening, because they were now in new country and only a few miles from the safe hut of a colourful man named Old Job Simms, whom J. H. frequently visited. Their guide from last night turned back.

With a hint of fabric at the shuttered window, Old Job Simms's dwelling was, even from the outside, a much more refined place than where they'd spent the night before. Men might live brutishly, but Job had a wife. He, an English convict, had met and made his peace with a woman of similar background, and they were the most reputable pair you would want to meet in any wilderness, and demonstrated again by their open-handedness that the great British tragedy might be that it had a ruling class. Job was very proud that this was the first place Tom Meagher had stopped when he withdrew his ticket and began his escape. Tom had shaved off his moustache by that very mirror there, Old Job remembered.

Mrs Simms prepared a genuine breakfast for which, famishing for a day, the travellers showed a powerful appetite. Then Job brought Mitchel a razor, looking glass, basin and soap, and he began to transform himself from the colonial farmer he had till yesterday been. He wrote a short note to Jenny saying how well he was and looking forward to reunion with her. Job Simms was going to have to take cattle across to Bothwell for their friend Mr Philip Russell the very next day and could drop it into the cottage. This man who had been a convict and was an Englishman would not betray that letter, Mitchel expected, for any fortune offered him.

And so they rode on in the direction of Westbury, Job riding with them for a few hours to show them the way to the ford of the river, one that flowed down from Lake Sorell. After that, after Mr Simms turned back, they kept on over another high cold mountain, a rough one too, but with at least a clear track on it. Most of these tracks were made in the first place by the Aboriginal people, sole proprietors of this place for some millennia.

They rode down to the house of a Mr Woods, whose son was anxious to help Mitchel in the manner of young J. H., and despite the fact of his father's magistracy. As they descended, they came to a sudden turn amongst tall trees, and met there with two gentlemen riders ascending the mountain. Taking the second man on trust, Mitchel asked the lead rider was he young Woods? He said yes, and Mitchel introduced himself.

Woods junior quizzed Mitchel for a while and turned to his slightly younger friend. He smiled. 'You know you cannot speak of any of this?'

And his friend said, 'And you know Denison wouldn't believe me if I did.'

This young man – the second one, whose name Mitchel never discovered – gave up his fresher horse to Mitchel and agreed to take Donald gently down to the Woods house to be looked after and fed and stabled. As for J. H., that young colonist from down Bothwell way, he was free now to return there, with Mitchel's thanks ringing about his ears. For he would have a hard ride to get back.

Then young Woods brought Mitchel by a more secret backtrack to the family's house. They were away from the mountains and their boulders. The Western Tiers were turning up a lowering purple as they rode around their base and came to the splendid house of stone and shingles. Only one hundred yards down the same road, however, Mitchel could see a police station and constables mounted in front of the door.

That night Mr Woods senior – Woods junior having gone off to visit a young woman of the district – had Mitchel as his guest at table. Like all the others, he complained a lot about the authoritarian policies of Denison and the man's opposition to democratic rule and just taxation. But Woods spoke in a measured way, as did his wife – they were no family of ranters.

'I admit my family could not have made their way here without convict labour,' said Woods, the magistrate. 'Although the raids by convict bushrangers, decamped into the wilderness, nearly drove us out before I was sixteen. The bushranger Howe smashed our best furniture and my father wanted to move to Sydney, but my mother said that after travelling so far from Lanarkshire she did not want to make one more move. In any case, the time for convict labour is gone now. We can afford to pay free men an honest wage and live without the stigma of being a penal settlement.'

For the sake of landing a blow on Denison, Mr Woods was kind and entertaining to the limit, and Mitchel slept with every confidence that no-one associated with Mr Woods would slip down the street to the police depot to report his presence. But when he woke the next morning, a little later than was usual, Mr Woods was waiting for him downstairs. He said that the police garrison at the station next door had been increased. He thought it would be safer for Mitchel if he went from the Woods' estate by a bush track to the farm-house of a young Irishman.

And so young Woods escorted him a few miles through the bush from Westbury to the Irish farm. The Irishman, Burke, was married to an amiable, muscular spouse, who, like many of her kind, had seen the advantages that arose from her transportation as a butter thief. Their farmhouse had a number of rooms and was comfortable, and carried an air of permanence about it, as if generations would grow here. As well, it had some periodicals and half-a-dozen books, a veritable library in terms of Van Diemen's Land.

Waiting to hear from Smyth, he was pleasantly ensconced there a little over a week. He rode each day to keep up his mettle, and re-read his old acquaintance Thomas Carlyle's *History of the French Revolution*. And then Mitchel got the expected letter from Nicaragua.

Nicaragua Smyth had ridden safely to Oatlands on the day of the escape, but was aware of being pursued by police. Poor Fleur-de-Lys, who was in a lather after the ride, he put in the stable, and made loud inquiries as to whether he could get a horse to travel eastward to Spring Bay. That night, he left the town and hotel by way of the garden, climbed over several back walls of houses, reached the road outside the village, waited for the Launceston coach, and so went northwards to confuse pursuit (although, admittedly, the fair Regan lay in that direction too). Nicaragua said Mitchel would not recognise him, since he had shaved and his hair was disguised by a new style. He would try to arrange for a ship leaving Hobart for Launceston, and then Launceston for the Australian mainland.

Mitchel's Irish host, Burke, meanwhile, told him that mounted police, having traced Nicaragua's tracks, found poor old Fleur-de-Lys in the stables in Oatlands: Nicaragua's loud questions about Spring Bay had paid off handsomely in drawing off many police pursuers. Some visitors from the south told Mitchel that Mr Davis had charged one of the constables with failing to grab him when he was called on to do so, and claimed also that the man had been bribed by Nicaragua, which in this case was not the truth. Davis dismissed him from the police service, and the man went over to the pub and was bought drinks, then came out into the street at a late hour outside the police station yelling three cheers for Mitchel. Mitchel knew this man was not, in fact, bribed. But he deserved a reward.

But meantime, Westbury being an Irish hotbed, the police were still patrolling it day and night. At his friendly Irish farmer's house, these reports, instead of making him feel threatened or hunted, exhilarated him and made him feel that he was destined to escape the mean power of men like Davis and Denison. They also simplified his choices: death or America.

He looked forward to the United States as to an idyll. He did not at that stage take account of the fact that America had its own sundry causes and divisions that would engage and bite at him. He saw his future Atlantic coast self as removed, as someone tending his garden, living a life rather like his Irishman lived here, in the city or, more likely, given his passion for the agrarian ambience and even his experience at Nant Cottage, in some smiling county of an as-yet-undisclosed and bounteous state.

In his week at the Burke farmhouse, he had a visit from a friend of Meagher's, O'Keefe, who'd set off from his house further north at dusk in one direction and then diverted to another bushy tangent to reach Mitchel. He was, in fact, forever to be honoured as having brought Meagher of the Sword through the bush and to Bass Strait, from which O'Meagher escaped and reverted to being Meagher.

Nicaragua's next letter was brought by one of his supporters from Hobart Town. Smyth declared in it that he was back in Hobart and negotiating with the agents for a ship named the *Don Juan*. *Don Juan*, which, like their earlier hope, was owned by Mr McNamara of Sydney, was apparently a very solid brigantine, two-masted, that is, with a full-shrouded mainmast up front to drag Mitchel to freedom – if arrangements worked out. They were keeping a watch on him, the colonial peelers were, said Nicaragua, but he was able to deal with that, since he had more craft than they did. The *Don Juan* was bound for Melbourne, and he hoped that it would be able to pick Mitchel up in some remote bay in the north of the island.

Two days later, another message came. The *Don Juan* would pick him up at Emu Bay, near the mouth of the similarly named river on the north coast. The distance was about eighty miles from where Mitchel was sojourning, and they were not the easiest miles to traverse. But no sooner did Mitchel have the word about rivers than torrents of winter rain began to fall. His Irish host assured him that, even if they were mounted on elephants, the surging rivers would sweep them down into open ocean – open ocean being Bass Strait. Mitchel was not fond of the prospect.

Mitchel asked was it possible to strike direct north and go along the coast in a boat. He was told that the police were watching the river mouths in their own boats. Mitchel used to daydream that Denison would be happy to see the back of him, but no, he was concerned that such a notable escape would bring mockery in the world's press and elevate him to page one of the *New-York Tribune* or *La Presse*, and the English papers too, as the imperial buffoon from whose grasp Mitchel had slipped.

O'Keefe suggested that, given the torrential rain, they should wait for *Don Juan* at a solitary beach between West Head and Badger Head, to the west of the mouth of Launceston's River Tamar – named for the ambiguous lady of that name in Genesis, whom Judah first wanted to put to death and then married. They could get to that point of Van Diemen's Land without having to ford any river except the Meander. Only one thing made Mitchel anxious about Melbourne, and that was that all arrivals were scrutinised, under suspicion of being escaped prisoners from Van Diemen's Land. However, he was sure he could disguise himself, and even then was partially disguised by the fact he kept his beard well-trimmed, like a gent's.

And he had heard from Jenny. That miracle of a woman. Mitchel would not expect even the bravest wife to take his escape as a given, but Jenny apparently had, so dear old John Martin told him in an attached letter. She had weaned little Rixy in preparation for her own exodus, and had advertised for a new tenant.

John Martin had written to O'Doherty in Hobart, asking if he could find some decent girl to accompany Jenny and the children to America. They were seeking someone not prone to seasickness beyond what was usual. Such a thorough embracing of what was only an ambition to Mitchel himself was beyond his merits, he believed, and a measure of her mighty soul.

As Jenny shared with him, 'Many ladies had come into Nant Cottage with the sewing and preparation for a voyage they knew is coming. Miss Reid and her friends the Cook girls are amongst them.'

John Martin had written as well to McNamara's agents to find out if the *Emma*, which went back and forward to Sydney, was fitted out with bedding for the berths, or whether passengers had to bring their own. Jenny, it was apparent, was selling up their household effects, including a good mattress, but might not if they needed to retain bedding for what would be a cold crossing to the mainland.

If Mitchel's determination needed reviving, this message did it. Not only was Jenny banking on his escape, but she and John Martin spoke of goodwill, of a kind to move him to tears, amongst their neighbours in Bothwell. In the process of selling horses, the whole district seemed to know what the situation was, and no-one took advantage of Jenny. They bought discreetly and above the asked-for price.

This Jenny Verner was thus a tigress, even though her parents had always seemed the incarnation of timidity. He could merely try to match her for valour. She behaved as if the complete escape was accomplished.

The *Emma* was due to sail from Hobart on 18 July. On the night of the move to Badger Head, Mitchel left the Burke farm in a party, and was led on his way by a profusion of Irish guides, who had volunteered to take him to the meeting place. It was a night of scudding cloud and as cold as any winter's night in Ireland, with all the recent rain frozen to the ground. Mitchel had accompanying him Mr Burke, his brother, two O'Keefes, and Foley, a powerful Tipperary man over six feet tall, as well as the Connell brothers ridden up from the Sugarloaf. They were all armed. And as well, they were to meet up with Mr Woods and his son at a point on the Westbury road.

They did so within an hour of setting forth, and from there they rode almost due north, the moon brightened up by hoarfrost, but they seemed to lose all light as they rode down into the valley of the Meander. On the further bank was the farm of O'Keefe. He had told Mitchel he immigrated there after Lord Hawarden in South Tipperary forced him and thousands of others, if you counted in the families, off their land. It was clear that his kindnesses to Mitchel were also a form of vengeance against Lord Hawarden. During the evictions, one old lady set her bees on the police and the soldiers, but they smashed down her roof like all the others and forbade her to come back. It was now going to take more than armies, he said, to drag him away from his secluded Meander farm.

They crossed the fiercely running river. Mitchel's horse was tall but the water came up to her chest and filled his boots with an icy shock. But soon they were over, and up the embankment and at the door of O'Keefe's bush mansion.

All his family were a-bed, so they stabled their horses, then crept into the house where the fire was stoked up to a blaze and huge lumps of steak were soon spitting in a big skillet. They drank a little rum and O'Keefe welcomed Mitchel formally to the hospitality of the bush – he hoped, he said, despite Mitchel's renown – for the last time. By the same cause, he wished the fugitive a thousand welcomes to the quiet place he had found, as he put it, 'a little removed from interference'. The Anglo-Scottish Woods, who had ridden there instead of sheltering in their splendid stone house, bore very sportingly O'Keefe's Irish speechifying, and with the appearance of robust Mrs O'Keefe, there was further oratory and appeals were made to the Mother of God to witness the honour Mitchel was doing her house, as a year before the mighty Meagher of the Sword had also done.

Soon, a little drier, a little warmer, they went outside and mounted again.

Mitchel had yearned to be out of the mountains, and so they were now. But the country at that end of the island was a terrain of hills divided from each other by marshes, and streams with crumbling banks. It was tedious and slow travel, that last forty miles to Emu Bay and Badger's Head, but Mr Woods and his amiable son and the Irish as well all remarked that it was no country in which you expected to see police patrols. Their horses could not manage it, they said. At one stage, O'Keefe, mounted on a heavy black mare, sank into a swamp and was in danger of drowning if he had not flung himself off the saddle. It was hard and long work, however, to heave and urge his mare out of the mud.

They arrived at a raging creek whose depth was inscrutable, its banks deep and of crumbling red soil, and the passage across the water choked by fallen logs. They searched along its banks for an hour for a place where there might be a ford. At last one of the Irish launched himself down the bank and across the creek, yelling confidently, 'Follow me!' Soon he was at the far bank, and his horse clawed at the slick, crumbling soil. But the soft earth gave way beneath the horse's hooves and forced him vertical, so that horse and rider were thrown backwards into the stream.

In the end they discovered a place to cross with some safety and came out of the foothills and found themselves at the estuary of the River Tamar, near a small town named York. They skirted the little scatter of buildings and made for Badger Head beyond. Darkness came before they were there, and in this country occupied by those curious animals named wombats – marsupials who dug burrows just the right size to take a horse's leg and break it – they bivouacked in a clump of bush, well-grassed for the animals. They roasted by a fire on forked sticks the last of the mutton they had brought from the O'Keefe farm and finished the supply of brandy; then they smoked pipes and lay on saddles for some sleep.

The *Don Juan*, if it had got the message to come, might have been lying off Badger Head during that night, but it was agreed that it would have had to stand far out to sea to avoid being blown onto rocks, given the strong onshore winds. At dawn they set out again, and through the marshes heard the raging of the surf and beheld Badger Head like a great barn of rock on the left. They climbed through a mile of sand dunes and neared the sea, and, coming round the point of Badger Head, saw a brigantine. They could not see McNamara's signal flag, but it certainly looked like *Don Juan*, and, asked Woods, what else could it be?

The whole party dismounted and gathered wood and lit a signal fire. Mr Woods opined it could be seen from thirty miles away, as they heaved logs and boughs on it. If so, the captain of the *Don Juan* did not notice it, nor did the ship depart from a straight course out into the Bass Strait and on towards Melbourne.

As it vanished, Mitchel felt ashamed that he had somehow compelled these men watching, commentating, surmising around him, for some days to accompany him, that they had abandoned their own business to help him, and that it had all been for nothing. But to give them credit they did not seem at all distressed except for his sake, though there were mutterings against Mr McNamara of Sydney and the mongrel captain.

O'Keefe and Mr Woods began discussing very practically what should be done now. Mr Woods' best suggestion was that he had a pastoral run in the mountains of north-west Van Diemen's Land, a barely populated wing of the country. Mitchel could spend the winter as a stockkeeper there. This being June, he would not be able to emerge until September. The prospect nauseated him and did not fit with Jenny's confident plans.

The signal fire burned down and they took off across more of the same country, and saw no-one. Mr Woods rode ahead to the village of Port Sorell, and a fellow who had a house in the vicinity, Miller, came riding back with him. Miller did not seem at all jaded or disappointed as they were and was good for all of them. He was the picture of a colonist as Mr Dickens might have imagined one – Welsh, and with a whimsical grin and a stocky build and mutton-chop whiskers. Above all, he seemed positively delighted to be involved with the helpless escapee.

Miller's house was off the road, he assured everyone, and separated from the town by a stream. Even so, Port Sorell itself – less than a mile away – sported a police station and a magistrate and the rest. Even a small place like that had all the dignity of a magistrate! The only person Miller had seen recently was a constable who'd ridden out to warn all the remote farms to be on the lookout for Mitchel. But the thing was that all visitors in any case – and certainly anyone bearing despatches from Launceston – had to call out across the inlet to have him come to fetch them in his boat.

The party was impressed by the security of the Miller estate, but O'Keefe – perhaps even a little jealous at the claim this non-Irishman was making on all their attentions – was somewhat dubious. 'Someone will report that we have

279

been through here,' he said, 'even though we might not be aware of having been seen, and in no time you could get a visit from an express force of police.'

The genial Welshman was unperturbed. 'But you see,' he replied, 'I would come across here with a bottle or two of spirits and take whatever despatch they had, and make them drunk. Or I can bribe the head peeler to return home and report he had delivered the warning, even if it was only *per me*. Or I could drown the lot of them in midstream, if you wished. Now I know the constables up this way. They are always having to cross water on the rivers here, and always looking for an excuse not to.'

Mitchel also soothed O'Keefe, reminding him that, for all they knew, the *Don Juan* might have been watched by the authorities and might come back for him tomorrow or the next day. He could see the open ocean from Miller's hut if the ship returned. On top of that, Mitchel declared, he was aware that his cohort once again were all busy men making their colonial fortunes, and that they must feel free to ride away after they had rested at Miller's. Their former host, Mr Burke, had agreed he would find and make contact with Nicaragua.

And so they rested in the sprawling bush haven of Mr and Mrs Miller. The next morning, before full light, armed with the Millers' telescope, O'Keefe and Mitchel set up a watching post in the sand dunes, well shielded from the police office in town by a thicket of stunted trees called boobialla. As they looked out to sea, they saw nothing.

After breakfast, all of Mitchel's friends rode away, anxious to be summoned to return if needed. Burke left his horse, the same one Mitchel had been riding all along. Mr Woods' offer of a posting as stockkeeper in the Tiers remained in place. When they had ridden off, Miller and Mitchel took to the dunes again, and late in the morning a sail came into sight. Miller clapped the escapee's shoulder. It seemed more to the Welshman's disappointment than to Mitchel's that the vessel turned out to be a three-master bark.

As for the Miller menage, that household also abominated — as a matter of principle, they said — the vice-regal rule of Governor Denison. Now that gold had been found in Victoria, the cry of men like Miller was: 'Why should we pay to keep miscreants in proximity to a goldfield, when free men in Britain and California are paying their way to get to it?'

Regarding Mitchel's escape, Miller came up with the most exotic plan anyone, including Nicaragua, could possibly have imagined. Mitchel was sitting in his screen of boobialla, worrying about Jenny and the children at Nant Cottage and wondering whether they should stay or go, sell or retain. Miller interrupted this melancholy with the news from town that there was a vessel fourteen miles to the west, in the mouth of the River Forth. It was filling up with sawn timber its owner intended to take to Melbourne for the city's gold-rush boom in buildings.

The point was, Miller had a brother he'd mentioned to the police and to others, who had recently arrived in Melbourne from Cardiff, the Welsh capital, and had promised to visit Port Sorell. Nicholls, the local police magistrate, and the chief constable there, would not be surprised if this brother turned up. If you would go along with this, Miller proposed to Mitchel, they could go across to the village the day before the ship was due to sail, and he could introduce Mitchel to the magistrate as that very brother.

'Nicholls will give you a certificate to go back to Melbourne on the timber ship,' said Miller, 'and he will ask us to dine. And then, later in the evening, we can ride across to the ship, along with the clearing officer himself, and you will go aboard as my brother, Henry Miller.'

Mitchel was, of course, attracted by the generosity and style and daring fun of this plan, but also afflicted with the fear it would be another chimera. Miller asked him would there be any police over there in the town who would be familiar with his appearance. Mitchel told him he could not guarantee that, as they were always moving police around. But he had had to change his appearance very much since the last time a policeman saw him, he added, developing a moustache rather along the lines of Nicaragua and cropping his hair more severely. That was enough encouragement.

Miller immediately ran to his boat and began rowing away like a Welsh imp. When he returned an hour later, he was even more puckish. He told Mitchel he had mentioned his brother to the chief constable over there, and said he had been only a short time in the bush of Port Sorell, but was already tired of it and wanted to go to Melbourne without the trouble of riding all the way to Launceston for one of the steamers.

'So I asked him, was there not a good vessel about to sail from one of the local rivers. And he said, "We have the *Wave* loading with timber in the Forth – it's just the ticket for your brother."'

Miller seemed delighted, and was already congratulating himself a little on having the final responsibility of getting Mitchel off the island by his own resources, where Nicaragua and all the Irish friends had until now failed. He dashed and told his pleasant wife about it, and she shared his mischievous glee in the whole enterprise.

It was early July and cold weather. Mitchel went out with Miller's son and his dogs, hunting kangaroos in the dunes. They saw the tracks of another human, which made them speculate, but Miller himself did not seem very worried. He was more concerned about some new eagles from the mountains behind who were hovering over his newborn lambs.

20

Jenny in Bothwell

In John's absence, Jenny had been concerned each chilly evening about where he lay his head each night. She hoped it was indoors, by a fire, and not amongst boulders and trees. The boys and Henty had been good at not asking about their father all the time, but Willy's question was why his father didn't take him – he would have been such a good messenger, he had said, and would tell the peelers nothing. As well as that, Willy would have been able to visit zones he never had before. As for the baby Rixy, a Mrs Russell, a capable woman who was once clearly a centre of bene-volence amongst the women of Calcutta, in India, when her husband Philip had worked there as an official, had a quite skilled convict woman, servant and seamstress. Between her and the seamstress, they were producing an entire layette for the youngest of the Mitchels.

Meanwhile, John Martin was as sturdy a presence as any elder brother. He was selling off the last of the Nant Cottage

hay that Jenny had feared they would have to leave as virtu-
ally a present for the new owners.

And a letter had arrived from that woman who had
done her best to represent the revolution incarnate –
Miss Jane Elgee or, as she would have it, Speranza Elgee.
Indeed, the letter was addressed to Jenny. She was curious
as to what Speranza might have to tell her. Jenny thought
Speranza might have considered herself too masculine in
her revolutionary ardour to address a wife, despite her taste
for fabric and mantuas fastened and festooned with golden
sheafs of wheat.

> You may remember me as perhaps an overenthusiastic
> presence at your table, but not only at your table, in
> your house. For I remember your two little boys and the
> little girl being very distressed when I told them one of
> my fairy stories. I remember it was about a changeling,
> the fairies having stolen the original child. And your
> little boy wanted to know how could he be sure he
> wasn't a changeling? – how he could be sure he was
> the true John Mitchel, the junior of that name? The
> other little boy frowned as if thinking, 'What a good
> question.' As fast as I could I said, 'You are not a change-
> ling because if you were, you would not understand
> the story.' There I was, even by your little boys' bed,
> starting more trouble than I could perhaps deal with.

Jenny wondered, was Speranza writing a sort of confession and apology? Early in their ambiguous friendship, at
gatherings at the Mitchel household, Speranza would begin
the evening talking to Jenny sincerely, earnestly. However,
she seemed to need to move deftly on to talking to men,

because ideas – to be implemented – would need executive force, and the men possessed that.

But I wanted to tell you that I brought no malice to your household, and I hope my later behaviour proved that. I brought a reckless enthusiasm when I was young, that was all.

Jenny remembered with an indelible fondness how Speranza had helped her in a vain effort the day Mitchel was transported.

I have recently heard that you have now gone to the end of the earth, that 'cold Van Diemen's Land' they sing about in ballads, to be with your husband John. I applaud you for doing that without knowing what hardship and degradation it might mean. And you have taken your children, including the little boy who was not a changeling. You were always wise and calm, and John Mitchel loved you and watched as you spoke, as few men do their wives the honour of doing. I believe I am now capable of assessing your bravery and of applauding it as well.

For you have probably heard I am myself a wife now. I married a man of genius, a celebrity, no less – a man eminent in his profession as a doctor of the eye and author of many books, both literary and scientific. He is Dr William Wilde. He is melancholic and hypochondriacal in the house and I think he married me just for my high spirits and the hope that they might lift his. I asked him once what would make him happy, and he told me, 'death', in all honesty. I said, 'Death will have you in the end. In the meantime, I have you.' And yet if some idea comes to him through conversation or other means he will take it up with an enthusiasm, in a rush of life. In the sort of life I had in the days I wrote for the *Nation*.

For I have a son now. His name is William, like his father's, and to know him is to fall back into childhood. I scarcely know myself. I fancied I could live in lofty abstractions, a woman who loved objects or the ideas they incarnated. I am utterly enthralled by Little William's minute hands. I do not want to write, I do not want to talk. My thoughts are all to do with the child. My soul is imprisoned within a woman's destiny, in that I am again pregnant. All I care about is William Wilde and his infant son and the child yet to be born. If a girl, it will have as styling the names Isola Francesca Emily. If a boy, Oscar O'Flahertie Wills. I would once have warned myself against becoming who I now am. I did not understand how a married woman is contained within her destiny like a woman in a runaway carriage. Husband worship is our duty. However we rail against it, a woman must always be doomed to the prejudices of society – it is her duty, and yet I hate myself for doing it.

Here I was writing to congratulate you on your bravery and turning the letter to my own trepidation. Smith O'Brien should never have been rebel leader. He was more a saint of liberty, but would not hack his way towards it, and above all would not shoot a pathway through police and military. Meagher understood what was needed. But it was your Mitchel who had the coolest head, the truest instincts of the rebel. I wanted to wish you well, as a brave woman locked in a hard destiny. May your husband and your children forever honour you and never grow away!

I send you the best of wishes, and I hope you do not think of me unkindly.

Jane (Speranza) Wilde.

This praise, so fully intentioned by Speranza, for some reason did not flatter Jenny as once it would have. Still, Jenny had Speranza's approval, she thought, and to her that was no hollow thing.

But what did it mean, in the layers of chance and outcomes in which she lived? What did it mean when destinations could not be predicted?

21

Mitchel on the Tamar

A few days before they were to meet the chief constable and catch the *Wave*, Miller's son ran in to report he had seen two horsemen approaching the inlet from the direction of Badger Head. Miller locked Mitchel up in his room and advised that he should see that his pistols were ready to fire. The two riders, in fact, proved to be the two Burke brothers. John heard their voices and emerged.

Ultimately – through Nicaragua, they told him – it had been arranged with a captain in Launceston that he would be taken to Melbourne. Mitchel was informed that he would be travelling in the name of Father McNamara, and the appropriate clothing would be provided him. He was to be in Launceston by the following night, go on board the *Wave*, and remain there through the dark hours until the vessel left at dawn. There was no time to be lost because there was a rumour getting round that he was still on the island.

Now he had an embarrassment of escape plans. The Burkes were suggesting that he go straight away to cover the distance to Launceston, somewhere between fifty and sixty miles. Miller, however, argued that Mitchel should follow his plan. But John believed in the end he must keep loyal to Nicaragua's proposals for escape, and indeed he thought of Miller's that it was a little operatic for the real world, and could be damaging to the Welshman himself.

After thanking Miller for his hospitality and invention, he ended by riding off with the Burkes. That night they stayed at a hut in the forest about twenty miles out, and all through the next day, which was wet and blowing a gale, they struggled on into Launceston. There, they went to the house of an Irish supporter at which Mitchel was shaven clean, as Irish clerics always were, and rigged out as a Catholic priest should be. He said goodbye to the two Burkes, and they told him that though they could never tire of his company, they hoped it was the last they saw of him.

The dismal message then came that the captain had lost his nerve and said he could not take Mitchel on board at Launceston, or anywhere else on the river on the way to the sea. There was too much searching going on. What Mitchel must do, said the captain, was to go downriver in an open boat that night, beyond Georgetown near the mouth of the river, to be picked up about three o'clock the next afternoon.

That proved to be an appalling night, though, to take to the river in a vessel without cover. To begin with, John was thoroughly tired, having ridden through torrents of rain and across rivers and through the marshes. In any case, at an agreed place near the Launceston pier, two boatmen were waiting for him when he got to the riverside.

Two Irish gentlemen, not rowers, who had been looking after him since he arrived in town earlier that day, insisted they were willing to go downriver with him, despite the foul night. Mitchel was so exhausted that, as soon as the party boarded the watermen's skiff, he fell into the bottom of it and went to sleep. It was a long pull up the right bank of the river to where it began to open up to the sea, and as it did they put into a house in the dark and hammered on the door.

A man named Barrett appeared, who seemed wide awake and ready to take Mitchel on. Mitchel knew that Barrett and his brother had transported Meagher out into Bass Strait to meet the whaler that got him to America, and Barrett seemed delighted to be of service in this case. 'A strike against old Denison,' he told Mitchel.

The Barretts had the sort of boat called a gig, and they used it for coastal work. Barrett would need to collect his four oarsmen to take the group out at first light. Meanwhile, he fed them all breakfast. He would command the boat himself, he said, to make sure Mitchel got away.

The oarsmen arrived and in dim dawn radiance they were all soon on their way down the last of the estuary, where the river was sometimes half a mile and sometimes three miles wide, amidst wooded hills. Opposite Georgetown, Barrett dropped Mitchel – now in his clerical rig – and one of his gentlemen in the woods on the west bank of the river. He intended that the rest of the party, including Barrett himself, would go into Georgetown to spread false reports about what errand he was on.

But almost before Barrett pushed off, leaving the two behind, Mitchel could see the black funnel of the *Wave* to the south, as close as three miles away. Barrett would need to be fast back to the pick-up further down the river still.

The usual practice of the authorities would be to delay the steamer about an hour at Georgetown as it underwent a final search, so Mitchel and his friend comforted themselves that Barrett would be back in time to fetch Mitchel to it. His guide and he were in the meantime to slog down the riverbank, he in his wet priest's garb, past the point a few miles on where the search and clearing of the vessel was usually done.

Mitchel and his Irishman were doing their part, slogging up the estuary to the final meeting with Barrett. But after the police boat came promptly out of Georgetown to inspect the steamer, the police, quickly satisfied, sent her on her way. Barrett's gig had not even left Georgetown, three miles south and on the far side of the river, yet on its return to collect Mitchel, he and his friend waited half an hour for the gig to come across, and the steamer began to dawdle down the river until they saw her stop by the lighthouse at the very heads at least another three miles further on. Barrett's boat, meantime, was finally coming for Mitchel, and he and the Irishman jumped in as it kissed the rendezvous point and put off again immediately, all eyes on the steamer.

They were too far off, though, to be visible from the *Wave*. The captain had obviously decided they hadn't been able to reach his nominated place, so the steamer began to move off as they looked on and yelled their protests into the wind. Mitchel's ship of rescue swept around the lighthouse on her way north to Melbourne.

There were reasons why everything had gone wrong – as there always were. The clearing officer, whose job was to confirm the vessel contained no unlawful passengers or contraband, had come down on the ship from Launceston and had finished his work by the time he got to Georgetown.

The job of the police boat then had been merely to remove him from the steamer. After the clearing officer was in the launch, there was no credible reason for the captain of the *Wave* to linger.

Mitchel was not involved in the oar work getting up the river again, but with all the oarsmen recovering from liquor imbibed overnight and perhaps even by Barrett in his Georgetown stop, it was demanding work against the tide as the rains sheeted down. Twice they came up on sand-banks before they reached Barrett's house in the small hours, dropped him off and then set out for Launceston.

John swore in geographic dudgeon that he would not trust the north of the island anymore, but would instead go to Hobart and cast himself on the mercy of some captain there. As they rowed up river again, the night estuary grew madder and shrieked with wind, and all they could see was the phosphorescence of waves. They pulled ashore into an inlet and lay on soaked earth amongst the trees, waiting for the tide to turn.

They got back in the boat at six and Barrett dropped the Irishmen and Mitchel about a mile from town. After Mitchel gave all parties, not least the oarsmen, much hollow thanks, he and his friends walked through the woods and into the streets to the house of the Launceston parish priest, Father Tom Butler, friend of Nicaragua and Terence Bellew MacManus now in San Francisco. On the way they walked right through the town, such was their sleep-starved daring. Mitchel dressed as a Catholic curate, with his two good lay attendants, came to St Joseph's, church of Father Butler.

———

Butler was nervous for him, and with regret for the weather hid him in the bell tower that day. For the priest was concerned that it would take just a single oarsman from Barrett's crew to start telling people of the night attempt to connect with the steamer, and in gossipy towns police might be informed and search the priest's residence. Altogether, the priest's suggestion that Mitchel catch the coach to Hobart still dressed as a clergyman – this time one named Father Blake – seemed the best idea. The change of name would operate in case police took the trouble to come searching for Father McNamara. Father Butler decided Mitchel was best concealed in the enclosed belfry of the Church of St Joseph until the coach was departing that night to take him on board for the one-hundred-and-twenty-mile journey. Given his lack of sleep, John began to believe that he would be an object eternally bouncing between north and south of the prison island.

One of his Irish supporters, a Mr Connellan, was already on the stage and beaming at him from the carriage window as he approached it that night in company with Butler. They shook hands. But then, on boarding, Mitchel had not expected that a lawyer friendly to the Governor, one Edward MacDowell, a man who filled the task of Colonial Attorney-General, would also be aboard. The man did not, however, seem to recognise Mitchel as he sought a corner seat. He did, though, try to engage him in conversation about the Catholic bishop of Hobart and some recent dispute with Father Therry over church lands, a subject on which Mitchel tried to say something – he had read a little in the papers, and it was a quarrel about real estate – but altogether to be shy and not to have a decided opinion either way.

Late in the night, they passed the point on the mail road that was closest to Bothwell. He felt a considerable guilt because beyond the immediate hills lay his family, sleeping through uncertain dreams at Nant Cottage.

Near dawn the coach reached Green Ponds, less than thirty miles from Hobart. Stretching himself before the inn Mr MacDowell greeted some early-rising constables who were there, perhaps to look at the coach and see that miscreant Mitchel was not on it. Mitchel had one hand on the door away from the inn and the other on the pistol in the pocket of his black coat. He moved his lips as if in silent prayer. But nothing adverse happened and the coach departed into a brightening morning.

There were police at Bridgewater too and Mitchel knew there would be more still at the Ship Inn terminus in Hobart, so he decided to leave the coach and take a room at the Bridgewater hotel. As Mitchel departed, his Irish companion, Connellan, in the other corner of the coach leaned over and told him, 'It was an honour to travel with you, Father Blake.' At which Mr MacDowell idly said to the Irishman, 'Your reverend friend doesn't carry any luggage, Mr Connellan.'

After exhausted and yet edgy sleep, Mitchel spent the day that then broke walking feverishly along the Derwent and through the bush, dressed as a priest still and still in character, as actors say, but wishing the sun to set. He was ready outside the inn when the night coach arrived next morning. Once onboard, and six miles short of Hobart Town, he saw Dr Kevin O'Doherty climb into the coach – as if simply to support his disguised Irish friend. Mitchel felt an immediate fever of gratitude for him. O'Doherty sat directly opposite him, without giving a sign of knowing the clean-shaven cleric.

Mitchel knew that Mr Connellan, from the earlier coach, had a house in Hobart Town. Father Butler had given him the address. So now Mitchel had the coachmen pull up at the right corner, and then walked down Collins Street to Connellan's address. When he knocked on the door, it was not Connellan but Nicaragua who answered. And Mitchel saw that he too did not recognise him. So John Mitchel asked Nicaragua Smyth was Mr Connellan in, and was told he was out on business. In fact, he had gone to Bridgewater to fetch Mitchel.

'And how are my wife and children?' asked John, advancing into the hallway. That was how Mitchel introduced himself to Nicaragua, but Smyth still took a great deal of persuasion. Later, when Mitchel identified himself to Nicaragua, the latter told him he had decided Mitchel had been somehow intercepted by the police and that his visitor was a disguised detective come to arrest him. But when John stepped into the middle of the lighted hall and took off his big clerical hat and began laughing, Nicaragua saw it was the authentic Mitchel who had arrived.

This was the first time the two had seen each other since they'd split up after the initial escape from Bothwell. And it became apparent that Nicaragua had been travelling nearly as much as Mitchel had. He told John that in the last three days he had called in at Nant Cottage and everyone in town was still dining out on, and revisiting, the story of poor Mr Davis. There was a song people were singing in the pubs about *Donald*, the horse which once belonged to Davis, and many believed that Mitchel had bought not just the horse, but the magistrate as well. By happy chance, Nicaragua had been treated by the authorities as if he were a mere spectator in the events in Bothwell.

When Connellan returned to his home, he was of the opinion that Mitchel could not safely stay at the house overnight, so Nicaragua and Mitchel took different routes through town to get to the door of McNamara's Hobart shipping agent. In consultation with that gentleman, the plan was finalised – Mitchel would go on the regular passenger brig, the *Emma*, due to leave within a week. Nicaragua would go to Nant Cottage the next day to help Jenny with the sale of stock and other matters, with the idea that they could all sail by the same vessel and, as free settlers, be cleared by the authorities. Mitchel would then join the *Emma* some miles down the river as contraband, and be incognito even to his own children.

22

Jenny, Winter 1853

The convict and the question of his or her status, and the general hatred of the institution of transportation, lay very lightly on the landscape of Bothwell. 'Convict' here meant Jenny's talkative Irish cook and Mrs Russell's seamstress, and also John Mitchel, who was, after all, to Jenny's mind – as well as to the minds of many Irish throughout the world – a genius and an ornament to any system of half-civilised life.

It was a very restless time now at Nant Cottage. John Martin, sage old helper, and convict, made dozens of trips between Bothwell and the farm, shopping for the oddments Jenny would need for a journey that must be coming. Sea trunks were half-packed: one for Jenny, one for the boys, another for the girls. Everyone in the family had been selecting the most precious mementos, but they did not even know if these items might need to be unpacked again, or at the end of the day, if – unthinkably – Jenny's John was retaken, they would be forced to reverse plans and would remain Van Diemen's Landers.

Willy, who was barely nine, had been going around the countryside with a notebook, sketching what he could not take a sample of, such as the wombat and the kangaroo and the little hissing carnivore named the Tasmanian devil, and then collecting samples of the botanical species – for example, leaves of the Antarctic beech. In the whole of the huge continent of Australia, he told his mother, it was the only species of its kind that shed its leaves and became at least partially bare in winter. The pencil pine and the white native iris were amongst his favourites. His brothers, though teasing him of course about his interests, if going on a ride to pass the time (for attempts at schooling ended when their father passed in his parole), would bring him samples. Henty as well, taking young Minnie on rambles around the farm, brought items home – all of which he earnestly studied and for which he thanked her profusely. His world was in his book of notes and samples, and Jenny realised they must not leave home for the migration without making sure he had it. Better to forget his under-drawers. That book was his moveable habitation.

The house was full of women every day – Miss Jane Reid of Ratho, Mrs Russell, Mrs Head – all accompanied by a useful servant, while they themselves were making sure that every aspect of the farm was in such order that Jenny could simply walk out of it. Jenny proudly kept her repute as a good housekeeper, even when always within an hour's notice of departure. Not all the sheep had been sold yet and barely a third of the stockfeed; stockfeed not being very scarce there.

Her heart leapt to see Nicaragua turn up wearing his long theatrical cape. She did not explain his appearance to the ladies except to say the Mitchels knew him in Ireland, and that after that he went to *The Sun* in New York. Jenny had thought it would be a good idea if he came and wrote about the island to which Smith O'Brien – and indeed John – had been consigned, since there was very little knowledge of Van Diemen's Land in the United States.

The women became more subdued when Nicaragua entered. They wanted to study him. He looked very much like a creature of a different New World from this one. Jenny whispered, though, that he was in love with a Westbury woman – severely smitten, like a man in a theatrical cape should be. All Nicaragua told Jenny was that she would be leaving soon, in a matter of days, for Hobart, as the first step on the migration. He also told her that he had found a young woman in Hobart – whose parents were both dead – who was looking for a means to get to San Francisco, where her brother was located. She was, he said, a sturdy Welsh girl.

Jenny asked Nicaragua was she good at sea, in case she herself wasn't, and he said that in his interview with her he had stated that as the first issue, and she claimed that after leaving England she had been once very ill and never since.

When Nicaragua left after appropriately helping Jenny dispose of her furniture, it seemed now that Jenny and her children might need to be gone almost without warning and the farm, previously loud with children, suddenly empty. Jane Reid seemed to become paler and paler, and her eyes hungrier and hungrier, since it was assumed by the press and the police that John, on the loose, had America in mind.

'I would never have met you,' said Jane, 'if it had not been for the sentence of an Irish court. The work of the Crown. The same Crown my husband served, and consid-ered himself a servant of, good fellow that he was. It is all so strange. Now it seems from what I have seen of your impressive husband, Jenny, that he is a brilliant fellow, but certainly not a servant of the Crown.'

'I am afraid he is not, and will never bow to it. The Famine, you see . . . for one thing.'

'Even here it is a confusing world. I wanted to say, though, you should tell your husband that there is often not as much reward in the service of the Crown as in rebellion.'

'I think he always knew that Downing Street's demands of their subject were always extreme. I think he feels the weight of things in his own body. Like a spur in his blood. Yet there is that in him that wants to sit and talk and be surrounded by his children too. I could tell he would not be easy in soul. And deliberately chose him.'

'When you met him?'

'Even then. Mind you, I did not know precisely it would take me to Van Diemen's Land. But how pleased I am it did.'

And here her friend Jane's huge bleak eyes filled with tears. Jenny reached out to her and said, 'I understand.'

'No,' said Jane, as if sturdily refusing easy comfort, 'I knew nothing of my husband, Lieutenant Williams. As a wife I was learning, and as a mother. In the Park Street Cemetery in Calcutta, there are all the young officers and mothers and their babies – including my angels, and my officer . . . sometimes feel I am there myself. I did not know that serving the Crown can be a death sentence too, just as thwarting it can be.'

'My poor girl,' Jenny told her and took her hand. But even then, Jenny thought impatiently, 'Will we be gone by the end of the week?' Meanwhile Jane's grief and disappointment and her new-stated theorem about loss worked away in her, particularly now, when it seemed she was about to lose Jenny.

But now Jenny had foreshadowed her going, it was essential that she should promptly go for Jane Reid's sake, because Jane was growing melancholy at the sight of her. But of course, if John were captured in the next few days, they would all be back here again, though then they could be friends for a long time yet.

23

Mitchel's Escape, 1853

Mitchel slept and awoke refreshed in a vacant cottage down the river a little at Bonnet Hill, where the shipping agent had placed him for safety. Nicaragua was in Hobart to greet Jenny and the children as they arrived, driven down to the port by the Russells' convict coachman, and Jenny was to catch the *Emma* with the children that evening. He felt a fever to see Jenny. Just to see her. That was to be enough for now. Anything beyond that was a reckless hope.

Late in the afternoon Mitchel heard a cry in the garden and, dressed ready for escape in his canonicals, went outside to look. He saw nothing in the garden, but a horse was hitched just beyond the gate. The shipping agent's horse, Mitchel presumed. But where was the man himself? Mitchel walked to the corner of the house and was gazing towards the bush beyond the garden when he felt a prod in his back.

'Ah, my dear Mr Mitchel,' said a familiar voice. 'Don't turn, I have you. Isn't that hilarity itself? I have you and I hold a pistol at your spine.'

'I'm not sure that I know . . .'

'You don't recognise the voice from our previous discussions, Mr Mitchel, sir?'

'You'll have to forgive me,' said Mitchel.

He felt the pistol, if that's what was truly there, withdrawn from his back.

'I don't take it personal, Mr Mitchel. You can turn about now, but be careful.'

He did that and standing in front of him with meritorious stripes on his policeman's uniform was Garrett from Bermuda. Mitchel was so astonished by the absurdity of this that he couldn't speak.

'All explained now,' he said, his pistol still on Mitchel. 'What odds, Mr Mitchel! What damned odds!'

'How are you, Mr Garrett?' Mitchel managed to ask.

'Oh Lord, I think it'll be Police Magistrate Garrett now! It'll be Superintendent Garrett! It'll be Gord Almighty Garrett of Hobart after this! What do you reckon?'

Mitchel could not see the humorous side of this. He could only see the cruel and ridiculous side.

'You wouldn't read about this in the best romances!' Garrett continued to rejoice.

'My associates are on their way from Hobart,' Mitchel told him uncertainly. 'You won't get past them.'

'Your average peeler wouldn't. But Senior Constable Garrett would! I would expect you to acknowledge, Mr Mitchel, that I am a man of uncommon fibre.'

'Since you have caught me, and the rest of your brethren haven't, I must indeed agree to that statement, Mr Garrett.'

'Within the limits of my duty then, is there anything I can do for you, Mr Mitchel?'

'If you have any mercy, you could shoot me now. I mean it, Garrett. His Excellency Governor Denison would be delighted with you too if you do, and cover you with civic honours.'

'I have a better proposition,' said Garrett seriously, no longer celebrating the oddity of what had happened. 'Could we go inside?'

Mitchel led him into the cottage and they sat at the kitchen table with Van Diemen's Land winter sunlight in a stripe across it.

'I am serious in my request about the shooting, Garrett,' Mitchel assured him as they sat.

'Mr Mitchel,' said Garrett, his pistol still playing in Mitchel's direction, 'doesn't it strike you that as inconvenient as it is for you to be captured by me, it is equally inconvenient for me. I have not been home for a day and a half, but watching your movements and deciding on my duty. I've been up at all hours, observing the Yankee Smyth too and making him jumpy.

'Now you wish me to shoot you, as if murder were easy to me. But I have never before done it! I have never shot a weapon into living flesh. So what I am proposing is that incompetent as I am in what you ask for, I'll wait here, evade being shot by whoever collects you here, and that I see you to your ship along with your friends, as if I'd been taken hostage. That is the only fruitful idea I have. I shall be praised for pursuing the desires of Governor Denison to the point of being taken hostage by the Irish ruffians! What do you think of that idea?'

'I think you are tormenting me,' Mitchel said.

'No,' said Garrett. 'And now I put my pistol in its holster and expect you not to take advantage of me.'

And he did it, knowing it was a serious step to take, and with not nearly as much irony in his eye.

'Are we cosy then?' he asked.

Mitchel could not dare hope in what he proposed, but said, 'We are certainly cosy at this end of things. But I cannot see that you seriously intend, Garrett . . .'

He raised his hands to stop Mitchel. 'You should hope, my good fellow. I was just joshing with you before. I love scenes like that, and cannot give them up even for kindness. But the joke is done with now and kindness is set in. And wisdom has too. I have made my proposal. I insist on seeing you off, Mr Mitchel. Seeing you off as a hostage. That is nearly as meritorious as actually stopping you!'

'Then,' said Mitchel, 'you should remove your blue jacket, since the shipping agent might shoot if he sees blue through the window.'

Underneath the blue jacket, Garrett wore a homely jerkin of knitted wool. It reminded Mitchel of domesticity and he asked, 'Has your wife joined you here in Van Diemen's Land?'

'Not yet,' he said, 'for the home authorities watch her too severely.'

'You must be lonely,' Mitchel said to him.

'But for Miss Susanna Harris, my convict companion, I would be. God had it to a T when he said it is not good for man to be alone. My wife has sent me, however, some remittances which are highly welcome, Mr Mitchel. I have invested in some land near New Norfolk and it is run by a competent manager. One day, methinks, I might try

California. Or stay here to be jovially torn to pieces by the two women.'

———

They heard the shipping agent ride up, and Mitchel went and explained things to him, as improbable as they were. The shipping agent came into the house and in no time was talking amiably, but still with a little suspicion, to Garrett.

When it was time to go, the same agent led them to a cutter dragged above the tide line on a beach nearby the cottage, and they all three fraternally pushed it afloat. Four oarsmen appeared at that moment from the hinterland to help. Garrett had left his blue jacket with his horse and took to the water as a mere citizen volunteer. Mitchel was dressed in his Catholic canonicals still. And in the last light of dusk, they pulled out on the large still river, poised between tides.

Soon Mitchel could see the ship bearing down. There was still some sharp dusk light as they approached it. Garrett had little to say at this stage. It was as if he had talked himself out and exhausted his whimsy as well.

The cutter pulled in under the ship's stern and neared the ladder in place for Mitchel. There were many faces at the railing of the poop deck.

'One of those your wife, Mr Mitchel?' asked Garrett above the sound of rowlocks and the creaking of ships.

Mitchel could actually see Jenny's face at the railing above the poop deck, frowning in her way, Nicaragua by her, and Johnny beside him, a cornstalk, as they called young colonial men, nearly as tall as Jenny. He could hear James's adolescent basso conversing with some passenger and the other children talking to each other in the chirping voices of childhood as their cutter bobbed against the boarding stairs. Mitchel could also hear a low register rumble from Nicaragua at Jenny's side.

'The dark-haired woman with the blue hat,' Mitchel told Garrett. 'Beside the tall fellow in the cape.'

'Oh,' said Garrett. 'She is a beautiful woman. You would have missed her in Bermuda!'

Jenny's eyes engaged Mitchel's. That she knew, and the three eldest knew, who this late-coming priest was, and must keep it secret, seemed a harsh restriction. The little ones did not know it was him, and thus were more carefree, since the man Mitchel was in that priest's hat and long coat and collar was much changed from the father they had known. And now he was about to rise to the deck, it was all better than begging Garrett to shoot him!

Mitchel shook hands with Garrett then, and then with the shipping agent, waved thanks to the oarsmen and ascended the stairs carefully, hobbled a little by the length of his coat. On deck the skipper, broad-bearded Captain Brown, another colonial Denison-hater, told him curtly that he was almost too late and that he had nearly despaired of taking him on board. Then he brought him down to the saloon cabin and introduced him to the passengers as Father Wright. Many of the good Protestant saloon passengers had no desire to meet a Roman priest.

The two elder Mitchel boys laid their weighty eyes on him. Jenny paled but not so markedly that anyone but John would notice. Nicaragua bade him the sort of greeting you would expect of an Irishman addressing a cleric. Mitchel wanted to rush across the room and embrace the family, and endured not doing so and was rewarded for the sacrifice almost at once when a great westerly seemed to arrive, audibly filling the sails. Now it would scuttle them away south-east until they tacked north for Sydney.

Mitchel was taken to his saloon cabin where Father Wright's modest possessions – the valise, an overcoat – had been put. He had the steward bring his evening meal to his cabin, too, which was agreeably ample in size. He knew he would not have an easy night – he so desired to be with Jenny to console her if she fell ill. But to his surprise he slept well, after telling himself and not quite believing he had actually got away, or that Nicaragua after all had got him away. And that Garrett could have stopped the operation entirely except it suited his humour not to.

From the portholes, Mitchel next dawn saw the receding spine of Maria Island where Smith O'Brien had been kept a time. In Van Diemen's Land with its forests and bright rivers, and with the penal system that oppressed souls and ravaged bodies! And from which he had emerged whole, without bearing its scars.

He went on deck, but Willy began trailing him with some indefinable suspicion, until his lovely mother and Nicaragua called him back. The Welsh girl with Jenny looked plump and nobody's fool, he was pleased to see, because as they headed into the strait they must cross before they reached the Australian mainland, there was an energetic swell beginning to run with foam on the crests of the waves, and Mitchel feared that Jenny would suffer soon enough from her sea malady.

In his cabin, he needed to remind himself: 'You have escaped.' Just an interlude in Sydney and then the absconding of John Mitchel would be complete. It could, however, still be cancelled if he were unfortunate in Sydney, which, whatever the colonists might claim, was still a transportation colony in the minds and laws of Westminster, even if the colonists had stood up and stopped it some years past, and the last convicts in the old sense of the word.

———

At a Confederate bivouac of the First Virginia Regiment on the Rappahannock River in ten years' time, Mitchel's son Private Willy Mitchel would tell his friend Lieutenant John Dooley that on the *Emma* he had asked Nicaragua if his father was on board. Nicaragua swept the child off his feet and forced his upper body through a port in the cabin. This in the Roaring Forties with the most strenuous waters of the world running beneath him, and him half-blinded by wind.

'Do you want to drown?' yelled Nicaragua from behind him.

Of course, Willy said no. He knew that he couldn't die in this universal ocean. If he died it must be for Ireland.

'Then don't ever mention your father's name on this ship.'

Willy promised frantically, and on that promise Nicaragua Smyth spared Willy Mitchel's life, dragging his slight body back into the habitable ship, and thus reserving it for a later immolation.

———

When the ship reached Sydney, a travelling band from Van Diemen's Land played as they entered and found moorage along the deep reaches of Sydney's harbour. Mitchel still did not reveal himself to the family. It was a bright morning, all the headlands and beaches glittering like freedom, but not yet the full accomplished reality.

On the morning of their arrival, Captain Brown took the customs officers and police to his cabin and fed them brandy, which reduced their level of punctiliousness about landing passengers. Before leaving the ship, Mitchel nodded surreptitiously to Nicaragua Smyth, and to the handsome Mrs Mitchel, to whom he had only briefly been introduced aboard.

The officials were still there in Captain Brown's cabin, in amiable and lengthy conversation, when the captain himself sneaked away to see Mitchel aboard his personal boat. Mitchel was taken ashore across a stretch of bright water, still in the persona of Father Wright. An Irishman met Mitchel and took him by carriage to the ship owner James McNamara's house in Elizabeth Bay, a wooded cove of blue water not far at all from the city and doing its best to imitate a wing of heaven.

He was kindly received by young Mr McNamara, who explained that his father was in Melbourne but that Mitchel would be safe there. John seemed doomed never to meet the mysterious McNamara, but was not surprised to find he had come there as a convict from Ireland for being involved in a peasant's attack on some landlord's property – hardly a crime in the Irish calendar of culpabilities.

James McNamara immediately went to his father's shipping office to see what was the earliest vessel that could deliver Mitchel across the Pacific. He and Nicaragua had decided that Mitchel should be transmuted into one Father Warren, in case someone happened to come looking for that Father Wright who was on the ship from Van Diemen's Land.

It was mid-winter in Sydney, but the weather was bright. The centre of the town seemed busy. Gold had been discovered to the west in New South Wales and ships full of miners arrived each day – even Californians seeking a fresher field. McNamara took Mitchel out to the South Head of the Harbour, where they saw the extent of that great embayment and looked across to North Head and to the Pacific beyond, which this Father Warren hoped to transit very soon. McNamara's inquiries had told him there was a ship named the *Orkney Lass* due to sail in three or four days for Hawaii by way of Tahiti. In Tahiti he could change to a vessel going to San Francisco. Nicaragua and his party of Mitchels did not have to leave quite as urgently.

Jenny went to see Mitchel next day at McNamara's. In meeting up again so joyfully with his wife, all Mitchel's doubts were diffused, as were all the mental confusion and agitation of his escape. She herself occasionally showed him a tautness. She could not avoid the fear of something going wrong, even here. After the normal intimacies, she told him how supportive of his escape the locals had been, and how helpful all the folk had been in aiding her disposal of horses and sheep and general tack. The furniture was probably overvalued, she said, by the English gentleman who'd insisted on buying it. The horse, Tricolour, was sold to Connellan of Hobart, who'd come up from his house in Collins Street to buy it, in between catching coaches.

'What have you told the children?' John wanted to know.

'That you are somewhere in the Pacific Ocean and free. Willy asked, "Is he in the cannibal islands?"'

Mrs Mitchel and the children stayed in a place named Woolloomooloo, thus one bay around from Sydney Cove itself. They were well set up with two rooms and the use of a parlour. Nicaragua himself was staying in an inn in the town.

The plans that were made for them were that Father Warren would depart in the *Orkney Lass* for Honolulu – by way of Tahiti – and an American ship, the *Julia Ann*, was due to come up from Melbourne and would take his family across the Pacific. But Mr McNamara could not give any very exact times, since half the crew of the *Julia Ann* had abandoned the ship in Melbourne to go to the goldfields, and the police had managed to bring only some of them back from there thus far. But the *Julia Ann* and the *Orkney Lass* then arrived promptly, within a day of each other in the great bright harbour, and John looked through the telescope on McNamara's verandah.

Dressed as a civilian – he had decided to travel now as a layman – Mitchel was taken by coach to a boat waiting in Sydney Cove and so was rowed out to *Orkney Lass*. Presenting himself to the officer of the deck, he requested he might inspect the ship in light of coming travel and so went on board, and conversed in the saloon with a few passengers from Melbourne. They were all lively types who would certainly have been inhibited by the presence of a priest.

He kept to McNamara's two more days and then boarded *Orkney Lass* in a business suit provided by McNamara. Once on board, he kept to his very adequate cabin.

The *Orkney Lass* departed that evening in early August, and there was a thorough search by water police of every possible hiding place aboard, but no-one looked at the tall gentleman in his cabin, his head in a book. The ship did not reach up the harbour and clear the great wall of sandstone at the heads of Sydney until the small hours. Out in the Pacific night, Mitchel watched the receding coastline with only lighthouses, no cities, to mark it, and knew now he was definitively away. Yet he was not disposed to make any gesture of triumph as he left the waters of the British Crown and entered the waters of the world. It was hard to appreciate the scale of what had been done.

———

As Mitchel emerged from his cabin, he found it was as lively a company on board as he had expected, the first ship in five years in which he was not a convict. They were carrying four loud-voiced and amiable histrionic actresses to the theatre of Honolulu. There was an American circus rider as well, a cowboy from Texas. The actresses told their fellow guests they intended to give a concert in Papeete, the main port of Tahiti, and were assured that the French merchants and government officials would give them a good house. A French lady of Sydney and her little girl were on their way to visit relatives in the islands. An English merchant, young but in bad health, meant to get to San Francisco, which, according to repute, would finish what was left of the poor fellow's health. There were a number of French merchants too, who had profited by selling their merchandise on the goldfields and buying new merchandise for sale in Papeete. And so on. And as if to confirm Mitchel's escape to himself, they were by dawn on the second morning so well into the broad Pacific that they would barely see land all the way to Tahiti.

Mitchel recreated himself on board. He danced with the English singers, celebrating the lively distance they represented from the dismal policies of Downing Street. There was a young man from St Malo in Brittany aboard and he had a cargo on this ship that he had bought onshore in Sydney. Calico, silk, satin, heavy shoes, rum, gin and claret. All of this he'd acquired duty-free from bond stores, and intended to impose, for a price, on the natives of Papeete.

John got to know a number of passengers and exchanged small talk with them, as they glided past far-off coral islands. Weeks were consumed in remaking him into a very sociable Irishman with no penal connections, going to work as some sort of broker in San Francisco.

The barbarous, exotic, decisive peaks of Tahiti came up sharply out of the sea, and those of Morea as well. From the ship, he could see the palm trees of the lowlands and in the foothills a great dome, which proved to be a theatre built by a former French governor who was an adorer of all things thespian. A pilot boarded and took the ship in through the reef, and the contrast between the lowlands and the great wild ravines running down from the mountains was very pleasing.

The women of Papeete proved statuesque, with flowers in their smooth dark hair. Coconut and breadfruit trees shaded the streets, where there were a number of French restaurants. Sadly, the concert of the four women in the dome was a failure, since many of the dignitaries of the island expected complimentary tickets and would not attend on any other terms. Mitchel attended, and observed that most of the audience were the colourful native women, whose swathes of loose fabric reminded him somewhat of Speranza. And amongst these women, outside the theatre before the performance, were Queen Pomare and her children. Mitchel's friend from St Malo took him to her and introduced him, and when the Frenchman invited her into the concert, she briefly told him, 'No dress!', even though she seemed to be wearing a perfectly fine one.

The following day, he went swimming with the captain of the frigate, the American circus rider and the St Malo merchant in the Fowtowa River, overarched by guava, lime, breadfruit and palm trees. He! The free felon!

As he disported himself like a commercial traveller, Mitchel wondered: where were Jenny and the children and Mr Smyth? With the St Malo trader, he went to a soirée that evening at the Queen's house, where the delightful band of the frigate played polkas and *schottisches* and the flower-crowned Tahitian women danced with French officers on the lawn. The St Malo man had somehow worked out, perhaps by worldly instinct, that Mitchel might very well be on the run from Australia, and he made jokes about an abandoned wife, a failed business or a prison. But with winks and secretive intonations he made a great play of assuring Mitchel he would be keeping the secret, and Mitchel hoped he could manage it, even though he was now in a French jurisdiction.

Late in the night, they met Queen Pomare's present but fourth husband, the former King of Bola-Bola, a large Polynesian man of great jollity and vast alcoholic tastes. But what weighed most on Mitchel in quiet hours was that nearly two weeks had already passed here before the ship's cargo was discharged, and before the man from St Malo was free to go ashore to his share of it.

Then, on the morning the *Orkney Lass* was to depart for San Francisco, an American-flagged vessel appeared outside the reefs, and a Frenchman nearby to Mitchel guessed it was the *Julia Ann*. Through a telescope he saw that she was lying off and did not seem motivated to try the passage in through the coral to the port. The Frenchman said it must be that she had no passengers or cargo for Papeete.

Soon, however, the boat put off from her side and came into the opening of the reefs. Could it be carrying antipodean officials? Mitchel wondered with an unthinking pulse of fear. But then he saw, sitting in the bows, James, his second son, his tanned face wearing the handsome frown his mother had as a schoolgirl. And Nicaragua beside him. The *Julia Ann* had, it seemed, in this vastest of oceans, called in to collect him! He supposed by now the news of his escape from Van Diemen's Land was everywhere, except perhaps in outposts like Tahiti.

A Yankee captain, who was both generous of soul and attracted to notoriety – for which Mitchel had heard Americans had a greater weakness than any other race – had indeed steered the *Julia Ann* in to port at Papeete for his benefit. Captain Davis of Newport, Rhode Island, happened to be the commander and a sturdy nonconformist like the Mitchels themselves. By that evening, then, John was able to mount the deck of the American ship and take off his hat below the Stars and Stripes. Here now at last he was even more definitively John Mitchel and could drop his pretence of being a future San Francisco broker.

The owner, a Mr Pond of New York, was on board and invited the Mitchels to dinner. The passengers and crew were also heavily American. And beyond Mr Pond and ready for his embrace, the embrace of a free man, stood Jenny and the children – and Nicaragua, the engineer of escape. As Mitchel accepted the cheers of passengers, and the crying out of his name – under which he had not been free to travel since he withdrew his parole in Bothwell – the British world dropped away from them and that day in the brilliant Pacific, he breathed in a new dispensation.

When Mitchel caressed his elder sons and Henty, he

thanked them earnestly for their part in rescuing him. He told them, 'Rescue would mean nothing if I were not to see you at the end of it.' Rixy tossed her infant head. She had Mitchel's mother's suspicion of facile emotion. They waited out his speech with their mother's eyes shining from beneath their foreheads at him, the same young eyes he first met in Jenny when wandering with aimless fervour around the hills of Down.

After a few rough days that unsettled Jenny, the reach to California was three weeks of carefree voyaging, a holiday in the truest sense, before they entered the Golden Gate. People speak of bustling ports. This one seemed deranged!

24

Dancing Liberty's Dance

Nicaragua and Mitchel went ashore first to search for the escaped MacManus, but ultimately learned he was fifty miles out of the town at a place named San Jose, where he had taken up a ranch. As they went round the streets inquiring for him, they were surrounded by citizens, Yankees and Irish, who had read of Mitchel's escape and heard from people on the *Orkney Lass* that he was arrived. Some of them called out particular details of it so that Mitchel could give them a conspiring, confirming nod and wink. 'Got away dressed as a priest!' they might call. Or, 'Going to see Meagher in New York, are we?' The story had been in the papers, with speculation about Mitchel's possible and ultimate return to Ireland.

Two city officials found them. They turned up in a carriage and offered it to Mitchel and Nicaragua for their own use. It took them to the Portsmouth Plaza. There was an extraordinary amalgamation of palaces and structures mostly made of lath and painted canvas. There were palazzos of painted canvas, in fact, as if they were not sure whether their Golden City was a habitation or a theatrical set for a play.

There had been many fires in the town, which was made of wood (and canvas), given the risk of earthquakes. Accordingly, the town burned regularly, so that there were always the blackened absence of a previous house in the city's streets. And gambling was everywhere. It had only been an American city for a few years, and before that a Spanish mission, but the gold had rushed it into being, and it felt halfway between an encampment and Athens.

They all stayed three weeks there in the main plaza, as they called it from the Spanish, and Jenny and the children loved it, as Mitchel himself did with his unfamiliar guarantee of freedom, of which he had to keep reminding himself. Interviewed by the San Francisco *Public Balance* and the *Alta News*, he told them that Ireland would next be able to rise when England had difficulty with an enemy in Europe or the Atlantic. 'Are you saying you would like America to go to war with Britain?' he was asked.

'Only if it suits America's interests,' he said.

The mayor had them to a public dinner, at which he pledged his readiness to go back to Ireland when such an occasion arose, and the Irish, who were numerous, indeed superabundant there, went wild with enthusiasm and cried they would go back with him.

Jenny had suffered her normal seasickness on the *Julia Ann*, but part of her recovery from any illness had always been to ride, and ride the Californians let them do. They spent a week with Terence Bellew MacManus at his ranch beneath noble mountains at San Jose, and he told them something amusing about one Captain Ellis, the captain who had been paid to rescue Smith O'Brien at Maria Island but had betrayed the escape to Denison. The Irish in San Francisco had formed a Democrat Party set of vigilantes, and they captured Ellis in a bar and took him to a large tree, where he would be tried and if necessary hanged. MacManus, still in the city then, pleaded for the defendant, arguing that the great O'Brien would rather Ellis be treated with contempt and deprived of any Irish trust, and any unloading of his ship or filling of his cargo hold.

MacManus's word had great authority, given that he had escaped so elegantly from the purgatory of Van Diemen's Land, that isle lovely for panoramas, appalling for liberty. Ellis, with the court's supreme contempt, was let go his way.

———

The people of San Francisco thought nothing of crossing Central America to get to New York. It carried no dread for them, and the ship the Mitchels and Smyth took for San Juan del Sur, the *Cortez*, was full of sanguine Californians, together with east coast Americans going home after a Californian sojourn.

They sailed down the coast of California, and the ocean was kindly to Jenny; often, the captain told them, being peaceful in the Eastern Pacific, to justify its name. They passed down the great mountainous peninsula of Lower California in Mexico and Guatemala and, further on, blue hills and tropic verdure and in the end the crescent bay of San Juan del Sur in Nicaragua.

There, they waited in the shade of white buildings around the wharf a greater part of the day for mules to be assembled for the transit to Lake Nicaragua, fifteen miles away. Atop those docile beasts, they made it by lush tracks through the pleasant coastal hills, and past cane farms cut out of the jungle and studded with banana and other trees. It was humid but the vistas were spacious, and the Nicaraguans had eradicated the bandidos, and did not seem to know that the Mitchel guardian Smyth had plans for the United States to annexe them. John carried on the saddle in front of him little Minnie, while two other gentlemen carried Henty and young Willy in the same way. Rixy rode in front of her mother like a veteran, though scarcely more than eighteen months old.

They were over the coastal hills and at the berth of the Lake Nicaragua steamer, at Virgin Bay, by dusk. The great lake stretched before them with extraordinary mountains of jungle all around, and even on Ometepe Island in the middle. They took the night to transit Lake Nicaragua, and once across from the steamer and the rest it offered, they boarded a further native-looking boat and entered the San Juan River. They journeyed until rapids caused them to disembark and walk a quarter mile to get below them and reach a very primitive hotel.

Though a little tired the children seemed to revel in all of it – the bright birds and the burros, the occasional python hanging from a tree. Before Mitchel fell asleep in this pilgrims' and voyagers' place halfway between Rivas and Greytown on the Atlantic, with the younger children billeted in John's and Jenny's room, he saw Willy make notes and sketches of the bright flowers he had gathered that day. The other boys called him 'the Professor'. He was like Mitchel's brother William, with his eye for small things.

Jenny seemed more stimulated than wearied by this, for they had left Van Diemen's Land so far behind, the Atlantic side of the world was quite close now, and all had gone well. They talked together that night. 'I've been wondering,' she confessed. '*To abolish and demolish and derange.* That was your motto in Ireland?'

John admitted it. He fancied himself as a force for demolition.

'But in the US, you won't have to be. It is your ideal republic.'

'I believe Meagher has found it ideal.'

'Do you mean to say you won't? Come, Johnny, you have lost your Downing Street for life.'

Could that be believed? Discussing this by lamplight with her, he was as yet, to Jenny's amusement, unwilling to declare himself fully at peace with America. He knew Jeffersonian America would delight him, the idyll, the prosperous farmlands for the ordinary man who need bow to no lord. But Jefferson was not president now. A handsome fellow named Franklin Pierce was admittedly a Democrat but a Northern one. Something told him that he must see first how America played out, before finally consoling poor Jenny and giving her a destination – this divine and supreme woman who married the maelstrom of John Mitchel. But he had adopted a tone that sounded like reassurance and conviction. It was what he had already seen and heard and scented of all-inventive, all-nineteenth-century booming Yankeedom which gave him pause.

The next day they were carried further down the river amidst jungles where plants had seemed to grow so close together that they had become the same green-coated vast vegetable. Alligators were everywhere on the river's beaches and the Americans shot at them with their California-bought Colt revolvers. And then the jungle ceased without a warning, and they found themselves in the wide bay of Greytown or San Juan del Norte, and thus all at once on the Atlantic. Ireland's ocean, after all.

In the port's few hotels, rooms were at a premium. Given that the New York steamer, the *Prometheus*, was not in, the Mitchels needed two rooms at least, preferably three, since Nicaragua preferred not to sleep with the older boys, and they got them at Lyon's Hotel. This was on the Mosquito Coast the British claimed and had never quite given up. But Nicaragua – the country itself, not Mitchel's rescuer – argued the British were a mere memory, and the mayor was Yankee, to prove that Nicaragua, the land, was an American phenomenon.

Prometheus came in all lit up on the next, hazy afternoon, with its many eastern American passengers all talkatively bound for California. Only a few years back, said the manager of Lyon's Hotel, it had been fired on by a British warship for not paying harbour dues.

They could not board until the next day, and so they sweltered in Lyon's and dined at a little restaurant run by a languid Frenchman of the type that never wants to see France again.

Mitchel knelt by Minnie's and Rixy's cots and sang them Gaelic lullabies in the humid night. And then rested in the ponderous air.

Next day they boarded. The newspapers on the ship were full of news about Turkey and the Tsars competing in the Crimea and Romania. England and France were said to be ready to intervene, to staunch Russia's ambition. But it seemed all too far to the east to involve or awaken Ireland.

On the Atlantic side of Central America, the anchors of *Prometheus* were raised, with the Mitchel family and

Nicaragua himself aboard. Mitchel's escape was in its last phase now, and it was fanciful for him to consider it a fragile thing anymore. Yet he still did in his edgy dreams.

He went on deck with Nicaragua that evening. Almost sullen, Nicaragua was missing Miss Regan of Westbury, who was brighter in his imagination than all the bright flora of his namesake country. And, off the coast, he reiterated his Nicaragua arguments. Argument 1: if the British, from the other end of the Atlantic, can have pretended to a claim against Nicaragua, why not the more contiguous United States? And it was the best route between oceans, and between east coast and west, and thus organically necessary to the Americans.

In an attempt to win the locals, the British distributed to the natives the cheapest and medicinally ill-advised brandy. The French did the same thing in Tahiti and then blamed Tahitian men for being drunken – having it both ways, as you can do if you own an empire. Thus, according to Nicaragua, 'I am against bad brandy, and for the next war!'

But sometimes he seemed almost to resent the fact that the Mitchels had brought him so far from his love, as if something had gone out of him the further he got from Van Diemen's Land. Their fraternity had gone a little stale since the escape was achieved and occasionally Nicaragua seemed bored by the escape party with whom he was travelling.

The ship docked in the Spanish colony of Cuba, for which the Mitchels and Nicaragua held no particular Yankee ambitions, though many other long-established Yankees did. In fact, nearly everyone on board whom Mitchel met in the saloon, especially Southerners, had an opinion that Cuba was necessarily part of the United States.

A Spanish warship hove in to meet them as the ship anchored in Havana. That night Nicaragua took the two eldest boys ashore to the opera, and the Catholic majesty of Spain had regiments drawn up before the Opera House in case of unrest and resistance to Spain. When the next day Nicaragua took Mitchel ashore, they met everywhere regular soldiers, and entered a debate with a local Yankee who said, 'If you ask the Spanish why these troops are here, they will say it is to protect Cuban people from Yankee fili-busters and raiders. And I say, if the Cubans are so proud of being Spanish, why do you need to protect them?'

That evening, on board again, the Mitchels were on deck as *Prometheus* edged away from that great imperial over-exertion to keep Cuba. The Gulf Stream swept them forward and the next stop was – at last! – their last. Once they turned to Florida it grew colder, but overcoat or not, Mitchel wanted to be on deck as they passed the eastward protuber-ance of Cape Hatteras, the point closest to Bermuda, that first station on his Via Dolorosa. But the freedom America was about to give was what he had never had on Bermuda – the freedom to take action.

The dawn following their last night aboard, Mitchel saw the heights by the Neversink River, then Sandy Hook, Staten Island and Long Island. Jenny and he bathed in the gusto of the returning New Yorkers, including Nicaragua, though he was as far away now from his love as he could be. Nicaragua saw the vast Hudson opening to them and became livelier and pointed out aspects of it to the children. Jenny and John could barely speak as they passed through the Narrows and then, abeam of Staten Island, saw the great mass of the fabled city reaching out to them. And hardly less august was Brooklyn to the starboard.

When they moored at the pier at the very base of Manhattan at Castle Gardens, the first on board were Mitchel's enthusiastic younger brother William, and Thomas Francis Meagher, whom John had last seen as a young husband at Lake Sorell. Meagher was pomaded and well-barbered and dressed at what Mitchel saw as the limit of fashion. His waistcoat shone with a silken gloss.

Immigration officers had come aboard and asked for the Mitchel family, and in the − except for them − now-vacated saloon, granted them with great ceremony and pride a permit to land. And so they landed then, and walked across a promenade bridge embraced by Willy Mitchel, who had a job as a federal official at the Washington Patent Office, and who had very likely organised the little ceremony with the immigration officers.

Mitchel saw Jenny take Meagher's hand. 'Do you have Benny with you here?' she asked.

His eyes flitted and he stood still amongst landed crates and machinery and bales of transhipped cotton. 'Benny was here. But she's now with my father in Waterford. You see, I have to go on a speaking tour.'

Jenny smiled, slowly, ruefully. 'I look forward very earnestly to meeting her again in this city, Mr Meagher,' she said.

Meagher shifted on his feet. 'Benny found life in New York very threatening in its way. After a time here, you might agree with her. She will give birth to our baby in Waterford, which is more Benny's style in towns than this one.'

He inclined his head like a man wanting a concession, and trying to look like an understanding husband.

There was a pleasure boat nearby to take Jenny, the children, Nicaragua and Mitchel, with Meagher and Mitchel's honest brother, straight across to Brooklyn. As the boat set out, bands drawn up nearby played some of Davis's songs and other Irish airs from embrasures around Lower Manhattan, and straight ahead, from cliffs on the Brooklyn side, there arose a boom of cannon, a notable cannonade all up.

'That's the Napper Tandy Artillery Regiment of the New York Militia,' Meagher told Mitchel with gusto, happier with artillery than with Jenny's questions. 'They intend to fire a twenty-one gun salute. To you, as President of our Irish Republic.'

Henty, who was beside Mitchel under the canopy and nursing a sleeping Rixy unawakened by the guns, said with piteous wonder, 'They are so happy to see us, father!' Girl though she was, she did not let events overwhelm her. But apart from Henty, the Mitchels were all creatures in a stupor. After the jerry-built San Francisco, and the tropic bays of Nicaragua, New York was a vast proposition to be presented with. What did the evicted Irish peasant with fever in his blood think of this monstrous phenomenon, Mitchel wondered, this nation unto itself? It was as if the future were making a bid for one's soul, and Mitchel was not adequately pleased with his own relations with the present to welcome that.

As the little coal-driven ferry they were in docked at the Atlantic Avenue pier at Brooklyn, a full military band in the Irish Confederate clubs uniform was stationed there playing a fast tempo 'Minstrel Boy', a raw, exuberant 'Garryowen' – the great Celtic march – and, as a tribute to Mitchel's Irish Protestant origins, 'Lillibullero'. The music from Manhattan and Brooklyn accompanied them as they walked onto the wharf, their legs still jumpy from long acquaintance with the sea.

As if anticipating Mitchel's escape, or perhaps to support her other son William in his patent dreams, their mother had taken a house a mere walk from the Brooklyn pier. She was financially secure, having inherited the Mitchels' ancestral home at Cumber Claudy in Derry, as well as some other of the Reverend Dr Mitchel's provident investments. And so maybe she had come to New York to greet John when he made the escape the world considered he would one day accomplish. But was she restless as well? Had she given her restlessness to her son? Mitchel thought so.

And as to her other son, William, an extraordinary boy whom she was energetic in protecting, with his obsessions with small devices and his own obsessively achieved design for a printing press, which might one day make him rich. She was very happy he had achieved a post as a clerk in the branch of the patent office in New York, and would travel occasionally to Washington.

There were neighbours on the pavement, and press milling by the gate and ornamental harps decorated the house, while the Irish tricolour, which Meagher had brought back from Lamartine in Paris, fluttered in orange and green and white above a little turret, keeping faith with Mrs Mitchel and the sisters, and declaring the fibre of the people within.

With a pulse of recognition John saw his mother, hands folded before her, and two of his sisters, Henrietta and Matilda, on the doorstep of that handsome Brooklyn villa in Union Street. It was Meagher, singing along with William to the music, who led them there. Meagher suggested Mitchel should inspect the band before going inside, and John did so, parading the ranks of bandsmen in the street with little Minnie in his arms. They all smiled, not least because Mitchel had Meagher at his shoulder.

Then they went inside for refreshments his mother and sisters had laid out, and all of the new arrivals felt they were citizens of Brooklyn by noon. And though the house was not palatial, his mother had a place for every child to occupy and for Jenny and himself.

In the evening as they were dining quietly, a number of their friends from Young Ireland, those who had escaped to America – including young Devin Reilly from the days of the *United Irishman* – began to arrive. Nicaragua arrived then too. He had spent the day reporting to the Irish Confederation, whose committee was rhapsodic, he said, about the escape. He sat a little beyond the company, though, as if having rescued Mitchel he almost wished to be a stranger to him.

They were all at tea, and in the distance the noise of 'Garryowen' could be heard competing with 'Boolavogue', 'The Wearing of the Green', 'The Rising of the Moon' and 'Roddy McCorley' in Celtic cacophony. Mitchel's friends smiled at each other and told him Tammany Hall and militia bands had found him out, and were descending on them.

Suddenly, in response to doorbell peals, the living room in Union Street was full of militia officers humbly begging the Mitchels, despite the night's briskness, to open the front windows and pull the sashes and greet the hundreds, if not thousands, of bandsmen from the company assembled in the street.

Meagher said, 'I hope no poor citizen is trying to get on with the business of dying with all these fellows outside.'

In the end, Mrs Mitchel did throw the front door open to receive all the representatives of various militia regiments and many civic and temperance society bands. This process of greeting militia, and waving at and greeting bands, went on so long that all the children, who began as witnesses, were found asleep on the upper landing when it ended.

So was set the pattern of Mitchel nights for quite a number of weeks to come. The Americans were not people to do things by halves. And with all the crowds of civic and military folk in Union Street, no policeman was seen or needed to be sent. The dignitaries from the city council and from Tammany Hall whom Mitchel greeted in the hallway and living room were more often than not accompanied by journalists taking down speeches. These exchanges were reproduced every morning, not only in *The Brooklyn Daily Eagle*, but in the New York *Evening Post*, *The New York Times*, and Horace Greeley's *Tribune*. Yes, even the *Tribune* listened. There was very little snide comment, even in those parts of the press that were considered Britanno-phile.

And still they came, one company of men with glittering axes – the ships' carpenters. Sundry benevolent societies, to whose speeches Mitchel was required to respond. All ridiculous – he knew it – but all tribal and delicious as well, and what he said . . . Well, what he said was that Ireland was half-dead but would rise when the opportunity came, and when that time did come, he knew the Irish in America would not be supine.

———

New York had a hard winter to greet them, with vicious frosts relieved only when it began to snow. And though it got very cold, the days were dry and, strangely, as bright as a summer's day in Bothwell. Brooklyn was lively by night, when in every living room there was someone singing – Poles and Russians, Irish, Germans, Danes, Italians, singing of the earth lost in Europe and reclaimed in America.

In this bright, crystalline winter, the Brooklyn Council held a solemn procession in Mitchel's honour and a reception in the City Hall. The mayor brought his carriage to Mitchel's door and took charge of him as they rolled through dense ranks of men, armed and uniformed, the militia and fire companies of New York. Mitchel, somewhat bewildered and puzzled by all this demonstration, wondered what recompense he might be required to repay.

While the mayor and Mitchel processed through the streets of Brooklyn, beautiful women waved handkerchiefs from their windows and threw bouquets of winter blooms into the carriage, and he picked these up, the mayor, and gave them to Mitchel. Good God, he thought, this is excessive.

Mitchel asked his friend John Dillon from Dublin later that night, 'What is the sense of all this, and what value can I give for it?'

Dillon laughed and told him, 'You don't have to give anything. They do all this because you are the gift. Because you offer them a pretext for all they love, public processions and speechifying. Just let people make capital of you. The capital they make of you is the point. Never you personally.'

And it was the same with the Irish as well, he told Mitchel. They were used to being treated there as the lowest of the low, and to see him so treated made them know that they were noble too.

And there were a great number of Irish arriving in New York – in the week the Mitchels landed, some eleven thousand other Irish arrived, which was in no way abnormal. There were even greater numbers of Germans and Italians, Danish and Swedes. And these people did not mill in the streets of New York and create mobs. Many of them were in a railway car by the evening of their arrival, bound for Michigan or Illinois or the banks of the Wabash or the steppes of Ohio. Thousands stayed, though, in the milling tenements of lower Manhattan, or uptown shanties.

At last Mitchel was considered to have shaken enough hands in Brooklyn and was thought to be ready for New York. He caught the Fulton Street ferry across with William and Devin Reilly, now working as a journalist. The steam ferryboat looked like a section of street cut off and floating, crowded with vehicles and wagons, and with at least three hundred passengers in the ladies' saloon.

They landed in New York at the foot of almighty Fulton Street. Fulton Street could take them fair across town, past the new City Hall and into Broadway. And there, all along it, was a great crush of vehicles loading and unloading every kind of merchandise. They stopped at City Hall, for the uncomfortable truth was that it was a day when he was to be welcomed by the Mayor of New York, Jacob Westerveldt, renowned ship builder from an old Dutch family, builder of fast clippers that offered a ten-day passage to San Francisco and occasionally delivered.

Many militia regiments were assembling in front of the hall, and there were bands tuning up. Robust fellows wore the rosettes of sundry parties and causes. And in the midst of it all, the Napper Tandy Artillery again gave Mitchel twenty-one cannon salvos from the direction of Battery Park. All these felicitations for escaping from Bothwell. Oh, what an honour and a chastisement that was! But yes, an embarrassment to the British proposition, and to the Downing Street consul who was said to be active in gathering intelligence in the port of New York.

The amiable mayor arrived. They were introduced, man to man, he in a fine suit but without the paraphernalia of mayordom common in Ireland. The bands again began their barely exhausted playing, as he offered Mitchel and Ireland itself congratulations on his escape and arrival in the land of the free.

When it came Mitchel's time to speak, he made the point about this event that, by its nature, it stood as a humiliation to the British authorities who had enslaved Ireland and John Mitchel. A journalist later took Mitchel aside and warned him that in honouring Ireland and Mitchel, 'These people do not mean any affront to the British government at all; they mean to pay you a passing tribute of respect; take it as it comes and best not to push it too far.'

Now from all he had observed, Mitchel thought Dillon and that Yankee journalist were correct. He felt better about all the fuss. And hence, by the complementary and friendly demonstrations, no pledge was made regarding Ireland. There was anger along the Atlantic shore of the United States when the Royal Navy highhandedly intercepted American ships on the open ocean, but never so sufficient as to cause war. Manchester was too dependent on Southern cotton for that, and the other way around, and there were millions of mechanical looms that would cease their work in Britain if a war ever came.

When, a little later, a great banquet was organised for Mitchel at the Broadway Theatre, and the pit was floored and covered with tables, and the boxes full of glimmering women, Mitchel took it for what it was – a passing tribute of respect, as the journalist had told him. And he gave New York the same. John Mitchel's tribute was that he took in and even marvelled at the city, but did not invest in all its propositions.

He discussed these matters with Jenny, of course. She still believed America would inevitably license some great Celtic Armageddon, when the Irish would return to reclaim their island. The rich rivers of rhetoric implied as much, and the air of the place did.

Mitchel told her, though, 'You must remember, Jenny, my love, that they are having sufficient business claiming America.' And, obviously, not all the states were of the one mind with each other!

After all the sentiments, they kindly took him home. But not before he knew what a grand and wondrous city New York was. And, having been brought there by Nicaragua's cunning, it would always be somehow alien to him.

Nicaragua was not at the Broadway Theatre event, though he did send apologies and it was characteristic that he did not intend to be applauded endlessly for rescuing Mitchel. He had other rescues to attend to, and a further name to make after he was done with them. Nicety – Mitchel hoped it was not embarrassment – kept him absent from many places where he would have been praised as a master plotter of escapes.

———

War between the British and the Russians had begun, over Istanbul and Ottoman holdings in Romania. There was a sacred objective in this struggle – the freedom of Christians in the Holy Land. Russia was to ensure the Orthodox rite by driving the Turks out of the East; Britain and France by making the Turks so safe they would be kind to the Holy Land Christians out of gratitude. The same holy cause from both sides!

None of them really gave a shilling or a dime for Christians in Jerusalem; for Christians, whether Romish or Orthodox. That was a mere adornment in the emporium windows of the British and French war endeavour, as in that of their enemy Russia. The war had been designed on the British and French side to prop up the Turks so that the Russians were not suddenly all the way to the Balkans and the warm water of the Adriatic.

So far, said the New York papers, it was a war in which the fallen had chiefly succumbed to fevers and dysentery. The war front was near the Black Sea and the shores of Romania and the environs of Istanbul. At first sight, it was a comfortable distance to prevent too much perturbation in Downing Street. But the forces of construction and destruction worked in mysterious ways in this world. The arena could be shifted, Mitchel thought.

Waiting for developments, he travelled with Devin Reilly to places and events that were necessary for Reilly to visit in his work for the *American Review.* As every young journalist should be, he was very interested in hypocrisy, and especially in the hypocrisy of an upstate manufacturer named Cadwallader.

Living in state in a palazzo in New Paltz, New York, Mr Aeneas Cadwallader was the chief owner of the Atlantic Molasses Company. His storage tanks were on Vesey Street on the Hudson. One evening that winter the tanks of molasses more or less exploded before filling Northwest Avenue with a wave of molasses. Some people were inadvertent to it to the last moment, and on it swept to North End Avenue and did not give up till West Street.

Mitchel subsequently visited the site with Devin, but they were too anxious to enter the morass of syrupy, claggy muck, or interpret the debris of molasses-choked cats and timber and household goods and general debris that marked the high tide of Cadwallader's molasses flood. Twenty-one people had been drowned. By molasses!

Cadwallader was recorded in the press as praising the dead. But compensating them? That was a usage too far for his impulses to accept – that, like bread, the working man's breath was an irreplaceable item of value. It seemed he had been warned that loading warm molasses from the Caribbean into cold molasses had been observed to create a trigger for tanks to explode. Cadwallader remained supremely innocent in most of the press and was further praised for his initiating a public fund for the families bereaved by his molasses wave.

What a nobleman! While Cadwallader called for the end to slavery, the streets were full of men and women and children, his industrial slaves, drowned by his tide of molasses. In the New York morgue, an attendant, who wanted to demonstrate what a good chap he was, depressed the chest of a drowned woman and saw the molasses surge out of her mouth, and some laughed, however nervously. For she had become a joke in the New York carnival. Come and see the woman drowned in molasses!

At some of the places Mitchel visited, he would meet Nicaragua, writing for *The Sun*. Smyth frequently came to Brooklyn for dinner on Sundays. He had been remarkably restrained in his manner and in what he had written since the escape, and had published a mere article or two on their crossing of Nicaragua. All his arts were bent to having Jeannie Regan join him, since, he now confessed to them, they had discreetly married in Westbury.

Nicaragua did not want to give the Regans any reason to delay consigning their daughter to her American-based spouse, but Jeannie's mother was concerned that she was not yet fit, after a congestive disease she had recovered from, to make the journey – either crossing Nicaragua, the country, on one hand, or travelling by way of hectic Cape Horn on the other.

As Mrs Regan of Westbury had no doubt read, there was near Civil War in Nicaragua between progressives and conservatives, and the US, which owned the route across the peninsula, licensing it to Vanderbilt, whom the Mitchels had had to pay for their crossing out of what the Irish Directory had given Smyth, might now take sides in the civil conflict to guarantee to Vanderbilt's Accessory Travel Company its right of passage.

Jenny and John were chastened that Nicaragua had kept faith with the Mitchels and escorted them when he might have travelled with his wife. They said so but he brushed it aside. If Irish lives were partway sane, Smyth would have been able to escort his bride across Nicaragua. As it was, he intended now to go back as a private person to bring Jeannie to that experience.

25

New York, November 1853

The Mitchels knew now why New York was the right city for Meagher. It too had a feverish spirit, a drumming in the blood. For there it was, just as Mitchel wrote about it to his friend in Bothwell, Vandemonian patriot Mr Alex Reid.

My Dear Reid,
It is like my going into your country again for me to write to Bothwell out of the very heart of this infernal hubbub. Neither Dublin nor London is half so busy as this place, where there does not seem to be half room enough for the work that goes on in it, although it is stretching itself and expanding its huge limbs with convulsive energy.

Were you in the business portion of the town, you would find the streets are all very narrow, but houses immensely high, and the earth is nonetheless burrowed out not only under houses but under the streets. While overhead, telegraph wires are running and crossing each other through the air, whispering what was the price of stocks at New Orleans and at Halifax five minutes ago – carrying the Congress bunkum-debates of this forenoon at Washington to the newspaper offices, where the fellows are setting up the speech in type before the orator has finished in the House 300 miles off. This, therefore, is not like Bothwell. New York is a nervous and feverish patient, hysterical, irritable, with a determination of blood to the head, and a decided tendency to *delirium tremens*. By comparison, Bothwell is a quiet and healthy shepherd, whose food is mutton and whose drink is Clyde water (not un-mingled with moderate brandy), lying on a sunny hill under honeysuckle, and listening to sheep bells. Is that poetical enough for you?

But seriously, I do assure you, that intolerable as was my condition in Van Diemen's Land when I thought on it, that here in New York I often almost long for Nant Cottage. Do you find that hard to believe?

And I shall prove that by my account of this place. But first of all, I need to confess that Nicaragua itself was crossed, with the incarnate Nicaragua Smyth as our guide, and so we are in Brooklyn, and if we did not know we escaped, we are reminded daily by processions and bands. I do not speak out of vainglory. I tell the literal truth. Processions. And bands. In denial of the truth of where and what Ireland is, men address me as Mr President as if I were the half-brother of Franklin Pierce, who is the President of these states and, of course, a good friend of my friend, Tom Meagher, recently of Lake Sorell.

——

Mitchel discussed with Meagher that early winter the possibility that they should initiate a newspaper together in New York. Meagher had, in the kinder environment of New York, remained the model escapee from tyranny, though Mitchel hesitated to invite him regularly to Brooklyn for fear Jenny would interrogate him concerning the highwayman's daughter, Benny.

'I have signed a contract to tour the West as a speaker,' Meagher told Mitchel in the Metropole, two escapees amongst the purple and the plush, except that this time Mitchel had brought Jenny. 'It has been my best means of earning a living thus far.' His deep-set, dark eyes seemed very troubled, but his suit and vest, his cravat and boots were not those of a man who had made himself a social recluse for want of the company of his dear wife.

'It was either leave her here on her own, poor girl, or take her on my harsh journey with me,' he shared. 'And so we decided, she would go back to Waterford with my father to give birth. Which I am happy to say she has just recently done. And to a boy!'

They congratulated him. 'Are she and the boy to come back?' asked Jenny.

'Yes, I hope so, Mrs Mitchel,' said Meagher with a brittle jollity, but his eyes were still wells of doubt. He was never at ease discussing his Vandemonian wife.

With the proposed paper in mind, Mitchel met with Meagher in his law office in East 8th Street, near his New York patron the esteemed Brady's booming office. What line would their paper pursue? Yes, *The Citizen* should first be a sophisticated journal of opinion and reviews. But of what opinions?

As they spoke, Meagher seemed a little distracted by his imminent tour of the Americas. It turned out that he would write about his travels in *Harper's Weekly*, and he had a mission to see if Costa Rica, south of Nicaragua, would be a suitable country for Irish settlement. He seemed bravely to draw his mind back to the paper every time Mitchel asked him about their editorial policy, yet it seemed a struggle for him.

The Citizen would be, above all, anti-Know Nothing. To the grief of the Know Nothings – the native-born who feared the Irish as an untamed and unpredictable force on their Yankee, Protestant society – there were eleven thousand a week of Irish still arriving in New York then, in 1854, near four years after the end of the Famine, if it ever ended fully. They were ungratefully fleeing a country to which alleged peace and plenty had been restored by Downing Street. But they were not welcome in New York. The people to whom they were not welcome were, in particular, the Know Nothings, and Meagher and Mitchel realised that whatever the two wrote, the Know Nothings would be the snakes in their garden. In exalting American republicanism in his years of imprisonment, Mitchel had tended to overlook these gentlemen, and the poor bigoted wives they harboured on their bleak hearths.

They'd got their name from the secret society-cum-political party they had founded to fight the threat of Papism, and their members were required to rebuff any enquiry about their organisation with the simple formula, 'I know nothing.' Their other names were the Nativist Party, or the Order of the Star Spangled Banner. As well as fearing the numbers of Irish Catholics being admitted to America so negligently through immigration, they feared too its impact on the Constitution and Bill of Rights. They believed that the Irish, one and all, were in a plot to undermine America and its institutions, and that the priests and bishops – in particular, forthright Bishop John Hughes, whom people called 'Dagger John' – were orchestrating a takeover of the entire Protestant Republic and a transfer of fealty away from the Constitution and the Bible to the Pope and the Popish religious entity, the Whore of Babylon, Rome and the Vatican, herself.

Know Nothingism had a hundred Congressmen in Washington and controlled eight state governments. Party members also called for deportation of foreign beggars and criminals, a twenty-one-year naturalisation period for immigrants, and the purging of all Catholics from the public office. In the past ten years three million immigrants, most of them Catholics from Ireland and Bavaria and Poland, had come through New York, and it was well many were illiterate, for greeting them on the streets were the posters of Know Nothings, proclaiming, 'All persons who favour the Catholic Church are vile imposters, liars, villains, and cowardly cut throats.'

Meagher took Mitchel one evening during that winter to the New York Democrats' shrine, Tammany Hall, from which the commissionerships and chief-ships were dispensed by the Democratic government of New York. The chief wigwam of Tammany, officially entitled *Saint* Tammany, and Tammany had been the chieftain of the Turtle Clan of the Lenni-Lenape Indians who was admired as a peaceful negotiator by William Penn of Pennsylvania. The wigwam, having no resemblance of course to an actual tent, stood solidly on the corner of Frankfort and Nassau streets, and was like some great bazaar of politics. On the ground floor was a large bar, where Mitchel admitted you could see some of the worst of the Irish, the tribe of the blather, sitting down hoping for a crumb from the table, a deputy commissionership of some sort with its ample salary, its chance to be a minor lord of New York patronage, and its undemanding labours. Many there were blatherers, and no-one there remembered where he came from – Belfast or the Baltic or Bristol or Bavaria. All of them were united in desire for an utterly American prize. And who could blame them, said the softer side of Mitchel; and what a tragedy, said the sterner Mitchel of longer memory.

The atmosphere of the place, he could tell, caused Meagher's eyes to gleam, because he could sniff the chances here, and because he was an unconquerable orator. There was something about this sale yard of potentialities that appealed to Meagher and repelled Mitchel. Here was the sort of America that Dickens had portrayed and despised in *Martin Chuzzlewit*.

And God knew Meagher had the gift to be king here if he wanted. He could walk in and take any commissionership. But his tour of the western US would outstrip even the fortunes to be made here in this bar. Indeed, men came up at the sight of him simply to pay tribute, and because to be seen to be a friend of Meagher's was to be seen to be a friend of Tammany Hall.

On the side of virtue, there were men here too who took the trouble still to meet every boat from Ireland, and turn the Irish into instant Democrats, runners and foot soldiers, while finding them places to live in New York's tenement tumult. This was the meeting between 'Old' New York and the latest arrivals, and God bless the Democrats, said Meagher, in that they were amenable to the Irish.

And here, he said, any fellow of native wit, toughness and eloquence could rise high without being asked what dung heap he came from. Here, in this bar, was one half or better of the political power of New York and New England! Well, Mitchel thought, looking around the brandy-flushed faces, on that basis democracy had imposed its cost, as well as its rewards. But it was still, perhaps, on a better basis than the old world's obsession with birth.

Upstairs was the large and ornate Council Hall, where meetings on Democratic policy matters were staged, as well as a number of offices. From one of them, as they were making their way to the stairs, came a massive-shouldered man at least ten years older than Meagher. He wore a tight brown suit, heavy boots with steel tips to them, and a hat pushed graciously down over his eyes. His upper body generally was enormous and his fists massive.

'Ah,' said Meagher, holding up an arm in his overly thespian way to hold Mitchel back. 'Captain, sir, may I introduce you to my friend, the eminent escapee from Van Diemen's Land, Mr John Mitchel? Mr Mitchel, may I have the equal honour of introducing to you the eminent Captain Rynders, commander of the Dead Rabbits. Captain, do you have time to drink a little brandy with myself and Mr Mitchel?'

'Sir, Mr Mitchel,' Captain Rynders replied, in a voice respectful and tender and surprisingly melodious, 'I sighted you at City Hall on the day you were justly honoured in that place. It is my great privilege to see you face to face. Mr Meagher, sir, one of my officers has called me to the post office urgently.'

'Then you must be away so, with our apologies for delaying you.'

With a tip of his little bowler hat, Rynders took to the steps, which rang under the steel concussion of his boots as he descended.

Captain Rynders? thought Mitchel. Of the Dead Rabbits? For he had heard rumours of such a body. It was said they had once taken over the post office and destroyed Republican mail in a bonfire on its main floor. A federal offence that went unpunished.

When they were down in the bar again, Meagher was surrounded by men who wanted him to drink with them. In part it was a desire to meet Mitchel, in view of his own notoriety. The twenty-one-gun salute from the Napper Tandy Artillery on Brooklyn Heights, recognising him as President of the as-yet-unproclaimed Republic of Ireland, had done excessive credit to Mitchel's name, but on top of that was the stylish and better polished credit of Thomas Francis Meagher. Meagher could have called on the entire bar and all its whiskified warriors to accompany him and Captain Rynders, on his way up to the post office on 23rd Street, for whatever valiant action was in process there.

It became clear that, because of interruptions, they would not have any further quiet talk on the proposed newspaper in that place, and Meagher told an easy lie that he had to get Mitchel back to Brooklyn and the formidable Mrs Jenny Mitchel, of whom he said, since they had never met her, that her verbal powers were such as to warrant unquestioning obedience.

He led Mitchel in the end to a nearby alehouse named the Morgue and Fiddler, where Irish waiters were delighted to welcome the two escapees as nobility. In Meagher's honour, and perhaps in Mitchel's too, the band struck up 'Garryowen', and men in all stages of intoxication supplied versions of the lyrics, some singing: 'But join with me each jovial blade, Come booze and sing and lend your aid . . .'. And others, 'We'll smash the window, we'll break the door, The watch knock down by three and four . . .' And others again, 'For debt no man shall go to jail, for Garryowen in glory!' It was a good vocal example of the Irish inability to sing one verse, let alone pursue one strategy. But they were not punished for that here in New York.

The two guests were led to a private room, where brandy and water was brought and light played cheerily at the panelling and the prints of famed thoroughbreds from Kildare and Saratoga Springs. The proprietor exchanged solemn and yearning Gaelic words with them along the lines of *'Ardchtully-Abu. Diabhal an sceal.'* Devil the news!

'Mr O'Hanlon!' cried Meagher in greeting. 'I recognise in your greeting the cry of the O'Hanlons, from when they were standard bearers of the Kings of Ulster.'

'Before the Mitchels ever came to the kingdom,' Mitchel himself said, to temper the Celtic enthusiasm.

'But you came at the urging of your masters, and knew not the brouhaha you were walking into,' said Meagher, with a wink. 'And soon enough the brouhaha captured you too. Ulster's noblest son.'

'You do well to pronounce that, sir,' said O'Hanlon, 'in brotherhood, and across the void that threatens every gesture of Irish fraternity.'

'Happily said,' sang Meagher.

He had the same impenetrable good humour he had shown in bush lodgings at Lake Sorell. O'Hanlon withdrew after telling them of the quality of the brandy he was providing. French – in fact, Armagnac – and *hors age*, distilled when Napoleon was still in power.

It was delightful, Meagher and Mitchel found when left alone. 'Armagnac is fruitier,' said Meagher, with the sort of conviction of a man who has tried all life's delicacies and, as it were, knew them by their first names.

They got onto many subjects but above all Mitchel wanted to know why Captain Rynders was going to the post office that night. 'The Know Nothings must be using the mail again,' Meagher explained. 'Sending forth their lies and their delusions with the help of the US post. We have men in the post office the captain is familiar with, and they let him know if anything untoward is happening. Sometimes the Know Nothing blackguards, led by their hateful captain, Billie the Butcher Poole, linger to ensure their mailed items are not interfered with. That is when Rynders and the Dead Rabbits need to grow more militant – and God is my witness, and so are many good Americans, that the Dead Rabbits are a force fearsome to confront.'

Mitchel wondered aloud where the battles occurred – in the street or within the post office – and Meagher said it was frequently within, on the marble of the main hall, after hours, or else in the sorting room.

The Democrats had Irish gangs to fight them, cudgel for cudgel, nunchucks for nunchucks, brass knuckles for brass knuckles and dogma for dogma. Mitchel found this astonishing but wished that Rynders and the Dead Rabbits had taken to the streets of Dublin the day My Lord Clarendon hustled him across Dublin to his ship of exile.

While the policy of the newspaper would be anti-Know Nothing, Mitchel pondered whether they were to be pro-Democrat.

'Of course,' said Meagher. 'We can't be pro-Whig, because they tied up with the Know Nothings.' What planks of the Democratic Party doctrine should they emphasise? 'Well, that it should rule for the common man. State sovereignty. Co-operative movements for farmers.'

Mitchel had to be aware, said Tom, that while Franklin Pierce and his group of Democrats favoured canals and railways, it was chiefly so that the small farmers of the hinterland could sell more of their goods outside the local market. Democrats supported the Independent Treasury, a federal bank whose aim was to spread prosperity, and they had rebelled against European high culture because they believed it was used to keep the common man in his place. The Democrats were trying to establish through writers and theatre a purely American aesthetic standard to do with the common man and woman – the tradition begun by Ralph Waldo Emerson in a famous speech at Harvard, and applauded by the poet Longfellow (though there were other areas in which the Democrats did not agree with Longfellow).

Meagher knew some Emerson by heart and warmly recited a little.

Think ye I made this ball
A field of havoc and war;
When tyrants great and tyrants small
Might harry the weak and poor?
My angel – his name is Freedom,
Choose him to be your king.
He shall cut pathways east and west
And fend you with his wing.

And then Meagher breathed, 'What a vision! What a vision!'

Most New York Democrats, he went on, agreed with the settlement of 1850, which restricted slavery to the South.

They were split, often North and South, on whether new slave states should be founded.

'Therefore,' said Tom, in a voice that had smothered yawns in it, 'we can publish articles on either side of Douglas's proposed Kansas–Nebraska Act, which seeks to allow the citizens of those new states to decide whether they should be slave or free. The problem is that slavery would thereby be introduced north of the magic line of 36 degrees 30 minutes, the line made by Mason and Dixon, the line dividing North and South. And you could argue that ambitions to make those states slave states unnecessarily rile up the abolitionists.'

'My line,' Mitchel told him, 'is that the capitalists are happy to profit from industrial slavery in the garment tenements of New York, working women more than ninety hours a week, then go carrying a banner for freeing the slaves. There is hypocrisy here, Tom.'

Meagher laughed. 'You didn't expect that?' he asked. 'Did you think the Constitution redeems human nature from itself? The truth is that in New York, the North and South are closer to each other than anywhere else. New York banks fund the cotton and sugar business, and in return the South makes New York boom! Despite the rhetoric, they are dogs who sniff each other's arses. It's said that grass will grow in the streets of New York if it were ever separated from the cotton and sugar businesses! On Sunday a man might be an abolitionist, but at his desk on Monday morning he votes for cotton and sugar, slavery and all. Even some Democrats are Sunday abolitionists.'

'What should I write about it then? That North and South tolerate each other?'

'Whatever you write on the matter, you annoy half the audience. But if you sign it, indicating it's a personal opinion of your own, I believe I am happy.'

Mitchel conceded that, even though he had only been a little while in New York, the tragedies of the winter had confirmed him in his opinions of Yankee capitalists, who with the backing of a bunch of Calvinist ministers, devoured their working people alive, toyed with abolition and went over to Brooklyn to attend the massive church of the Reverend Beecher, supreme abolitionist.

The molasses tide, of course, had killed innocents in early winter. And another disaster: Mitchel was meeting a manager at a commercial printery, with the prospect of entering into a contract for the printing of *The Citizen*, when a huge pressure attacked his eardrums. This pulse of tension in his ears came from a calamity that had just occurred three blocks away, when an exploding boiler lifted an entire building eight feet in the air and brought it back to the earth in fragments.

When he and the printer rushed out to see what had caused the sensation and the noise, they found that entire slabs of stone had projected themselves across the street, killing two elderly folk seated by their windows, and a hundred were buried in the rubble of what had been the Taylor Hat Factory. At the site, as near as they could get to it, Mitchel could hear the unearthly voices from beneath all that ruin. One woman's voice announced she was cold. But these unexcavated voices would die down that night, never to be revivified. Another wonder of the ninety-hour working week and factory life was here achieved.

When, that same season, a suit factory caught fire in Cortlandt Street, the seamstresses dropped from the eighth storey like bouquets, their skirts ballooned to above their knees. They lay on the pavement for a time before workers arrived to place them in coffins, which remained open on the pavement for wailing families to arrive and claim remains.

While an Episcopal dean at Christ Church, out in the New York countryside, railed against godless agitators demonstrating for a forty-hour week on omnibuses, on his way to and from the Brooklyn ferry Mitchel found women weeping; mature women. They were going to or returning from some site of industrial mutilation in New York. If one inquired or offered sympathy, one found out that the casualties of American capital were numerous and daily.

And as of the Peculiar Institution itself – slavery – some people in New York, as Meagher had said, while condemning slavery, still lived off processing the accounts and providing the shipping to take the cotton of the South to England and Europe. If New York business was not to do with financing cotton and with shipping it away and lending the capital to expand the industry and building the railways of the South . . . well, asked Meagher, what was it about at all?

'One thing to beware of,' said Thomas. 'Some Northern people assume that anyone who accepts slavery in the South approves of slavery in its grossest forms – the violation of men and women, the separation of families, flogging, and all the rest. Does the industrialist concern himself with lighting in the slave quarters of the labourer, in the hovels of the miners, in the squalid little hutches of the canal builder? One black slave flogged in Louisiana means more to the North than one hundred buried Paddies in a landslide!'

The brandy they drank worked well on Mitchel and seemed to smooth the slide of Meagher's ideas into his mind.

'I am pleased,' Mitchel said, 'to see that we seem to be at one.'

Meagher, taking one more dainty sip of the Armagnac, warned Mitchel. 'But be careful of the slavery issue. Let us say we accede to and recognise the Compromise of 1850. You don't need to know what's in it. But it can stave off battle with either side. As for slavery, it is also safest simply to report events and not to push opinions.'

Being such a fast learner, Mitchel already knew what that compromise was. California had been admitted to the Union as a free state – the California state convention had voted that way – in return for the enactment of a new and severe fugitive slave law throughout the country. The slave state of Texas was admitted to the Union and had its national debt paid by the US, in return for giving up its claim to New Mexico and Utah. Southerners retained hope New Mexico and Utah were open to becoming slave states. The slave trade in Washington D.C. was abolished, but could flourish just across the Potomac, in Alexandria.

'Very well,' Mitchel agreed. 'The Compromise.'

'Bravo,' said Meagher, and joined the side of his glass to that of his friend. 'It is a matter of regret to me that I shall be away when our new journal raises its head.'

Mitchel assured him that his name alone was sufficient lustre. For Meagher was not by nature an editor, and more an orator than a newspaperman. Whereas Mitchel felt in himself that night the power to write an entire weekly, and to write it again, and again.

Last thing that evening, John offered congratulations again on the birth of a new little Meagher in Waterford.

'Assure Mrs Mitchel,' said Meagher, 'that I know certainly Benny is my wife. Your wife is a fearful woman, Mitchel.'

'Not to me,' said Mitchel. 'If I ever give her less than the truth . . . then, I would fear her.'

———

Meagher left for the West immediately after the Mitchels' first Brooklyn Christmas. Press stories began to appear about the forthcoming *Citizen*, in a season spent with great hope and joy in Union Street, Brooklyn, but with a lingering foretaste of dread about battles inevitably to be joined, old Irish battles, and new American ones. *The New York Herald* and its prissy editor commented that it took a great deal of side from Meagher and Mitchel to call themselves any sort of 'citizen'. And were they British or Irish or American citizens? And in any case, certainly, they had not been here long enough to rattle the word *Citizen* in the faces of Americans. So Mitchel felt obligated to write an editorial on that subject for the first issue.

It was in the hope of investing ourselves and our children with the proud attributes of citizenship that we selected America as a place of refuge, and finally, it was with the sincere desire of aiding our immigrant countrymen to appreciate the responsibilities and rights of citizens, and to discharge the duties of citizens, that we established this journal. Because to become thoroughly and intensely American will be, for our readers, the best way of ripening and fulfilling the destinies of Ireland. The privileges of citizenship in America give Irishmen the right to arm themselves as they drill and prepare for revolution in Ireland. Under the Crime and Outrage Act of the United Kingdom in 1847, all individuals without police permits were forced to surrender their weapons. Not so in the United States ... As to the Irish in America, the more fully they are absorbed into existing American parties, always excepting the Know Nothings, and the more lost they become among American citizens, the better.

A Young Irelander of twenty-four years asked to work on *The Citizen*. John Savage, who had dined at Ontario Terrace – something of the playwright and a likeable boy who got away from Ireland when a British warrant was out for him in 1848 – became Mitchel's copy subeditor and began to produce articles of his own with a very sharp eye on Democrat politics. He presented Mitchel one day, in the rented editorial offices in Fulton Street, with a little piece he had written, a piece that did have a little irony to it, about Rynder's recent set-to at the 23rd Street post office with the Know Nothing gang led by Bill the Butcher. For there was a stalemate in that: neither the Democrats nor the Know Nothings could now mail election materials with safety.

Savage had been very useful to Mitchel by reminding him that, before his transportation to Bermuda, not all Irish had accepted the Famine to be the fault of British government, as distinct from their own fault or the will of the deity or bad fortune. Now, he argued, the ordinary Irish immigrant to America took it as a given that their enemies had been in Westminster, and that men in power had been complacent about the death of the ancient society, the ancient race. 'God did not despise them,' said Savage. 'Westminster did!'

Young Savage was a thorough Democrat himself and quite a student of the party. He was in love too, with the daughter of a ship's captain. But in the meantime, he and

Mitchel and other early promisers of material for *The Citizen* had the beginnings of the English war with Russia to celebrate, and the hope that it might bode some good for Ireland to add a glow to the first edition.

The war was in abeyance, though, and very much remote in the East. The French and English had taken the Christian Orthodox regions of Moldova and Wallachia back from the Russians and given the Turks back their power over the region. Things seemed static for the moment, and though people in London were baying for new victories on the shores of the Black Sea, fever had killed their young soldiers. With all that volatile enthusiasm pressing on the British generals, anything could happen, some grand mistake. And what if a Russian fleet took a Russian army from the Baltic to the west of Ireland? What if . . .

And so Mitchel initiated the paper, he and Savage running between the editorial office in Fulton Street and the printery in Pearl Street. Mitchel had in the meantime written to the Russian ambassador in Washington, while the first edition was a-printing, and had offered to visit him and discuss ways in which the Irish might be able to assist the Russian cause to the chagrin of Downing Street.

The advertising sales manager, McClenehan, told Mitchel that his repute was such that everyone Irish would want to have space in the first *Citizen*. There were, indeed, pages upon pages of classified advertisements bought by bar owners and bowling alley proprietors, undertakers and drapers and accommodation suppliers and dry goods merchants, billiard-hall owners and wholesale butchers, all with solid Celtic names that bespoke grateful industry – and all taking solid lumps of page to congratulate the immortal Meagher and Mitchel, escapees from British penal colonies, and humbly drawing the reader's attention to the merits of their own services.

On the first editorial page was the editorial statement of intent. Mitchel did not resent that at the moment of its appearance, Mr Meagher was somewhere in the Gulf of Mexico, charming four-fifths of the Irish from the Atlantic coast to the Mississippi and beyond. And based on the advertising, Mitchel was, on the strength of the first edition, on his way to a financial glory he had never dreamed of nor desired. And it was as well, therefore, that in the end he had no room for slavery amongst all the other issues raised by *The Citizen, Volume 1, Number 1* in mid-January 1854, his baptism in the American newspaper business.

The principal conductors of this newspaper are, in the first place, Irishmen by birth. In the second place, they are men who have enjoyed years of penal exile at the hands of the British government for attempting to overthrow the Dominion of that government in their native country. In the third place, they are refugees on American soil, and aspirants to the privileges of American citizenship.

The principles and conduct of their new journal will be in accordance with their position, their memories, and their aspirations. They refuse to believe that, prostrate and broken as the Irish nation is now, Irish independence is utterly lost. They refuse to admit that any improvement in the material condition of those Irishmen who have survived the miseries of the last seven years – if indeed any improvement there be – in any way satisfies the honour, or fulfils the destiny, of an ancient and noble nation.

That first edition of *The Citizen*, which appeared on a snowy Saturday in January, sold 50,000 copies, to make an august opening. Mitchel felt exultant to be about his normal work again. To be back in the business of ideas and politics and cultivation, back to the sweeping many-claused argumentation of the editorial. And how he turned the exclusive Americanism of the Know Nothings on its head. Bryce, the national leader of the Know Nothings, had written to Mr Wise, the Democrat Governor of Virginia, to claim that no-one was more dedicated to freedom of religion than his brotherhood. Mitchel made great irony of Bryce's claim.

He wanted *The Citizen* to be a journal people read for the reviews and opinions, whether one liked the editorial policy or not. He took pains to publish reviews in that first issue of Schiller's *History of the Thirty Years' War* in a new translation, of John Ruskin's *Stones of Venice*, and of *The Life of P.T. Barnum, Written by Himself*. The boys and Mitchel had been to Mr Barnum's museum and they had liked it greatly, but he had reservations.

Humbug is lifted out of the mire, where an ill-informed public sentiment and longing looked down upon it, and elevated it to its proud position as one of the humanising arts of life. To fix the tail of a fish to the torso of a monkey, to advertise this as a mermaid captured at the Fiji Islands, to induce men, women, and children, under that representation, to come and pay their money for permission to see the thing – this and similar operations which would certainly have, even one generation back, brought the operator under the penalties of criminal law, are related by Mr Barnum not with an apology, not with an unbecoming boast either, but with a modest and manly pride, and evident absence of self-reproach, and a transparently clear conscience, as humble efforts of his in supplying his dear public with what the public really wanted.

For the first edition Meagher wrote for publication and sent to Mitchel one of his transparently sensible 'Letters to a Know Nothing Acquaintance'. 'The Know Nothing Order is nothing but an arrangement made by one set of Christians to hunt and persecute another set of Christians according to the ancient sporting traditions of true religion.'

Additionally, Mitchel made a sober account of the Russian campaign to hold onto the duchies of Romania. But it was not what was in *The Citizen* by which Mitchel and Meagher were judged, but by what was not. The pair had escaped detention in Van Diemen's Land, and yet, as avid as they might be for Ireland's liberation, the former prisoners were accused of not seeming anxious about the forced detention of American slaves. This attracted a number of letters to the editors asking their position on slavery, given that they had both demonstrated themselves notable champions of liberty.

The potentialities that the war on the borders of Asia Minor might move itself to northern Europe was the more pressing matter, though; so pressing a matter, indeed, that Mitchel went to the terminus and entrained on the New York–Washington line, making his way to offer the Russian ambassador in the capital a prospect of Irish help. On the train south he read Dr Cartwright's pamphlet on drapetomania – running-away mania – entitled *Diseases and Physical Peculiarities of the Negro Race*. Like various other scientific works of the era, it questioned the slave's capacity to exist in open society and took slavery as the normal and compassionate usage of the Negro race. Cartwright's work, like Gobineau's, the Frenchman's, was ultimately compassionate to the African race. Mitchel knew he should emphasise compassion for the African race more strongly. For that surely was the point. That the institution had the African's own welfare as the headline of the book of slavery!

26

Dancing Liberty's Dance (2)

For the first time Mitchel saw something of the farmlands of New Jersey and the city of Philadelphia, and then the great conurbation of Baltimore, before coming to Washington itself. That is, he saw something of the scale of this country, which was considerable, the line of his journey being barely more than a quarter of the North–South immensity of the continent, let alone the even greater extent of the East–West lines to the Mississippi and beyond.

In Washington overnight he stayed at the Willard, believing America was about to enrich and elevate him purely through its scale. In the morning he rose early and hired a sulky and driver to visit Alexandria across the Potomac, in Virginia, and its slave pens. These pens in Duke Street were often large and well-made buildings, even though the term implied something less than that, something of the farmyard. The buildings with high-washed wings often enclosed an entire town block. He had exactly the talkative driver he needed, who named the establishments and boasted of the large houses and slave pens of Armfield and Franklin. The driver claimed they had sold a million slaves into the deep South, including New Orleans.

'Given the price of slaves, I wish I could sell myself,' said the driver.

'What are you worth?' Mitchel teased him.

'My wife would sell me for a few dollars,' he replied, 'but I would reckon on $1000.'

As they rode by, Mitchel would hear an occasional black voice from within, but the atmosphere of the pens, which were often called 'slave jails', was one of good order under the sun. How Mitchel wished he had time to attend and meet the slaves for sale.

'Why, they're getting $1500 for a young mulatto woman,' the driver told him. 'It's a rich man's business, sir.'

There had been institutions like this in Washington itself till a few years back, but the District of Columbia had had them removed as part of that 1850 Compromise Tom Meagher was so keen on.

They rushed back to Georgetown to the Russian ambassador's house. A black servant admitted him. The ambassador was a courtly young man, and very welcoming, and when they went to his office a child intervened, speaking in an American accent and asking him to settle some dispute between himself and his sister. The baron was married to an American, a Miss Howard, and his name was a Germanic one, Stoeckl. The Stoeckl child stared at Mitchel as the father wrote some judgement down on paper that he wanted their nurse or their mother to enforce.

When the child was gone, in the good humour created by the incident the ambassador asked Mitchel about his escape and his own family, and then the circumstances in which he saw himself intervening in this conflict. Irish brigades, the ambassador said he knew, had fought for the colonists and the heroic Bolívar against the Spanish. There might be room in this war for such a brigade, he said, if recruited from Irish-America.

'But that is merely a regiment. I came to offer far more than a regiment,' said Mitchel, and the ambassador sat forward. 'I envisage something more strategic than that – that the great mass of Irish would be delighted to collaborate with any Russian force that landed in Ireland.'

'Ah,' Stoeckl said, shaking his head, 'you surmise our fleet would survive a battle against the British if we emerged from the Baltic.'

'Tsar Peter the Great would have loved such a test,' Mitchel suggested. 'Isn't it why he built a fleet? Isn't that still the ultimate test and theory of your imperial navy?'

'Our navy has protection from the forts of the Gulf of Finland,' said the ambassador. 'I am not sure they would choose to operate belligerently beyond the range of those guns. I have the honour to represent my imperial master, Tsar Nicholas I, who, if he were here, might say that he is rather fully engaged as it is with France and Britain.

'Look at the reality by which we are constrained, Mr Mitchel. England can claim slabs of earth on the globe, especially in the sub-continent of India, and is never criticised for it! France seizes Algeria from the Ottomans, but that is permitted by the High Priests of World Order. But we, the Russians, invade Wallachia and Moldova to assist Orthodox Christians under the heel of the Ottomans, and it is a world scandal for which blood must be shed! I shall certainly report our conversation, Mr Mitchel, but I cannot be certain that the Tsar and his government are not fixed on Romania and the Black Sea as the arena in which, offence having been offered, remediation must be made.'

'Irishmen in this country are already trained as militia-men and would go to Ireland if appealed to, and fight beside your Cossacks . . .'

'And called to arms by men such as yourself and Mr Meagher.'

'We are not lacking in the authority to do so. It would be very likely that the cost would be met by various Irish bodies, including the Irish Directory of New York and the Emmet Epitaph Society. They would spring into action at a word!'

'Emmet,' he said and began to quote, '"When my country takes its place amongst the nations of the earth, and not till then, let my epitaph be written." Let me say that our navy, the centre of much brave adulation, poetry and music, has still to order ships as modern as Lord Napier's. But we'll see. Am I right in saying that, despite your American existence, you would be instantly ready to call on Irish militia and to lead them?'

'Yes,' Mitchel assured him. 'To accompany them anyhow. To give them their moral force! My prayer has always been, "Send us war in our time. And at our door!"'

———

Mitchel returned to New York the next day, with much to write about, and not simply the war between Russia and Britain.

But the issue of slavery awaited him. A Quaker merchant, James Haughton of Dublin – whom Mitchel had known in Repeal in Dublin, and at that distance from America an abolitionist – had written to him, asking him publicly to take up the abolition issue in his and Meagher's newspaper, accusing that if they did not, 'By your silence you will become a participator in their wrongs.'

Haughton was one of those who had been attracted to Repeal by the Liberator's sympathy for the American slave. Mitchel's view was that many a famine victim and many an industrial worker would have chosen the slave life, if offered it – the life by which you were owned, certainly, but in which most human needs and questions were answered. For one thing, you were never starved!

But abolitionists would say, the slave has no choice, and that is his tragedy. The science of human groups and phrenology, Mitchel believed, showed that it was not within the talents and power of the slave to choose either way. Indeed, all science, claimed Dr Cartwright in his book on drapetomania, suggested that the African slave was not constructed for freedom.

As well, Professor Blumenbach, the German, said there was monogenism, that all races had a single origin; that is, that all races other than the Caucasians had undergone forms of degeneration that made them lesser. The African, asserted Blumenbach, could not compete with the Caucasian or enjoy the same life. And there was a lot of further expert commentary on this, whether the scientists believed in one or different origin events.

Scientific opinion, marshalling evidence from the analysis of different skulls of humankind, also proved the limitations of the black man or woman. To turn them loose in the world of capital enterprise, of which New York was a fierce demonstration, would be to make them as good as slaves anyhow, believed Mitchel.

Now in walking about New York and looking into the laneways and alleys, one occasionally saw one of the freed black men who lived in the city. He was always the helper, the spare man, and never the teamster. The white workers hung onto that privilege, and were not above using violence to maintain it. The freed black man was free to be a menial in New York. And even the supreme abolitionist Mr Beecher, for all his gesturing, would surely not give up his preaching chair to such a man. The Caucasian suffered from the evils of capital and its inequal field of enterprise – imagine how the slaves would, if given their supposed liberty. No friend of the black man or woman would fill either of their heads with the facile concept of freedom!

The challenge from Mr Haughton had been published in *The New York Herald* – much to Mitchel's irritation, he had sent his missive both to *The Herald* and *The Citizen* – and so within a few weeks Mitchel and company were being pushed again into the great abolition question without seeking it. It was appalling, he reflected, to imagine the undeveloped consciousness of a black man or woman being subjected to the same oratory, the same pressures.

Mitchel knew that Meagher would not appreciate being challenged by this gentleman in this heavy-handed manner. Put on the spot now, and although his colleague had said they should not be drawn into this question, he felt entitled to make his own opinions clear to Haughton.

Because Mitchel believed the paper had no choice now, he began writing a large piece on the issue for the next Saturday's edition. He knew he had a tendency to answer arguments he considered fatuous with levity and with overstatement; and he was inflamed, suddenly, and wanted to mock the whole controversy. When finished he was full of confidence and satisfaction, yet had a lingering sense that he had baited the bear Meagher had suggested he ignore. He wrote that he could not speak for Mr Meagher, whom everyone knew to be travelling, but he could declare his own views, having been harried for them, and even used the editorial 'we' in stating them.

We, *The Citizen*, venerate our African brethren whose labor generates wealth in the South and in the North. Their Coloured Churches are throughout the South, as we have heard, where our African brothers and sisters invoke the same merciful Christ as the rest of the population and with the same fervour if not greater. But if they came North and wanted to worship in the same church as the mill-owner and the sweatshop proprietor they would not be admitted. Nor, despite the braying of the abolitionists, would they be welcomed to the New York Bar or Delmonico's steakhouse! The freedom the Reverend Beecher would have imposed on them would be the freedom to occupy the cellar of society, and to step off the pavement into the gutter when whites approach. If they were offered the same freedom as us, and were they capable of engaging with it, I would be an abolitionist.

But as it is, I am not an abolitionist, no more an abolitionist than were Moses, or Socrates or Jesus Christ. I deny that it is a crime, or a wrong, or even a peccadillo, to hold slaves, to buy slaves, to keep slaves and make them work within the limits of humanity and needful coercion.

Not 'even a peccadillo' was, he would later admit, a touch too far.

> But what right has this gentleman to expect Thomas Francis Meagher or myself to take up this wearisome song which they always refused to sing at home? As for being a participator in the wrong, I for my part wish I had a good plantation, well-stocked with healthy Negroes, in Alabama. There now! Is Mr Haughton content?

Still greatly annoyed at Haughton for sending his letter not only to him but to *The New York Herald*, John read the galleys of this piece to Jenny in the editorial offices one day when she was visiting Manhattan.

'Do you think they can tell you are joking?' she said, doubt on her forehead. 'Because you don't want a plantation in Alabama! It's the last thing you want.'

'Damn the lot of them,' Mitchel asserted. 'Let them take a joke!'

She was right to ask the question. Readers' sense of irony was not necessarily at the same level as Mitchel's, or if it was, they were pleased to take him at his word.

The advertising man, McClenehan, was delighted with the controversy, since advertisers liked controversy. On top of that success with advertising, Savage had proved himself invaluable in dealing with the printers, and *The Citizen* had stood pretty high with them after that first week.

There came, on top of Haughton, chastisement from two Frenchmen. These men, condemned for political crimes, had escaped to America from the penal settlement at Cayenne, operatically known as Devil's Island. They wrote to Mitchel about his opinions, particularly taking the time to publish their letter in *The Evening Post*, in case Mitchel wanted to evade their message.

They began with flattery:

Sir – Democratic Europe loved to place you in the first rank of the champions of Liberty. In you, the defender of the rights of injured Ireland, every people and every race saw a defender for themselves. You yourself have been, for a long time, a martyr in the cause, and inseparable from the cause, of universal humanity. Was it not natural to hope your sympathies belonged forever to the martyrs of every human wrong? This hope, one might say this certainty, has been strangely annihilated, by the second number of your *Citizen*.

The claim ran on over several future editions, that it was inconsistent for one John Mitchel to bless slavery in America when wanting freedom for the Irish.

However, as Mitchel protested in a further article, 'You have not seen Ireland! You have not seen men who would sell their souls and perhaps even their children for the dish my slaves would receive at regular hours and routinely in Alabama.'

That deathly *clachan* in the Comeragh Mountains, the one he had tramped to with Meagher, recurred as he wrote. And he deepened the argument by resort to the Bible. When St Paul met a runaway slave, Onesimus, while they were both in prison, he wrote a letter to the master of the slave, one Philemon, who lived in the town of Colossae. 'I appeal to you for my child, Onesimus, whose father I have become in my imprisonment. I am sending him back to you, sending my very heart. I would have been glad to keep him with me, in order that he might serve me on your behalf during my imprisonment for the gospel; but I preferred to do nothing without your consent in order that your goodness might not be by compulsion but of your own free will.'

After further issues of *The Citizen*, Mitchel found himself acclaimed a champion of the South in Richmond, Virginia, which he had never visited to that point, and being something of a pariah amongst the abolitionists of New York. Where he lived!

27

A Visit from
Mr Beecher, 1854

One of those appalled by Mitchel was the famed clergyman brother of a certain novelist who had herself produced
a sentimental book for the abolitionist cause. This clergyman was the brother of Harriet Beecher Stowe, whose *Uncle
Tom's Cabin* was acclaimed in parts of the North, though not
quite as robustly in New York as in Massachusetts. Reverend
Henry Ward Beecher, an equally theatrical creature and
pastor of a huge Congregational Church in Brooklyn, was
the famed clergyman.

Beecher was the P. T. Barnum of religion. Molly Tunstall,
a friend of Matilda Mitchel and Jenny's, had told them
without any amazement or disapproval that he preached
from a stage, sometimes on his feet, sometimes from a large
easy chair. *An easy chair?* Only in America could the pulpit
be supplanted by a well-upholstered chair. God forgave him
because he, the reverend, believed above everything else
that God was an indulgent and forgiving father, and of all

the divine qualities, clemency towards the frail human was supreme. And who amongst all the sinners of New York did not want to hear that God was more merciful than vengeful?

First in a sermon and then by article, this board-treading or easy-chair-sitting divine condemned Mitchel. Again, the main argument was that it was inconsistent of him, a champion of freedom and Ireland, to champion slavery in America.

———

As a summer came, Mother Mitchel and Jenny had got on very well in Brooklyn, as they had in Dublin before John was transported. There could have been mutual accusations: 'You, Mrs Mitchel the elder, raised him with too much indulgence for his wild ideas!'; 'You, Mrs Mitchel the younger, let him become irresponsible and did not remind him he had children.' But no conflict on that scale arose. Instead, there were minor domestic irritations. Mrs Mitchel the elder told her once that she was amazed that after such wanderings, the children were so urbane, but that the boys must be introduced to various sports to absorb their animal spirits. She loved especially Henty, who had come through all her adventures still fit to shine in any parlour; however, her affection did not exclude the younger, wilder girls, Minnie and the Van Diemen's Lander Rixy.

The two women and the sisters habitually met up for luncheon at midday, unless one of them had other business, and one day Mrs Mitchel senior told her a visiting card had been dropped at the door by the Reverend Henry Ward Beecher, the notorious preacher of Plymouth Congregational, Orange Street, Brooklyn. Mother Mitchel abominated the man's church, with its great blunt modern front, which she said looked more like a theatre than a church.

Though she and her eminent husband had come from the same tradition of Presbyterianism as Beecher, that building offended her as did the size of the congregations; not honest hundreds but spurious thousands attended Plymouth Congregational.

'They say that he fits four thousand of his devotees into that great barn,' she complained. 'Our Divine Lord himself never preached to such a mob!'

The sisters, though, were full of suppressed excitement. The famous Beecher? At their door?

On biblical evidence, Jenny could have argued with Mrs Mitchel senior about the size of Jesus's crowds. But to her mother-in-law, such a number as four thousand was obscene, comparable to crowds at theatres, football matches or Orange marches. The Reverend Dr Mitchel would never have countenanced such a gathering, said Mother Mitchel, because after a while crowds meant that doctrine was watered down or turned into a cult, like the virgins and saints who set the uncritical Papists processing in the streets.

Molly Tunstall had observed Beecher regularly. She told Jenny and Matilda that she saw through his vanity and yet forgave him, because he said himself that he was an impossibly vain little man but that God forgave him for it. It was rare for preachers to parade their own sins. So rare, in fact, that at least half the congregation, said Molly, came across from Manhattan on Sundays to listen to him preach on love and mercy.

'Because,' she said, 'it's simply that he preaches that hell doesn't stand up in the face of the mercy of God. A lot of his congregation will need mercy, and the Reverend Beecher does himself, with all his interest in other men's wives. Yet the congregation is more than happy to hear the gospel of forgiveness.'

Matilda also told Jenny with a little amazement that he used slang in his sermons. From various sources, Jenny was getting a rounder version of the preacher.

Whatever was said about Beecher, Jenny knew it was her Johnny's good opinion of slavery that had brought him to their door. John was, in fact, teasing half of America with talk of his desire to run a slave plantation in Alabama. As if it were the very next thing he would do with himself! In fact it would never happen, any more than Johnny would lead an expedition to the Arctic. She would not stand for it to begin with. She had no vocation for a parish of plantation Africans. But they did not know that, and had swallowed his joke as a declaration of intent.

The Mitchel girls were bouncing with suppressed excitement about the impending visit. The Reverend Beecher was, after all, claimed Matilda, absolutely the most famous man in America, and much more so than any president.

'Well, well,' John said at dinner, and his eyes were a-gleam too. 'He shows an honest intention not to shy away from his adversaries.'

Mitchel wrote to the reverend immediately, inviting him to visit in two days' time at four o'clock in the afternoon.

On the day the distinguished critic visited, the sisters and Mother Mitchel did not try to impose themselves on the meeting.

That day when the Reverend Beecher called, John Mitchel himself insisted on opening the door to the man so they would stand, opponent to opponent, from the start. Jenny could hear John disposing of the reverend's overcoat and hat in the foyer cupboard, the two of them engaged in weather chat and predictions of snow. In drowsy Bothwell, amber heat would at this time be drenching the valley of the Clyde, she thought, and in the Caledonia Hotel a local was no doubt enlivening the hour for a newcomer by telling the story of Mitchel's escape.

But then the Reverend Beecher claimed the space around her. Though small, the man who entered the front parlour seemed to require considerable air, for – as he came in – he sucked some fair part of what the room contained. Drawing breath, Jenny saw his huge limpid eyes, and a rather ravaged-looking face, as if life had not been easy. But all this came with the extreme, sportive liveliness of his movements.

John conducted him to a chair. The air settled as he did, and the Reverend Beecher moved those large eyes, full of conviction, from John to Jenny, and back to John.

John talked him into having a sherry, and poured sherry for all three of them, both men saying it was an honour to meet the other.

'And your valiant wife, Mr Mitchel,' added Beecher, 'who joined with you in imprisonment and escape!'

John said that his father would have been very interested to meet a fellow pastor from America. However, Mother Mitchel would have been very angry with him for saying so for, as John himself had said, Beecher appeared to believe himself the purveyor under contract to that divine manufacture called forgiveness. And his sanctuary on Orange Street, Brooklyn seemed not so different from Barnum's on Broadway between Spring and Prince.

To Jenny, the striking Mr Beecher declared again that he was pleased she was sitting with John, since he highly approved of women being involved in exchanges of political and theological ideas. His church favoured the franchise for women, he said. His huge eyes dwelt on Jenny with something akin to regret, as if it were somehow her fault they had not met to this hour.

'Too many men dismiss their wives from their counsels, whereas I believe that women, if encouraged, can shed new light on many questions and see through what is merely pompous. As it is, should the slavery issue cause a war, women will be asked to yield up their sons to it, but that should not happen without their being asked for their opinions first!'

'Surely no war, Mr Beecher,' Jenny suggested.

'Indeed, God forbid! In any case, meanwhile, my church supports the suffrage of women to be a necessary and future reform. Yet there are holy men who consider this blasphemous, and contrary to injunctions on the servitude of women in the Scriptures.'

But then he turned those same reproachful eyes on John. 'My congregation contributed to the American grain shipments sent your way during the Irish famine.'

'My way?' asked John, a little whimsically this time.

'I think you know what I mean,' enunciated the Reverend Beecher from beneath those admonishing eyes. 'As we felt the moral necessity to succour the Irish as fellow children of God, we feel the necessity to extend freedom to the slave. My congregation has raised money again and again to buy slaves from their masters. The first time was some seven or eight years ago, and now we are in the business regularly – of buying slaves into uncontested freedom!'

John said quite honestly and without a trace of his ordinary debating humour, 'I do not see the connection between the two. God has meant the Irish for freedom, just as he has meant the slave to serve until the master extends liberty to the slave. It goes without saying that the misuse of slaves is a great sin, but so is the misuse – one could say the criminal and homicidal misuse – of Irish labour by some of your manufacturing gentlemen. I do not hear many pulpits exhorting rich barons of steel or coal to kindness. The kindness of industrial masters, and indeed the appearance of God's favour towards them in their very wealth, is taken as a given fact! Why not then the plantation owners' kindness? That I would say for openers, Mr Beecher . . . It is not *Doctor* Beecher, is it?'

Mother Mitchel would have been proud of her son for that question – the late Rev. Mitchel had had his Doctorate in Divinity.

'It is plain Mr Beecher, Mr Mitchel, since I was not a gifted student. I consoled myself that our Divine Lord Jesus lacked a doctoral degree also.'

Some impulse in Jenny, which may have been an attempt to keep the reverend defensive, made her ask, since he was all for women shedding light on the councils of man, 'Is it true that you send rifles to the Free State settlers in Kansas?'

'Only for their protection against the Southern zealots, Mrs Mitchel.' He developed a crooked and uncomfortable-looking smile, but he was not hapless, she could see, and he was accustomed to discussing things with women: there was no condescension in his manner. 'People are kind enough to call them "Beecher's Bibles".'

'Do you think that is perhaps unkind to honest slave-holders?' Jenny asked him. She found him an engrossing little fellow of whom she was suspicious. She was aware that Beecher was trying to entrance her as he entranced others, and that it was partially working.

'After all, sir,' John reminded him, 'the rights of slave owners are guaranteed by the compromise of a few years back, just as abolitionists' freedom of speech is.'

'I cannot see 1850 as more than a satanic compromise, Mr Mitchel, which is capable, as it now seems, of extending the evil of slavery into previously unaffected parts of the Union. But as God calls on man to take joy in the world, God calls on man also to be free. Especially in this advanced age.'

'Advanced age, sir? I have never found it very advanced. The Irish Famine, sir, was a phenomenon of disgrace, yet underwritten by political economists, philosophers and the high priests of the market.'

This humbug, that everyone was better simply because of the various mechanical applications men had devised, always infuriated Mitchel, though he felt he controlled his contempt well.

'Sir, you would have not thought the age so advanced if you had visited the Famine *clachans* of Ireland and seen the ghastly dead,' he continued. 'That is, people who had died according to the latest fashion of political economy and utilitarianism. Doctrines that go along with the mechanical mill and the steam engine! In the shade of these supposed benefactions, both philosophical and mechanical, people have died who would have lived if fed half as well as are the British convict or the American slave!'

John had held up a pedagogic finger, and it stopped America's greatest preacher with his mouth open. 'And let me tell you about the true slaves of America! To advance the mine and the mill as exemplifying God's will would seem to me, Mr Beecher, a morality highly selective in its objects of concern.'

And John made something like commas in the air to signify to Mr Beecher, who would rarely have to await permission to speak, that the Mitchel podium was free.

'Ah, my dear Mr Mitchel, and Madame Mitchel,' the preacher declared, putting his disturbing eyes fully upon Jenny, 'you must know that we do not stand for crushing the bruised reeds of industry at Plymouth congregation!'

'Yes,' John charged him. 'But you do not think that workers should strike for better pay? Do you think we should fight a war for that cause? For a forty-hours week? You see the industrial slaves suffer numbly and with pursed lips. You praise their patience. But you take no action and are willing to pray for the day when your God will move their masters to give them enough to feed on, man, woman, child. If you sent rifles to the mill workers, I would be more impressed by your "Beecher's Bibles".'

'I have indeed,' said the reverend, sitting forward, 'called for patience and fortitude, as the masters of industry accommodate themselves to the new wonders of machinery and are educated by that very experience and by the influence of Christianity. The new machines bring justice implicit with them. A mill or mine can be run on moral principles, whereas there will never be redemption for the slave–master equation; an equation that makes it somehow to be admirable that fellow children of God should be owned as chattels and auctioned like land or items of farm equipment.'

Jenny was planning to speak here, not least to justify the strange Mr Beecher's faith in the tempering wisdom of women, however John intervened with an 'Ah', before she had her sentence ready.

'You see engineering and the cleverness of it as the beginning of a new morality,' John continued. 'I see it as the beginning of a decline to a new barbarism. And in that decline, the sufferings of the Irish farmer and his family were indeed the early signs of that new barbarism, not of a coming liberation. I see it here too, in America, in the confidence that those unjustly killed by the machine of capital will be replaced by the next boatload of hapless Irish.

'Such are the slaves that concern me, Mr Beecher. Such are the girls packed into open coffins, their humble clothes ripped and open to the condescension of the vulgar gaze – such are my slaves, whom I would liberate! And if the innocent African slave were freed, as you want him to be, and committed to this slavery, what would become of him and his wife? It is because I would save them from worse fates than they presently need to face! The black man would be destroyed by the industrial model, whereas he is not destroyed by slavery.'

The preacher now clapped his delicate little hands together. 'Sir,' he said, 'your historic certainties seemed to be an excusing factor in your defence of slavery. Do you think we are in need of such defenders? The very Constitution from which our freedom flows pretends that it gives the same weight to slavery as to the freedom of the individual. This is a hopeless contradiction, Mr Mitchel, and will tear our nation in two as clearly as any contradictory impulses will.' And while he spoke, he kept his strange broad eyes on Jenny, and the strange, terribly tolerant reproof that they contained – apparently for failing to say something before her orator husband had.

Jenny gathered herself, seizing the chance to tell Beecher, 'I have to admit I am not as certain as is my husband on the value of the peculiar American institution of slavery.' She felt she must assert her own belief and doubts. 'I am not sure that with time we might well be able to dispense with slavery. But you have never mentioned the sciences.'

John took up Jenny's theme. 'Given what the scientists like Gobineau tell us of the limitations of the African race, how could you be halfway certain that liberation burns in the brain of the African slave as you say it does? Is it not true, and do not scientists such as Blumenbach say it, that the African is a degeneration of the model of man and that his skull proclaims it?'

'May I say,' Jenny intruded, not quite finished with the matter of science, 'we Mitchels take joy in these realities. But that zealotry on the matter of abolition is not only ill advised but seems, indeed, to contemplate the sundering of this country; as well as being indeed a denial of what men as eminent as Dr Linnaeus says of the African race.'

'An African slave,' John concluded, 'could thus plead for liberty without knowing what he asks for.'

Mr Beecher had time to nod, and nod again.

'Madame,' said the reverend, reproving Jenny again with his eyes, 'while agreeing with you as to the possible coming tragedy, I do ask you earnestly whether a temple can stand which is half-divine in impulse and half-debased. This is the pass at which we have arrived in America. But I assure you I do not revel in its potentialities.'

'We simply do not accept your description of the temple as half-debased, sir,' said John, like a friend and in a calmer voice. 'At least not in the terms you define it. You task me with the duty not to mention Washington and Jefferson, the builders of your temple. In the span of your history, these men are barely dead! Jefferson not three decades gone.' He held up a hand as Beecher rushed in to help him, the foreigner, with the dates. But even if a foreigner, Johnny was a quicker one than that. 'You tell me that the temple he built is no longer suitable for you, sir, or your congregation.'

Jenny saw John's hand tremble and thought that all the arguments of the day, including the ones he had had with himself, were having an effect on the sinews of his admirable arms, and on the nerves that had knit them.

'I would like to know on what basis,' he continued, 'you believe yourself better qualified than Jefferson to place the columns in the temple of liberty?'

Jenny thought, if only John could convey the naked truth of Famine to this half-actor, half-pastor, who saw the hungry and the sick from the windows of carriages! Who did not catch omnibuses, as John did? One thing she didn't say: other Christian countries would have considered the Reverent Beecher's eminence and lustre very suspect. The Church of England and of Ireland would have unleashed on it the finest artillery the archbishop's palace at Lambeth could muster. But then Beecher turned his gaze on Jenny. He seemed full of infinite want, like a child. What did he seek? She did not think it was as abstract as liberty.

'I do not consider myself superior to any man,' he told the Mitchels, moving his eyes from John to Jenny. 'Like all the children of Adam, I am a child of sin.' This frankly acknowledged sinfulness – as previously observed by Jenny's friend Molly Tunstall – was a novel element in Mr Beecher's array of pastoral tools. Jenny was sure as he said it, permitting something unrehearsed into his face, he spoke of his own imperfections. He seemed to have substantial sins in mind. According to Molly, they were specific sins to do with members of his congregation. But his august presence made Jenny wonder if that might have just been her friend misreading signs or jumping to callow conclusions.

382

'But,' he continued, 'even as we acknowledge our own imperfection, we are also aware that there are flaws in the very foundation of the temple. For our republic, Mr and Mrs Mitchel, elevated freedom to the highest apogee of civic and religious honour, and at the same time left the Africans, our brothers, bereft of it.'

'Yet as my dear wife says,' John declared, 'read the scientists and learn from them. The flaw of slavery was overlooked in the excitement of a new state, but the very existence, the breath of the nation itself, demanded then that this fatal irony be attended to with reason. That is all we are about, Brother Beecher.'

Jenny got the impression now that the reverend's eyes were threatening to bleed from their sockets in front of her. An extraordinary impression, only one of many he could propel at people.

He said, 'You do not know, and I do not know, when this contradiction will strike us in our body and in our blood, and in the body and blood of all Americans. But it will not leave us, you understand. It will not let us rest.'

'What if the South wins the argument, Mr Beecher?' Jenny asked. 'Would you accept that? The decree of war?'

'And,' said John, and Jenny had the sense that he was tiring of this dispute, 'there are Christian leaders in the South, I believe, and soon hope to find by investigation, who are perfectly happy to receive their congregations without any sanction being laid on them for their owning slaves. Amongst them, I am told, it is taken as truth that the African origins of the slave make a very poor preparation for the civil life of Europe and the Americas, and that the pagan African culture or even the limitation of their souls require Americans to offer their African slaves a different nurture, a nurture inherent in slavery, rather than wave them off to the mine and the plant. Remember, Mr Beecher, one does not say they are not God's children, but as St Paul wrote to Philemon . . .'

'Do not stretch yourself, Brother Mitchel, on the letter to Philemon, since I have had it quoted to me by every Southern advocate I meet. But with St Paul, sir, you are reaching back – unlike with Mr Jefferson, to antiquity – and since we are not of that antiquity but are of American modernity, I cannot see how the letter to Philemon applies.'

'And so St Paul was wrong to send the escaped slave Onesimus back to his master in Colossae? For it seems a large reach by any pastor to find his conscience superior to that pillar of Christianity!'

'St Paul was a man of his time, as all of us are. I am a man of my time, that is all I claim for myself, and my time is the time of liberty, at least here. If we deny its force and are happy to live part slave and part free, the malign contradiction will consume us. But I am beginning to repeat myself . . .'

They all looked at each other then, as if for offerings, and for a moment Jenny saw her Johnny the debater and wondered for a moment how profoundly placed was his belief in this whole business of slavery. Had he found himself forced in it by his own playfulness? For what cause was he arguing? He didn't own a slave, and was unlikely ever to do so. Indeed, he would never own one while she lived. Jenny would feel reduced if they ever had a slave, and so where did all the fervour of the Mitchels – his, hers – come from?

'I can see you are sincerely set in your arguments, Friend Mitchel,' the Reverend Beecher conceded. 'In that situation, I wonder would you do me the honour of confronting me in my den, of visiting me at Plymouth congregation just down the road a little? No notice taken and nothing assumed. Simply the willingness to praise God.'

Jenny wanted to agree to attend – she, Madame Mitchel – because of the uncommon way the famous preacher had stung her sensibilities. She felt almost refreshed by this afternoon of discourse.

She said, 'Would you tell your congregation I would feel most wronged if they devoured him alive.'

The Reverend Beecher gave a compelling smile. 'My congregation will not subject him to the slightest discourtesy, least of all to cannibal aggression.'

John smiled at her and said, 'We must do this, Jenny, on one of our Sabbaths. Do you think the congregation is ready for our six little God-fearers, especially Rixy? And would the Reverend Beecher permit me to address his congregation?'

'I am afraid, Mr Mitchel, I cannot give such an undertaking.'

'We'll be along,' said John, 'as soon as you make that concession.'

Beecher smiled and stood and thanked Jenny handsomely for having him at their residence. And so they parted, more or less as respected friends. When he'd left, the Mitchel sisters crowded into the room, having of course heard the entire exchange, and somehow excited by the Mitchels' resistance to him, even though they wanted to argue some of the main points themselves.

John said, 'They can free them if they want. But the abolitionists themselves will treat them like inferiors. It's madness.'

They would never go to Plymouth Congregational, of course. John mentioned that night, without malice, that he could tell the reverend had enjoyed Jenny's company, and had addressed many of his questions to her, perhaps wanting to divide his opponents but in a way that showed he was attracted to her spirit.

'Who could blame him?' John Mitchel asked. 'For you are a beautiful woman in your prime. But you must have heard from some of your friends that women who enchant the Reverend Beecher do not in any sense fare well from it.'

Jenny became a little gruff at this, as if she were perhaps being accused of flirting with the preacher. At that moment, to tell the truth, she would have welcomed a fight. On reflection, however, as the mesmerism of the Reverend Beecher wore off, she saw that indeed there was no woman who could benefit from association with him. In truth, the names of those who had tried to were known amongst the congregation, and their husbands were known to frown thunders, and what was the point of it all? Jenny realised how patently she would prove herself flippant if she changed her principles just because of the power of Beecher's gaze.

She knew how fortunate she was not to have the normal, much-approved dictatorial husband. John did not issue edicts to her. Only to history. There would have been great fights had it been otherwise.

Still, she lacked any vocation for owning slaves and undertaking their care.

———

There was a sentence amongst what the reverend had said to them that remained after the frenzy. He had said something which suddenly seemed a genuine warning, and it struck Jenny as such even that happy afternoon, when arguments still were innocent and did not yet draw blood.

'You do not know, and I do not know, when this contradiction will strike us in our body and in our blood, and in the body and blood of all Americans.' Was it just a mere point in all the debating? Yet it was memorable for her, with more force than all the rest of the argumentation. Perhaps it was the invoking of body and blood – as if John and she were counted in, and not exempt at all simply because of their recent arrival. They had certainly thought they were listed and doomed to pay high Irish costs, and had done so! But the Reverend Beecher was rounding them up into the American congregation, into the liability of paying large costs.

There would be many times when, in tiredness or low spirits, the idea would recur to Jenny and make her uneasy for her children.

———

Affluence came now, after all the travels and all the perils. And who would begrudge the Mitchel family? The children got measles in the spring, and it took two months to run through them, but even before the discomforts and demands of that, shared by John's amiable sisters, the Reverend Beecher's visit and the strange weight of his eyes were forgotten by Jenny.

Meanwhile, in Italy, the men trying to unify the country in those days, the Italian politician-unifiers and the general, Garibaldi, were complaining that the Vatican States, such as Lazio, Umbria, Marche, Romagna and a few other areas, lay across the Italian Peninsula like a primitive gag. The Catholic clergy and the Archbishop of New York, John Hughes, a muscular priest, worried about the impact the loss of those states would have upon Catholicism and on the authority of the Pope.

When this matter arose and John applied himself to it, his honesty, let alone annoyance, had a capacity to offend Know Nothings and clerics in one swipe. 'The very existence of the Pope and the vitality of the church,' he wrote in *The Citizen*, 'is endangered by his standing between the triumph of popular liberty, and the overthrow of despotism in Italy and in all the Catholic countries of Europe.'

Why did the Pope have to be a temporal leader of a state in Italy? asked Mitchel in one of the early issues of the newspaper. Dagger John – that is, Archbishop Hughes – and the Catholic clergy condemned John Mitchel now for raising the proposition the Holy Father might be a better spiritual prince if not encumbered with these Papal States.

The archbishop, a refugee from County Tyrone as a child and a seminarian in Philadelphia, from which point he came in due course to clerical prominence, knew the Church and the Irish were inseparable, and, as far as Dagger John was concerned, were not to be sundered. From the reaction of this Archbishop of New York, it became apparent that Mitchel was taking on a broad spectrum of the world in those early editions of *The Citizen*: the abolitionists and the British government, and both the Know Nothings and the Catholic clergy. However, the survivors of the Famine themselves, ordinary Catholics in Ireland and America, were willing to stand behind the Prince of Rome since he was *their* prince, and displeasuring Dagger John was dangerous to the circulation and authority of *The Citizen*.

There was another piece John wrote at the time Jenny might have advised him against. 'The Irish here will be good and loyal citizens of this republic,' he had asserted, 'in the same proportion that they cut themselves off, not from religion, but from the political corporation which you call the Church of God.'

Jenny sensed that most Catholic Irish could not or would not make the distinction. Some priests accused John of being a Know Nothing, and of having reverted to his native Orange-ism.

'There is far more of the Orangemen in you than I have,' John protested to the archbishop. 'That is, you possess a narrow ferocious spirit; but if there be any class of persons whom I abhor more than Orangemen, worse than the Know Nothings, it is the Inquisitors.'

28

Meagher Back in New York, and John Mitchel Goes South, Spring 1854

Until now, Mitchel had been assumed by other Protestants to have been all in favour of the spiritual rule the clergy had over the Irish, or else to recognise it as a given of the world. In the tide of ultramontanism — that is, strident devotion to the Prince of Rome as source of truth and the prince as well of the Papal States — he was influenced and pleasantly distracted by a piece he read in the *New-York Tribune*. It was about the growth of a little town named Knoxville at the eastern end of Tennessee, hard up against the Great Smoky Mountains.

To begin with, few people there owned slaves. No-one owned factories. The mountains there breathed out a vapour — hence their name — and it seemed the vapour of honest survival and homeliness and self-sufficiency.

Mitchel always felt he belonged in the land of mountains and farmers, being by upraising a man of Down, where farms and mountains were the summary of what Down was.

Meanwhile, as the spring broke in New York, sales of *The Citizen* remained solid, though some priests forbade their congregations to buy it, under pain of damnation, albeit in a free society people tended to make their own decisions on that. After all, Mitchel had begun publishing excerpts of his journal of imprisonment and then of his escape in its pages – his *Jail Journal* – which most Irishmen were quite intrigued by, and in the reading of which they did not let the archbishop govern them. The condemnations of Mitchel by Mr Beecher diminished in time, and even Dagger John got sick of damning Mitchel from his pulpit in Fifth Avenue.

And now John was invited suddenly by the Council of Richmond in Virginia to visit their city, and at the same time by the University of Virginia to give their Commencement Address. He asked Jenny would she like such an excursion, a visit of investigation, and held out the concept that besides visiting the capital of Virginia, nearby Charlottesville, they would visit its university and the house of Monticello – both of them, house and university, designed by immortal Jefferson. Mitchel was aware that in some way Jenny had been unsettled by the extraordinary Reverend Beecher, and persuaded towards expecting a gloomy and perhaps bloody outcome for the United States and its families, whose future she had till then considered largely gleaming.

Mitchel said, 'All nonconformist clergymen in County Down that one could have met aren't a preparation for the entirely American Mr Beecher.'

'It is true,' Jenny admitted. 'But if you are to be made a pariah for the South's sake, you should at least lay eyes on the South.'

Jenny and Mitchel travelled to Washington by train, transferring to fresh carriages at Exchange Station in New

Jersey and seeing another side of America, the New Jersey and Pennsylvania farmlands, which delighted her. They then took the steamer along the Potomac to the point named Aquia Creek, where the Richmond, Virginia and Potomac Railroad ran south through splendid country unmarked by factories and their darkness and squalor. As happened with Mitchel when he'd first travelled this way to see the Russian ambassador, Jenny knew at once that they now lived in a nation of considerable scope, expanse and variation. A nation into which Ireland would have fitted twenty or even a hundred times.

They arrived in Richmond, an amiable town in those days of far fewer than it later came to hold – perhaps less even than twenty-five thousand – on the west bank of the James River. It was to be two or three days before the promised mayoral dinner, and the university's commencement would precede it, so they would have time to look at the buildings they had come south to see; namely, those designed by the immortal Jefferson.

The plantation house of Monticello was a little run down, but its rotundas and colonnades were a memorial in stone to the order of Jefferson's mind and of the order of society – as in coming and going there they looked at the black people labouring in the fields of this most wonderful of states. The whole scene, felt the Mitchels, declared a pleasing and orderly hierarchy. Here was order. Look elsewhere for the voracious machines of capital!

And if elsewhere men simply piled stone upon stone, striving for effect, here there was a hierarchy in stone, a hierarchy of society's skills applied in the one nobility of architecture. No such message emerged in the North, where the most skilful man built railways and textile factories and mines of consummate ugliness, debasing to owner; above all, to worker. Here was a landscape that was in balance with itself and the elements of which were reconciled with each other.

'People can hear themselves think here,' Jenny remarked to John, and he understood what she meant. Mitchel had the disquieting feeling, as they looked at Jefferson's symphonic structures, set in sylvan places, that perhaps he had been rushed into taking postures in the great ferment of New York. This had been, in part, the newspaper acting as a hastener of – and a catalyst for – his adopting attitudes. You were required to state who you were in New York. People felt entitled to the full balance of the ideas you wore like the bright colours of teams or factions, and to which you were required to nail your name. No teasing was allowed, no humorous overstatement could be tolerated, no mischievous wordplay.

Mitchel had arrived in New York through the ministrations of Nicaragua, innocent as a babe, uncoloured by anything but an obvious lust for freedom. But he could not be allowed to remain a babe in the arms of the great republic, and to take his time with deciding on the shibboleths of the society. New York lay in his imagination as a place where bands never ceased playing to allow reflection, where men of supposed worth congratulated drum-majors for militant music forced on sensibilities. All New York shouted, and bands shouted. What is America? Tell us what you think of slavery, quick! And hammer your flesh to that mast of opinion!

Here, in the boskiness of Virginia, where nothing, not even birdsong, had the strident assertiveness of New York, the garment of opinions in which he had already covered himself in front of the American native-born seemed almost accidental, a costume he had simply picked up and worn.

As for the University of Virginia, its buildings had been kept up, as they say, and the impact of the place on his nervous system and Jenny's came as another form of relief from the New York fever. The quadrangle amongst the rotundas and the Corinthian colonnades at Charlottesville made Mitchel envious of those who were young enough still to be called students. He remembered the coldness and lack of colour of the Easter Commencement at Trinity, the iron gates that allowed graduates entry into the theatre, the march of the Fellows, all following a Puritan appetite for grimness and an ambition for at worst dun, if not stygian blackness. No meaningful music. And graduates were told that if they wanted their graduation certificates, they could collect them at the porter's lodge whenever they chose!

Since Jenny and he approached the university by way of a broad avenue with woods and vistas either side, its obvious spaciousness overwhelmed the memory of the cramped space of Trinity College Dublin, crammed into its small acreage. And even from the steps of the Rotunda itself, designed by immortal Jefferson, one could see the vistas of farming land stretching off southwards. Whereas, what vistas were evident from Trinity? Blunt walls weeping with rain!

As Jenny and he promenaded down the quadrangle at the University of Virginia, amidst the elegant low buildings, a tentatively smiling man in academic gown approached the Mitchels. He was young, and spoke in a melodious accent from somewhere else, perhaps the Carolinas.

'Excuse me,' he said, 'but we are always grateful for visitors from abroad. Could I be of any assistance?'

Jenny challenged him first on the grounds for his thinking her foreign. 'Do I look like a foreigner, young man?' She was wearing a bombazine dress that had come with her from Van Diemen's Land.

'Madame,' he said, covering his tracks fairly well, 'perhaps I have been premature in my judgement. I do not mean . . .' But he did not define what he meant, instead setting himself to defining what he did. He gave up at last and said, 'If I can be of any assistance, I am Dr Darcy Prendergast, professor of history in this university.'

'Well, we are the Mitchels.' Jenny, knowing that she and John were here for a conquest, smiled. 'You must have heard my husband is here to give a commencement address . . . he escaped from the penal colony of Van Diemen's Land but is editor of the New York *Citizen* . . .'

'Oh my God, so you are our hero, sir!' declared the professor. 'A hero in Ireland, a hero in your escape, and now in defending the South!' He laughed heartily and in undisguised joy. 'Oh my heavens, is it really you, Mr John Mitchel?'

John could always depend on Jenny to produce this trick of proud announcement, which cut through a great deal of introductory palaver.

'Mr and Mrs Mitchel,' Professor Prendergast enthused. 'I believe you knew the immortal Davis? And you are said to be a familiar of Carlyle himself?' Then he declaimed a bit of Davis, for good measure. 'Alas and well might Ireland weep, That Connaught lies in slumber deep . . .'

And Jenny responded. 'And hark, a voice like thunder spake, The West's awake, the West's awake!'

Young Professor Prendergast clapped his hands in delight. And immediately he took them off to meet the faculty at their midday dinner in a long, panelled dining room. A black waiter brought meals for the Mitchels as Prendergast, his face agleam, introduced them. Another professor cried,

'But, Prendergast, you lucky devil, you have come to our Commencement a day early. You mustn't abuse your good fortune by quizzing the poor man about the substance of his speech.'

'All of Virginia will be here, for heaven's sake!' another reminded them. 'Starting with Governor Johnson. And here we have the champion that has taken on the abolitionists in his New York journal! Surely, gentlemen, it won't offend Mr Mitchel if we ask for a tiny presentiment of his speech.'

For once Mitchel was a little reluctant. 'I can tell you that, as is appropriate, I speak on the broadest possible subject, the question of whether this century is the capstone on the past and whether the march of progress has benefited us. I have called it "Progress in the Nineteenth Century".'

He did not want them to think that he would deal with accessible, with easy and applaudable subjects, such as the intrusion of federal government into states' rights.

There was in any case a round of polite applause from the dons' tables. And so by the end of the lunch hour the Mitchels had more Southern friends than they would have thought possible and Jenny, her full girlish face flushed with a glassful of sherry and with her own triumph amongst the scholars, smiled at Mitchel, her cheeks as rich as fruit. Splendid nights and resonant speeches seemed to hang in the air, and altogether in another world, a world that was not the Yankee world, a world where there was space to breathe, a world of agriculture and craft, instead of machinery and heartlessness.

On the forenoon of the appointed day, Mitchel was part of the procession into the stately Rotunda, and beyond it into the theatre. The benches within were already crowded by women in summer fabrics, each fluttering a fan, a rustle like flocks of birds in the seconds before they take to the air. The upper end was a handsome carpeted platform, occupied by scholars and generals of militia and judges and politicians. And in the gallery at the rear, a band had been brought in from Baltimore to provide appropriate music – not the bombast of bands in New York.

Then, when the moment came, Mitchel rose to begin with his thesis.

'It is taken for granted, perhaps it should not be, that every advance in machines is for the better and is servant to the greater happiness of humankind. Where is the evidence? Is humankind happier than it was thirty centuries ago? There is no denying in a temple to the scholarly spirit that the printing press had brought with it the broader literacy of humans, with happy results, such as are evident in the Rotunda today.'

Mitchel did not denounce the great machines of convenience, and could praise gas and steam, upholstery and telegraphs as well as any man, but along with them came other machines whose results could not be as fulsomely praised. The boilers whose explosions filled the streets of American cities with the coffins of the desecrated. The children who managed the doors or clappers in mines and never saw the sun, living and dying under the ground. Those infants and folk of small frame maimed by the machinery of textiles. Those buried when embankments on tunnels gave way and barely mourned before further legions of men and women, arriving at the dock of New York and Boston and Philadelphia, filled the gaps of the industrial soldiery awaiting the next industrial calamity, which would be as certainly perilous as artillery was to the soldier. There could be no advance for humankind unless, along with the inventions of machinery, there came a greater wisdom amongst those who used them. As his friend Carlyle had said, machines had taken human destiny out of the hands of the individual and even those of God. By machines wealth was created, according to the story all were fed, but as Carlyle wrote, '. . . of our successful, skilful workers some two millions, it is now counted, sit in work-houses, poor-law prisons or have "out-door relief" flung over the wall to them – all justified by utilitarianism, the idea that society shall create the greatest happiness of the greatest number! How does the doctrine of the equality of man stand in the face of such opportunism?'

There being no system of legislation or compulsion which called forth wisdom, there being no law except the prejudices of the present moment in which people lived to make them any wiser or better than we had been as wanderers and journeyers upon the face of the earth, there was no sagacity that demanded that innovation in machinery and thought must occur for the benefit of the mass of humanity rather than of the wealth of some industrial slave driver. We could not argue, he continued, that our era was one in which the mass of our race was advanced and cherished. Things had diminished since the day of Jefferson, and the expeditious machines of capital had overtaken the original dream of homesteader and patriarch, and had overridden the dignity of man and woman.

Wisdom was not in the works of those historians like Macaulay, Mitchel went on further, who thought that the tragedy of earlier centuries was that they were not the nineteenth century. In fact, for many humans it is that the tragedy of the nineteenth century is that it was not like any *other*. Only by returning to Carlyle's 'Everlasting Yea', to the divine in humankind, could universal happiness be achieved.

There was polite and even enthusiastic applause, though Mitchel thought that in their way his listeners were secretly admirers of the century. Professor Prendergast, in thanking him for the revelations he had offered those about to graduate, and to the scholars and people of Virginia, praised him for realising that a commencement ceremony should not be taken up with tales of the South Seas and with thrilling escapades.

Quite a dinner was held that night, and many accolades offered Mitchel, despite his controversial speech. The next day, after rest, John and Jenny decided that on their way home they would traverse the wonderful vein of the Shenandoah to Harpers Ferry, from which they could make their way to Washington.

When they returned to New York, travel of a full two-and-a-half days, they found Tom Meagher was back from his absence.

———

On his return, Meagher insisted on taking Mitchel to dinner at Delmonico's at South William Street. In a sense the glittering Delmonico's showed the gulf between the two men, for it was three floors of dominant glass, and its ground floor colonnades were said to come from Pompeii. These were details Meagher considered significant, and even more appropriate for the democratic use the Delmonico family made of them in the New World.

They had a small room to themselves, a solid, secret cocoon amongst all the sparkle and refraction of light and marble.

'Dear old fellow,' said Meagher, as soon as the waiter left, and with a complaisant smile on his lips, 'when I abandoned the editorial drift of the paper to you, I did not expect you to pick such mighty fights with abolitionists and Archbishop Dagger.'

His suntanned and handsome face transmuted into a frown. Mitchel awaited a chuckle to accompany it, but there was not one. It was a genuine reproach.

Mitchel felt a surge of anger. Naturally, he was close to saying, 'If you want *The Citizen* to reflect you, write something for its pages!' But he swallowed, and said instead, 'It's true what Jenny says. When I write I give way to exaggeration and teasing, and to irritation too. I don't want to be a plantation manager in Alabama any more than you do. But it's the sort of excessive sentiment people here take as the literal truth.'

He inhaled and resisted begging for pardon. Meagher shook his head, paused, and unexpectedly let go of a bark of laughter. 'Now I am back, Dagger John will not attack you. I had better declare my own colours on these matters. And old fellow, worse things do happen. I remember how your Jenny begged us to take action the day of your sentencing. If you will forgive my failure to do so, I shall forgive your being encouraged into stating things as you see them.'

Mitchel thought there would an expansion of that statement and was already thinking that he loved Meagher for his spontaneous gesture. But his astonishment was that Thomas now began weeping at the table.

'Benny,' he explained. 'It is poor Benny!'

Mitchel leaned across to take his wrist, all pique at an end.

'Benny is dead at my father's place in Waterford. You must surely know that.'

'No,' Mitchel declared. This was a shock and news that did not reflect well on Meagher, for whom he felt a surge of annoyance at his inept marriage, as well as for the loss of young Benny.

'I was not in the office today,' said Meagher. 'It will be in the papers tomorrow. All the Anglophiles will scoff at my poor colonial marriage, of course. The troubles Benny and I had between us: this city simply too massive for her. But the poor girl is gone. I shall wear black for her and make an offering to Archbishop Hughes to say a solemn requiem in St Patrick's. May she rest in peace, poor child.'

Mitchel could not say anything coherent. Meagher both wanted – and knew he did not deserve – sympathy.

'It was typhus,' he continued. 'Not that your Jenny would take that as exonerating me in any way. And indeed, why should she? Those who said I was rushing into an association in Van Diemen's Land were right! It was not a marriage that could survive my escape. I did not wish her death. God forbid! Yet there it is.'

'I am very sad for the girl,' Mitchel stated. 'She may have made an excellent New York wife in the end.'

'Come on, Mitchel, you can't mean that. And the fact that you and I and everyone says that, fixes her more firmly in her place as a Van Diemen's Land convict's daughter. But she won't stay there. She is with me here, the highwayman's lovely daughter that New York terrified. Mother to my son, but dimly remembered at this remove from Lake Sorell. Shamefully distant altogether is what she seems. Yet she'll always be there. A great reproach to me. And yes, I think your wife is right in her suspicions of me.'

'My wife is frequently right in her suspicions,' said Mitchel.

'But you see,' Meagher declared, 'she cannot condemn me in the terms I already condemn myself. I have done Benny terrible harm.'

It was bewildering to see Meagher so troubled. Speranza, who had thought him such a darling, laughing boy, 'an engine of joy, untroubled by doubt', as Mitchel remembered . . . Speranza honking with her own blend of innocence and knowingness. But she was married now, and it was too late for them.

Meagher said, 'Catherine Ann Bennett, born Van Diemen's Land, 1832, died of typhus, Waterford, Ireland, May 9, 1854. *Requiescat in pace.* May her sleep, poor girl, be with the angels. *Solas mhic dé ar a n'anam.* Our infant son is still there, Mitchel, in Waterford.'

'But you can bring him here.'

With a little tremor of the head, he agreed. 'I can, I can. To be decided, I suppose, by my father. He would have the kindest of nurses, and my sister as well, tending for the dear little fellow.'

'But you are the father, Tom.'

'And he's the father of the father.'

Meagher drank a deep draft of burgundy wine, sighing afterwards for the partial absolution it gave.

'Now, Mitchel, this is not unconnected to the other matter.' He laughed a little and shook his head. 'The fact you went full blast right into the slavery business, as I said. In the second issue, no less. I did warn you.' But chastened by loss, he again decided to laugh, this time with fondness rather than chastisement. 'Some men might peer about them a little longer before going into battle against the Dagger Johns and the Beechers and the Know Nothings in the one hit. You are courageous to a fault.'

'I was challenged by Haughton and the Devil's Island prisoners on that matter.' Mitchel thought Meagher meant nonetheless a complaint with his 'courageous to a fault'. But he pretended in the circumstances that Tom was complimenting him.

'We were even visited at home,' Mitchel said, 'by that Barnum of preachers, the Rev. Beecher.'

And for a while Meagher laughed along with Mitchel and shook his head.

'He met your Jenny?'

'He met my Jenny,' Mitchel said, and was willing happily to imply that Jenny had summed Beecher up with the same ease she had brought to summing up Meagher himself.

'The slavery thing,' said Meagher. But he did not say anything further to illuminate the matter. Then, 'I have a spiritual adviser, a Jesuit, Father Clunes. I have been with the Jesuits all my life.'

'The Know Nothings,' Mitchel observed, struggling to contribute something, 'consider the Jesuits an especial danger to the Constitution.' For bigots considered Jesuits the most sinister guerrillas and filibusters of Papism.

Meagher shook his head at this common knowledge, Benny's inescapable death colouring still all that he said.

The Jesuits had, in fact, been mentioned by good Protestants, even at the academic banquet in Charlottesville. They had heard Mitchel's father was of the Unitarian Presbyterian ilk, and therefore felt free to share with Mitchel some of their fearful perceptions of that famed order as the Satanic cavalry of Rome.

'So,' Meagher continued, 'I have been up to Fordham today, in the Bronx. Up to see Father Clunes, the professor of rhetoric. What can a spiritual adviser do about a bad

403

marriage? And a bad conscience? So I wept for Benny up there with Dr Clunes! I knew I had to meet you, of course, not least as a business partner, but for a time I did not think I would be able to stop grieving enough. But it's a particular kind of grief. It's not that I could not go on living without Benny. Because, to be honest, I could. It was my guilt for using the girl.'

Mitchel contemplated this, a lifetime's penance for a marriage tidied away by the hand of typhus. The first child in its grave in Van Diemen's Land. The wife dead in Ireland.

Meagher seemed to weigh his responsibility a while, and said, 'Meanwhile, there's the slavery issue. And you seem to write with great certainty on the matter, John. I think it's time we tried to shed new light on what seems a settled subject. That we understand the full scope of the matter. Do it for Benny's sake, if you must. For I believe we must moderate the editorial policy we've started off on. I know you will believe what you will believe, Mitchel. And believe it immovably.'

'Not necessarily,' John confessed. 'Because recently, on the journey South and into the country . . . I was wondering for a time what I do believe. One is forced into postures in New York.'

'Yes, yes, isn't that true,' said Meagher, still the bereaved husband.

John mused, 'I wondered if I do want to be an Alabama plantation owner. I don't, I believe.'

'New York,' Meagher told him solemnly, 'is a particular form of theatre.' And then, 'But you and your wife will attend the Requiem mass? Saturday? St Patrick's at ten.'

'Of course.'

Meagher shook his head, as if dismissing previous ideas. 'Will the grass really grow on the streets of New York if the business of the South ever stops? I do not think the Union of the United States should be split apart to liberate the slaves. But the question of liberation in itself . . . No man should be content to speak on that, I believe, without having heard comments from the slaves themselves.'

'Of course, slaves themselves will complain and speak of liberty,' Mitchel said. 'The way soldiers complain. The way sailors do. While enduring their lot. But there is a difference. Slaves want freedom because abolitionists mention it tirelessly.'

'You really believe that?'

'I do.'

'The Compromise of 1850 we all say we hold to . . . Believe me, Mitch, it cannot itself hold.'

'You are probably right,' Mitchel conceded.

And so it was arranged – they would visit the Jesuit together. It would be a form of useful research. Mitchel had not seen before the acreages of forest and farmland in upper Manhattan, and the cascades of the north end, nor crossed into the villages of the Bronx. 'Of course, I'll come,' he told Meagher.

'Then,' said his friend, 'may we drink deep to poor Benny?'

——

In the week following his evening with Meagher, Mitchel received a summons from Baron Stoeckl, residing appropriately at the new St Nicholas Hotel on Broadway, a vast hotel famously complete with steam heat. The baron told Mitchel in his letter that he had received orders from his masters to talk further to him about the idea of a Russian flank emerging in the Irish Sea.

After the doubts plaguing Mitchel from his journey to the South, he again felt the exhilarating pulse of great strategies and massive events. Stoeckl wanted John to meet him amidst the palms and fluted marble columns of the hotel's great lobby, itself bigger than a rail terminus. When Mitchel arrived there he was greeted by a young Russian secretary, a slight fellow named Duderow, his hair and beard done in the French manner, like a facial Versailles after the uncropped hairiness of many New Yorkers. Duderow led him to a meeting room, all velvet hangings, gilt mouldings and vivid sconces, where in a shining blue vest and a dazzling-sheened jacket, the ambassador could have passed as a Southern planter visiting town.

Duderow nodded, directing him to a place by the baron's right and himself took a seat by a supply of paper adequate for a novel, and inkstands primed with India ink to make notes.

Stoeckl congratulated Mitchel on the emergence of the *Jail Journal* in *The Citizen* and in his stance in defence of Russia's honour in the matter of seeking to liberate Christians within the Ottoman Empire from the rule of the Turks.

'You skewer the hypocrisy of the British and the French,' said the ambassador. 'But I ask merely as a would-be philosopher – you disapprove of the works of empires when it comes to their subjects. Don't you? Do you not secretly disapprove of our Russian imperial reach too? Will *The Citizen* newspaper seek the opinions of a native of the Kirghiz Steppe or of a Tashkent separatist? To a revolutionary like you, does the destruction of the British Empire cry out to God more loudly than does a similar fate for the Russian Empire?'

Mitchel had not expected to be presented with such an abstract question.

'But I was hoping to hear a reaction from your govern-ment, Count Stoeckl,' he said, with plausible neatness, 'whereas I am all too familiar with Downing Street's reactions.'

'Yes, indeed, and you should be. I simply wondered . . . Would you indulge me? Every empire could be seen as a series of inflicted wrongs to subject peoples. Do you love us Russians at all, or only love your Irish?'

Mitchel thought for a while. But soon decided, to hell with abstractions of empires.

He said, 'I never pretended other than to be a man of an oppressed nation. This gave me brotherhood with the despised of my country. And the despised were the greater number of them. And the extent to which they were despised was demonstrated by the famine deaths. This was not the work of your empire. Now I could abominate your empire, sir, if it imposed similar suffering, but even so, that suffer-ing was not imposed on my brothers and sisters. Thus, in defending yourself from Britain, you are my friend. That is the extent of what I can tell you. The hour does not permit abstract questions, if I may be so bold.'

The secretary was writing away. There was silence. Outside, a porter was crying out in the lobby for a Mr Jimmy Ticehurst of Augusta, Georgia.

At last Stoeckl said, 'That is an interesting and honest answer. And I must tell you I have had communication with the Imperial Secretary for the Navy, Prince Alexan-der Sergeivich Menshikov, and with Foreign Secretary the Honorable Karl Nesselrode. They are both grateful for your suggestion of Irish aid, but cannot as yet formally record their thanks, of course, in part for your own benefit. There are two questions they have, though. The first is, what is your realistic estimate of the capacity of the land to support a Russian army?'

'If you landed a military expedition in mid-to-late summer, the harvest would sustain you as you advanced into the country. A student of British statistics would show that the Irish harvest, ignoring potatoes which are the peasantry's staple, is capable of feeding eleven million souls. After the calamity of the last ten years, there are barely more than five million left on the island. I know that armies plunder. But there would be little need of plunder. My friend Mr Meagher, Meagher of the Sword, as they call him, could document these figures for you.'

The secretary wrote fiercely. The baron smiled at Mitchel and waited for him to finish. At last, he asked the second question.

'What are suitable landing places on the west coast? That is, if cannon, horses, armaments, wagons and men were to be landed?'

'Again, I can provide these more authoritatively from the New York Public Library.'

'No need, my good Mr Mitchel, we have our own researchers.'

'In that case, the Dingle Peninsula is an admirable landing site in country where you would get great popular support from the peasantry of the south-west in Munster. For landing of the equipments of war there are ports at Dingle itself and further along towards Tralee, and behind the promontory of Derrymore, fine beaches for landing men in sturdy boats. On the lower promontory is Kenmare too. And then in Cork, Bantry Bay. And Kinsale, where the Spanish once kept an enclave. These are all splendid places, though Dingle should be closely examined. Would you like me to make a list?'

'My secretary Duderow is familiar with British and Irish nomenclature.'

'And of course,' said Mitchel, 'the French revolutionary government attempted a landing in 1796. But that was in a season of westerlies. At a kinder time of the year, conditions would be better.'

'But as Prince Menshikov says, so would be the capacities of the British Navy.'

'Not,' Mitchel asserted, 'if you had already defeated them in the Baltic . . . In any case, there are numberless places on the west coast, from Munster to Ulster.'

'These are all helpful suggestions, Mr Mitchel. You must realise that for us the key is emerging from the Baltic, when the British have such interests in Norwegian woods for topmasts and Eastern Baltic tar and pitch for the Royal Navy. However, all I can do is report to the cabinet. It would be true to report that your interest is chiefly Irish advantage, not Russian opportunity.'

Mitchel said, 'I would be deceitful if I said I loved a nation I have never seen.'

'Understandably,' the baron agreed. 'I know we don't need to ask you to prevent any whisper of this meeting being reported in your Irish *Citizen*.'

Mitchel felt hopeful, perhaps too much, as he walked out onto Broadway and into its press of citizens passing beneath the sizzle of the overhead wires. What had exhilarated him was that the baron had asked for the names of landing places. Mitchel had a joyous image in his head of Cossacks watering their horses on the rural banks of the Blackwater, and being greeted by Irish peasants somewhere in Kerry, Cork or Waterford, while to the east, Britain quaked.

29

Greeting the Slaves

Jenny was of course shaken and appalled by the news of Benny's death. It was as if she half-suspected Meagher of conjuring it up for his own convenience. She was given to tears for Benny when they attended the Requiem in the new St Patrick's on Fifth Avenue, in the pleasant, less over-built part of the town, not far from the uptown shacks of the immigrant Irish. Benny's seemed a great tragedy, and it was as if the very scale of her husband's world excluded her.

Many observant Catholics greeted the Mitchels as friends, overlooking the conflict between *The Citizen* and His Grace, Dagger John. Some whispered behind hands at the strangeness of having John Mitchel and Archbishop Hughes in the one building.

The archbishop spoke well of Tom Meagher and Benny, united in mutual consolation in a penal colony which, by its very existence, testified how the children of Roisin, the poor old woman who symbolised Ireland, Mangan's 'dark

Rosaleen', bore exile. And even here, in a happier place, the exiled sons and daughters of Roisin were so numerous that to pay tribute to Mr Meagher and his deceased wife, they packed the cathedral's pews. They were there, said His Grace Dagger John, as a salute to that great escaper and bereaved son of the Church, Thomas Meagher. Here was a man whose history and brilliance had placed him at the fore with the Irish of New York, and justified the crowd gathered in grief for him at the Holy Sacrifice of the Mass that sad day. The archbishop must have been pleased with himself, since it had been announced that a new and grander cathedral was to be built in the revived Gothic style, which, given all the old architectural devices – stained glass and effigies and gargoyles – was sufficient to make the Know Nothings froth impotently.

At the words describing Meagher as 'a son of the Church', Jenny smiled ruefully, shaking her head, as if it were a sign of the tenderness the Church was determined to treat Catholic Meagher with, but not Presbyterian Mitchel. After his experience in the uprising, Meagher himself did not love the clergy outright. But the priests could not afford to fail to love him, since their congregations certainly did. Meagher could survive any heresy and not be spurned by the archbishop. Mitchel, a non-conformist Protestant, could not. This was the reality of which Jenny was too well aware.

The archbishop declared that they all knew Mr Meagher, and some amongst the brethren had fought with him in Ireland's cause. They did not, most of them, know Catherine Bennett, but they could guess her character to be such as to make Meagher of the Sword's burden of grief heavy indeed. For she, though born in the New World and in a penal colony, child of Irish exiles, was the irreplaceable *bean an tí* of the Irishman's hearth.

'And of her own hearth,' murmured Jenny, like a prayer, beneath her breath. 'A tragedy from start to finish,' she had told Mitchel. Jenny considered Meagher a subtle killer by omission. Why had he not set Benny up in comfort with an Irish housekeeper in New York – to give birth securely, or as securely as it was ever the lot of women to do? If John had told her that in a few afternoons' time he would be off with Meagher to see Jesuits in the Bronx, she would have taken it as yet another sign of Meagher's levity.

———

Meagher collected Mitchel with a well-polished little buggy and driver, both borrowed from his lawyer, the eminent and affluent James Topham Brady in Broadway. Topham Brady was the man working to get Meagher admitted to the New York Bar. His odium as an Irish Roman Catholic was not moderated by the fact he was an enthusiastic member of a committee to promote warm relations between the Jewish and Irish societies of New York. But he was such a performer in the courts that few could afford to be his enemy.

On the way to see Meagher's Jesuit in Fordham, an excursion Mitchel hoped would not be a waste of time, Tom and he kept to Broadway, then turned off northwards on Third Avenue. The driver went as far as the solid habitations lasted, and continued their passage into the area of hovels and encampments beyond 45th Street. They passed many pleasant farms before seeking and crossing the 6th Avenue bridge. The country roads and open grounds, with children herding small mobs of cattle for milking, gave Mitchel once again the yearning for something smaller than the city, and raised in him that appetite he had always had for the smaller places of simpler equations than the demonic enigma of industrial cities.

He liked the farms around Bloomingdale, where Meagher said a friend of his from the Democrat Party owned a place. It was hard to believe that in this landscape Know Nothings and abolitionists and even Jesuits were at any ferocious work to alter the fabric of things, or to cast clouds over the bountiful earth.

It was less than an hour after leaving that they rolled across Harlem Creek and in amongst the farmlands of the Bronx, undulating away to ridges from one of which Fordham College would welcome them. The village of Morrisania looked prosperous and ideal, and Mitchel was cheered by it as he always was by well-ordered country. The farm workers passing them, the sun on their faces, looked well, and a sight less ragged than the Irish peasantry at the best of times. There were men, said Meagher moved to sudden conversation, whose families lived here and who worked in the city all week, returning to their hearth on Saturday afternoons and for the Sabbath. And if you went south in the Bronx from here, he said, it was all their fellow countrymen, Irish shanty towns with *shebeens* and Irish speakers from Donegal, Mayo, Sligo and Kerry and the wilder parts of Cork.

Mitchel could not help thinking of the work piling up in *The Citizen* office, and was even a little resentful that Meagher, having still – Mitchel supposed in some senses reasonably enough – not contributed many words of copy, would now be attempting to influence its editorial policy while having ruled out any reportage of this evening's excursion as newspaper copy at all. Well, it was too late now, to grieve or argue over it, since they were coming to the streets of the little town of Fordham.

On a hill with a circular drive and a scatter of pleasant buildings, some neoclassical and some with religious nods to the Gothic, sat the university. These American colleges, Mitchel began to see, had a particular arrangement, and did their best to seem to imitate some of the style of the University of Virginia. The fields for militia training and sport were not on the periphery but in the midst of the academic circle, so that one wasn't sure whether the grounds nearer to the buildings were meant for Socratic strolling or for the struggles of lacrosse. As they rode along the circular drive, a clocktower announced half past three in the afternoon. The carriage pulled up in front of the central rotunda.

Inside, a Jesuit scholastic, an as-yet-unordained young man, greeted them, and greeted especially Thomas Meagher as a regular visitor. Mitchel knew that if he were a New Yorker for fifty years he could not be as familiar to people, and as easy in people's company, or as much a habitual part of every scene, as Meagher was. The scholastic led them down a scrubbed corridor and knocked on one of the heavily panelled wooden doors, august in its claims on the best local hardwoods. A lively voice told them to come, and they did so, entering a room with its own library and fire and a view of the playing fields. There was a small ruddy-faced priest with a pipe in his hand.

'Mr Meagher,' he cried.

This Father Clunes would have heard Tom's confession, Mitchel thought, and Tom would have confessed the failure of his marriage, and his connection to women of the great city. But whatever he had confessed, it seemed not to have made a dent in the little priest's respect for him.

When Meagher introduced Mitchel, Clunes stood back a moment, inspecting him more or less, and gasped out the sentiment, 'I did not know I'd have the honour of ever meeting our great lightning rod, John Mitchel. You are indeed enthusiastically welcome, sir.'

'He is a remarkable fellow, my friend John Mitchel,' Meagher assured the priest.

'Of that I have no doubt at all. And I believe, sir, you are willing to accept this afternoon's proceedings on a confidential basis.'

'I believe they are the terms, yes, father,' Mitchel told him.

'Then, have you heard of the UGRR, Mr Mitchel?' the priest asked, tapping his pipe out on an ashtray.

'I am not sure. Is it a movement?'

'You could say so. The Underground Railroad. And according to bad law which I feel no necessity to uphold, we will all be guilty of not reporting these slaves on the run.'

'Yes, of course,' Mitchel admitted, but feeling it was a large concession.

The priest was holding his two small fists out but not in aggression, more in invoking Mitchel's silence. 'I can introduce you to two slaves, who have been on the UGRR, that rescue arrangement for runaway slaves. We will shelter these people in the New York area until they can be moved on to northern New York State and then to Toronto in Canada, where of course their slavery will be null and void. Again, I am breaking man's law by helping these souls along in any way, but I consider I am not breaking God's. Mr Meagher is convinced that as a newcomer to America, you, Mr Mitchel, will benefit from hearing the aspirations of such people expressed in their own tongue.'

He offered his guests refreshments before they faced the slaves, but as much as Mitchel would have welcomed tea, he was too anxious for the illicit meeting to begin – the proposed learning exercise. Meagher and Mitchel sat in chairs placed around the priest's desk, while Clunes went to the door that connected to the next room, opened it and called, 'Mr Jenkins, sir!' As he stood by, a hulking black man appeared, wearing a checked jacket and narrow pants, an ensemble perhaps provided to him by the priest's friends, by his fellow members of the notorious UGRR. Mitchel was quite fascinated to see the man, who had a big upper body and a much-scarred face but was not yet old, and certainly moved with some vigour. He paused by a chair put in place for him. This was Mitchel's first Southern slave in the flesh, when he had been so certain on slavery as a principle.

'Would you care to take a seat, Mr Jenkins?'

'I would not much mind that at all, thank you, Reverend,' Jenkins told the priest in a silken African voice.

He settled quickly and with only a modicum of fiddling with his unfamiliar clothes.

'I am reminded,' said Father Clunes, 'that you have had a considerable wound in your arm.'

'I was afraid of the lockjaw, father,' said Mr Jenkins, lifting the offending left arm painfully, a few inches off the chair.

'Yes. You took the full impact of a loaded gun on the left arm. Isn't that so?'

'Shot by slave hunters three days out from Martinsburg, Virginia, Reverend. That shot just ploughed up my arm lengthwise and raked the flesh off the bone. I was greatly afraid at the idea of lockjaw, but praise the Lord, I must say through mercy and the treatment of good folk who got me help from a doctor in Baltimore, the wound held true. When I go to work in Canada, people will ask me what's the meaning of that strange scar? I will tell them straight, it's where the Angel Gabriel held me as he led me out of slavery!'

'It's very likely the truth,' the priest told him, and looked at Meagher and Mitchel then as if he were concerned the idea sounded too fantastical for worldly men. 'But a doctor treated it with maggots, isn't that so? To prevent the poisoning of your blood.'

'I had that too, Reverend,' Mr Jenkins confirmed. 'The creatures of the grave singin' along with the angels of freedom, sir.'

'Do you have many wounds on your body, Mr Jenkins?'

'More than a soldier, Reverend Father,' said Jenkins, almost amused.

'Would you enumerate them? I mean by that, tell us where they are?'

So encouraged, Mr Jenkins obliged, touching through his clothing the places where – under the fabric – the scars were located. So the first time, at the age of eighteen, he had been shot in the meat of the shoulder while refusing to co-operate with a flogging. This had given him a reputation, he said, and the word got around that if people saw him at large, it was easier to shoot him than flog him. His master argued against the idea, given that he was worth $1500 – the same master had told him that, some years back. In any case, when he was twenty, a sheriff shot him in his head with squirrel shot, and then he had a flogging while getting better. Another man shot him in the leg when he was twenty-one.

'And thereafter,' Jenkins told us, 'I always took the trouble to walk with a limp, so people would think I was less of a subject for firing at.'

Meagher laughed – a rare laugh of this time of his life.

Jenkins took up his narrative again. When at last he decided to run away and try to make contact with the railroad, not only was his master dead but also his mistress, and her estate about to be settled. He was thus about to be inherited by his mistress's son-in-law, one James Bailey Esq., who on visits to his in-laws while the old couple still lived, promised Jenkins that as soon as he himself took possession of the estate, they would test out this proposition that it was so hard to make him submit to flogging. Or else he would talk about selling him to someone cruel for a large amount.

'He always managed to make me boil with rage, sir,' admitted Jenkins, 'and I had thoughts a Christian shouldn't.'

There were two other slaves, unmarried brothers, on the farm with Jenkins, and they too did not wish to become the property of Mr Bailey. And Jenkins had been talking to these two brothers about the Underground Railroad in Canada, which was a place of snows, but where slavery was against the law.

The last day of December they all decided to run off together. Between them they had life savings of $30, which they had promised to pay to a white man Jenkins had met once on a journey to town for his mistress. This man professed himself to know a great deal about the underground railway. They met, on the day of their escape, this supposed expert, and handed over to him all the money they had on earth. However, the man delivered them not to any underground railroad but into an ambush of slave hunters two miles beyond town.

Jenkins, with his arm wound, escaped them somehow, stumbling off into woods, and the two young men surrendered and went back to the mercies of the son-in-law. Jenkins hid himself in a drainage hole and did something of pure desperation the next morning: he had heard the minister in a place named Charlestown had made a stir by preaching a sermon which urged his parishioners to dream of a time in the future, when by their kindnesses and influence, the African slave might be ready to enjoy liberty. Jenkins walked through the forest to the village, entered a church consecrated to white worship, and hid behind the altar. The Episcopalian minister found him in the late afternoon, which was the beginning of escape true and sure; for even in Virginia there were people of the underground, and the minister had been earlier approached by some of them and knew them. That was how Jenkins was rescued and passed along the railroad.

Smuggled into Baltimore in a load of goods, his arm now treated with maggots, he had gone into hiding there. After some months, the Underground Railroad people asked Jenkins whether he was willing to go aboard a steamship bound for Philadelphia. It would not be an easy passage, they told him, but Philadelphia was at least in the North. If he could land there, he would be free, although if his master used the courts to get him back, the courts were obliged to hand him over. Thus, Philadelphia was the half-freedom that preceded the full liberty of Toronto.

Jenkins told his protectors that he embraced the chance. They warned that the escape space he might take to in the ship was cramped, but he assured them there was no hiding place so dark or small he could not tolerate, nor fail to will himself into. Late one night, he was smuggled aboard the steamship *City of Richmond*. A free black sailor introduced him into the boat and took him below to a place of concealment directly over the boiler. The sailor doubted Jenkins could fit himself in, in that dark cavity where he would get very warm. He applied himself to getting in there, though, and as he said to the sailor, he had heard that the voyage to Philadelphia was only a day and a half.

When the ship left on time with Mr Jenkins so hidden, all seemed well. They were halfway to Philadelphia when the headwinds hit them and blew madly for a number of days, and when the winds went off, the fog set in, disappearing only on the eighth day as *City of Richmond* made her way at last into the estuary of the Delaware, and on to Philadelphia. All that time he had to be smuggled into and occasionally let out of that cavity above a boiler, and was never caught.

Jenkins was well on his way to freedom now, he told Meagher and Mitchel in an earnest but celebratory voice, a voice warm with gratitude and thus touching. There was no mistaking the hope that was a-fire in him here in the Bronx. He said he dreamed his wife, who was with another master near Harpers Ferry, could one day be persuaded to take the course he had himself taken.

When the Reverend Clunes dismissed Jenkins, he stood and bowed. 'Sirs all,' he told them melodiously. As he left the room, neither Meagher nor the priest looked at Mitchel for confirmation that he was touched. He was. His sense that the world was broad in its malice had not been diminished. And Jenkins certainly, with his own story and convictions and wounds, was an eloquent case. Meagher was right. A person had to hear from someone like him to get the rounded story of what it was to be a slave. Jenkins's irony and narrative powers were also more than Mitchel had expected.

Meagher said to him at last, apparently casually, as they waited for their next meeting with a woman slave, 'What do you think, Mitch?'

'It is an affecting tale, no question. I was surprised by how well he delivered it.'

But what had impressed Mitchel above all was Jenkins's developed sense of freedom; that it had reached such a high level of clarity. It was true that some defenders of the Peculiar Institution, such as Dr Cartwright, declared the Negro slave could not understand the principle of personal freedom. Whether Jenkins had been instructed by his rescuers to make that very point, it seemed to be a sincere and unprompted desire within him.

In the door by which Jenkins had departed, there next appeared, without her being called for, a raw-boned young woman, tall, with a regal nose and a warrior's jaw. She wore a frown that even to Mitchel seemed to anticipate imminent recapture.

Father Clunes declared, 'It is my honour, gentlemen, to introduce you to Miss Adelanta Cunningham.'

He then invited her to sit, and asked a few questions about her origins, leading of course to her embarking on the UGRR. She, like Jenkins, came from Virginia, though the southern end, from Portsmouth. She had been born into the household of one Mrs Barclay and her widowed sister, under whom she and her mother and brothers had always served. Some of the white men they employed could behave with viciousness, but the sisters were kindly disposed, she said, and she added winningly, 'I had not been used as hard as many others.' This detail of course arrested Mitchel's attention, especially since she did not go on to gild that particular lily or to elaborate.

She and her two brothers had talked endlessly of the railroad. The brothers had taken it themselves and had reached the great whaling town of New Bedford, Massachusetts.

Adelanta herself had remained hidden a long time in Virginia after her first run from her owners. She did not say by whom she was sheltered, but it was for a period of seventy-five days, longer than Christ was in the desert. She brought out of her pocket a torn piece of the newspaper, advertising her brothers and herself, and offering an award of $1000 for her recapture.

Adelanta said that the advertisement had still been running in the paper when her protectors, fine Quaker people, offered her a chance of escape north. This again was by way of a steamer – in her case, *The City of Charleston*, Philadelphia-bound. The news was that she was to dress as a man, and present herself on the wharf at three o'clock in the morning. When she left hiding and reached the wharf, it was raining torrents. She was greeted by a crew member, a young black man who was a hired-out slave and who worked the decks. He took her to one of the holds and hammered her up into the box and its dark space. Within two days, the ship docked in Philadelphia – it was evening – and the box was unloaded, put on a wagon, and delivered to the Railroad's Vigilance Committee in Philadelphia.

She did not tell the listeners what arrangements she made to attend to nature in the two days of seaborne darkness. Her brothers, she had heard in Philadelphia, had by now gone on to Toronto, after rebuffing the idea of becoming whalers on a New Bedford ship for fear it would put into Southern ports. She herself had discussed with goodly white people about getting her brothers' wives and children onto the railroad. She was certainly a sturdy soul, Mitchel had to admit to himself.

When Adelanta was finished, and they bade her goodbye as she disappeared, the Jesuit offered both men the hospitality of the university.

'Enough for you to know,' said Father Clunes, 'our two fugitives were brought here specifically to meet you both, and have now been carried away into the evening by friendly spirits. Not that either of you gentlemen resemble slave hunters in any way.'

Meagher addressed Mitchel from his chair. 'It is a sobering thing to hear the escaped slave speak, don't you think, John?'

'It gives one some pause,' Mitchel agreed. 'Definitely, some pause.'

Father Clunes nodded, but there was little of the evangelist in him: no moral gloating.

Both Meagher and Mitchel claimed they had to be back in town. On the way home in the cold rural dusk, Meagher said to him, 'I saw enlightenment reach you, Mitchel, as you listened to Jenkins.'

'That it was all enlightenment, I can't deny,' Mitchel admitted.

'The common cry is that Africans can't understand freedom and need not be bothered with it. But Jenkins and Adelanta certainly showed a sharp sense of it, wouldn't you say?'

'Exactly my thoughts,' Mitchel conceded. '*The Citizen* must never sell them short on that score.'

'I must tell you I have had that experience once before,' Meagher admitted. 'Meeting two other runaways in Father Clunes's premises. It has made me more careful in what I say. I suppose I admire them, the escaped slaves. But I do not necessarily want to die for their freedom.'

'Do you support the railway?'

'In small ways,' Meagher admitted. 'Through Father Clunes.'

'But you are a Democrat, Tom, and believe in states' rights and tolerance for the institution.'

'But Mitch, I am not a Southern Democrat.'

It was time for Mitchel to confess what he had found to be the limits of the experience. 'The thing is, should slaves be encouraged to think of freedom? Is it not like whites desiring wealth? I, who am fortunate in any case, might want as many riches as an ironworks owner. It does not mean I am entitled to them, or desire to spend my life managing mill workers.'

Meagher looked gloomily out of the carriage window and sat forward wearily, but as if to challenge Mitchel.

'Why do you say an ironworks owner? Do you mean to imply someone by that?'

He was prepared to become angry at the outcome of the question, to the utter bemusement of Mitchel, who pressed on.

Mitchel said, 'Ironworks, cotton miller, textile factory owner . . . I don't know. I was reaching for examples.'

'Forgive me then,' he said. 'I am very touchy at the moment . . . Benny . . .'

'I must be clear about this matter of slaves, though, Thomas,' said Mitchel.

'Please, go on,' Meagher invited, but with a smothered yawn.

'Substitute Mr Jenkins,' suggested Mitchel, 'with a private in the United States Army. The soldier is like a slave, and has his freedom limited by military requirements and the commands of the state and his officers. Some officers are fit to command your man in the ranks, others may never be. The soldier, like the slave, is sometimes misused, and separated from his wife or his mother and father, but without an underground railway for soldiers he cannot decide that with the help of kind citizens he is entitled to flit from the ranks and disappear to Canada. There might even be a Soldiers' Underground promoting freedom, so of course he takes up the cry, "Give me freedom!" If such a man deserted tonight and presented himself to you, invoking freedom, would you help him to escape to Canada?'

'I could not, not if he were American. But I can't say exactly why not. You would correctly say, it is against the law. But having sat and listened to escaped slaves, all without informing their masters I have found them – that too is against the law.'

'So the soldier has volunteered . . .' Mitchel suggested, pursuing the argument.

'Probably while tipsy and not in his right mind,' said Meagher. 'However, he has volunteered himself, and, after his time, is free to re-enlist or become a civilian. I don't see how you can compare that with Jenkins' situation. The soldier volunteers for service. The slave, born of his mother, has no choice from the moment of birth. He is no volunteer. It is a clear difference to me.'

But Mitchel was not persuaded. Tired as they now were, they nonetheless could not leave the subject alone.

'So Jenkins and the young woman both have their grievances,' he declared, 'and want freedom from some of their suffering and hardship. But again the soldier has his tyrannous sergeants and sergeant majors who have a rod for his back and are likely to use it. The soldier is fired at, as the slave sometimes is. But – once more – we do not rush in to save the soldier.'

Meagher made a mouth of disapproval.

'No, Tom,' Mitchel insisted, returning to his main theme. 'Despite being touched by what I've seen, I do wonder why citizens feel they must help the slaves move north by surreptitious means. Is there not enough industrial misery and misuse in New York to occupy all our philanthropy? The victims of the Famine had far more horrifying tales to relate, but who other than the Irish was interested in those? And in the popular press of New York, our people are depicted as orangutans.

'Does your Underground Railroad feel bound to intervene and protect the Irish? The Irish worker has complaints most justified in terms of the dangers of his work or the callousness of overseers. Are we smuggling factory workers or miners to happier climes? Does that interest your Vigilance Committee? I know that those who died in the Famine would have accepted the life of Adelanta with open hands, and would have lived out their slavery with thanks.'

Meagher, shaking his head a little, as if driven more by tremors than by thought, now seemed too tired, too dispirited to answer.

'I was considerably frank and mischievous in writing on the issue, Tom,' Mitchel conceded. 'If I were writing it again, I would have said – without referencing my experience of this afternoon, of course – that many tell me, and I accept, that African slaves can show a considerable taste for liberty and can seem to understand what it is they have been deprived of. It would be very peculiar if they did not cry "Liberty!", given the choirs of abolitionists who keep singing the idea to them! But in this fallen world, many people are deprived of what happier groups have. There are immensely worse things you and I have seen, Tom, than Mr Jenkins and Miss Adelanta, and we have not finished crying out together against them.'

'We must disagree a little then,' Tom said. 'I will contribute my income from *The Citizen* to causes that seem valid to me.'

'That is your right,' said Mitchel, 'since your name has added lustre to our paper. It is taken for granted that those, like me, who prescribe slavery as essential, are not moved by malice to the African. We recognise that by his background and his origins he is not fit to face being exploited in industry, and that it is contrary to his interests to throw him into that stew. What happens to Jenkins if he takes a job in a plant? If he is paid less, the white worker wishes to attack him for lowering wages. If he is paid the same, the white worker is outraged! And that outrage can express itself viciously. But it is only natural that, having heard their freedom constantly invoked, slaves would desire it.'

'It is a little curious that I'm involved with these people,' Tom Meagher sighed, bleary-eyed now with fatigue and the burden of his young, dead wife.

'I would never have guessed it,' Mitchel admitted in a conciliatory tone.

'It is because Clunes is my spiritual adviser and my confessor,' said Tom. 'I seek redemption, though Jenny does not believe it. Anything that priest is conscientiously engaged in has a claim upon me.'

Then Meagher seemed to put his head back and become still, and Mitchel did not know whether he was asleep or not. When he next made a sound, it was as if he were speaking with the remnants of consciousness.

'I am still a Democrat, nor do I subscribe to the belief of Mr Beecher, who wants a cleansing battle, a blood climax for America's young. The men who talk that way rarely offer their own blood as part of the settlement. Whereas, I could foresee liberation making its gradual advance, by reform perhaps, by the scales falling from Southern eyes. Or more likely, a fall in the price of cotton.' He sniffed and extracted a handkerchief from his pocket. 'None of which seems likely now,' he murmured.

Mitchel asked, 'Have you read Dr Cartwright, Thomas?'

'You know I am not scholarly like you, Mitch.'

'He depicts the running away of slaves as an illness of the mind brought on by endless talk by abolitionists. What did Jenkins say, and the woman too? They ran away only because they heard rumours of your railroad!'

Meagher even looked shrunken in his sleepy corner of the carriage. He yawned again and said mournfully, 'Yes, I am too serious a sinner to die for the slaves.'

And with that he did fall asleep.

30

Broaching the South,
Late Summer 1854-55

Throughout that summer Mitchel began to speak to Jenny about the South and the ease with which they could live there. McClenehan had undertaken to organise for him, if Mitchel were to leave and give up *The Citizen* into his hands, a winter lecture series that would give them a year's income, whether any farm they bought returned them adequately or not. Jenny seemed cheered at the prospect.

'But,' she said, 'I do not wish to live in the heart of the big plantations. I have tasted one extreme of what it is to be an American. I don't want my nose rubbed in the other version.'

She thought there must be a world in between, where American virtues were not skewed by extremes. A world reigned over by the spirit of Jefferson. And the idea of John giving up his part in *The Citizen* – that would be a relief, she told him, since occasionally women had confronted her in stores and chastised her for his editorials.

Jenny's desire was also amenable to a village perhaps, since she did not want to be dropped into the turmoil of a big Southern city – Charleston or Savannah or New Orleans. 'Somewhere there is no slave trade,' she said. 'Are there such places in the South?'

Mitchel assured her there were.

He sought information about the healthy towns of Appalachia, and read in Dr Ramsey's *Annals of Tennessee* of the piedmont town of Knoxville near the Appalachian Mountains, which in Tennessee they called the Great Smokies. It was a settlement far from the big plantations and not much characterised by the Peculiar Institution.

Mitchel was enchanted by that wonderful book of Dr Ramsey's, which did due honour to all actors – settlers, Choctaws, Shawnees, Cherokees. He was interested that for survival the settlers had entered into treaties with the Indians, which the colonists of Van Diemen's Land never had with their native people. Ramsey's chief love was for the country itself, a country, Jenny would be pleased to find from Ramsey's pages, for settlers; for small, free farmers; for rustic virtues unimpeded by any landlordism, and farming carried out without slaves. The people of East Tennessee had fought and defeated the British at King's Mountain, just up the summit track, and indeed a touch over the Tennessee border in North Carolina, as early as 1780. Most of these settlers were Highland Scots and Irish trying to stop General Cornwallis's campaign into the mountains and its crucial passes. From fighting that campaign, they had great respect for the Union.

Knoxville had been the capital of Tennessee earlier in the century and thus harboured the state's university. The Mitchels had not found their harbour, the rewards of their escape, in New York City. John could tell that Jenny was no more at ease there than was he. The angels sang 'Knoxville' and Jenny and he were listening.

'In New York,' she had complained, 'people are so moved by pretence.' She nominated in the one breath the Rev. Beecher and Tom Meagher as masters of pretence. She was ready for Mitchel to break up his relationship with Meagher. 'That's a sly man!' she said. 'He'll be reconciled to Benny's death before the month is out. Soon we will see him in the papers with this or that hoyden.'

Jenny was so certain that she kept a watch on the papers, and less than three months after Benny's demise was announced in the New York press, she showed John a picture taken in Saratoga of a group of people, most of them couples, but two of them not so. One of the latter was Meagher and the other a full-faced and apple-cheeked woman named Libby Townsend, the daughter of the Townsend Ironworks, a woman of perhaps Meagher's own age, who stood in the group with the confidence of someone who knew her own mind. Mitchel remembered Meagher's sensitivity to a remark he had made about owners of ironworks on the night of their visit to the priest's stretch of the Underground Railroad. So he had known her already, at that time. Perhaps even before Benny was dead.

'He is a dog,' said Jenny in conclusion.

Mitchel did not tell her, for fear she would forbid him from their home, that Meagher had planted at least one foot on the UGRR.

'I am sure,' he told Jenny, 'that inconstant men live in the South as well. That is a male plague unrelated to politics or the design of society.'

'Of course,' she crisply answered him. 'I know that. But when a so-called friend . . .'

She did not need to supply the rest of the sentence.

'If we go,' she said about Tennessee, 'we must stay for a time, a good time. For we have barely been more than birds of passage. Think of our boys and our daughters! They've lived on three continents!'

He made his pledges, believing that they would become rustic people there, in the Great Smokies. They would be happy, complete, close to the sky. The boys were strong and would carry a small farm on their shoulders. As for Henty, she could stay in Knoxville with a good family and pursue her music studies – or so they decided.

———

As the summer came on, John wondered whether the Russians were still weighing their launching an expedition from the Baltic. The Mitchel enterprise in the South could occur only if he and Meagher did not have the higher duty of going to Ireland on the heels of a Russian invasion, and taking a hand in the arrangements of a new Irish state. The wonderful thing would be that the Russians, in invading Ireland, had no desire to acquire a possession, and were moved above all by a desire to march in Piccadilly, as once, at the end of Napoleon's reign, they had marched in Paris!

Since the United States was, above all, an enlightened platform from which Mitchel could enter Ireland when the politics suited, for a brief few weeks there was an extraordinary hope in Mitchel of a Russian emergence from that Baltic Sea. But the opposite of what he wanted occurred.

A swift manoeuvre carried out by new steam-powered warships of the Royal Navy spoiled the dream.

This British fleet arrived off the Aland Islands in the Gulf of Finland and destroyed any forts that would have allowed the Russians to move. The Russian fleet emerged from its ports only when it had cover from its coastal batteries, but many of those were promptly destroyed by Vice Admiral Napier's long-range guns. French marines would capture the Bomarsund fortress in Aland, deep in the Baltic between Russia and Finland, by summer's end. A Russian expedition into the Atlantic, and a landing in Ireland, was now a daydream again.

Mitchel was depressed by the reflection he might never have in his life a similar opportunity. There would be no Cossacks on the Dingle Peninsula. Carlyle was right: large events were triggered by the swift decisions of rulers. The decisiveness Mitchel hoped for from the Tsar – Nicholas I now in old age – was not available. The Tsar was stupefied with authoritarianism, and could not move quickly, almost considering it ungodly!

By autumn, Mitchel was a less confident and more wary man. The death of the dream of Muscovite outbreak was like the loss of a dear, consoling friend. He and Meagher continued to publish, and Mitchel, on whom the management continued to fall, took time to opine in *The Citizen* that Russia's naval inferiority would lose them the war. He also helpfully suggested that, in the future of the world, Russian ambitions would be restricted to the Euro-Asian landmass if they did not keep up with the Carthaginian Fleet!

———

As for *The Citizen*, the readers were getting used to it. Sales did decrease under the continued preaching of Beecher on the one hand, even if on the other the archbishop and his corps of priests regretfully began to reconcile themselves to its existence for Meagher's sake. To McClenehan's discontent, they dipped to a circulation of thirty thousand a week by the end of June 1854, seven months since its inception.

'Good Christ, man,' he said, 'you have run out of your shock power. And just like that!'

'I can't speed up the chapters of my escape,' Mitchel told him. John was continuing to tell the tale of his escape in weekly chapters people loved to read. Many young women were said to read of its excitements in secret.

'Nor should you. Spin it out! It looked for a while the chief work of Dagger John seemed still to protect the faithful from our *Citizen*. Irish wives warn their men against buying it. Fortunately, and as in all areas, not all the men obey their spouses!'

Thirty thousand copies a week was still affluence, and influence, in itself. In fact, people were so taken with Mitchel's journal of imprisonment and escape from Van Diemen's Land that Irishwomen themselves secretly bought the paper – 'For God's sake, Patsy, don't tell the archbishop!' McClenehan's all-important advertising revenue picked up in the autumn, and so did circulation.

———

At year's end, Christmas in Brooklyn was a pleasant time, with the seasons being what Mitchel could not help but think of as 'the right way around'. He had Yuletide visits from Savage, from Meagher and his companion, Miss Libby

Townsend, from the Dillons, whom the Mitchels had known in the Dublin days, and indeed from so many of their old acquaintances that Mitchel half-expected Speranza to walk in, talking furiously. But each Christmas, he supposed, would tease them with memory. They had had no chance of a return to Ireland. They had needed daring from the Russian court. But there was none.

Meagher told the Mitchels, when he introduced them to his 'walking-out' companion, that robust and amiable Libby Townsend's ancestral ironworks had forged the giant chain that was stretched across the Hudson at West Point during the Revolution, and thus excluded the Royal Navy from striking deep into the New York hinterland and its neighbouring colonies. He seemed to be claiming this as if it was one of many factors that would make their ultimate nuptials suitable and approvable. The New York daily press all said the Townsends looked without much joy on their daughter marrying such a man – a man who was 'not their type'. Even so, Libby Townsend, who sometimes seemed a little under-engaged with the Mitchels, would suddenly want to know details of Meagher's past. And would ask Jenny about it. There was a sense in which she was strangely engaged in all Meagher had done in his youth, and in what he might yet do.

Jenny liked Libby. Indeed, it was normal for Jenny to forgive pleasant women, if forgiveness was necessary, for the men they attached themselves to. Behind everything, Libby had a kind of ruling Yankee innocence in her, and so she passed that test, Jenny saying, 'She has fewer pretensions than the big Irish families.' Big Irish families being in sentiment big British families too.

But the midwife of Mitchel's freedom, Nicaragua Smyth, was not amongst the Christmas gatherings. He had vanished from New York, without much noise from him – to the amazement of many, including Downing Street. Nicaragua was said to be in the act of liberating two people from Van Diemen's Land: his wife Jeannie Regan and, if at all possible, Smith O'Brien himself. And such was his repute that as he approached the Australian colonies, the British government of Lord Palmerston felt compelled to make a statement about Mr Smith O'Brien.

Palmerston was a Whig and even a liberal, and was a dreadful Famine landlord who sent so many cargos of his fever-ridden Irish peasants to New Brunswick that the Canadian legislature complained. Nothing much was done about the complaint, of course, and now there was this statement to clear the way for pardoning Smith O'Brien, and thus preventing another famous Van Diemen's Land escape.

Palmerston knew that Nicaragua, whose part in Mitchel's escape was well known through his *Jail Journal* published each week, presented him with a problem. If Smyth entered Van Diemen's Land – the about-to-be Tasmania – in disguise, he would again have many of the democratic elements helping him. But arresting an American citizen, which Nicaragua had decided to become, would attract the wrath of citizens of the United States, particularly of the American Party's President of the US, Millard Fillmore.

However, if Palmerston pardoned Smith O'Brien before Nicaragua could get to him, that would relieve everyone of further escapes like Meagher's and Mitchel's. It would also be an act of pretending the Famine was now a settled matter, not an ongoing grievance. Palmerston had already declared that Smith O'Brien had acted like a gentleman over his parole, and might be considered for a pardon if he sought one. This made Nicaragua pause and attend to his personal and marital endeavours, instead of liberating prisoners of state in Van Diemen's Land.

Mitchel wondered if a pardon would flow too to his old friend John Martin, and to the medico Kevin O'Doherty and to O'Donoghue. The rumour was that to honour Ireland's supposedly settled condition, they would be let free as well. That winter Mitchel received letters from dear Martin about all this, and Smith O'Brien's wife and family packed up in Cahermoyle in Limerick, intending to join him in France, since Martin presumed the pardon would be conditional on Smith O'Brien not returning to Ireland.

The story of Mitchel's fellow prisoners filled the pages of *The Citizen* and gave it an admirable revival. Anyone reading that newspaper knew that the supposed British mercy was a deceit and a card trick. A conditional pardon did reach John's former fellows in Van Diemen's Land that northern winter, during which the Mitchels themselves celebrated the New Year in Brooklyn. Before the pardoned men left Van Diemen's Land, the colonists gave them a feast in Launceston and another in the gold city of Melbourne when they reached that place.

Martin wrote to Mitchel, 'Contrary to our expectations, the "pardon" was not attended by any conditions whatever other than the geographic one.' That is, the one by which Martin and O'Brien and the others would need to live on the Continent; Holland, maybe, or France. Martin, rightly as it turned out, predicted this restriction would, one day soon enough, be unobtrusively waived. Meanwhile, in Westbury, a mere American named Smyth collected his bride and began to consult the best means of reaching New York again in her amiable company.

The next spring, after a long winter producing *The Citizen*, Mitchel turned the running of the newspaper over to McClenehan, that young man of both editorial and advertising skills. There was another farewell to his mother and sisters and the young patent enthusiast, his brother William, but Mitchel assured them all he would be back the following winter to lecture in the city.

His mother asked, 'Are you sure, John, that this is not simply more of bouncing your wife and children around the world? For the sake of not settling?'

His sisters in the living room had paused at this question, for it was a crucial one. He assured them, 'I have revisited the issue with her so often.'

'As you should, John,' Matilda told him.

'And we wonder, John,' said Henrietta, after whom Henty was named, as she acutely examined the surface of her cup of tea, 'about such things as education, of which you had the best your parents could provide.'

'Believe me,' John consoled them, 'I do not move my family about as an act of autocracy. I have tried to make all my intentions clear, and in return I expect to be governed by any misgivings Jenny has. Thus far our schooling has been adequate for the children, but I have sworn to Jenny we will need to attend to the others as they come to a certain age. And I would like to say that you will encounter no lack of literacy and informed intellect in my children.'

'Your Jamie,' his mother conceded, 'is a consistently charming boy in company and your young Willy is already an accomplished scientist and knows two-thirds of Linnaeus's system . . . As for the rest, I know that John C. is going for a railroad engineer . . . But seven hundred miles. You are removing from us by seven hundred miles!'

What was true was that, due to his lecture tours, Mitchel's own departure was not as absolute as it was for Jenny and the children. And even though lectures that only he could give would keep them affluent and well established, he would feel miserable leaving the farm to Jenny and the second son, Jamie, Willy, who was now ten years, then Minnie, and Rixy, who was nearly three, and was described by them as 'spirited', a condition they admired but feared could skew her in unwise directions if the only influence on them was mountain people. As well as that, Henty was the best pianist in the house and in Brooklyn and the world as well, at least her grandmother believed so. Even if special arrangements were to be made for her to continue her piano studies, the Mitchel sisters lamented that her music would fade from their lives altogether.

Indeed, there were factors that would limit their numbers in the mountains. John pointed out that, despite suspicions to the contrary, he wanted to have his children acquire formal skills. They had decided that Henty should stay in the town at Knoxville at some good house and pursue her piano skills at the Knoxville Female Institute. And John C. had his job with a railroad that would see him trained as a railway engineer – a full-scale builder of great spans, not a driver of trains – as honourable as that latter craft might be.

Mitchel told his mother and sisters what he had so often repeated to Jenny. From their farm, wherever it might be in the mountains, it would be at most thirty-five miles from the Athens of the South, Knoxville, and its university and academies.

———

Packing up in the late winter of 1855, the family of John and Jenny at last took a ship to Charleston. After four days of calm passage, for which Jenny was grateful and which served as an omen, it entered that long harbour of that Southern city and skirted the mass of Fort Sumter, which looked like a rather French jewel box of a fortification. They moored at one of the northerly docks within a walk to the centre of the town. The Mitchels' move south had been projected in *The Citizen*, and so *Charleston Mercury* journalists met the ship and asked him questions on everything from the war in the Crimea to his eccentric taste for being an American farmer and occasional lecturer. It was refreshing not to know many folk within that city, and not to have to prepare for the artificial exultations of a civic dinner, but nonetheless, John and Jenny were told that a public reception had been prepared in their honour in Columbia, once they reached it by rail, by the mayor to honour John as Southern and Irish champion.

Who remembers train journeys when they are over? They were hauled by slow locomotive through farmlands and by South Carolina plantations. The Mitchel young passed the children in the fields, working with their parents, carrying panniers of cotton or armfuls of cane towards the crusher or the gin. In Columbia as the train arrived, brass bands played and they were greeted by the mayor, who rejoiced that the legendary John Mitchel and his admirable family, having tasted the daily life of New York, had chosen now to acquaint themselves with a different, purer model of American life, the ethos presented by the South.

Then it was across a hilly section of Georgia to Chattanooga in Tennessee, and so into a delightful, verdant little town named Loudun, on a vast bend of the Tennessee River. Here the rail line gave out and, again, they found themselves unknown to all, and all unknown to them, traversing strange but lovely forests. Those bound for Knoxville to the north-east – only two other gentlemen apart from the Mitchels – were loaded in a big wagon called a carry-all.

The two little girls, Minnie, who was eight years, and Rixy, were querulous as the ponderous carry-all traversed dense woods, heading for their destination, a journey which took them all of one day and some hours into the night. Thus, they were utterly lost in America, and thus Mitchel felt utterly freed.

As they progressed, Jamie often left the big, slow wagon to go on foot and hunt for botanical and insect samples for Willy, and would then sprint back to the conveyance with his pockets and hands full of leaves and beetles of bright colour to entertain Minnie and Rixy. Shooting stars, Willy assured them, and Solomon's seal, redbud leaves, American holly and sourwood. Willy had been given a guide to the botany of the region by a kind woman at the reception in Columbia, who had read about the little fellow's passion for nature. He was by now an expert. To match a plate with a still-living specimen was the height of life for dear Willy, and his enthusiasm soothed the others.

Their carry-all ground down over the Henley Street bridge at last, with the buildings of the University of Tennessee looming ill perceived in darkness on their left. They found lodgings in an establishment named the Coleman House, in a town whose features were as yet teasingly unknown to them. Henty, exhausted herself, sang her little sisters asleep, for she was a noble girl.

The next day they slept late, breakfasted leisurely, and suffered some inroads on their anonymity. For that morning Mr Swan, mayor of the town of Knoxville, visited them with other luminaries, including two young stars of the city, a Mr Mabry and a yet younger gentleman named McAdoo, who had the honour to be Attorney General for the state of Tennessee.

Swan, like his friends, proved to be an amiable, generous man, bright and municipal, and Mitchel liked him for his warmth and his vigour and the pragmatic political air he carried so easily. The mayor offered to show any who had the energy to join him in a promenade through the dimensions and details of his town. Parts of it were heavily wooded, and across on the other bank of the Tennessee River, there was no town at all. In walking the streets they saw some slaves – Swan pointed them out and they were undistinguished from black freed men and women. They were often engaged in business, loading and unloading wagons in particular, but they did not seem notably oppressed, thought Mitchel, and had no air of grievance.

Knoxville in any case, as John had promised Jenny, was not a great centre of slavery. The farms at this eastern end of the state were smaller, and up in the mountains beyond the town, apparently smaller still. Thus, they did not see the chained contingents of plantation slaves that haunted the imaginations of men like Beecher.

The atmosphere of Knoxville was very rural and settled and peaceable and pleasant, but Mr Swan said it had been wilder ten years past, when mountain dwellers and Cherokees, availing themselves of liquor and old grievances, shot each other dead along Main Street. Now the thoroughfares were about to be paved and there were trenches dug for gas lighting, which would banish all dark deeds. The pipes lay on the edge of the road in pyramidal numbers. Mr Swan was proud of what he was showing them, but was prouder

442

still of the future. The railway was on its way too, he said, and it would connect them to Georgia and, northwards, ultimately to Washington.

Swan's rhapsody to his city reminded Mitchel a little of Dr Ramsey's *Annals*, which had moved Mitchel to visit the region in the first place. Indeed, Swan declared, he could introduce him to Dr Ramsey, who lived near Emory Square in this very town.

Swan did understand fully that it was Knoxville's unapologetic rusticness that drew Mitchel, but Mitchel had to forgive the man for praising the non-primitive aspects: gas lighting; railways. The mayor pointed out the site of a new Catholic church, since the Irish and Italians had flooded Nashville and were now coming in tribes to Knoxville. He told Mitchel the Know Nothings in town believed that the new chapel was to be a secret fortress built to store Jesuit gunpowder for eventual suppression of American freedoms, and for setting up the Inquisition in Tennessee. There was also a rumour that Mitchel's arrival was somehow part of the Papist capture of the South. To their honour, Swan, Mabry and McAdoo laughed with Mitchel over this ludicrous assumption. He was a little disappointed to find such ugly thinking, and the presence of Know Nothings, in such a pretty town.

'Do they know I am the Protestant child of a Presbyterian Unitarian minister?' Mitchel asked him.

'Such perceptions as theirs,' said Swan, honest Democrat, 'are not susceptible to reason.'

McAdoo the lawyer had read some of Mitchel's *Jail Journal* as republished in Southern papers, and considered it, from its first printing, a classic. He kindly rode with Mitchel and his two eldest 'farm-sons', Jamie and Willy, as they scouted the district for places to settle. For his friends in Knoxville all said, 'Don't go to the mountains, settle here in the foot-hills where life is far more convenient.'

They arrived at Clinton, twenty miles from Knoxville, another pleasant, wooded town on the banks of a rapid river, the Clinch, a tributary of the Tennessee. Mitchel found the town thickly settled, though. It lacked all the advantages of Knoxville and yet none of the advantages of isolation.

On the way back to Knoxville they stayed in the big but not showy house of a gentleman named Joe Black and his wife, an authoritative-looking older but not aged woman with remarkable eyes. They were all at dinner with the Blacks, in the middle of eating pork, when Mrs Black suddenly extended her right arm into the air and let out a penetrating scream. No-one but the boys and John seemed shocked. The host and Mr McAdoo continued eating, and Mrs Black lowered her arm and took up the conversation with an air of august respectability. Mitchel had nearly convinced himself the scream had been a delusion of his own.

But on their next day's ride to Knoxville, Mr McAdoo explained to the boys and Mitchel that this was a common symptom of many people in that part of the country. It was called 'the jerks' and was caused by attendance at camp meetings, very fervent tent affairs in which Southern prophets stimulated the most restrained people to shout and call out loud and let the Spirit speak in tongues through them.

As Mitchel searched for a place to settle, he continued to indulge fantasies of the Great Smokies. Going there would be an utter break with the familiar world and he retained in his imagination the name of a place he had read of in New York, in Dr Ramsey's *Annals of Tennessee* – a vast nest and embayment of open farmland named Cade's Cove.

They left the Coleman House now to dwell in what was a proper family residence at Mrs Duncan's. The structures of Knoxville seemed very modern, but built on a generous scale in a town that seemed spacious. Mrs Duncan's house was that of a well-read woman of about forty years, and she and Mrs Coleman had made time in Knoxville very pleasant for Jenny. Jenny found it hard to restrict herself to carriages, but liked to walk about the town and achieved a better knowledge of the little city than Mitchel himself had. It was about the size of Banbridge. And she loved it, she told John.

Mitchel nonetheless suggested that he should go up and look at the mountains, taking Jamie, and Jenny was open to that idea. On a spring day, Jamie and John set out on foot from Knoxville, carrying satchels and blankets, determined to sample and explore the country as walking pilgrims. The pleasant country road eastwards ran through forests one could not help but think of as American, and occasionally there were glades where a small town had taken root around a mill for grain or timber. The air seemed utterly free of that tyranny of precedence and landlordism which was the poison in the old world's veins, and free of the inhuman Yankee capital. Even if fortunes might be modest here, there was a liberating sense that hopes were lush. It was that promise that lured and rewarded the emigrant and, even, the escapee.

As they approached Sevierville in the mouth of the mountains, the forests, particularly, were rich with everything that the book of American botany, carried by Jamie today, contained, from hickory to firs. At noon a farmer in a clearing happily greeted them and took them indoors for stew, telling them he had not expected that day to meet

445

right strangers who wanted to become Volunteers, which was one of the titles East Tennesseans went by.

Walking on till sundown, seeing an occasional elk but not yet any bears, John and Jamie came over a wooded ridge and saw below them the beautiful valley, or cove, they had been promised. Cade's Cove, a farmer passing on a mule confirmed for them. Beyond there, beyond the sorghum crusher that helped to make molasses at the end of the cove, there was Rich Mountain and then Tuckaleechee Cove. A Cade's Cove settler was happy to feed them and let them use his storeroom for accommodation. When they stepped out in the morning, the air and light, and the way mist hung like sulphur fumes about the mountains – it was all intoxicating.

'Making molasses from sorghum?' Mitchel asked Jamie. That seemed a symbol of a departure from the normal. Indeed, it was a cove, an embayment amidst a sea of ancient foliage and primeval forest. And there seemed at the ends of this embayment to be mountains emitting smoke, as if from volcanic flues at the base of the hills, and it was clear why they were called Great Smokies. Particles rising from the trees, Jamie told his father, clung to moisture in the air to give this appearance.

From a 'bald', which was what the locals called open ground on a ridge, stripped clear by grazing cattle, they saw generous farmland ahead and a man ploughing with a cow. Wits in Knoxville had warned Mitchel that farmers in the 'coves' of the mountains used their wives as plough animals, but the scene ahead put the lie to that. John and Jamie walked on through the valley and discussed the design of the local houses. If they were two storeys, the upper floor seemed better built than the lower floors and better caulked against the weather. They passed a shed with what looked like a cider press, but surmised it was the sorghum press of which the farmer had advised them.

It was a testing rise to the pass over Rich Mountain, and they were feeling weary now. They were willing to make their own camp that night – they had their blankets, though in this country anyone who saw them was likely to invite them into a house.

From the pass, through screens of foliage, they could see further cleared land below, and a spacious cabin, the gaps in its planks caulked with a clay that so much as shone in the late light. It was a fine scene, empty of labourers at this hour, and the ploughed soil in the valley below seemed deep, alluvial, promising.

This was isolation if one wanted it, and they did – Jenny and he and the children – seeking their own Judea like a tribe from the book of Genesis. This American garden could not be stolen from them by British perfidy, or even by Know Nothing idiocy and all the rest of it! Mitchel felt that if living in the world of ideas was always to have bad ideas imping-ing on your reason; if living in the world of invention was to have the equal ground between men ground to dust by it; if living in the world of politics was to be surrounded by plausible starvation and barbarity; then this cove offered rescue from the tedium of the world's malice.

They got to the farmhouse below as daylight faded, and knocked at the downstairs door. It was answered by a woman about Jenny's age, though in no way as exquisite, for the labours of the place had deeply seamed her face. She had a clay pipe clenched in her remaining teeth and her forehead was wrinkled. Her apron was homespun, but her dress, though a faded blue, was shop bought. Mitchel introduced himself and asked could he and his son stay overnight on the edge of the fields? He was quite excited to have a chance to inspect the night sky up here.

She would not have it! They could be fed corn and stew for dinner, and given the spare room. So they entered and shed their valises in the room below, then followed her up rough-hewn but well-planed stairs. They could hear male conversation above them. The woman stopped at the head of the staircase in a big room with a loft, a kitchen at one end, and a dining table in the midst.

'These are jaspers I bid in, Mr Edmonds,' she announced mysteriously to the male authority in the room, who was, as it happened, her husband. 'It is what we have here, Mr Mitchel and his son Jemmy.'

Both visitors nodded to the man of the house, a big-jawed fellow who sat at a bench pulling on boots, apparently in their honour. He rose and greeted them soulfully to his home.

'We have the greatest interest in jaspers,' he assured them. That meant, as they would find in time, strangers. But for the sake of what was cooking in the kitchen and its meaty flavour, Mitchel did not enquire at the time. He was Frederick Edmonds, the farmer told them.

As they thanked him for his generosity in taking them in, two lank, barefooted sons looked on, a sullenness in their faces, as if they wanted the guests to prove more threatening than the Mitchels were, so they could then reach for the ancient squirrel guns and other armaments that lay in corners. Their suspicion was the suspicion of innocence.

Beyond the end of the table in a chair large enough to be a rustic throne sat an old big-jawed man, and the jaw was working – he was chewing tobacco.

'Hello, sir,' the Mitchel men called to him.

He reached for a jar and spat tobacco juice into it. He said, 'Sir, are you them angels of change we hear so much about these days?'

'No, Daddy, they're just walking through here,' said his daughter-in-law, before offering the Mitchels a meal of cornbread, corn and stew.

The two sons sat down as if this were a feast involving Macbeth and Duncan, and the Mitchels had come to kill them in their beds.

'Hello then, gentlemen,' said Jamie and they warmed to him. They asked him what his country was, and he said, without hesitation, though he had not been consciously primed by his father, 'Ireland!' Then, again, he told them the English had sent his father as a criminal – which he was not – to Van Diemen's Land, but that Mitchel had famously escaped across the Pacific and come to New York.

Under their eager questioning, he described Van Diemen's Land. 'Indeed,' said Jamie. 'It's a very pleasant land, rather like this.'

Mitchel thought, how apt. There was something of Bothwell's three-mile vista here, in this cove. Was that it? That he was seeking the place he had already escaped?

Afterwards they ate some pie and molasses, and then everyone sat around the fire: the woman herself, the husband, two lank sons and the old father. The man of the house, very weathered and with brooding eyes, asked Mitchel, 'So you have crossed the ocean's seas to get here, Mr Mitchel?'

'We have,' John admitted.

'It is time we crossed seas,' Mr Edmonds said, 'or at least rivers and mountains. But we have been nowhere and seen nothing but this.'

'You shouldn't yearn for strangeness, Mr Edmonds,' said his wife. 'You should be grateful for what the Lord provides right here.'

'I agree with your wife, sir,' Mitchel told him.

'Is it true, mister,' he asked, 'that the seas are all brine?'

'Are they all brine, James?' Mitchel asked his son.

'Every mouthful between Tasmania and the United States,' said Jamie, grinning away. Mitchel's ambassador. But John was now fascinated that these people had been American for so long that they had lost all the memory of their original Atlantic crossing.

'Well, I do wonder!' said the farmer and sat back in his chair to contemplate this. Both of the sons, barefoot by the fire, spat tobacco juice gently into their respective jars. 'So you will return to the seas of the earth one day, Mr Mitchel?' asked Mr Edmonds further.

'Perhaps to go to my homeland,' Mitchel said. 'But we have seen the country in Cade's Cove and Tuckaleechee here, and that is enough. Is there any native of this valley who wishes to sell out, Mr Edmonds? Here or Cade's Cove?'

The sombre-eyed farmer consulted his wife. 'We do not believe so,' she said.

She was, he had observed, possibly no older than Jenny, but a hard life and the loss of teeth had not stripped her of decisiveness. Her mouth, however, folded in an aged way.

———

John and Jamie slept in the loft on palliasses, and the entire family disappeared behind curtains at the far end of the hut. In the morning after breakfast Mitchel told Mr Edmonds that he would go and look again at Cade's Cove, but that if he received any news of a farm for sale, Mitchel would be grateful to hear from him. They walked some miles along Tuckaleechee, though Cade's was vaster still, eleven miles in circumference, while Tuckaleechee seemed at most two thirds of that. Both were limestone country, with caves in the mountains that sheltered plentiful wildlife. There were four such large coves in the Smokies, John had been told. That afternoon, as the Mitchels turned back through Tuckaleechee towards the Black Mountain ascent, one of the boys of the family came running towards them from the far side of the corn crop.

He stood panting before Jamie and John. 'My pa has agreed to go and farm at Gatlinburg with Ma's brother.'

Jamie asked if Gatlinburg was the town he and his father had passed through on the way, but Mitchel said no.

'Why, it must be two thousands of people,' said the boy. 'Grandpa can die a more popular death there. And Pa can read newspapers. Ma has been telling father for years on end that she can abide it if he will go to farm with uncle Ogle. He says to tell you $10 an acre. There's one hunnert and forty acres here and fifty under cultivation. And the house and the barn. We take the wagon. Pa was very anxious I catch you with the offer today.'

Mitchel felt a sudden huge stimulation in his blood, and an exaltation such as he had never before felt. For this was Eden before it was spoiled with ideas gone rancid, and the Edmonds family wanted to sell it up. Mitchel saw that Edmonds was a man cramped for choices, and wanting to expand his world, even if it was only partway down the track that ran towards North Carolina. Jamie could see the excitement in John and rightly warned, 'Father, you've said you would speak to Mamma about it.'

451

'Yes,' he said. 'Yes, but she will be happy, I know it. I know how she will love it.'

'You watch the Parton women, who will set their minds to marry your sons,' the boy said. 'The Parton girls are sly and a right nuisance.'

Mitchel exchanged a smile with Jamie.

'I will certainly watch out,' said Jamie, smiling.

'I will ride up in two days' time with my answer and, if we proceed, the money,' Mitchel said to the boy. 'Tell your father.'

The grandfather had asked, 'Are you them angels of change we hear are on their way?' But Mitchel did not see his work as changing things. He would be a recipient. His heart threatened to burst with the possibility of what he would receive in this lovely valley.

'My God, Jimmy,' he cried, 'I believe I am happier than at any time since the judge sentenced me. This is liberty, James. Unargued and unassailable. And by the valley-ful!'

He half-closed his eyes and through his lids the valley indeed might have been Newry.

Or Tasmania. But constrained by no parole. Utterly without chains.

Author's Note

I must thank my ever-fine primary editor, Judy Keneally, and then my agents, Fiona Inglis, Sam Copeland and the legendary Amanda Urban. Two English friends advised me on this book – Sue Burton, a wandering Novocastrian in Australia, and Maggie Gabbe, an amiable woman of Kent. They made sure my post-colonial Aussie-ness did not offensively assert itself. For their dedication to this text, I must thank Meredith Curnow and the kite-eyed Patrick Mangan.

To John Mitchel himself, I must say your classic work *Jail Journal*, and your Irish and American journalism, are frankly presented here in terms intended to echo but not abuse their original intent. May you and your remarkable Jenny rest in peace.